THE SOWER
OF THE
SEEDS OF DREAMS

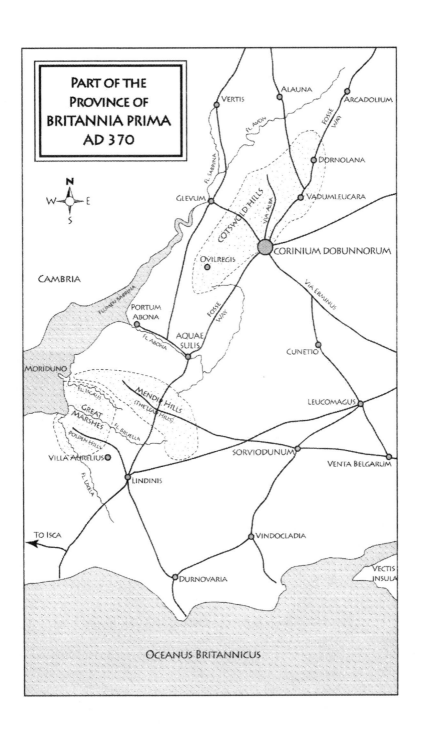

PART OF THE
PROVINCE OF
BRITANNIA PRIMA
AD 370

N
W — E
S

VERTIS
ALAUNA
ARCADOLIUM

FL. AVON
FOSSE WAY

DORNOLANA

FL. SABRINA

GLEVUM
COTSWOLD HILLS
VIA ALBA
VADUMLEUCARA

OVILREGIS
CORINIUM DOBUNNORUM

CAMBRIA

VIA ERMINUS

FLUMEN SABRINA

PORTUM
ABONA

FL. ABONA

AQUAE
SULIS
FOSSE WAY

CUNETIO

MORIDUNO

FL. ISCALIS

MENDIP HILLS
(THE LEAD HILLS)
LEUCOMAGUS

GREAT
MARSHES
FL. BRUELLA

POLDEN HILLS

VILLA AURELIUS
SORVIODUNUM
VENTA BELGARUM

FL. URELA

LINDINIS

TO ISCA

VINDOCLADIA

VECTIS
INSULA

DURNOVARIA

OCEANUS BRITANNICUS

CHAPTER ONE

January AD 370

He still hears her screams, even now. Once he thought that time would fade them into silence, but he was wrong.

It is night in the Long Limestone Hills, one of the endless nights of midwinter, moonless, although when dawn comes a new moon – her moon – will rise unseen in the south-eastern sky. Inside the villa, opening off one of the long corridors, is a bedroom with brightly frescoed walls and a mosaic floor portraying Bacchus surrounded by dancing maenads and satyrs. An ornamental bronze brazier stands on tripod legs, the glowing charcoal in its deep tray softening the January chill.

A woman, young and beautiful, sleeps peacefully beside him, but his own sleep is fitful, his head turning from side to side, his feet pushing against the blankets as he tries to move away from things that only he can see.

'*Canio! … Canio!*'

Her screams make the pictures inside his head expand to unbearable vividness and suddenly he is awake, suddenly still, staring upwards into a darkness relieved only by the glow from the brazier and the faint starlight seeping in around the window shutters. Slowly he sits up, breathing heavily, scenting the air like a wary animal.

'Marcia? … Marcia, are you here?' he whispers.

But now the woman too has woken, and sleepily she asks what troubles him. 'Was it those bad dreams again?'

'Did you smell it?'

'Smell what?'

'Honeysuckle,' he murmurs, but so softly that when she replies he realises that she cannot have heard him correctly.

'It's only the charcoal in the brazier,' she whispers huskily, leaning over and gently rubbing his shoulder as though comforting a child, her body warm against his own bare skin. 'You know how the smell of anything burning can set off your bad dreams.' Still only half awake she stifles a yawn with a cupped hand. 'Now go back to sleep, and when you open your eyes again it'll be morning and all the dreams will be long gone.'

But he does not sleep. He lies there – his body unmoving, his mind churning – until long after the woman has drifted back into oblivion. Then he swings his long legs out of the bed, stands and dresses quickly, almost noiselessly, in warm outdoor clothing. He throws a cloak of beaver fur around his shoulders, closes the bedroom door quietly behind him and starts walking down the long corridor where oil lamps burn in niches set into the shadowed walls. He waves away a sleepy maidservant, waits until she has gone back to her room, then unlocks and slips out of a side door and makes his way towards the stables. It is a bitter night for a long journey, but that scent of honeysuckle is still strong in his memory, calling to him, summoning him.

He both longs for her to be there and dreads her being there.

CHAPTER TWO

Mid June AD 368 – Eighteen Months Earlier

'House of Hades, there it is again! Even you heard it that time, didn't you, *Acting* Primicerius?'

Canio twisted around in Antares' saddle. 'For fornication's sake, Peltrasius, it's only some damned dog.'

'Dog? I've never heard a dog make a noise like that. It sounded more like a wolf to me.'

'It can't be a wolf – didn't I hear Galenus say that your *Comes* Theodosius strangled them all with his bare hands when he got bored with slaughtering barbarians?'

'Oh, very funny, *Acting* Primicerius. But dog or wolf, that's the fourth time I've heard it in the last mile, louder each time. The damned thing's beginning to get on my nerves – if I catch sight of it I'll skewer the bastard.'

'You do that.' *And see if you can skewer yourself while you're at it – I could do with a laugh.*

There were three soldiers – himself, Peltrasius and Galenus – riding a desultory patrol through the green summer countryside, following the line of the Fosse Way back towards Corinium, although they were still more than five miles south of that city and it was already late afternoon, sultry and oppressive, the threat of thunder in the air.

Canio was bored, and as he rode his mind began wandering back over the events of the past long year, the year of the *Barbarica Conspiratio,* those seemingly co-ordinated invasions by the Scotti and other Hibernian tribes, by the Picts, the painted people from north of Hadrian's Wall, and by Saxons and Franks from across the Oceanus Germanicus. He gave a bitter snigger as he recalled the opening words of the recent proclamation from the Praetorian Prefect of the Gauls, declaring officially that the *Conspiratio* was at last over, something that Canio and just about everyone else had known for at least two months.

It had begun, as far as he could remember, *"Due entirely to your vigilance, wisdom, valour, skill at arms and the terror of your name, most sacred emperor Valentinian, those few barbarians who evaded the might of your sword have now been driven back into the sea from whence they crawled, howling for mercy ..."* Canio hadn't bothered to read it all: he knew a work of fiction when he saw it. He had written several himself over the past year.

These current patrols, of which he was more than a little weary, were a response to the continuing depredations of roving bands of army deserters and runaway slaves, which the chaos of the *Conspiratio* had both spawned and cloaked.

But as Canio, his thoughts now turning to his favourite Corinium *taberna* and pleasant female company, as they often did, started to pull ahead of his two companions, Peltrasius called out, 'What's the hurry, *Acting* Primicerius? We're still waiting to hear that story of how your brave Prefect Aemilianus charged a hundred savage Hibernians all by himself.'

The request irritated Canio. 'Go suck your sword, Ganymede. At most there were no more than fifteen or twenty of the bastards. Besides, you've heard the story before, so why in the names of the Mothers of the Hills would you want to hear it again?'

'Why? Because Galenus has never heard it – have you Galenus? Not from Aemilianus's loyal second in command anyway.'

Canio breathed an obscenity, then shrugged. 'All right my brave lads, I'll tell you what happened that day.' He let Antares slow to an amble. 'If nothing else it'll pass the time. And everyone who hears it laughs like a donkey, especially those who've ever met my glorious leader.'

They were now in an area of open woodland alongside the Fosse Way, still heading north towards Corinium. 'You know, Canio, I find it surprisingly easy to picture all your friends laughing like donkeys, particularly your lady – '

At that moment the unseen dog howled again, now startlingly loud and close. But before Canio could so much as curse, he saw a man burst out of hiding from behind the massive trunk of a pollard oak not fifteen yards distant and begin running wildly away.

He rapidly lost sight of him among the trees, although not before noticing that the man was dressed much as he himself was, in a long tunic and loose trousers tucked into soft leather ankle boots, but without the helmet, scale cuirass and long *spatha* cavalry sword he wore.

'It's another of those damned deserters!' Peltrasius shouted, lashing his horse forwards with the free ends of the reins. Galenus followed. Canio hesitated, then reluctantly decided that he'd better do likewise.

The man ran like a hare, but after a wild gallop through the woodland, swerving between bushes and trees and ducking under low boughs, the three horsemen managed to corner him in a grassy clearing.

As the horses' flanks jostled the panting captive into an ever-smaller space, Canio ran his eyes over the man. He looked to be in his middle twenties, quite tall and well-built, but there was a travel-stained and unkempt air about him which suggested that he'd seen some hard living in the last few weeks. 'So, what's your name, soldier?' he asked. 'And tell me, what unit are you hurrying back from leave to rejoin?'

The man did not reply immediately. He stood, chest heaving, his head moving from side to side, trying to peer between the horses as if something beyond them was a source of greater anxiety than the soldiers themselves.

'Come on, don't be shy, tell us all your name,' Canio demanded impatiently.

The man looked directly at him for the first time. 'Orgillus, sir. The name's Orgillus.'

'Don't call him "sir;" he's only a lousy civil guard.'

Canio ignored Peltrasius. 'And your unit?'

'Unit?'

'Yes, soldier, your fornicating unit. Or have you been gone so long you can't even remember what it was?' Thus Peltrasius's further contribution.

'The *Numerus Moesiacorum*. I'm sure you've heard of them – we were one of the units that fought under the command of *Comes* Nectaridus in those desperate first days of the *Conspiratio*.'

'Ah, the late lamented *Comes Maritimi Tractus*. I heard he got a spear in the back, running away from a rabble of Saxons. Is that true?' Galenus asked.

'That's a damned lie! He fought like a lion, just like the rest of us did.'

But dead heroes look just like dead cowards. I've seen enough of both to know that. 'Where are you supposed to be stationed now?' Canio asked.

'I'm stationed, temporarily, at the port of Noviomagus, on the south coast of the province of Maxima Caesariensis.' Orgillus shot another uneasy glance around him.

'I know where the lousy place is; been through it a couple of times myself.' Canio's eyes instinctively followed Orgillus's own and he looked all around and then at the heavens, where in an otherwise blue sky a dark mass of thundercloud was towering upwards. 'Well, we won't detain you much longer. Just give us all a quick look at your furlough pass and then you can go on your way.'

'I … haven't got it any more. Got set upon by a bunch of damned deserters a couple of days ago. They took my pass, money, sword – just about everything except the clothes I stood up in. That's why I ran when I first saw you three: I thought you might be part of the same pack of wolves. Once bitten, as they say,' Orgillus added.

'Indeed they do,' Peltrasius agreed. 'But if you've got no pass then we'll have to search you, won't we, *Acting Primacerius*?'

Canio shot Peltrasius an exasperated glance. 'Yes, I suppose we must. Sorry, Orgillus, but it's standing orders. For all we know you might be a deserter yourself.'

Orgillus looked as if he might protest, but Canio and Peltrasius were already dismounting and handing their reins to Galenus. He shrugged. 'If you've got your orders then I suppose I mustn't complain.'

'Hands behind your head and spread your legs. I'm sure you know the drill,' Canio said briskly. His thoughts were still on that *taberna* in Corinium.

'I'm no deserter,' Orgillus said, slowly raising his arms. 'But would it really matter if I should have been back from furlough a week or two ago? I mean, everybody knows that *Comes* Theodosius has issued an amnesty for all deserters and furlough men who've overstayed their time.' His eyes went from face to face, but it seemed that those faces were giving nothing away. He sighed. 'Look, the truth is I met this woman in Glevum and stayed a little longer than perhaps I should have done. Haven't you done the same once or twice, brother?' This to Peltrasius.

'No, never,' Peltrasius replied coldly.

Canio grinned. 'No use pulling that teat. I've heard he only joined the *Jovii* because he thought he'd meet some fellow Ganymedes in that outfit. Wouldn't know what to do with a woman, even if you dangled a naked one over his bed.'

Peltrasius coloured at the insult. 'But haven't you heard?' he hissed at Orgillus, 'Theodosius's amnesty ran out at the end of May, and here we are now in sunny June. Looks like you've got a problem, brother.'

Unbuckling the flap of the large leather pouch hanging from

Orgillus's belt, Canio began ferreting inside. 'Oh, shame on you, saying they'd taken all your money,' he scolded as he counted out a dozen little silver siliquae. 'And what's this?' he added a few moments later, as his probing fingers emerged with a small fabric bag from which he proceeded to pour out six gold solidi. 'Oh, well done; you've managed to save a whole year's pay. That lady friend of yours must have been a damned sight cheaper to keep happy than most of the tarts I've known.'

'Is that all there is?' Galenus asked, craning his neck to get a better look.

'That's the lot, apart from a few bits of cloth.' Then Canio's fingertips felt something beneath. 'Wait a bit though, there's something wrapped up in them.' He drew it out and peeled off the rags.

'It's gold, isn't it?' The excitement showed in Peltrasius's voice as he stared at the figurine of a woman cradled in one of Canio's large hands. She was about five inches high and almost black, except for one area on the drapery which gleamed bright yellow.

For a long moment Canio stared at the lady, as the bitter memories came flooding into his mind. The lady's blank eyes stared back.

'What do you think?' He suddenly tossed her high into the air for Peltrasius to catch.

'No!' In the instant before Peltrasius could react, Orgillus, quick as lightning, had sprung forwards and caught the figurine himself. Then, dodging between the horses, he started running madly into the depths of the encircling woodland.

'Come back here you bastard or I'll gut you!' Peltrasius bawled and started racing after him.

'Oh, let him go!' A few moments later, when Peltrasius showed no sign of heeding him and had disappeared among the trees, Canio shouted, 'It's not –'

A piercing scream shattered the summer calm.

'Gold,' he concluded quietly. He felt a muscle in one cheek

twitch: he had heard screams like that too many times over the past year, and each one had brought back bad memories of his years on the *Limes Germanicus*. 'Stay here,' he muttered to Galenus, then walked across the glade and into the trees.

Orgillus was sitting slumped on the ground. He was moaning softly and clutching his belly with both hands, his face as pale as the elder blossoms that smothered several of the surrounding bushes. Between and over his interlaced fingers the bright red blood was trickling in several thin rivulets and soaking through his tunic. Canio guessed that he had turned, intending to plead with his pursuer, and then Peltrasius had stabbed him. If the wound was of any depth then he was as good as dead.

Indifferent now to his victim, Peltrasius was examining the object for which Orgillus had risked his life. Canio looked first at the stricken Orgillus, then at Peltrasius. Almost without conscious thought his right hand slid towards the hilt of the scabbarded *spatha* dangling from his left hip.

Peltrasius was scratching at the metal with a fingernail, and as he did so his face contorted with anger. 'It's not gold, only some sort of *orichalcum* – damned worthless brass!' He spat the words out in disgust, then with an obscene oath hurled the figurine away into the undergrowth.

Canio ignored him. He turned to Orgillus and asked, 'So what was so special about it?' But Orgillus said nothing, his eyes staring intently at the ground, as though trying to control the waves of agony that must have been pulsing through him with every beat of his heart.

Peltrasius was still furious. 'Damned cretin: you'd think a grown man could tell the difference between brass and gold.'

'Yes, only someone with less brains than a shit-fly would confuse the two,' Canio replied, not even trying to keep the contempt out of his voice.

Peltrasius looked sharply at him. Canio returned the stare. *Go on – go for your sword. Give me the excuse.*

Peltrasius turned away, muttering something inaudible.

'Have you got him?' came Galenus's voice.

'Yes, I got him all right. We're done here,' Peltrasius called back. 'Come on, *Acting* Primicerius; don't you want to get back to Corinium and your feather bed?'

Canio watched him walking away, then looked down at Orgillus, who looked back with seemingly unfocussed eyes. He hesitated, then turned and followed Peltrasius back to where Galenus still held their horses.

'So where is he?'

'Back there. Dead, or as good as,' Peltrasius replied brusquely.

'Christus, did you have to kill him?'

But Peltrasius was already remounting and didn't bother to reply.

* * *

The three soldiers began riding northwards again, Canio silent or answering only in monosyllables, Peltrasius describing to Galenus his own techniques for thrusting a sword into the body of a man in such a way as to miss any bones which might turn or blunt the blade.

After half a mile, Canio, who had been increasingly lagging behind, swore loudly and reined in. 'Damned horse is going lame again.'

The other two halted.

'It's nothing serious; all it needs is to rest awhile. I wanted to exchange him for another mount when I was last in barracks, but the spare nags there were even worse. You go on – I'll meet you back in Corinium.'

Before either could object, he added, 'Here, have the first drinks on me.' He lobbed each soldier one of the siliquae he had taken from Orgillus.

They caught the coins, then fixed him with ironic stares and waited motionless. He gave an exasperated sigh and divided the rest of the money ostensibly fairly equally between them. But Peltrasius and Galenus only received two solidi each whereas Canio, who had managed to retain one inside the bag when he tipped out the other six, kept three.

'Do you really think I'd cheat fellow soldiers?' he asked as he handed each his share of the spoils. He didn't wait for an answer. 'I'll meet up with you back in Corinium,' he repeated.

'Whatever you say,' Peltrasius replied, and parodied a salute as he and Galenus started off. 'See you there then, *Acting* Primicerius.'

'Unless I see you first, shit-fly,' Canio breathed as he waved back. He slid out of the saddle, crouched, and began carefully examining one of Antares' front legs. He was still doing so when Peltrasius and Galenus disappeared from sight, and for a little while afterwards, just in case they returned. Then he remounted and cantered back towards the woodland.

To his surprise, Orgillus was not where they had left him. He searched and soon found him, sitting with his back against the deeply fissured bark of an ancient oak. His eyes were closed, his breathing rapid and shallow. But his hands, red and glistening with his own blood, now clasped the figurine. What agony it must have cost him to retrieve it, Canio did not care to imagine. He dismounted and saw the dying man's eyes slowly open and look towards him as he approached.

Canio wondered if he could actually see him. 'Want a drink?' he asked, holding out the small goatskin that had been hanging from his saddle.

Orgillus shook his head weakly.

'Probably just as well. Water can be bad for a man with a belly wound.' Canio hesitated, then asked, 'Is there anyone ... anyone you want told?'

Orgillus was staring down at the figurine. Then he spoke, slowly and deliberately, as though every word brought more pain. 'No. There's no one, not now. The hound – is it still here ... have you seen it?'

'I've seen no hound. It must be long gone.'

'Good ... Good ... I thought she was my protector, but I should have thrown her into the lake. That must have been what she wanted. In the lake, with the gold.'

'The gold? What gold?' Suddenly Canio was listening very hard.

'The gold we threw into the lake. You can have it all, if you take her back.'

'To the lake? Where? Where is this lake?'

'On the far side of the Great Marshes.'

'What? That's way south of the Lead Hills.'

'Yes.' Orgillus nodded as vigorously as the pain would allow. 'But there's enough gold in that lake to make you a very rich man.' Canio saw his face tighten as another wave of pain hit him. 'Swear you'll take her back ... for pity's sake, swear you will,' he pleaded.

Canio looked into his eyes and saw the terror of death staring back at him. 'All right: tell me exactly where this lake is and I'll go there.'

'And take her?'

'If that's what you want.'

'You'll never find the gold without her. Only she knows where it lies now.'

'How do you mean – "only she knows"?' Canio asked, suddenly uneasy.

For a long, long moment Orgillus's eyes closed, as if he were summoning up the last reserves of his strength. Slowly opening them again he said, 'There were five of us ...'

'Who?'

'My comrades. Together we carried the gold from the villas and the temple where we ... most came from the temple.'

'What temple?'

'Just a burnt shell now.'

'But where was it?'

'Down in the South Country. Far away in the hills. We'd never have found it by ourselves.'

'Was it near the lake?'

'No. Not near. A long day's walk away to the west.'

'So why did you throw the gold into the lake?'

'Because of the dream. We were camped at the lake, out of sight of the road, when she sent it to Rautio. He said he saw us weighed down by the sacks of gold we were carrying, scarcely able to move –'

'There were sacks of it?' Canio interrupted, scarcely able to believe his ears.

Orgillus nodded weakly. 'Rautio said that in the dream he saw soldiers riding towards us. But we couldn't run away because the sacks were so heavy, and all the time the soldiers were coming closer. And then he said he saw her, the Dark Lady, standing beside the lake, pointing at the water, showing us what to do. And afterwards, after we'd emptied the gold out of the sacks and thrown every lump of it far out into the water, then we were able to run like the wind. Faster than the soldiers' horses, Rautio said. And when he woke in the morning he told us about the dream, and what we had to do to save ourselves.'

'And you actually believed this Rautio?' Canio was sure he wouldn't have.

Orgillus nodded. 'He convinced us. And the dream came true – because soon after leaving the lake we saw soldiers ride by. They were the same soldiers from the dream, Rautio said. We were hiding in the reeds, but we knew they were looking for us, because that damned priest was with them, looking this way and that.'

'Priest? What priest?'

'The one who led us to the gold. And to her. He wanted her, but I thought I heard her whisper to me inside my head that I shouldn't give her up, and if I didn't, then she'd be my protector. The priest cursed us then, but we chased him away. I wish we'd killed the bastard like we killed the others. He must have been the one who told the soldiers. Damn him! Damn him!' Orgillus's feeble anger flared and then died, crushed by the pain.

'So why didn't you go back for the gold after the soldiers had gone?'

Orgillus slowly shook his head. 'Soldiers everywhere. Rautio said we should split up. Go our separate ways. But before we parted we swore an oath that we'd all meet together at that lake on the first new moon after midsummer and recover the gold.'

Orgillus's face was now a white mask beaded with sweat. 'I should have thrown her into the lake with the gold. That must have been what she wanted: I know that now. If I had … But if you do it for me – for her – then I know she'll save me.'

Canio said nothing, and Orgillus, as if terrified that he still might not understand his meaning, went on, 'Don't you see? If you throw her into the lake for me, then, even if I seem to be dead, she'll bring me back to life again. She can do that, I know she can. Please, I'm begging you – swear you'll do it!'

'If that's what you want.'

Orgillus seemed to sense reluctance still, seemed too to guess the reason. 'Look, I'm certain the gold is still there in the lake. It must be there – nobody saw us throw it in, and a week ago I met a man I'd once known in Londinium. He told me that Rautio and one of the other men who were with me at the lake were dead. He'd heard that they'd been killed when they tried to raid a villa down near Durnovaria, so it's almost certain that the others are dead too.'

'All right, I'll do it.'

'You swear it? Swear it in the name of whatever god or goddess you truly believe in?'

Canio was well aware that those who knew him, or thought they knew him, might have said that there was no such a deity. Or perhaps suggested either Bacchus or Venus as the most likely candidates. 'Rest easy, brother. If it means that much to you then of course I'll swear it.'

'Swear on her! Hold her and swear!' Orgillus held out the figurine with shaking hands that were sticky with blood.

Canio hesitated, uncertain now, a voice in his head screaming a warning. But all that gold … He crouched and gripped the head of the figurine hard between the thumb and forefinger of his left hand. 'I swear it.'

'Say it all,' Orgillus pleaded. 'Say you'll take her back and throw her in.' His voice was rapidly growing feebler now and death was in his face.

Despite himself, Canio felt a surge of pity for the dying man. 'All right, you have my word. I swear I'll take her back to that lake, and I swear I'll throw her into it.'

Orgillus gave a great sigh and the hands gripping the figurine dropped back onto his lap.

'But where exactly is the lake? If I can't find it …'

'On the south side of the Great Marshes,' Orgillus began, his voice barely audible now. 'Several lakes, near a road. But go there. She'll show you which one.'

'But that's … how will she show me?'

But for Orgillus, time had almost ended. 'Remember … Always remember … She heard you swear to take her back … If you don't, her vengeance will be terrible. It's you she'll be watching now.'

'But how will she show me where the gold is?' Canio pleaded.

Orgillus struggled to speak, but he was so weak now. 'She'll be there … She, or …' His voice trailed away, his head slowly sinking onto his chest. He appeared to be trying to say something more, but death was overtaking him too rapidly and whatever words might have been forming in his dying brain emerged only as a faint and meaningless slur of sounds.

* * *

Canio waited, hunched and motionless, until he was sure that Orgillus would say nothing more. Then he rose quickly and walked away to a place where he could see the southern horizon and the vastness of the blue summer sky with its skeins of high, white clouds. The thundercloud had vanished. He needed space

15

and time to think. He wanted that gold, and was determined that nothing was going to stop him from getting it. It was only that little figurine that made him hesitate. But slowly the sunlight and the bright sky soothed his doubts and fears, and his mind filled with thoughts of all the wonderful things the gold could buy. Yet however hard he tried he couldn't stop those same thoughts from returning to that damned figurine.

He strode back and prised it free from the dead fingers that still held it so tightly. Snatching a couple of large hazel leaves from a bush he used them to wipe off the sticky, congealing blood, and holding it in a shaft of sunlight that came slanting between the trees he examined the figurine closely for the first time.

The lady wore an ankle-length dress with long sleeves, loose and flowing and gathered at the waist by a belt from which hung what appeared to be a coiled whip. Her arms were bent at the elbows, a flaming torch held upright in one hand, a short sword in the other.

Her face was unsmiling, grim even, and curled protectively around her feet and forming the base of the figurine was a great hound, its lips drawn back to reveal cruel, pointed teeth. Canio could almost hear the growl.

And he knew who she was: had known from that first moment when he took her from Orgillus's pouch. When he had last seen her she had three heads, but one or three, he knew her. She was the goddess Hecate.

And as Hecate stared unblinkingly up at him there came a memory from childhood. A memory of a woman's husky voice whispering to him beside a small altar in a cold room in a cold city.

'I love her, but I fear her too. She is the goddess of wildernesses and wild places, of the darkness of the night and its terrors. And she is the Queen of Ghosts, guiding them across the frontiers between this world and the next. One day we will sacrifice to her, you and I, standing together at dawn in some *lonely place where three ways meet and a new moon is rising unseen.'*

For a moment he felt his eyes prick with tears. Then he swore and shook his head. Angrily he began tossing the figurine high into the air. Each time higher than the last, higher and higher, and each time snatching it out of the air one-handed as it fell. Finally he grabbed it one last time, strode over to where Antares was tethered and thrust it carelessly into the depths of one of his polished leather saddlebags.

Decided now, he went back and squatted once more in front of Orgillus. He had to be sure. Raising the man's chin with one hand, with the other he eased up an eyelid and saw that the eye was filming over, the light behind it gone forever. With a confirmatory grunt he let the dead man's head loll back onto his chest.

'It's you she'll be watching now!' The words were only inside his head, but so loud that for a fearful moment he thought that the dead man had actually spoken them again.

He decided to bury Orgillus, prompted partly by conscience but mostly by a furtive animal instinct to hide anything which could indicate that he knew of the gold. Walking over to Antares he unstrapped the entrenching tool from the saddle and began hacking out a grave in the centre of the glade. He chopped and dug into the rooty soil until the hole was about three feet deep, then dragged Orgillus's still-limp body over to it, flopped it in and began backfilling. Suddenly he stopped.

Will I look like that one day, as someone carelessly shovels the earth back on top of me? If anyone bothers to bury me at all.

It was an unwelcome thought, but one which would not go away. Over the years he had seen too many bodies lying unburied, horrible things that some comforting part of his brain had tried to pretend had always looked as they did, had never been living men like him at all.

Reluctantly he conceded to himself that the grave was

distinctly shallow, although probably deep enough to deter wolves and foxes. He hesitated, then impulsively stepped down into the grave, one foot on either side of Orgillus, and placed one of his own solidi under the dead man's tongue. 'If you should ever meet him,' he muttered, 'pay the ferryman – and put in a good word for me while he's rowing you across the Styx.'

Vaulting out, he grabbed the entrenching tool and again began shovelling the rich, crumbly earth back into the grave, trampling it down until Orgillus, who had so recently been alive under the sun, was hidden forever in the chill darkness of eternal night. Finally, he scraped leaf mould back over the raw earth and scattered it around until he was satisfied that the grave site appeared no different from the surrounding area.

That done, he had no wish to linger there. After strapping the entrenching tool back behind the saddle he mounted Antares, broke clear of the woodland, and set the horse trotting briskly northwards, keeping well clear of the Fosse Way. He had resolved not to look back, but when he had gone about half a mile and was approaching the crest of a small ridge which would have shut out the last sight of the trees under which Orgillus lay, something – he could never have said what – made him stop and do just that.

The large black hound was some two hundred yards away, out on the open grassland. In the brief time before his eyes properly focused on it, Canio was almost certain that it had been moving straight towards him through the long grasses. Now it just sat on its haunches, looking in his direction. From that distance there seemed nothing remarkable about it: simply a very big dog, black as jet. Except that Canio couldn't shake off the suspicion that it had been following him.

He flicked the reins and rode on, over the ridge and down the other side. There he reined in behind a large hawthorn bush, turned and stared at the crest of the ridge. He waited until his eyes hurt from the brightness of the southern sky. Nothing came. At last, vaguely angry with himself, he set off again for Corinium. Several times on the journey he found himself unable to resist looking back, but never caught sight of the hound again.

CHAPTER THREE

In the long summer evening Canio reached Corinium. He had never rejoined the Fosse Way, having no wish to meet Peltrasius and Galenus on the road, unlikely though that was given the time interval between them. Like a cat guarding its new kill, he wanted no company but his own.

As they loomed ever larger, grim and stark and almost black against the skyline, he studied the line of large ballistae which had been hurriedly mounted on top of the city walls in the early days of the *Conspiratio*. Even now, at the insistence of Governor Laetinianus, their regular army crews still manned them day and night, relieving the boredom of the long watches by squinting down the arrow channels of the giant crossbows and taking aim at anyone or anything that moved on the little plain beyond the walls. A few weeks before they had amused themselves by shooting several sheep in a small flock being driven into the city, then taking bets on which stricken animal would be the last to show signs of life.

Clattering under the echoing arches of the Calleva Gate he nodded to the sentries, then trotted up the wide street until he reached the forum and the guards' stables. There he turned Antares over to Bupitus, the head ostler.

Bupitus, morbidly inquisitive, wanted to hear more about the killing of the deserter, which he had overheard Peltrasius casually mention to another soldier when he arrived in the late afternoon.

'Tell you later,' Canio muttered as he walked rapidly out of the stables, having first extracted the Hecate figurine from a saddlebag while Bupitus's back was turned.

As he walked into the main dining hall of the barracks he saw half a dozen soldiers and civil guards lingering over a late supper, desultory conversation alternating with crude jokes. He was less than overjoyed to see that Peltrasius and Galenus were there, sitting with young Quintillus of the civil guard. He returned a couple of salutes, then sat down at one of the massive oak tables, its surface grain raised by the innumerable swabbings it had received over the years.

Out of the corner of his eye he noticed Peltrasius nudge Galenus. 'And a good evening to you, *Acting* Primicerius. Tell me, how's your horse?'

Canio gave him a look calculated to say that he would much prefer his space to his company. 'He's well, Peltrasius, in fact he's very well. Turned out the trouble wasn't his old lameness after all, just a stone wedged in his hoof. Which reminds me, he asked me to give you a message.'

'You don't say.'

'He did, truly. Although, strictly speaking the message was only from one part of him. Now, what was it that he said? Oh, I remember now. He said, "*Salve*, Peltrasius … greetings from one horse's arse to another." At least, that's what it sounded like at the time. Maybe it was just the oats talking.'

Peltrasius gave a guttural snarl and his right hand twitched down towards the hilt of his sword. Canio bared his teeth in a mirthless grin, while all around the various conversations faltered.

In the resulting silence Peltrasius hissed, 'And what about his illustrious master? How's he feeling at the end of this fine summer's day? Does he think that the gods are smiling on him as warmly as the sun did?'

Canio sensed something coming, but didn't really care what it was. Lack of sleep can act like wine. And besides, his mind was on other things.

Why Hecate? Why her? Of all the gods and goddesses that it could have been, why did it have to be her?

'His master's never been better, Peltrasius. He's touched by your concern. And how's yourself, my hero? Managed to stab any more unarmed men in the guts since we parted company? No? Sad. Never mind, there's always tomorrow.'

Canio didn't wait for a reply but turned to Quintillus and asked, 'And what masterpiece of the cook's art is Deuccus tempting us with this evening?'

Quintillus pulled a face. 'Well Primicerius, to be honest, it looks and smells like something your horse itself might have produced. On a day when he was off his feed.'

'In that case I think I'll deny myself the pleasure and get something better on the way back to my room.' He stood up, kicked his chair back under the table, threw the assembled company a mocking salute and started towards the door. The Fighting Cocks *taberna* was where he wanted to be anyway.

But it seemed that Peltrasius was not to be cheated of his retaliation. 'Have you met him yet?' he asked casually.

'Met who?' Canio replied impatiently. Mentally he was already halfway to The Fighting Cocks and the first cup of wine of the day, always the most delicious.

'Why, your new primicerius, of course.' Peltrasius appeared surprised at Canio's ignorance. 'Haven't seen him myself yet, but I was told that he was here in the city last night, looking around and getting the feel of his new command.'

'I don't believe you, shit-fly.' Canio turned from Peltrasius and looked straight at Quintillus. 'Tell me that's a damned lie.'

Quintillus gave an exaggerated shrug of apology. 'I'm afraid it's true, Primicerius. Like Peltrasius says, he was here last night. Didn't Prefect Aemilianus tell you?'

'How the fornication could he? I haven't seen the man for the best part of a week. Anyway, who is this "new primicerius"?'

Galenus coughed. 'His name's Aulus Ulpius Marullinus. And – this is the bit you're really going to like, Canio – they say he's a cousin of Aemilianus. That's what the rumour is anyway, although I must admit Aemilianus hasn't said so himself.'

'No, I'll bet he hasn't, the bast...' Canio just managed to rein in his tongue. There were too many ears about nowadays – ears belonging to men he couldn't trust, fellow soldiers or not. 'So where is he now?'

'Who, Aemilianus? He's over at ...' Peltrasius began.

Canio just stared at him, moving his lips soundlessly to spell out an obscene phrase.

'Oh, your new primicerius. On his way back to Londinium Augusta, I suppose. He was on the Vicarius's staff there. Still is I suppose, until he takes up his new duties in ... how long did Aemilianus say it would be, Galenus?' Canio was sure that Peltrasius hadn't really forgotten.

'Four weeks, I think he said. Or was it only two? Can't remember,' Galenus replied.

'Four, two? Well, which was it, Quintillus?'

'I don't know Canio, sir, and that's the truth. I wasn't around when Prefect Aemilianus came in.'

Canio exhaled in noisy exasperation. 'And just what did this Marullinus do on the Vicarius's staff? Does anyone know that?'

'Well I heard, and this is only a rumour mind,' Peltrasius said in a stage whisper, glancing from side to side as if he didn't want anyone else to hear, 'I heard that he looked after the Vicarius's pet dogs. You know, fed them their dinner, took them for walks on leads around the streets, cleaned up any little offerings and libations that they happened to leave in the sacred halls. Those sorts of things. But in the end,' Peltrasius sighed, 'the worry and responsibility of it all became too much for him and he begged the Vicarius for an easier job. So, they demoted him and gave him yours instead, Canio. Sod of a life, isn't it?'

Galenus laughed out loud, but Quintillus made heroic efforts to keep a straight face, right up to the moment when it became impossible to do so. Then, to hide the unstoppable grin, he snatched up a cup and gulped down the watered wine that remained in it. A mistake. A moment later it all came flying back as the laughter that had been welling up inside him finally erupted. Fortunately for his relations with his acting primicerius it was Peltrasius and Galenus who caught most of the choking blast. As he left, Canio could hear Peltrasius cursing Quintillus for a cretin.

Abandoning thoughts of The Fighting Cocks he instead called at The Twin Serpents. There he "bought" a full goatskin of good wine from Reburrus, telling him to charge it to his account, although both men were well aware that in local folklore the phrase, "When Canio pays his account", had already become synonymous with "never".

* * *

Back in his room, which was Saturninus's old room above the Verulamium Gateway, Canio took the Hecate figurine out of his belt pouch, gazed at it, then stood it on the small table beside his bed. Sitting on the bed he unstoppered the goatskin and took a long draw of the neat wine, before leaning back and contemplating the figurine again. Time passed, evening turned into night, and after stoppering the now nearly-empty goatskin for the last time he fell into a doze. And as he slept, the long-suppressed memories began to bubble up from the depths of his unconscious mind.

He sees again the bleak plain that lies outside the high stone walls of the cold city. He sees the trampled grass speckled with frozen snow, the tall stake and the bundles of brushwood piled around it. And he sees the lone woman, her wrists bound in front of her, walking slowly towards the stake. He hears the harsh, jeering voices of the great crowd of people on the plain, but they must be somewhere behind him, out of sight. For Canio, there are only two people on that plain: himself and the woman. Ever closer she comes, and when she is no more than a dozen yards from the stake he sees her turn her head towards him and hears her scream his name.

'Canio! Canio! Give me the goddess. If I can hold her then she'll save me – I know she will. Please ... please ... let me hold her before it's too late!'

He looks down and sees that he is clutching a little three-headed figurine of Hecate Triformis. All he has to do is run to the woman and thrust the figurine into her hands, and then the goddess will somehow spirit her away. But fear has paralysed his limbs and he stands as immobile as the stake itself. He can only watch as the woman approaches nearer and nearer to that terrible stake. Again she turns her head towards him, and again she screams his name, so close to him now that he can clearly see the terror in her eyes as they stare directly into his own.

He clamps his eyes shut, time blurs, and when he opens them again the woman is bound to the stake and the flames are crackling and roaring up around her, shrivelling her black in the fire's orange heart.

I couldn't do it, Marcia! I tried – I tried – but something froze me like ice. Say you believe me! Just once, say you believe me ... please!

He woke. It was night and he was both sweating and shivering with cold. Confused, with wits still fuddled from the wine, he lay in the darkness looking towards the narrow windows of the room, which glowed with a pale light that seemed to be coming from below. A dull, irritated bewilderment possessed him: it was June for pity's sake, so why was it so damned cold? He sat up on the bed and almost vomited as a wave of nausea hit him and the room started spinning around.

If that bastard Reburrus slipped something into that lousy wine I'll geld him with a rusty saw!

But slowly the room settled, and he levered himself up and staggered over to one of the windows.

Leaning heavily against the icy stone sill he stared disbelievingly out at a monochrome winter landscape of pristine white snow dotted with a few stark black trees, a landscape which stretched away into the far distance under a moonless sky that glittered with countless stars. Unable to believe what he was seeing, he closed his eyes for several moments then opened them again, only to find that it was still deep winter, still bone-achingly cold, each exhaled breath a short-lived cloud of white mist.

It was only then that he noticed, out on the snow, the great black hound and the woman in the pale, ankle-length dress and hooded cloak. The hood was folded back on her shoulders, revealing a face of severe, glacial beauty and abundant dark hair tightly coiled on top of her head. They stood in the snow, seemingly no more than fifty yards from his window. Perhaps, he thought, it was only an illusion created by the featureless snow, but both woman and hound seemed to be of greater than mortal size. And they were so unnervingly still.

Why he had not spotted them the moment he looked out puzzled him. They stood side by side, motionless in the silence of the intense cold. Suddenly, with a stab of something very close to fear, Canio realised from the tilt of their heads that both were staring directly up at him.

Shivering, he stepped quickly back and turned away from the window. As he did so something caught his eye, a tiny green light glowing in the darkness on the far side of the room. He watched, fascinated but wary, as the light seemed to sway almost imperceptibly from side to side, like a miniature candle flame. Cautiously he began walking towards it. Even before he was close enough to be sure he had guessed that it was Hecate's torch, lighting his way towards her in the darkness. Up close, the flame was bright enough to cast a faint green glow over the entire figurine and onto the palm of his hand as he stretched out his right arm towards it. Feeling a strange compulsion to do so, he lowered the tip of his middle finger until it was almost touching the torch. For a moment he felt nothing, then ...

'Merda!' He snatched his hand away and sucked the smarting fingertip, the cool saliva soothing the burn.

The pain died almost as quickly as it had come, and into

Canio's still-muzzy brain there crept the thought that this too had to be a dream. Nothing else made sense, even though it did all seem so real – the cold and the woman out on the snow and the green fire. He wondered if it were possible for a man to be aware that he was dreaming while still trapped inside that dream?

Impulsively he thought of going back to the window to check if the woman and hound were still there, but the possibility of encountering again those black, baleful stares made him pause. Then another wave of nausea swept over him and suddenly he'd had enough. He flopped down onto the bed, shut his eyes and wriggled under the blankets. At that moment it was the only course of action he could think of that even came close to making sense.

* * *

It was not long after sunrise when he became aware of a quiet tapping at his door. At first he ignored it, but it persisted. He gave a slurred roar of, 'Go away, damn you! Can't a man get some sleep around here?' then rolled away from the light and buried his head in the pillow.

'Primicerius Canio … can I come in and talk with you for a little while?' There was a pause, then the voice said, 'I knew your predecessor, Primicerius Saturninus.'

The voice sounded female; young female. Canio slowly sat upright, then waited for his head to fall off. It didn't. He cautiously opened his eyes and stared down at the middle finger of his right hand. To his relief there was no sign of a burn. It seemed that the glowing torch and the figures in the snow really had been nothing more than another bad dream. He heaved himself off the bed, walked unsteadily to the door, unbolted and swung it open. The woman standing at the threshold was indeed young, no more than sixteen he guessed, although she wore a long hooded cloak that left little but her head, hands and feet visible. The hood had been eased back to reveal abundant dark red hair swept up and coiled into a tight bun on the top of her

27

head. Her face was pale and strangely attractive; beautiful even. Canio liked what he saw, although with him dishevelled and smelling strongly of wine he was aware that it was unlikely that the sentiment was reciprocated. Aware too that his long face, close-cropped black beard and slightly gaunt six-foot frame combined to give him a distinctly wolfish appearance.

The way she recoiled ever so slightly at the sight of him suggested that the young woman shared that awareness. 'May I come in, Primicerius Canio?'

'Just you?' Canio asked, craning his neck around the door frame and peering down the stone-flagged corridor.

'I'm quite alone,' she said, quickly recovering her poise.

'Then welcome to my lair.' He waved her into the room, indicated one of the room's two chairs, shut the door behind her and then sat down again on the bed. He had to: his legs felt as weak as peeled withy wands.

The young woman settled herself into the chair, smoothed her dress and then drew the cloak around her in a defensive gesture that was possibly unconscious. Or perhaps, Canio reflected, she was aware of his reputation with women.

'So, what brings a pretty young thing like you to my room?' Realising that the words sounded more leering than he had intended, Canio smiled to reassure her, forgetting that nature had designed his smile with intimidation rather than reassurance in mind.

'My name is Vilbia ... Did Primicerius Saturninus ever mention me?'

'Ahh, no, I don't think so. Not that I can recall anyway. Had you known him long?' He pressed his eyes with both palms in an effort to make them focus properly.

'No. I met him for the first and only time a few days before he disappeared.'

'Oh yes,' said Canio. 'And where was that?'

'I met him at the temple of Leucesca, up in the north of the Hills.'

'Ah, I remember now: Saturninus did go that way to see ... who was it that he went to see?'

'He came to see Gulioepius. But you knew that, didn't you?'

'And did he see him?'

'He saw us both.'

'You old Gulioepius's granddaughter?'

'No, I'm Leucesca's priestess.'

'Since when?'

'Since Leucesca made me so.'

Canio thought she sounded slightly offended by the question. 'So how is Gulioepius these days – not that I ever met him?'

'Gulioepius is at peace,' she said quietly. 'His life ended last November, when the first frosts whitened the land. The goddess let him slip away into his long sleep and spared him another winter.'

'Is that so ... tell me, just what did Saturninus find out at that temple of yours?'

'Didn't he tell you?'

'Probably – but that was a long year ago. Tell me again.'

'We looked into Leucesca's spring together and saw what the goddess was willing to show us. Strange things ... frightening things,' she added, looking down at the dusty elm floorboards.

'Things like Caelofernus?'

She looked up at him sharply. 'So Saturninus told you about his dream?'

'Yes, he told me.'

'But we didn't see Caelofernus – at least, not the Caelofernus he saw in his dream, the Caelofernus he thought was going to kill him. Truly,' she added, as if reading disbelief in his eyes.

'I believe you.'

'That Caelofernus is dead though, isn't he? ... Several months ago I chanced to meet one of your men, a soldier called Vernatius. Vernatius said that Saturninus told him that he did find and kill the Caelofernus from his dream, although the man was going by the name of Carausius. Is that true – did he kill him?'

'Saturninus wasn't the sort of man to lie about a thing like that.' Canio looked at her, wondering through the wine why she wanted to know?

'I'd also heard ...' she hesitated, 'that there was another man with you when you went after Carausius. A man called Magnillus, who was centenarius of the Vadumleucara guard post? Vernatius went into his shell like a startled snail when I mentioned his name. Is he still in the district?'

'Magnillus! If he values his life he's not even in the province. That son of a whore disappeared months ago, and when he went he took something he shouldn't with him.'

'And what was that?'

'Oh, just a few stolen trinkets whose rightful owners I was trying to find when the *Conspiratio* interrupted matters,' Canio replied, choosing his words with care.

'I see. Saturninus though ... I heard that there was a woman called Pascentia with him when he was last seen. Was there?'

'Who told you that?'

'Eutherius. He said he heard it from you.'

Canio was uncomfortably aware that she was looking intently at him now, as if the information she sought could be drawn out of him by the power of her will alone. 'There were rumours,' he said cautiously, wondering exactly how well she knew Eutherius. The mention of Eutherius's name had disconcerted him: that old man always seemed to know too much. He lay back on the bed and looked up at the stone-vaulted ceiling of the gateway tower. 'Apparently there was a woman with him on that night of the May full moon last year, when he left Ovilregis and headed towards the Sabrina.'

Oh Mercury, to think that it really was only a year ago. It seems so much longer. He sighed. 'Did you know that most of the Ovilregis garrison got themselves killed trying to stop the Hibernians from landing when they came sailing up the estuary?'

Vilbia nodded.

'After that there was so much chaos that it wasn't until weeks afterwards that I heard about Saturninus meeting the woman. And yes, her name was Pascentia, or so I was told by a man called Necalames who runs The Golden Cockerel in Ovilregis.'

'So he did find her,' Vilbia murmured.

'Was he looking for her? I was told he called out that name one night about four days before he disappeared.'

'I think they were looking for each other. But tell me what else Necalames said?'

'He said that Saturninus met Pascentia there at Ovilregis that night, although they didn't meet as strangers. He reckoned they'd known each other from way back. Apparently they talked for some time in a room at The Cockerel, and then he rode off westwards towards the Sabrina Estuary under the full moon. People assumed that she went with him, because neither of them was ever seen again.'

'So you've heard nothing of Saturninus since? Nothing at all?'

Canio thought she sounded disappointed. 'No, nothing. The Hibernians from that first scouting curragh that was seen on the Sabrina Estuary must have got both of them.'

'No! I can't believe that.'

'Why?'

'I just don't.' As if to stop him objecting, she asked quickly, 'Is Necalames still living at Ovilregis?'

'After a fashion. He was still there a month or so back. I saw him myself, though not to speak to.' Canio yawned, then added, 'He's not been right in the head since the *Conspiratio*.'

'Even so, I think I'd like to speak to him. Perhaps, as the memories of the *Conspiratio* fade, then he'll remember more about Saturninus?' She hesitated. 'Do you miss him – Saturninus, I mean?'

The question took Canio by surprise. 'Yes ... No ... Oh Hades, I learnt long ago that it's best never to get too fond of people. One way or another they always seem to vanish out of your life, and the more you liked them the harder it hits you.'

Vilbia nodded slightly as if in agreement, then stood up. As she did so Canio realised that her attention seemed to be caught by something beyond his left shoulder.

It took him several moments to realise that she was staring at the little Hecate figurine standing on the table on the far side of his bed. He thought she looked puzzled. Inwardly cursing himself for forgetting to hide it before letting her in, he turned his own head towards the figurine. The amount of wine he had consumed was still affecting his brain and preventing his eyes from focusing properly, but as he turned he could have sworn that the lady was smiling at Vilbia.

'Thank you for your time, Primicerius Canio.'

Confused, he turned again, first to see Vilbia moving towards the door, and then back to the figurine, which was now as he remembered it, the face grim and unsmiling.

'I hope we'll meet again sometime,' he heard Vilbia say. He tried to stand up to see her out, before realising that his legs still would not properly support him. So he simply waved as she thanked him again and left, opening and closing the door almost soundlessly behind her, something which Canio rarely managed. He waited a few moments, then rolled over and looked at the figurine, wondering if he would see her smile again. She did not. But nevertheless several ideas were beginning to form in his steadily clearing brain.

In his imagination he could still see the little goddess smiling. Not at him, of course – she would have no love for him, he was certain of that – but at Vilbia. And Vilbia was a priestess. If the figurine was the key to the location of the gold, then was she the one who could turn that key? If so, then perhaps her coming here today wasn't just chance? And another thing: there was something vaguely familiar about the girl, although he was certain that he'd neither seen nor even heard of her before this morning.

CHAPTER FOUR

Vilbia trotted down the stone staircase of the Verulamium Gateway tower, smiled at the gateway guard, who almost smiled back, and began walking down the long, straight street that led to the Aquae Sulis Gate on the south-west side of the city. Well before she reached the gate she turned into a side street which led to the house of Eutherius the apothecary. At the door she heard voices inside. She waited patiently outside until the door opened and an old woman emerged clutching a tiny clay pot. The woman carefully dropped the pot into one of the pockets hidden in the folds of her dress before hurrying off down the street.

Vilbia watched her go, then rapped softly on the door and entered. As usual, Eutherius sat on his throne-like wickerwork armchair, bathed in the glow of a charcoal brazier which was the room's only source of illumination, the window being closely shuttered.

'Welcome back, my daughter,' said the old man. 'And was the illustrious Acting Primicerius able to add anything of significance to what I'd already told you?'

'Not really, I'm afraid,' Vilbia sighed. 'He was somewhat drunk.'

The old man grunted in amusement. 'At this time in the morning? That's unusual, even by his standards.'

'Is it? You don't have a very high opinion of him, do you?'

'Oh, he could be worse I suppose. At least he has a few good points.'

'Such as?'

Eutherius appeared to reflect. 'Well, beneath a cloak of lechery, drunkenness, idleness and apparent belief in nothing in particular there is ...'

'What?'

'Just lechery, drunkenness, idleness and apparent belief in nothing in particular. No, don't smile. Far better that than a conscientious zealot.'

'Meaning, I suppose ...?' She drew a chi-rho monogram in the air.

'Correct.'

'Well he's certainly not that. Though I'm not so sure about him believing in nothing.'

'Indeed: why?'

'Well, when I was in his room I saw a little figurine of a woman. She held a torch in one hand and a sword in the other, and there was a dog curled around her feet. I'd never seen anything quite like her before: do you know who she could have been?'

For the first time in their acquaintance she saw Eutherius's impassive mask slip and he looked almost startled. 'I'm not sure,' he said cautiously.

She waited, but when it became apparent that he was not going to say more, she said, 'It was standing on the table next to his bed, the place where a man might keep the image of his protector god or goddess to guard him against the dangers of the night.'

'How very strange,' Eutherius mused. 'Canio, of all people. And what was she made of, this little goddess?'

'Metal of some sort, but it was black with age, except for one little patch which had been polished bright. It was probably orichalcum.'

'Did you pick her up?'

'No, I never touched her.'

'Pity.'

'Why?'

'Oh ... no particular reason.'

Vilbia narrowed her eyes slightly in what she hoped was a look of shrewd disbelief. Eutherius never asked a question without a reason behind it. 'Well, whatever she was made of, she was a strange little thing. As I was leaving ...' She hesitated, not wanting Eutherius to think her foolish.

'Yes?'

'Oh, nothing.'

'It must have been something.'

'Well, it's just that as I was about to leave I imagined I saw her turn her face to me and smile.'

Eutherius said nothing and Vilbia, feeling embarrassed, quickly added, 'But it was only for a moment. I'd probably breathed in too many of the Primicerius's wine fumes – I remember feeling a little faint and light-headed at the time.'

Eutherius remained quiet and utterly still, apparently deep in thought. At last he said, 'How many heads did she have?'

'Just the one, of course. Why?'

'Which suggests she's old, very old,' Eutherius mused. 'Did Canio happen to mention how he had come by her?'

'No. He never mentioned her at all. I don't think he was even aware that I'd noticed her. Who is the lady?'

'Oblige me: go back to Canio and find out as much about her as you can.'

'Now? But I'm on my way to Ovilregis. According to Canio there's a man there called Necalames who was one of the last people ever to see Saturninus and Pascentia on the night they disappeared.'

'Yes, I knew.'

'Did you? But you never told me – not about Necalames.'

'At the time it didn't seem relevant,' Eutherius said blandly. 'Anyway, surely seeing Necalames can wait for one more day?'

'I've waited too many days already, Eutherius; far, far too many. I should have gone to see Canio months ago, and would have done, except that ...'

'Except that you didn't want to tell Canio that you thought Saturninus had escaped to Gaul before the Hibernians arrived?' the old man suggested.

'Perhaps. And I'm still certain that Leucesca was protecting him and that he will come back one day, or at the very least send word to Canio ... or somebody. But – '

'But if you're certain that Leucesca protected Saturninus,' Eutherius interrupted, 'then why do you need to go to Ovilregis?'

She didn't want to give an answer to that question: or want Eutherius to supply one. 'I just feel that I have to, for my own peace of mind ... you can understand that, can't you?'

'So you are having doubts?'

Oh Eutherius, don't badger me! Surely you of all people can understand why I need to be sure? 'I'm as certain as I can be that Leucesca protected him,' she answered defensively.

Eutherius said nothing, but she sensed that she was disappointing him. 'Look, I promise to go and see Canio again immediately I get back. And anyway, by now I'm sure he'll be so drunk that he won't even be able to remember his own name.'

Eutherius sighed as if all the breath were leaving his ancient body. 'Oh well, I suppose another day won't matter, not after so long. And the chances are that it's not the real one anyway. There were fakes made.'

'Fakes – of that figurine? Why? What is "the real one"? And who is the lady?' she asked again.

'I'll tell you when you return from Ovilregis.'

'If you tell me now I might have more reason to hurry back,' she replied, slightly piqued.

Eutherius considered this in silence. And then he told her a story that was already old when Rome itself was nothing more than a few hovels on the banks of the Tiber.

A story which she was to recall with increasing frequency in the days that followed.

A story which he was to bitterly regret ever having told her.

* * *

Vitalinus, clerk to Aemilianus – prefect of the Civil Guard and Canio's immediate superior – was not where Canio expected him to be, which was sitting behind his desk in the corridor antechamber to Aemilianus's office. Impatiently he began hunting through the echoing labyrinthine corridors and rooms of the *praetorium*, moving steadily upwards through pools of sunlight and shadow until he arrived at the top floor. Hearing what he thought was Vitalinus's voice he drew back into the shadows, just in time to see his quarry come out of Marcellus's office. He almost burst out laughing: the coincidence was near-miraculous. Marcellus was a *rationalis*, one of the civil servants in charge of the provincial treasury, particularly the administration of the collection of taxes and their ultimate remittance to Londinium Augusta, the capital of the diocese formed by all the provinces of Britannia.

Vitalinus, an old young man, thin and intense, raised his right hand in a silent farewell to the unseen Marcellus, then started walking away down the corridor. Canio followed, stalking his prey down several flights of stairs, along another corridor, and on through the hall of the notaries, where five clerks sat at their large desks, endlessly making copies of official letters and other documents to be sent by couriers to distant corners of the province or to Londinium.

At last they arrived back at the wide corridor, the far end of which formed the antechamber to Aemilianus's office. Hiding in a doorway, Canio watched as Vitalinus halted beside the great double doors of Aemilianus's office, glanced furtively around, then stooped over the lock. He just caught a metallic click before Vitalinus opened one leaf, slipped inside and closed it quickly behind him. Canio counted to ten, walked silently up to the double doors, rapped and walked straight in.

'*Salve* sir,' he boomed 'I've been thinking, now that it's official that the *Barbarica Conspiratio* is finally ... Vitalinus?' Not without a certain malicious glee he observed that the effect on Vitalinus, who was standing on the far side of the desk, was dramatic. The clerk slammed a drawer shut and recoiled backwards, almost falling over Aemilianus's chair as he did so.

'Canio! What in the name of the Evil One are you doing here?'

Canio put on an expression intended to convey surprise and hurt. 'That's a fine welcome, young man. Where's our esteemed leader – have you come to see him too?'

Flustered, Vitalinus fell into the trap. 'Yes, that's right. I was just ...'

'Waiting for him?' Canio finished his sentence. 'We'll wait together then. Unusual, isn't it?'

'What is?'

'Aemilianus leaving his door unlocked like that. These days he usually behaves as though there's a legion's pay chest stored in here. Still, I suppose he's only slipped out to empty his bladder. Must be on his way back from the latrine right now. What's he like, this new primicerius? Have you seen the man?'

'Er, yes. In fact, Prefect Aemilianus himself introduced us. Ulpius Marullinus, I can tell you, is a *honestus*, a man from a good family.'

'Yes, Aemilianus's good family, or so I've heard,' Canio couldn't stop himself from remarking.

'Quite so. It will be quite a change to have ...' Vitalinus stopped.

'A change to have a gentleman in the post, rather than a misbegotten bastard with only one name?' Canio asked silkily.

'No – of course I didn't mean that!'

Canio smiled. 'Just joking. I know you didn't.' He sighed deeply. 'Oh, to tell you the truth Vitalinus, I can't pretend that I'll be sorry to be quit of this job.'

'Won't you?' Canio got the distinct impression that Vitalinus suspected he was lying, but didn't dare say so.

'No, not sorry at all.'

'Why not?' The suspicion was still there.

'Because, Vitalinus, I'm a soldier, not a damned clerk – no offence intended. You see, being primicerius during the *Conspiratio* was real soldiering, more or less. But in peacetime what is it? Nothing but endless inspections and reports and creeping around behind our beloved Prefect. Yes sir, no sir, and may I have permission to kiss your glorious arse, sir. Hades, Vitalinus, that's no sort of life for a man like me.'

'Is it not, indeed?' Vitalinus said coolly. 'Well, I really think that I should be going now. I have some important things to do before – '

'And there's another good thing about handing over the burdens of the primicerius's office to someone else: I'll have more time to look into all these rumours of bribery and corruption that have surfaced over the past year. Worrying rumours, really,' Canio added, scratching his bearded chin.

'Bribery, you say?'

'Mmm. And corruption.'

'So what exactly do these rumours say?' There was, to someone listening for it, just a tinge of anxiety in Vitalinus's voice. And Canio was listening as keenly as a musician tuning a lyre.

'Well – and this is in strictest confidence, mind – I've heard from several usually reliable sources that someone has been using Aemilianus's official seal cube to grant some distinctly unofficial favours. For a little ...' Canio rubbed his right thumb and index fingertip together.

'What sort of favours?' Vitalinus asked. His voice was giving nothing away now, but Canio knew that he was hooked.

'Oh, the usual sort. I'm sure you know them all as well as I do.' Canio settled himself comfortably on the edge of Aemilianus's desk and counted them off on his fingers. 'There's exemption from paying taxes for men who don't qualify for the privilege; there's permission to send private letters by the *cursus publicus*. And then of course there's everybody's favourite – permission to stay at *mansiones* up and down the province without paying so much as a single bent *centenionalis*.'

Vitalinus looked as though he were about to speak, but before he could do so Canio quickly continued, 'Yes, I know what you're going to say – that those things are nothing more than the little kindnesses that men do for each other to soften the cold winds of this cruel world. Scarcely even misdemeanours, not to my way of thinking anyway. But the trouble is,' Canio sighed again, 'I'm sure you've heard what our revered emperor, Valentinian, thinks should be done to people who commit such misdemeanours.' He clasped his own throat with one large brown hand and stuck his tongue grotesquely out of the corner of his mouth, simulating, in his mind's eye at least, the appearance of strangulation, and watching Vitalinus all the while as he did so.

Vitalinus shuddered ever so slightly; but not so slightly that Canio failed to notice, or to feel the fierce pleasure of the huntsman who has cornered his prey.

'Well, now that I'm back here in Corinium I suppose I'd better start the investigation. My best informant said – and remember, I'm telling you this in confidence – that one of the *rationales* is in it up to his neck ... That's an unfortunate phrase in the circumstances, isn't it? ... So I suppose I'd better start with him.'

'Who?'

'Who what?'

'Which *rationalis* is it?' Vitalinus sounded anxious now.

'Oh, he didn't say. My money's on Marcellus though. I've been hearing whispers about him for years. They used to say that he dipped his sticky fingers into all the tax bags that passed through his office. That was before they started the system of random checks, of course, and it became too risky. So, maybe he's found another little scheme to enhance his salary.' Canio yawned and stretched. 'It's been a long, hard year Vitalinus, and

I'm damned if I want to start an investigation like that just now. It's always a nasty business, and you can never predict just where it will lead to or who'll get caught in the net.' He gave what he thought was a splendid grimace of disgust. 'You know, Vitalinus, what I'd really like right now is a long, lazy, month's leave. Just to go somewhere far, far away from Corinium and forget the cares of the world for a few short weeks. I'm sure Marcellus doesn't know that I suspect him, so he'd have no reason to take advantage of my absence to dispose of any evidence. In fact, he just might get even more cocky and make a few silly mistakes. Then I'll really have him.'

'Well then, why don't you take some leave? You really do look tired – I've thought so for months – and you've certainly earned a furlough.'

Suddenly, Canio thought, Vitalinus seemed genuinely concerned for his welfare. He stifled a grin. 'Why? – Aemilianus, that's why. Can you remember – can anybody remember – when he last granted anyone a furlough? The man's scared stiff that if somebody didn't come back from leave then he'd be accused of aiding a deserter.'

'But you wouldn't desert, would you?'

'Vitalinus, the thought would never even cross my mind. First thing tomorrow though I'd better make a start on finding out who's been sinning with Aemilianus's seal cube.'

'Aren't you even going to try asking him for a furlough?' Vitalinus sounded almost indignant.

'What's the use? I'm not exactly Aemilianus's favourite person, now am I?' Canio murmured, turning to leave.

'I could ask him on your behalf,' Vitalinus said quickly.

'You would? Why?'

'Why not? We've been colleagues for several years now, haven't we?'

'True,' Canio said reflectively.

'So as soon as I think the moment is right, I'll speak to Aemilianus.'

'Oh, all right, if you really think it'll do any good.' Canio yawned again. 'Dammit, I really am tired. I think I'll go back to my room and lie down for a little while. If, by some miracle, you should persuade Aemilianus to let me have a furlough, then I'm sure you'll let me know, won't you, old friend?'

Vitalinus appeared to force a smile and assured Canio that he would.

Canio returned the smile and ambled out of the room, carefully shutting the doors behind him.

Vitalinus waited until he could no longer hear Canio's retreating footsteps, then opened the tightly curled fingers of his left hand to reveal a small bronze cube engraved with a different design on each of its six faces. For several moments he stared at the uppermost motif, a man on a galloping horse, as he weighed the cube in the palm of his hand. Then he dropped it into his belt pouch and gave the nearest leg of the desk a savage kick. Re-locking Aemilianus's doors behind him, he went scurrying away down the broad corridor, muttering dark, angry words as he went.

Canio, hiding behind a pillar, watched and grinned.

**

But Canio did not go back to his room. Instead, he strolled around the city until he came to The Fighting Cocks, a *taberna* located two *insulae* blocks north of the Calleva Gate. There he rapped on the polished marble counter and ordered a large cup of their best wine. The barmaid, youngish and with a certain animal promise, enquired whether she should put it on his account, or did he perhaps wish to pay for it there and then?

He decided to surprise her by holding up four copper *centenionales* for her inspection. Dodging her outstretched hand, he hooked her neckline with one finger and dropped them down the front of her dress, one by one, then threatened to retrieve them, she wriggling and shrieking prettily all the while.

After a visit to a barber to have his beard trimmed to his preferred stubble length, he then spent some time playing dice with Bupitus and a couple of off-duty soldiers in the barrack stables. When he did eventually get back to his room he found, pushed under the door, a four-week furlough pass bearing carefully applied stamps from what he knew to be the correct two sides of Aemilianus's seal cube: at the top a pair of clasped hands and at the bottom the emperor in a chariot drawn by four horses galloping towards the beholder. Canio grinned as he inspected it, then kissed it and tucked it carefully into his belt pouch.

He spent much of the rest of the morning carrying out with unusual speed and efficiency some of the irksome administrative duties that went with the post of primicerius and which even he could not wholly evade. At the same time he told everyone who mattered that he would not be around for the next few weeks. Aemilianus he somehow chanced not to meet, but obviously the Prefect must have been aware of his impending absence since the man had stamped the pass himself – as Vitalinus would doubtless remind him in due course. He sniggered as he pictured the conversation between the two men.

He then spent some time trying to find Vilbia, until discreet enquiries established that she had left the city for Ovilregis quite early that morning. Surprised, and slightly disconcerted, he hurried back to the barrack stables and told Bupitus to get Antares ready, saying that he would be leaving in less than an hour. Even as he said it he was well aware that neither he, Bupitus, nor anyone else could really judge how long a twelfth of the time between sunrise and sunset actually was. But it sounded the sort of order that a primicerius ought to give.

The sun, that ancient time measurer, was high in the southern sky and warm and bright in his face as he picked his way through the bustling crowds and creaking ox-drawn wagons in the city streets. Passing beneath the great stone arches of the

Aquae Sulis Gate he began trotting Antares away from Corinium south-westwards down the Fosse Way, past the sprawling cemeteries that bordered both sides of the road just beyond the city walls.

The Hecate figurine was stowed deep within one of his saddlebags. He did not want to carry it so close. In fact, he did not want to carry it at all. And when the gold was safely inside the sacks which were also stowed in those saddlebags, then the lake would be more than welcome to it: he would never want to see it again.

But before he had reached the high, grassed outer bank of the near-derelict amphitheatre, which lay some two hundred yards beyond the Sulis Gate, he spotted movement out of the corner of his eye. Reining to a halt, he watched as a small procession of people came walking slowly towards him, picking their way between the graves on the north side of the road. All were poorly dressed, some of their clothes patched and even ragged.

A grim-faced man in front held the hands of two silent children who stumbled along beside him with downcast eyes. Behind them walked an elderly woman who sobbed uncontrollably, her hands wiping away the tears. Another man and a woman followed, holding hands, and in front of them all walked two thickset men who carried between them a long bundle swaddled in coarse sacking.

The children looked up curiously at Canio, but the adults ignored him as they crossed the Fosse Way in front of Antares and made their way into the cemetery on the south side of the highway. Glancing across, Canio saw several mounds of raw earth and innumerable weed-covered hummocks, some with sad wooden markers in various stages of dereliction and decay. And amongst them all he spotted the dark gash of an open grave and the handles of two spades sticking obliquely up out of the spoil heap beside it.

He was well aware that only yesterday he would not have

allowed the crossing of his path by a corpse to bother him: he had seen enough dead in his twenty-nine years. But that was yesterday, and today he remembered the superstition that an enterprise whose path was crossed by Death could never succeed. And remembered too that other superstition, which said that it was Hecate who guided the dead across the frontiers between this world and the next.

So he waited silently until the funeral party had passed, calmed Antares as the horse whinnied restlessly, perhaps scenting a faint perfume of corruption, then turned the horse and rode back into the city. There he threaded his way through the side streets until he reached the Calleva Gate on the south side of the city, where a large gang of stonemasons were hard at work constructing yet another projecting bastion against the outside face of the city wall to widen the field of fire of the ballistae mounted on it.

From the Calleva Gate he circled round to rejoin the Fosse Way well south of the amphitheatre. The dead themselves could not harm him; of that he was certain. But if the Hecate figurine really did possess a malevolent power, then he reasoned that power might come from something which could itself never die.

Corinium receded behind him, and shortly after the second milestone he branched off the Fosse Way and onto the track that led to Ovilregis, some fourteen miles away to the south-west. It was only then that it occurred to him that he was travelling the same road, towards the same destination, as Saturninus a little over a year before, although then it had been the evening when the May full moon was due to rise. Suddenly he remembered that this coming night would also see a full moon rise. He shook his head; it was simple coincidence, nothing more. He urged Antares into a canter, but the miles seemed to pass maddeningly slowly.

CHAPTER FIVE

Even so, it was only mid-afternoon when Canio arrived at Ovilregis. Unlike Saturninus, he decided to keep well clear of the civil guard post, not caring to make his presence in the town widely known. At The Golden Cockerel he asked after Necalames.

'Not here,' said a thin man holding a wine strainer.

'Where then?'

'There's a high tree, way over in that direction,' said the man, waving towards the west with the wine strainer. 'These days, if he isn't around here then the chances are he's sitting up there, keeping watch in case the Hibernians come again.'

Canio suspected that in Corinium this explanation might have caused a few sniggers among those who chanced to overhear it. But here in The Cockerel no-one laughed. Glancing around he recognised several of the people sitting at the tables or lounging at the bar, people who could have given eye-witness accounts of the terrible things that happened in the first days of the *Conspiratio*. And there would have been precious little humour in those accounts. After one quick cup of watered wine he re-mounted Antares and rode off to find Necalames.

Westwards from the town the land first rose almost imperceptibly to the skyline, then started falling in a series of broken coombs down towards the plain of the Flumen Sabrina. On that skyline stood a row of great ash trees, and as he came closer Canio saw a rope ladder hanging down from the tallest. From underneath, looking up through the curtain of feathery leaves that shivered in the freshening breeze, he saw a wooden platform built in the cleft where the trunk branched some thirty feet above the ground.

'Necalames?' he shouted. 'Are you up there?'

There was no reply, but Canio was fairly sure that he could make out, through the dancing leaves, two feet dangling over the edge of the platform. He shouted again, but still there was no response.

With a muttered expletive he dismounted, tied Antares' reins to a low-sweeping bough, tested the strength of the rope ladder by giving it a sharp tug and began climbing up towards the platform. By the time he was halfway up he was certain that someone was there, but even when he was level with the platform and its occupant was in full view, all that Necalames did was to glance at him, nod in uncertain recognition, then resume his vigil, staring across to the south-west.

'That's the way they came last time,' he murmured, as much to himself as Canio. He had a sallow face framed in jet-black hair and the shrunken appearance of a once-plump man who has lost a lot of weight in a short time.

'And that's the way they'll come again, eh?' said Canio, thinking to humour him.

'That's the way they'll come,' Necalames echoed. 'But when they do, I'll see them before they see me. They'll never again take me by surprise. Never again, never again, never again,' he chanted, as if the words were a charm that could themselves keep evil away.

'Did a girl come to see you today? A redhead, young and quite pretty?'

Necalames did not reply, so Canio continued, 'Name of Vilbia? She came to me early this morning asking questions about Saturninus's disappearance on the night before the ...' he stopped himself just in time. 'You remember Saturninus, don't you?'

Necalames gave no sign of comprehension. 'I thought they were coming back last night.'

'Who – Saturninus and Pascentia?'

'The Hibernians.'

'Sweet Rosmerta – why would you think that? What did you see?'

Necalames slowly shook his head. 'Nothing. I saw nothing, I heard nothing. But I knew that something strange was out there, far away on the Sabrina Plain. I sensed it was there. Perhaps it will be there again tonight. Watching. Waiting.'

'Waiting for what?'

'Ah, who knows? The full moon, perhaps?'

'Jackass,' Canio breathed. 'Did she come to see you?'

'Who?'

'The girl, Vilbia.' Trying not to let his impatience show, Canio squatted down with his back against the ridged grey bark of the old ash's trunk so that his head was at the same level as Necalames' own.

'Oh yes, the girl. I remember now. She came when I was in The Cockerel. She asked me what I could remember about the night when your Saturninus disappeared.'

'And you told her?'

'Everything I could remember.'

'So where is she now?'

'Gone.'

'Gone where?'

'To the place where they found his horse wandering, out there on the plain.'

'That old cemetery near the Sabrina?'

Necalames nodded slowly, his eyes still on the horizon.

'Will she be coming back this way?'

'She didn't say. Best go there yourself if you want to be sure of finding her.'

'I just might do that.'

Necalames did not reply. Canio patted him on the shoulder and could not resist saying, 'If you do see the Hibernians coming, be sure to run and tell me first.' Then he climbed down the tree and rode back to The Cockerel.

He did not stay there long. It wasn't like the old days: there were too many dead people watching him from the shadows, people who had not made it through those first few bloody days of the *Conspiratio*.

Necalames did not return to The Cockerel while Canio was there, but then he hadn't expected him to. Mina, his wife, said that he often stayed up his tree on lookout all night, particularly on summer nights like this one coming, when the moon would be full and bright. He would not, she added, be returning to The Cockerel until well after sunrise. She said this casually, quietly, moving close to him so that no one else could hear, but not looking directly at him.

Canio let his eyes glide over her. In her mid-twenties, she was younger than Necalames and not unattractive, sharing with her husband the dark eyes and olive skin of the lands around the Eastern Mediterranean. He whispered that he had to ride down to a place near the Sabrina that afternoon, but that he should be back by nightfall.

She asked if there was anything he particularly wanted for his supper when he returned?

He replied that he rather fancied something warm and spicy.

'Warm and spicy is one of my specialities,' she murmured as she drifted away, smiling at another customer who had just walked in.

❈❈❈

Sitting on a small mound in a sea of flowering grasses, her cloak lying beside her, Vilbia watched as the lone horseman trotted steadily towards her across the undulating plain that lies between the Long Limestone Hills and the wide estuary of the Flumen Sabrina.

She waited, curious, as Canio raised a hand in greeting before dismounting and tying his reins to a nearby tree stump.

Determined to show no sign of nervousness, she smiled and said, 'I thought I recognised you, Primicerius, even in the distance. What brings you here ... and are you fully recovered now?'

'Recovered from what, my pretty one?'

'You seemed unwell when we met early this morning in Corinium.'

'Oh, that. It was just tiredness – the pressures of command, you understand.'

'Of course,' she replied tactfully, although was unable to resist adding, 'but happily the medicine you had been drinking appears to have revived you.' She decided against asking him again why he was there: by then she had thought of other questions. 'Tell me, where exactly did you find his horse? ... your horse, I should say. Necalames remembered someone – perhaps it was you – saying that it was somewhere close to this spot, but he didn't know exactly where.' She was trying to imagine how the place must have appeared in moonlight.

Canio sighed. 'Ah, poor old Necalames. He's not the man he used to be.'

'So you said.' *Although I don't think that anyone who lived through that time of wolves will ever see the world quite as they did before.* 'Saturninus's horse though, where – ?'

'Antares was just over there, about a hundred paces from where you're sitting now. The morning sun shining on his coat made it look as red as fire.'

'I suppose that's why Saturninus called him Antares,' she murmured. Seeing a look she took for uncertainty on Canio's face, she added, 'It's the red star of summer – '

'In the constellation of The Scorpion – it was mentioned to me once.'

'By Saturninus?'

'No, strangely enough Antares himself brought it up in conversation one day.'

She smiled tolerantly. 'Did he still have his saddle on?'

'Saddle? He did, yes – saddle, bridle, boar spear, saddlebags ...'

'But nothing in the saddlebags?'

'There was his cloak and the usual odds and ends; that's all I can recall. Why do you ask?'

'Oh, it's just that someone in Corinium told me that he put something else in.'

'Something like a lyre?'

'So you knew?'

'Bupitus told me. But it wasn't there. It must have been lost when ...' he gave an apologetic shrug.

'You still think it was the Hibernians from that first scouting curragh who killed them, don't you?' she gently chided him.

Canio's face took on a sardonic look. 'What else can I think?'

'Then why weren't their bodies ever found?'

'At the time they reckoned the Hibernians must have thrown them into the estuary, which makes sense to me.'

She shook her head. 'I heard that when that scouting curragh was last sighted, on the night *before* the full moon, it was already coming down the Sabrina, probably on its way back to report to their main fleet. Didn't they suppose it had only come to find out whether there were any war galleys from the *Classis Britannica* stationed in the estuary?'

'Some thought so.'

'So by the following night, the night when Saturninus came to Ovilregis, it should have been long gone,' she continued patiently.

Canio appeared unconvinced. 'Well, if it wasn't the Hibernians that got them, then what did?'

'I don't think that anything got them.' Before he could object, she asked, 'It's not far from the estuary to here, is it? Not far for a horse to wander?'

'About half a mile, I suppose.'

'And at the estuary it would have been easy enough to board a ship coming down the Sabrina.'

Canio blew out a long breath. 'Well, I suppose they could

have done, if they'd really been minded to. They could have used the old jetty that was built to load the grain ships. But Saturninus wouldn't have just sailed away with his sweetheart, not if he thought the invasion was coming.'

'But why would he have thought it was coming? One solitary curragh, which nobody at the time was even sure existed, doesn't make an invasion.'

Canio still looked doubtful. 'But this supposed ship of yours – it was night, and ships don't sail down the estuary at night for fear of running onto the mudflats.'

'But there was a full moon to see by, remember? And if they'd sailed on down the west coast of Gaul, then it would have been weeks before Saturninus even heard of the *Conspiratio*.'

'Gaul? Now why would Saturninus have wanted to go to Gaul? Did he or his sweetheart have kin there?'

Vilbia hesitated, fingering the large copper coin of the emperor Julian that hung, medallion-like, from a thin cord around her neck – the coin that Saturninus had given her for safe keeping three days before he disappeared. Looking down, first at Julian's bearded face and then at the great bull standing beneath its twin stars, she said, 'I heard that Pascentia spoke of a villa in … in Gaul, somewhere. A place surrounded by endless rows of vines in a rolling countryside. Perhaps, after Saturninus had talked with Trencorix, the fisherman who claimed to have seen that curragh, they came across a ship taking on or setting ashore other passengers.

'And so they simply decided to go, there and then, while that magic full moon was still lighting their way, before the dawn could come and break its spell. Maybe, as they stood together on that jetty in the moonlight, the thought came to them that the ship had been guided there by some god – or perhaps even by Leucesca, the goddess I serve – and that if they didn't go then, such a chance would never come again. Don't you think that's at least possible?' she asked. She was awkwardly aware that she had perhaps revealed more of her own thoughts and hopes than she had intended.

'Well, it could have happened that way. And perhaps it did,' Canio conceded. 'At least that would account for why no one ever found their bodies.'

She smiled, but Canio was looking eastwards. She thought she understood that look. 'It won't take long to get back to Ovilregis, not on Antares. Plenty of time to finish telling me what happened that day.'

'Oh, I will, don't worry. But I promised someone that I'd be back there by nightfall.'

'Do I know the lady?' some imp prompted her to ask.

Canio gave her a sly look. 'Tell me, just why are you so interested in what became of Saturninus? Were you a sweetheart of his too?'

She should have anticipated the question, but she hadn't. 'Oh no, nothing like that ... I only met him that once, at Leucesca's temple.' Her face felt suddenly hot, and she looked away from Canio. 'He promised that, if he cheated the death he saw in his dream, then he'd come back and tell me how he'd done it – and tell me too if he found Pascentia.' There was a slightly awkward silence, and to end it she said quickly, 'What happened at Ovilregis when they heard that Saturninus's horse had been found wandering here?'

'There was something of a panic. Ulpius Vassedo – he was centenarius in charge of the garrison there – set off at the gallop with four of his men. And me.'

'But why were you in Ovilregis? I heard you'd been sent to Glevum the previous day?'

'Did you now – you're very well informed. And so I had been sent to Glevum, but one thing leads to another. When I got back to Corinium –'

'The following morning, wasn't it?'

' – I heard that Saturninus had made it back to Corinium, and then gone off towards Ovilregis and the Sabrina Estuary, all alone. So I came after him. As it happens, there was something else that I wanted to see him about.'

'And what was that?'

'Oh, just those trinkets I mentioned back in Corinium. Nothing that matters now.'

No: time changes our perception of what matters and what doesn't. 'Necalames said that afterwards you went to Aust Cliffs with some of the men from Ovilregis.'

'I did. And we waited there, me and a couple of troopers called Bassus and Maenalis, until late in the afternoon, when the other two turned up. They'd been searching along the shoreline, looking for Saturninus.'

'And found nothing?'

'Not a trace. But it wasn't long after those two arrived that young Maenalis nudged me and said, "See over there – what do you make of that?" And we looked to the south, over towards Abona, and there was smoke, thick columns of it rising up from two places a mile or so apart. They wanted to go and investigate, but I said no: I knew trouble when I saw it. So we waited and watched, and by and by another fire started, further east than the other two. Just a small drift of whitish smoke it was at first, but it soon grew thicker and darker like the others. And then we saw them.'

'The Hibernians?'

Canio nodded. 'The beginning of the *Conspiratio*. The sun was about a foot above the horizon when Bassus suddenly shouted out, all excited, "Will you look at that!" and pointed down the estuary. And there they were – hundreds of those damned curraghs coming out of the sea haze, across almost the full width of the estuary – and it must be all of two miles wide downstream from the cliffs.'

'And that was late in the afternoon,' she mused aloud. 'So if Saturninus and Pascentia were on board a ship that had come down the estuary during the previous night, they would have been well out to sea long before the Hibernians arrived.'

'Yes, I suppose they would. Always assuming, of course, that your goddess had been watching over them,' Canio added drily.

'I believe Leucesca was – and still is.'

Canio just grunted. 'Anyway, I'm sure you know the rest. We warned everyone in Ovilregis, but what could we do against so many?' He stopped and glanced towards the north-west, where the sun was already beginning to sink below a line of distant Cambrian hills.

She too gazed at the setting sun, wondering if Saturninus and Pascentia were watching that same sunset in far-off Burdigala, the shared experience uniting them and her across the long, estranging miles. Then she smiled at Canio and slipped down off the mound. 'I'm sorry: I've kept you too long from your appointment at Ovilregis.'

'Oh, it's not that important. Besides, I've a little business proposition that I'd like to put to you.'

This was unexpected. 'Now? Can't it wait until later? I'd rather like to be alone here for a little while ... I can't explain exactly why,' she concluded apologetically.

Canio looked as though he were about to object, then appeared to change his mind. 'All right, if that's what you want. But will you will meet me at The Cockerel later tonight?'

'Yes, if you wish. And you can put your little business proposition to me then.'

'Fine ... Oh, and if I don't happen to be in the main bar when you arrive, just order a meal and tell them to charge it to me. I won't be far away.'

She waited until Canio had re-mounted Antares, waved farewell and ridden out of sight. Then she strolled over to the old cemetery, which lay half-hidden in the lush greenery of midsummer some two hundred yards from the spot where Canio said Antares had been found wandering a little over a year before. Tall flowering grasses grew there, just as they grew all around, their feathery heads trembling in the cooling breeze. Catching a faint, delicate perfume she glanced around and saw a tangle of dog roses trailing over the top of the nearest of the ancient tombstones. Impulsively she reached up, picked one of the deep pink, five-petalled flowers and breathed in the rose's heady fragrance, intense after the heat of the day.

Still holding it, she began wandering through that peaceful place, trying to picture Saturninus and Pascentia travelling past a year before, imagining what they were murmuring to each other in the moonlight as they planned a new life together. Now and then she paused and looked more closely at the time-blurred image of a long-forgotten man or woman, or at an inscription cut into the mellow, sun-warmed stone.

Then she noticed, on the far side of the cemetery, one stone which stood slightly apart from the others. From where she herself stood only its blank back was visible, and as she gazed at it there came a vague curiosity to learn what was written on its other side. She walked over to the massive stone, as tall as a man, nearly three feet wide and a hand's span thick. At first she was unable to make out any words, most of the once-crisp lettering having been degraded by the frosts of countless winters, or obscured by great crusted blotches of yellow and orange lichens.

And then her searching eyes stopped abruptly as they found the one legible part of the name of the long-dead man above whose ashes the stone was raised, the part over which the surrounding lichens seemed unable to grow. She read and re-read the name, and as she did so the rose slipped from her fingers and dropped unnoticed to the ground. She reached out and slowly traced, one by one, all eleven letters with her fingertips, unwilling to believe what her eyes told her was true. But the name really was CAELOFERNUS, the name that Saturninus had seen in his dream carved on the stone which, in that same dream, he had seen come to life and kill him.

In bewildered fascination she stared at the name, as one by one the questions without answers stumbled into her mind. She stood there, still as the stone itself, while the light slowly faded and submerged the letters back into the blank anonymity of its face.

At last, long after the red sun had sunk completely below the far-away Cambrian hills, she whispered, 'Oh Saturninus, what was it that you said about your dream? ... That it might have been like a dog barking in the night at something hiding out there in the darkness – something that it heard but couldn't see? Did you see something terrible come out of the darkness, here on that night a year ago? Come back and tell me ... *please.*' She waited, almost as if expecting a reply, but of course none came.

The night breeze was rising, and as it sighed mournfully through the grasses and the old stones she heard, mixed in with the wind, what sounded to her like laughter, mocking and cruel. Gazing warily around in the deceptive twilight she imagined that she saw something move among the stones. A scream rose in her throat, yet from somewhere courage came and she waited, silent and still, for whatever it was to come closer. But nothing came, and then the breeze itself faded and died. Her face set and taut, she began edging backwards, then turned and started walking quickly away from that place, back towards the dark line of the Long Limestone Hills from which she had come.

And above those hills, in the south-eastern sky, she saw a huge full moon silently rising, its ancient all-seeing face lit glowing gold by the light of the vanished sun. It was a face familiar and loved since childhood, and now seemingly so close that she could stretch out an arm and touch it as it floated there between the earth and the stars. But her childhood was gone, and now she knew that moon for what it really was: an alien land, unknown and unknowable, its dark other face forever hidden. As if it were itself a dream.

Leucesca, Leucesca ... when I was a child you promised to protect me from the demons of the dark. But if you couldn't protect Saturninus, can you protect me?

CHAPTER SIX

It was at first light, before the new sun had even risen above the north-eastern horizon, when Canio walked Antares out of Ovilregis, mounted and began trotting him towards the west. With rare tact, or perhaps even rarer conscience, he avoided Necalames' tree. He rode along one of the peninsulas of high ground that extended between the coombs until, some three miles from Ovilregis, he came to the edge of a steep scarp at the end of the peninsula.

And there, sitting not a hundred paces away, he saw Vilbia. She sat motionless as a rock, staring out across the sheet of mist which hid the plain below and through which only the tops of the tallest trees projected, appearing for all the world as if they were growing out of clouds. Her eyes seemed fixed on that point on the south-western horizon below which the full moon had disappeared.

Dismounting, he began walking towards her, leading Antares by the reins. She gave no sign of awareness of his approach, so he called her name. He saw her start violently, twist around and scramble to her feet. The rising sun was behind him, illuminating every feature of her face and cloak with minute clarity, while keeping him in semi-silhouette.

'Saturninus! Saturninus, is that you?'

Canio saw her shield her eyes with both hands and peer towards him.

As he came closer she realised her mistake. 'Oh it's you, Primicerius Canio. I'm sorry, I thought ...'

'I can't be Saturninus, not even for you. Did you want me to be?'

'No ... I mean ... it's just that against the sun ...'

But Canio had heard the excitement in her voice, followed so swiftly by disappointment. For a moment he felt something close to jealousy, an unusual emotion for him. 'You never came to The Cockerel last night. What happened?'

'Things happened,' she said slowly. 'Strange things.' She turned away and gazed again towards the point on the horizon where the moon had set. 'Did you know that in that old cemetery near the Sabrina there is a tombstone bearing the name Caelofernus ... the name of the man who Saturninus dreamed would kill him?'

'No, I didn't know that. Are you quite sure?' This was a complication that Canio most definitely did not want.

'I saw it with my own eyes. I even touched the carved letters in the dying evening light. But what does it mean, Primicerius Canio? That terrible man that Saturninus killed called himself Carausius. I know that Saturninus thought his real name was Caelofernus, but what if it wasn't? I mean, he and I both saw a man in the waters of Leucesca's spring who answered to the name Caelofernus, but who wasn't the man he saw in his dream. So what *was* the real meaning of his dream?'

Canio didn't even want to guess. 'Well, we knew Carausius was just an alias: obviously the man's real name was Caelofernus – why shouldn't there have been more than one man with that name?'

'But don't you see? Saturninus dreamed that a stone bearing the name Caelofernus would turn into a man, and that man would kill him. And there it was, that stone, at the place where they found his horse. That *must* mean something, mustn't it?'

Canio was thinking rapidly now. 'I know what it meant! What Saturninus dreamed of was the death of his old life. It must have been near that cemetery that he and Pascentia finally decided to sail off to Gaul together, just like you thought.'

'Yes, I did wonder ... oh, I truly wish I could believe that, Primicerius.'

'So why don't you then? It makes perfect sense to me.'

'Why? Because I can't shake off the suspicion that something terrible happened to them there.'

'But if you're so sure that the Hibernians didn't kill them, then what logical reason have you got for thinking that something else did?' There was an intenseness in her face that was beginning to make Canio feel uneasy.

'Because there's something strange about that place, something I can't properly put into words,' she said awkwardly. 'And yet I was so sure that Leucesca was watching over and protecting Saturninus, and Pascentia too. But if something terrible did happen to them, then I just don't know what to believe any more.'

'Look, stop worrying.' Canio paused for dramatic effect, then said, 'I *know* that nothing happened to Saturninus at that old cemetery.'

Vilbia stared at him. 'How can you possibly know that?' She sounded sceptical, but her face pleaded to be convinced.

'Because that's why I'm here. You know I went back to Ovilregis last night? Well, while I was there I happened to mention to several of my troopers that someone had been asking about Saturninus. And do you know what one of them, a man on secondment from the *Jovii*, upped and said?'

'About Saturninus?'

'About Saturninus. He said that not much more than a week ago, ten days at most, he had actually seen Saturninus with a squad of regular army cavalry camped at a lake down south.'

Canio saw a strange, wondering look appear on Vilbia's face. 'Was he sure?'

'Well, he said he was. Said he'd seen Saturninus once before, a couple of years ago.'

'But did he actually speak to Saturninus? Did he find out where he'd been?'

'No, he never got the chance. He was riding out of the camp just as Saturninus was riding in. You see, he'd never known that

Saturninus had gone missing, so he thought nothing of seeing him there. It's my guess that when news of the *Conspiratio* reached Gaul, then Saturninus felt that he had to return and help fight the bastards. It's just the sort of thing that he would have done.'

'But was he sure it was Saturninus?' Vilbia persisted.

'Well, like I said, he'd only seen Saturninus the once before, so it's just possible that he was mistaken. That's why I'm going down south to investigate for myself.'

'What, now? Straightaway?'

'That's right. I was on my way when I spotted you. By a lucky chance I'd just been granted a few weeks leave, now that the *Conspiratio* is officially over.'

Seeing what he took to be uncertainty still lingering in her face, he explained, 'I always felt guilty about letting Saturninus go off alone after Caraus ... after Caelofernus like I did. I know he'd ordered me to stay behind and help guard the prisoners at Duboceto Wood, but even so ...' Canio shrugged apologetically.

'Where exactly was this lake where your trooper saw Saturninus?'

Canio scratched one ear. 'Well, that's the problem: I'm not entirely sure. "On the south side of the Great Marshes," was the best description I could get out of him.'

'Didn't he know the name of the lake?'

'No. I asked him that, but he was only there the one night and never heard the name mentioned. Perhaps it hadn't got a name. Shouldn't be too hard to find though.'

'Can I come with you? I could help you search.'

'Did Saturninus mean that much to you? I thought you only met him the once?'

'I did. But if I were to see him again with my own eyes then I'd know for sure that my goddess had been protecting him. And that would mean so much to me ... do you understand?'

'Yes, I think so, and of course you're welcome to come with

me. But you do realise that Saturninus might not be at the lake by the time we get there? Although even if he isn't, there may be other people around who can tell us where he's gone,' Canio added quickly.

'Yes, perhaps there will be.'

He noticed that now she was looking uncertainly back in the direction of Ovilregis. 'Is there a problem?'

'No – I want to come with you. It's just that I had been intending to go back to Corinium. There's someone there whose advice I wanted to ask.'

Eutherius? Canio wondered. *Not a good idea.* 'Well, if you really do need to return to Corinium I can wait for you here. It's just that with every day that passes ...' He made an expansive gesture with his hands.

'No ... no, you're right. And in any case, it doesn't really matter now. That report of Saturninus being seen has changed everything.'

Canio smiled. 'Well, lets be off then – first stop, Portum Abona.'

She brushed at the limey earth stains on her cloak. 'By the way, what was the business proposition that you mentioned yesterday evening?'

'Oh, that? It was nothing that matters now. We've got more important things to do.' He paused. 'You look tired.'

'I am.'

'Never mind, you can get a good night's sleep at the *stabulum* at Abona. Where did you sleep last night?'

'I didn't sleep. I sat here, watching the moon.'

Canio looked at her curiously, but she did not explain why and he decided against asking. Together they stood for a little while, wordlessly looking over the Sabrina plain from which the strengthening sun was already beginning to burn away the mist.

Then, in single file, with him leading Antares, and Vilbia following at a cautious distance behind, he picked his way down the steep path to the plain, the horse occasionally skidding on the loose gravel that had been washed into drifts by the winter rains.

***

By noon, Canio had realised that the effects of the previous long day and sleepless night had at last caught up with Vilbia. So much so that, at his pragmatic insistence, she had wrapped herself in her cloak and slept for several hours in the shade of a wayside oak.

In the late afternoon, when they were still six or seven miles north of Portum Abona, she was riding a drowsy side-saddle, Canio leading Antares by the reins. As they passed along a track which skirted a large uncut hay meadow, the warm air vibrant with the drone of insects, he gradually became aware of the sound of distant voices. He stopped and began looking around for the source of those voices. The break in the swaying rhythm of the horse roused Vilbia.

She shielded her eyes against the sun with one hand and pointed with the other towards the next field. 'Over there,' she said quietly.

In the far corner of that field Canio made out a group of five women dressed almost identically in plain brown robes, which covered them so completely as to leave only their heads and hands visible. Nearby, in the shade of a large ash, a donkey stood patiently between the shafts of a two-wheeled cart with a hooped canvas roof.

As he drew nearer, Canio realised that the women were gathered around a wayside shrine, which two of their number were attacking with small hammers. They seemed to be making little impression on the stone. The other three women stood with outstretched arms and upturned palms in the manner of *orantes*, chanting what even he recognised as a Christian hymn.

'Greetings, soldier-brother,' said the nearest of the three *orantes*, a strikingly handsome woman in early middle age.

63

'Have you come to witness the destruction of this heathen abomination?'

Looking closely for the first time, Canio saw that the shrine bore the figures of Mercury and his Celtic consort Rosmerta, both carved in bold relief on a recessed panel on the front face of the chest-high shrine. Although weathered, Mercury's winged hat (the wings, he realised, now looking suspiciously like a pair of small horns) and the serpent-entwined staff he carried in one hand were still clearly visible, as were both the ladle which Rosmerta held and her magic tub which stood between them.

'No,' he replied casually. 'We were just on our way south and wondered what was happening.'

The rate of hammer strikes slackened and the chanting died.

'I trust that you approve of our actions?' said the handsome woman. 'As I'm sure you know, it was our blessed emperor Constantius, now with The Lord, who actively encouraged the destruction of such idols.'

Canio caught the note of suspicion in her voice. 'Of course I approve,' he assured her, on guard now. 'Although, alas, there are still many in this province who would not,' he added in a tone intended to make it quite clear that he was not among their number. 'It's strange work for women though. How do you ladies come to be doing it?' He had let his eyes rove over them all and concluded on the available evidence, especially the accent of the handsome woman and the large gold ring set with a purple gemstone which she wore on her left hand, that they were probably *honestiores*, not people usually found doing manual labour.

'We were called to it by the Good Shepherd himself, after our husbands' earthly lives ended during the *Conspiratio*. But the destruction of idols is not our real work. If we should chance upon them then we do The Lord's bidding, but we do not seek them out.'

'So what is your real work then?' Canio felt obliged to ask. He could not help noticing that the baggy robe which the

64

woman wore could not entirely hide the curves of the body beneath. 'Incidentally, my name is Marcus Ulpius Italicus, and this is my wife, Claudia,' he said, nodding back towards Vilbia, who raised her eyebrows fractionally and then bestowed a cool smile on the women.

'And mine is Gaia Valeria Aeterna – may the Good Shepherd's blessing be upon you both. Our calling is to find and give Christian burial to the mortal remains of those who perished at the hands of the barbarians during this last terrible year.'

'What, even the bodies of non-believers?' Vilbia asked. Canio couldn't tell by her voice if her apparent surprise was genuine or ironic.

'When a body has lain for months under sun and rain, who amongst us can say whether it was the earthly vessel of a believer or not? We give them all burial according to the rites of the Church, and in so doing we re-claim their souls for Christ,' Aeterna replied.

'A noble purpose indeed,' said Canio solemnly, noticing for the first time the three iron-tipped wooden spades strapped to the side of the cart. 'But doesn't it worry you that you might bury a barbarian by mistake?'

'Of course not,' Aeterna replied, seemingly surprised by the question. 'It is only by bringing the barbarians into the fold of the Good Shepherd that we will be able to live in peace with them.' Canio said nothing, but realised his face must be betraying his incredulity. 'You see,' Aeterna continued, 'it was in the very act of carrying the word of The Lord to those we now call barbarians that our husbands perished.'

'They tried to convert the barbarians? That was ... a brave thing to do,' Vilbia said. 'Though some might call it unwise.'

'No, it was holy wisdom!' cried one of the women who had been attacking the shrine. She had long, uncombed dark hair, beginning to grey, with bird-bright eyes that stared earnestly into Canio's own. 'The heathens of the *Conspiratio* were a plague sent by The Lord to punish us for not striving diligently enough to banish all pagan beliefs and practices from this world. But consider this: if the barbarians were to be converted to belief in The Lord, then they would never again attack us. Indeed, what reason would they have for doing so?'

Canio could think of several reasons, among them loot, lust and the sheer hellish joy of killing people and destroying everything they could not carry off with them. He guessed, however, that such objections would not be favourably received by the women. 'You certainly have a point there, ladies,' he nodded approvingly. 'We will draw strength and inspiration from your example, won't we Claudia?' he said, turning to Vilbia and giving her the ghost of a wink.

'Indeed we shall, Marcus,' she agreed, her face expressionless.

'You share your husband's faith, of course?' Aeterna asked, frowning slightly. 'I only ask because I could not help noticing that you wear a coin of the apostate Julian around your neck.'

Canio breathed a silent curse, but before he could think of a suitable lie, Vilbia said quickly, 'Indeed I do, sister, and for a very good reason. It serves as a constant reminder that the powers of darkness and those who do not share my beliefs are all around me, and therefore I must forever be on my guard against them.'

The answer seemed to please Aeterna. It certainly impressed Canio.

'That is so very true, sister. And, although it grieves me to say it, I fear that in this province, perhaps more than in any other of the entire empire, those powers of darkness are still greatly exalted.'

Canio was beginning to find Aeterna distinctly unsettling. If she could identify a coin hanging around Vilbia's neck, what else could she see? There was too much fervent energy about the woman. 'Ladies, I've detained you from your noble work for too long, and we must resume our journey to Portum Abona where my father should be waiting for us.'

'And your mother too?' Aeterna asked.

'Alas no,' said Canio, almost without thinking. 'She has been with the Lord now for nearly two years,' he added, with what he judged was appropriate sadness.

'May the Good Shepherd keep her soul,' Aeterna replied. 'Abona is only some seven miles from here. You should get there by early evening at the very latest.' She appeared to hesitate, then said, 'Although if you are in no great hurry to reach Abona, then you would be most welcome to join us for a simple meal of bread and wine. We have plenty of both.'

Canio thought of the goatskin of wine nestling in his own saddlebags. If that were to be combined with whatever Aeterna had … He gazed into their earnest faces and there came into his mind, unbidden, a vision of all five women hopelessly, riotously, intoxicated and capering stark naked around him, like maenads around Bacchus. He tried not to grin.

'That is most kind of you Aeterna,' came Vilbia's voice from behind him, 'but my dear white-haired father-in-law was expecting us to arrive this morning, so we are late already, aren't we, Marcus?'

'Yes … I suppose we are, Claudia. Duty before pleasure,' Canio added, shooting Vilbia a sly glance. He thanked Aeterna for the offer, then tugged at the reins and started southwards once more. Vilbia smiled sweetly at them all, and a little later turned and waved, before distance and the scattered trees hid them from view.

'Why, Primicerius Canio, I had no idea that you felt such enthusiasm for the new religion,' she said, her voice so neutral that he was again uncertain whether there was irony there or not.

'I say and do whatever is necessary to survive,' he grunted. 'And yourself?'

'The same,' she replied.

For the first mile Canio expected her to ask why he had not given their true names to the women. But she never did.

CHAPTER SEVEN

Canio knew Portum Abona quite well, particularly its eating and drinking establishments. It was an unwalled town standing on a small plain on the north bank of the Flumen Abona, some four miles east of that river's confluence with the ever-widening estuary of the great Sabrina. In the early evening he found himself looking down across its clustered buildings from the high ground to the north.

'Well, there's the old place again,' he remarked to Vilbia. 'Have you ever been here before?'

'No, never,' she replied, as she slowly surveyed the landscape all the way from west to east and then gazed down at the town itself. 'I've never been this far south. Is it still used as a port?'

'It certainly is – one of the biggest in the province. It got pretty badly mauled in the first days of the *Conspiratio*, but the river's still here and so the ships still come. Look – you can see two of them from here.' And he pointed beyond the rooftops to where two tall masts were swaying almost imperceptibly in the Abona's current.

It had been several months since his last visit, and as they drew nearer he looked around to see how the reconstruction was progressing. Along the riverfront stood a row of large, two-storey warehouses. Even from some way off he could see that their timber walls were new, the boarding still bright from saw and adze, although their roofs were covered with a random mixture of new and old clay tiles, the new ones raw orange-red, the old ones weather-darkened and lichen stained.

Behind the riverfront warehouses was the remembered

confusion of more warehouses, workshops, houses, shops and hostelries. Most of those buildings that had survived the *Conspiratio* were built of a variegated reddish-brown and grey stone. Few of the old timber buildings had escaped the Hibernians' torches. All that was left of some were low foundation walls of fire-blackened stone surrounding irregular heaps of smashed roof tiles and other weed-grown debris. Sticking out of this debris he noticed a number of jagged lengths of timber which had been so badly carbonised as to make them not worth salvaging. They seemed to cast an air of desolation over the entire town.

He continued on downhill until they reached the stream which formed the western boundary of Portum Abona. It wound down from the north before its once-bright waters merged anonymously with those of the Flumen Abona. There was a timber bridge across the stream, a bridge strong and wide enough to take the biggest wagon that might trundle across on its way to or from the warehouses. Its decking appeared to have been recently renewed in massive planks that had shrunk and warped in the June sun, creating gaps through which he glimpsed flashes of the water below as Antares clopped slowly across.

The first inn they came to was The Guiding Star, a large two-storey *stabulum* he had patronised a couple of times before. Beneath a large plaster panel painted with a yellow, eight-pointed star, the double doors of the establishment stood wide open. He went inside, leaving Vilbia sitting up on Antares, but soon returned, propelling before him a rumpled youth who led them round to the stable block at the rear. There he helped Vilbia to slide wearily down, before unsaddling the horse. He waited long enough to satisfy himself that both the feed and water which the youth was proffering were of acceptable quality, then heaved up both saddle and saddlebags and walked with her back into the *stabulum*.

The large main room of The Guiding Star was fairly well lit by a row of unglazed windows set several feet below the high coffered timber ceiling, their shutters hooked back against the walls to let in the warm breezes of the June evening. Long ago, or so Canio reckoned by their somewhat faded appearance, some journeyman fresco artist had painted the plastered walls with scenes of idealised seascapes, in which ships in full sail moved serenely over small blue waves where dolphins, octopuses, hippocamps and other strange sea-monsters sported. The floor was covered with plain stone slabs, worn and slightly sunken in places, and on it were arranged a dozen or so tables and three times as many chairs and stools of diverse designs, ages and states of repair.

There were about as many people as there were tables in the room, mostly men but with a couple of women, although since the people sat around in little groups of two or three the majority of the tables were still unoccupied. By their clothes and the snatches of conversation he overheard, Canio came to guess that most of the men were either merchants or some of the crew from the two ships tied up at the wharf.

'I *thought* it was you, Canio, you old dog!' came a bellow from a shadowed corner of the room. 'What in sweet Rosmerta's name are you doing down in this part of the world?'

Canio swung round to see two soldiers sitting at a corner table, each cradling a large beaker of green glass. The speaker was a burly man of about his own age with a bushy black beard. 'Primicerius Canio to you, Victor, you old sinner,' he replied. He grinned broadly and hoped that nothing in his voice would make Vilbia suspect that he was not best pleased to have encountered the pair. He dropped the saddle onto a table but kept the saddlebags slung over his shoulder.

'*Acting* Primicerius Canio. We must address everyone by their correct rank, mustn't we, Victor?' scolded the other guard humorously. He was older than Victor, mid-thirties perhaps, smaller but tough-looking.

'Indeed we must, Mettus, Shit-Shoveller Third Class. Are you well? Are you sober?'

'I'm very well indeed, Canio. And who in the name of Hades wants to be sober at this time of day? Who's your young friend?'

'Would you believe that this is my niece, Claudia?'

Both guards pantomimed their efforts of trying not to laugh.

Canio grinned again. 'No, I didn't think you would. The truth is, she's just a very good friend of mine,' he said with the air of a man who, this time, did expect to be believed.

'Of course,' said Victor gravely. 'We believe you, don't we Mettus?'

'Absolutely,' Mettus agreed, straight-faced. 'Wouldn't doubt it for a moment.'

Vilbia seemed less than amused by this banter. 'Primicerius,' she whispered, 'I'm very tired. Could you please arrange for our rooms.'

Canio raised one hand in temporary farewell to Victor and Mettus, then strolled over towards the bar that ran down most of the left hand side of the room.

'Oh, she's very *tired*, Canio. Don't keep her waiting!' Victor called after them. The man must have had the ears of a bat.

Canio did not turn around, but made an obscene finger gesture over his shoulder in Victor's direction. 'I want two good rooms for the night, Eucarpus,' he said to the sleek man behind the bar.

'Two, Primicerius?'

'Two,' Canio replied firmly.

'Of course, Primicerius. This way please.' Eucarpus walked the length of the bar, his height suddenly dropping by six inches as he stepped off the low platform hidden behind it.

'Keep an eye on my saddle; I won't be long,' Canio called out to Victor.

Victor smirked, and Canio guessed that he was on the point of observing to all present that the Primicerius must be intending to go for a ride that night. He gave Victor a hard look, intended to persuade him that such a remark would be distinctly unwise, at least in Vilbia's presence.

71

Eucarpus led them up a broad timber staircase to the upper floor, where a gloomy corridor ran the full width of the *stabulum*. On each side of the corridor were four doors. Eucarpus lifted the latch of the first and ushered both Canio and Vilbia inside. There he saw a bed covered with what looked like reasonably clean sheets and blankets, a small table and a couple of chairs. On the table was a bowl and water jug, both of red pottery, and a linen towel.

Eucarpus trotted over and pulled back the bedclothes. 'Examine that bed if you will, Primicerius. If you can find so much as one single, solitary flea, then both yourself and your lady can stay the night for nothing; I won't charge you a single *centenionalis*.'

Before Canio could reply, Eucarpus had reached down to the very bottom of the bed. 'And here, Primicerius,' he announced, 'is the reason why you won't find one. Fleabane!' With the triumphant air of a conjuror he pulled out and proffered several short lengths of a herb with wrinkled, pale green leaves.

'When it's in season I have a fresh basket delivered twice a week, and come the autumn I dry whole sackfuls of it to see us through the winter. And, by Mercury, it works too! I guarantee that any flea found in this establishment will have come with one of the guests – not yourselves, of course. But it won't be staying long, not with this stuff about.'

Canio looked at Vilbia, who raised her eyebrows. Perhaps, like him, she was wondering just how Eucarpus could possibly establish the provenance of any particular flea found loitering on the premises? However, he decided against asking the question. 'I thought it was the smell of the flowers that was supposed to keep the little bastards away – and you won't see any of those for a month or more.'

Eucarpus waved a dismissive hand. 'Don't you believe it, Primicerius. With or without flowers, there's not a flea in the province that can abide this stuff.'

'I'll take your word for it,' Canio replied. 'Well Claudia, what do you think of it?'

'It's fine, Primicerius. I think I'll sleep now.'

'Don't you want something to eat first?'

'No, not now thank you. Later perhaps, or in the morning.' She turned to them and smiled, and Canio and Eucarpus both took the hint and retreated. As they descended the stairs, Canio heard her shoot the iron bolt on the inside face of the door.

Back in the main dining room Canio ordered a meal. He had intended to have a roast chicken, but when Eucarpus told him of a brace of sea bass that had been brought in fresh by a fisherman from the mouth of the Sabrina Estuary that very afternoon he decided to have one of those instead.

'You won't regret your choice, Primicerius. It will be delicious. My wife, Paula, has a recipe that's been passed down in her family for generations. She rolls the bass in a mixture of salt and crushed coriander seeds, browns it in a skillet over an open fire and then bakes it in the oven inside a pottery dish with a tight-fitting lid, so that it cooks in its own juice. Once tasted, you will remember it for ever.'

While he waited for the unseen Paula to work her wonders on the fish, Canio strolled over to Victor and Mettus's table with a large flagon of good wine, a beaker and a freshly baked loaf of bread to stifle present hunger. He did not really wish to socialise with them, not on this particular evening anyway, but realised that it might appear distinctly odd if he did not.

'So, what's been happening since I was here last?' he asked as he topped up both their beakers from the flagon, before filling his own to the brim.

'Oh, nothing much,' Mettus replied. 'A week or so back there was a bit of a pitched battle on the wharf between the crews of two ships tied up there.'

'Seems there was an argument between their captains over who should carry a cargo of fleeces,' Victor added.

'How did it end?' Not that Canio really cared, but he thought he ought to ask.

'Don't really know, to tell you the truth.' Victor appeared slightly embarrassed. 'They were in nobody's way down there, so we thought we'd just let them get on with it and pick up any pieces after they'd done.'

'And were there any pieces?' Canio asked.

'Who knows? By morning both ships had gone. Sailed away into the night as if they'd never been there at all.'

'But there was blood on the planking. I saw it myself,' said Mettus.

'But no bodies?'

'No bodies that I saw,' Victor hedged. 'If there had been any, then they either took them on board or dropped them in the Abona there and then.'

'That's what I like; self-solving problems. Another refill?'

Both men looked tempted, but Victor said, 'Better not. We're both expected back on duty soon. Will you be coming to the guard post later, Canio?' he asked casually.

'I might,' he replied, 'just to check that you're not tucked up sound asleep in your little cots. But officially I'm on leave at the moment.' Seeing the incredulity in their faces he added, 'It's true, fellow slaves; I actually got a month's furlough out our beloved leader.' The incredulity deepened, so Canio delved into his belt pouch and pulled out the pass. 'Here, see for yourself,' he said and tossed it across the table to Victor.

Victor picked it up and examined what he must have realised only too well was a very rare document.

'See those two stamps?' said Canio. 'They're from Aemilianus's own seal cube, bless him.'

'As we frequently do,' Victor replied. 'So how in the names of all three little hooded gods did you manage it?' he asked, as he slid the pass back across the table.

'I simply asked him nicely, that's all. He's a good fellow, when you get to know him.'

Mettus nearly choked on the last drops of wine which he was swallowing at that moment.

'It's true I tell you, and this proves it,' Canio protested, tucking the pass back into his pouch.

'So will we see you at the guard post later?' Victor asked again.

'Maybe. Maybe not.' Canio grinned maliciously.

Mettus said nothing, but looked upwards and studied the ceiling.

'She's just a very good friend of the Primicerius,' Victor reminded him.

'So she is,' Mettus replied. 'Do you think I could get a friend like that?'

Victor shook his head gravely. 'Not on our pay you couldn't.'

It was Canio's turn to say nothing. He was off on a spree with a valid pass and a pretty girl. That was what they would tell anyone who asked, and that was fine by him.

***

After Victor and Mettus had gone, Canio started tearing fragments off the loaf and slowly eating them, washing them down with several more cups of wine. His sea bass came on an antique dish of glossy cherry-red Samian pottery, a large crack in its rim skilfully mended with thin strips of lead riveted through neatly-drilled holes on each side. He ate the fish slowly with knife and spoon. It was very good, and he told Eucarpus so.

Well fed, and mellowed by the wine, he got into occasional conversations with people at the adjacent tables, some of them local men and women who now and then drifted into The Guiding Star to drink and talk. The long summer evening slowly faded into night and Eucarpus began bustling around lighting the little pottery lamps on the occupied tables, using as a taper a long reed soaked in wax.

Gradually Canio became aware that the coming of darkness was turning the talk of the locals back to the first day of the

Conspiratio, the day when the Hibernians came. From what he overheard he realised that even now some of them, like Necalames, were still haunted by the fear that the barbarians might one day return.

As the cups of wine and barley beer were emptied and refilled, so their contents and the presence of Canio and those merchants and sailors who were strangers or near-strangers in Abona seemed to act as a catalyst, prompting the townspeople to tell their stories. And in the act of telling, perhaps to exorcise for a little while those year-old ghosts that, he guessed, would come creeping inexorably back in the dark and lonely hours before dawn.

After those ghosts had been exorcised for another evening, some of the birds of passage present – the merchants and sailors – started telling their own favourite tales. Canio wondered if they were telling them in an attempt to lift the gloom that the memories of the *Conspiratio* had brought? Whatever their reasons, he heard stories of narwhals and hippocamps, and of a giant squid bigger than any ship that the narrator had ever seen. This last tale produced several sceptical jeers from the listeners.

'Ah, but the world is changing, and few believe in real wonders any more.' The speaker was Flavius Helius, who had already informed everyone present that he was a trader in sheep fleeces and came from Bononia, on the north coast of Gaul. But Helius had already drunk so much wine that Canio couldn't tell whether he was being sympathetic or ironic.

He heard a chair scrape and turned to see a merchant he'd heard someone call Decibalus standing and raising his hands as if to implore silence. 'Well I still believe in wonders, although I call them miracles. Listen all of you – listen to what I actually witnessed with my own two eyes.

'It was almost two years ago, and we were sailing back to Londinium after delivering a cargo of hides to Rotomago, that city on the river Seine. By then we were far out on the Oceanus Britannicus, the day fine and clear with a light wind from the south-west in our sail. And then we spotted them – two of those long, sleek-hulled galleys with which the accursed Saxon and Frankish pirates infest the seas. They were half a mile or so astern of us and we tried to outrun them. But they were built for speed, with oars as well as sail, and soon they were only a hundred yards behind us – so close that we could see the fierce, cruel faces of their crews and hear their hellish screams as they worked themselves into a fury of bloodlust. So certain were we that our last hour in this world had come that I, and every man on my ship, fell to our knees, lifted our arms and our eyes to heaven and prayed to the Good Shepherd to receive our poor souls into his everlasting empire.

'And then the miracle happened. It was, as I've told you, a fine, clear day. But suddenly, when the heathens were no more than ten yards behind, so near that we could almost smell their unwashed, stinking bodies, there came down as if from heaven itself a wall of dense mist, right in front of our bows. The next moment we had sailed into it, only to find that it was like no other mist I had ever encountered, before or since. It wasn't dark or damp or chill, but bright and warm – like a cloud with the sun shining through it. And in the midst of it I heard singing coming from high above, singing as sweet as I imagine the voices of angels to be.

'How long we were in that mist I cannot say for sure. Not long, I think – indeed, it might have been only moments before we were emerging from the other side. I looked at my crew and saw the terror on their faces as they stared back towards the stern, expecting at any moment to see the gaping-jawed monsters carved on the high prow-posts of those heathen galleys come flying out of the mist to devour us. But they never came. And when it was about a quarter mile behind us, we saw the mist dissolve as suddenly as it had come, leaving nothing but an empty sea. Of those heathen galleys there was no trace, and we never saw them again. Which was proof to me, as it should be proof to you all, that the Good Shepherd does truly watch over and protect his own flock.'

Helius snorted his derision. 'Decibalus, it proves nothing – except that perhaps the prospect of your imminent company so horrified your so-called "Good Shepherd" that the sending of that mist was an act of divine self-defence.' Helius's voice was slurred, and Canio noticed that he was staring down into his wine cup.

In the ensuing laughter he took the opportunity to glance around the room, wondering if he would recognise any of those people who had slipped in unnoticed after nightfall. As he did so he saw Vilbia, sitting in the darkened corner behind him. Their eyes met and she nodded to him. He felt slightly uncomfortable: the watcher hates to find himself watched. Taking the wine flagon, his own beaker and a spare beaker from an adjoining table he slid over and sat beside her.

'I didn't realise you'd come down. Have you eaten yet?' he asked, filling both beakers and pushing one towards her.

'Thank you,' she murmured. 'No, not yet. Strangely, I don't really feel hungry at the moment. Perhaps later. Or in the morning, if there's time,' she added, sipping at the wine.

'There'll be plenty of time in the morning. Have you been down here long?'

'Not long. But don't you want to be off at dawn?'

'No: it's best to wait for the high tide. Easier to get the horse into the ferry,' he added by way of explanation.

'Ferry?' She sounded surprised. 'Won't we be taking the road that runs east from here to Aquae Sulis along this northern side of the river?'

Canio wondered how she knew of that road, if she had never been to Abona before? Perhaps she had been wandering the town while he had thought her safely tucked away upstairs. And if so, what else might she have discovered?

'Now why would we want to do that, my pretty one?' he asked cautiously.

'Because at Aquae Sulis we could join the Fosse Way as it heads down towards Lindinis. Wouldn't that be the quickest

78

way to get to the south side of the Great Marshes – from the eastern side?'

'Perhaps. Perhaps not,' Canio said slowly. 'You never know who you might meet on the highways these days. They can be dangerous places,' he added. 'Anyway, I think the western route I have in mind will be quicker.'

What he couldn't tell her was that, as time passed and the distance from Corinium increased, he was developing a paranoid suspicion that Vitalinus just might have been tempted to inform Aemilianus that his cherished furlough pass was a forgery. That he had been seen sneaking out of the Prefect's office, seal cube in hand. The clerk was cunning, and in Canio's absence he and Marcellus could have found a way to accuse him without incriminating themselves. Aemilianus was certainly fool enough to believe whatever lies that pair could concoct, particularly as he would not be around to defend himself. And if the Prefect were to send an order for his arrest to the patrols on the Fosse Way, the road down which he had been seen leaving Corinium …

Fortunately, Vilbia appeared satisfied with his explanation.

He had already told himself that she was forbidden fruit, at least until he was safely rid of the Hecate figurine, and if he had been completely sober he would never have done it. But by then he was far from sober. And so, under the table, his fingers began gently stroking Vilbia's knee through the soft cloth of her dress. Slowly his fingers started moving higher in a smooth, circular motion, working slowly inwards.

'Strange, isn't it?' she said quietly, looking straight into his eyes.

'What is, my pretty one?'

'To think that she might have been here, little more than a year ago. Here in this room, sitting at this table – perhaps even sitting in the very same chair that you're sitting in now.'

'Who?'

'Why, Pascentia of course.'

The name sobered Canio quicker than a bucket of cold

water. 'Now why in the world would you think that?' he asked.

'Because when she came by ship from Gaul she landed here in Abona, before making her way north to Ovilregis. Didn't Necalames tell you that?'

Canio slowly shook his head.

'Oh well, that's what he told me,' she said lightly.

Canio studied her face, now in motionless profile as she surveyed the other guests in the lamplight. He could read absolutely nothing in that face. 'I suppose she could have come this way,' he said, trying to sound casual.

'She might even have drunk from that very same cup that you're drinking from now,' Vilbia mused. 'Think of that, Primicerius.' She turned her head and looked him full in the face again.

Her gaze discomfited him. Those eyes seemed to see too much, to know too much. *Eutherius's eyes.* He hurriedly stood up. 'Well, I'd better be off to bed – it's going to be a long day tomorrow. By the way, if I'm not here at The Star in the morning then I'll probably be down on the wharf.'

'Until the morning then, Primicerius,' she replied, raising the beaker to her lips for another sip.

⁂

That same evening, in his little house in Corinium, Eutherius was peering anxiously into the green flames that hovered above the pulsing charcoal in his brazier. He already knew that Vilbia had left Ovilregis at around noon on the previous day and had not returned. Also, that Canio had been seen there too, before he had ridden off in the same southerly direction that she had taken. But where were they both now? And were they together?

After staring into the flames until long after the sun had set – although night and day were much the same to him – he at last caught a glimpse of dark, shimmering shapes that could, he told himself, have been a man and a woman travelling together. The vision lasted only for a moment and then was gone. He took another pinch of powder from one of his small silver bowls, sprinkled it onto the glowing charcoal and waited. But the dark shapes never returned. Perhaps, he reflected fretfully, they had never existed outside his head, simply the children of his fears. But he had to act on those fears.

Much later that night, when the moon was hidden behind clouds, he stood, a cloaked and hooded figure darker than the night itself, near the Verulamium Gate. In the shadows cast by the flickering torchlight he waited, motionless, until the sentry had changed position to stand under the far pedestrian archway of the four-arched gate. Then he crept silently up the stone staircase until he reached the passageway outside the locked door of Canio's room. A few stealthy scraping noises ended in a soft click, and moments later he was standing inside the tomb-dark room. Slowly and methodically he worked his way around the room, searching, by touch alone, first the table, then the bed, the chest, the floorboards, and finally even the walls themselves, stone by stone, in case one was loose and could be pulled out to reveal a hiding place behind.

But it was all in vain, and eventually Eutherius murmured to himself in the darkness, 'So it would seem that he took it with him. But where is he going? And why? Take care, my daughter, take care.'

CHAPTER EIGHT

Although Canio woke too late to catch the sunrise, he was at least in time to see the great white moon dissolve into the brightness of the south-western sky. Leaving Vilbia finishing a simple meal of bread, goats' cheese and watered wine, he strolled around to the stables. There he gossiped with the ostler and made sure that Antares would be groomed and ready in time to catch the tide. He then made a few enquiries in the town and bought some supplies, before returning to The Guiding Star for his own breakfast.

'The horseflesh situation here in Abona is just as bad as it was at Ovilregis,' he announced to Vilbia, between spoonfuls of mutton broth in which he had floated small chunks of bread. 'There's not so much as a three-legged mule for hire, not here or anywhere else so far as I can discover. It seems that over the last year my fellow heroes in the army have helped themselves to just about everything that they could throw a saddle on. I'd hoped to hire a donkey for you to ride,' he added.

'Thank you for the thought, Primicerius, but I'm used to walking. And now that I've had a good night's sleep we'll be able to move much faster.' Her somewhat cool tone made him wonder if she suspected that his primary motive for wanting the donkey was speed of travel, rather than her comfort. Which, admittedly, it was.

As soon as he had finished breakfast he paid Eucarpus what was owing, then carried his saddle and saddlebags back to the stable. There he saddled Antares himself, so ensuring that the ostler had no opportunity to investigate the contents of the saddlebags. Then, with Vilbia at his side, he walked the horse down to the wharf.

It was a fine, bright morning with scarcely a cloud in the sky, and Vilbia noticed how the sun made even the muddy brown waters of the Abona sparkle, particularly where its surface was chopped into wavelets and tiny white horses by the wind which funnelled up from the Sabrina Estuary. Canio had already told her that the river was still tidal at that point, and that its width varied with the state of the tides.

It was some forty yards across when they arrived at the wharf, and she found herself gazing down at the sloping banks of grey mud on both sides, their desolate surfaces fissured with the snaking channels of tiny watercourses made by the high tide waters draining back into the river. On the opposite bank, above the bare mud, was a narrow strip of white flowers which, when she asked, Canio informed her was scurvy-grass. Beyond the scurvy-grass stood a band of waist-high reeds.

The wharf itself was a masterpiece of crude carpentry. Peering down between the gaps in the decking she saw a criss-cross framework of massive baulks of timber that had been laid in the mud and built up to form a level base. Over this framework planks had been laid and fixed down with great square-sectioned iron nails. The decking creaked in a few places as they walked on it. An old man, sitting in the sunshine on an upturned barrel, cackled as she hopped quickly back from a plank which had groaned ominously beneath her.

'Don't you worry – them boards are a good three fingers thick and don't break very often. And even when they do, a body hasn't far to fall before the mud catches him,' he assured her cheerfully.

Looking down the length of the wharf she saw, arranged haphazardly on the planking, dozens of barrels, small hills of bulging sacks, and three or four stacked crates of pottery bowls packed in straw.

The two ships whose masts she had glimpsed on the previous evening were still riding at anchor out in the current, long gangways connecting them to the wharf. She had seen their like only once before, at Glevum docks. They were sea-going cargo vessels, both at least a hundred feet long and broad in the beam, with high, curved prow and stern posts and large dirty-white mainsails, which now were furled and hanging in swags from their cross-spars high above the decks.

Under the vigilant eye of an overseer, lounging against the side of a warehouse, four sailors were sweating and swearing as they humped heavy bales of sheep fleeces out of the warehouse and up the gangway of the nearest of the moored ships, before dropping them through the open hatchway into the hold. There, hidden from her view but making their presence known by the roared curses that accompanied the bales which just missed their heads, it seemed that other sailors were dragging and stacking them around the hold.

The ships fascinated her, and she would have watched them longer if Canio hadn't patted her on the shoulder and said, 'Come on, let's find old Charon.' So she followed him to the upstream end of the wharf, where a large flat-bottomed ferry barge was moored. Handing her Antares' reins, Canio then thumped on the door of what she had taken to be just another warehouse, shouting, 'Vindex! ... Vindex, you old rogue, you've got customers waiting!' He paused for a few moments, then hammered and called again, but there was still no response so he tried the door and grunted with exasperation on finding it locked.

'Merda!' he muttered. 'Where's the old bastard gone?'

Leaving her holding Antares he walked back, spoke briefly to the overseer of the fleeces, and then stomped further away down the planking. Vilbia watched him weaving in and out of the barrels and sacks, until at last he turned abruptly into another warehouse. Shortly afterwards he emerged, accompanied by a tall, thin man wearing baggy trousers and a smock-like tunic which reached down to his knees. Studying him as he approached she thought he might be of any age between thirty and forty-five, having the look of one of those people who seem to pass directly from childhood to middle age and then stay there for many years, virtually unchanged.

'Claudia, my young friend, this is Vindex: ferryman by trade, dicer, wine lover and I will not make you blush by saying what else, by choice. Vindex is going to carry us over the Abona, aren't you Vindex?'

'That I will master, as soon as the tide's high enough.'

'It looks high enough already.'

'Not yet it isn't,' Vindex declared flatly. 'You see, young lady, when they built that landing stage on the other side they made it higher than this one here,' he explained, pointing to a large timber platform jutting out from the reeds on the opposite bank. 'Don't ask me why, because I don't know; it was done before my time. So, unless I wait until the water level is just right, my passengers have to jump out onto the mud, which doesn't please them at all I can tell you.'

'How much longer have we got to wait?' Canio asked impatiently.

'Oh, still a way to go yet.' Vindex smiled at Vilbia, revealing his lack of front teeth. 'What I'll do though, young lady, is tell you a story to pass the time.' He sat down on a barrel and motioned Vilbia to do the same.

'I've heard a few of your stories,' Canio grunted. 'They'd make a satyr blush.'

'Didn't stop you laughing at them though, did it, Canio?'

'Primicerius Canio to you, you old goat.'

'Well this story's clean; I'd swear it on my father's grave.'

'You mean you've at last discovered who he was?'

Vindex ignored Canio. 'There once was a woman,' he began. 'A goddess, I should really say, called Aurora ... Have you heard of her, young lady?'

'Of course: she's the goddess of the dawn.'

Vindex nodded approvingly. 'Well, one day, as Aurora came peeping over the horizon bringing the new day, she saw this wonderfully handsome young man and straightaway fell madly in love with him.'

'Women don't function that way,' muttered Canio dismissively. 'They need ...'

Vilbia turned her head and looked enquiringly at him. 'Need what?' she asked.

But it seemed that Canio had second thoughts about sharing his accumulated wisdom on the subject, and he simply shrugged.

'Aurora was a goddess,' Vindex reminded him. 'They're not like other women.'

'If you say so.'

'The handsome young man's name was Tithonus, and he was the son of a king of Troy, whose name I've forgotten for the moment, and a nymph called ... something.' Vindex muttered an obscenity under his breath, apparently irritated that his memory had failed him.

'That's what comes of taking it unwatered too often,' Canio grinned, shaking his head.

'Laomedon – that was the king's name,' Vindex announced triumphantly. 'Anyway, Aurora was so madly in love with Tithonus that she straightaway carried him off to her palace, which lay as far away to the east as you can possibly go without falling off the edge of the world. And there she made him her husband.'

'Which is a polite way of putting it,' Canio observed to Vilbia.

'But the problem was that although his mother was a nymph, Tithonus was still only a mortal man, while Aurora was an immortal goddess. So she went to Jupiter and begged him to grant Tithonus the gift of eternal life, so that he could live with her for ever. And that is exactly what Jupiter did, he gave him eternal life. But he's cunning is old Jupiter, and what he didn't do was give him eternal youth to go with that eternal life. And so, as the years passed, Tithonus, who once had been so beautiful that a goddess fell in love with him, became old and ugly. But he didn't die, and couldn't die, not even if he'd wanted to, because he could never renounce the immortality that had become a curse.

'At last, when poor Tithonus was no more than the withered husk of the man he once had been, his once-fine body looking like the black and shrivelled pod of a horse bean just before it's harvested, Aurora at last admitted to herself that she had lost him forever. And in despair she turned him into a grasshopper, so that in summer he sang to her all day, and every spring he greeted her with a new, perfect body, all glossy green ... There, what do you think of that story, young lady?'

Vilbia looked out over the dark waters of the Abona. 'To come to look upon immortality as a curse – how strange and terrible that must be,' she mused.

'Not a curse likely to bother any of us much,' Canio muttered. 'Hey, do you think that's what happened to old Eutherius? Perhaps one day long ago, when he was young and handsome – that takes some imagining, doesn't it? – he had his wicked way with a goddess too. Maybe one of these days I'll go into his shop and see a big green grasshopper sitting in his chair, wearing his clothes and chirruping away. Or perhaps I already have, but never noticed the difference.' He sniggered.

Vilbia, distracted, her thoughts wandering down a long and lonely road, said nothing.

'River's about high enough now,' said Vindex, looking across the water.

Gazing across the Abona again, Vilbia saw it swirling and eddying quietly, menacingly, as if down through those muddy depths the normal flow from the east and the incoming tide from the west were meeting once again in their age-old conflict.

'Right, then let's be off. We can't hang around here all day listening to silly stories,' said Canio briskly.

Vilbia wondered if he was annoyed because she hadn't even smiled at his joke about Eutherius.

Vindex got down off his barrel and walked over to where the ferry barge was tied to one of several piles that stuck out of the water at the edge of the decking. He took hold of the mooring rope and clunked the side of the ferry right up against the timbers of the wharf and held it there.

'Ready?' asked Canio.

'Ready,' said Vindex.

Keeping a tight hold of the reins, Canio stepped into the ferry, then turned and tugged. Antares seemed reluctant to follow.

'Come on you old bastard, you've seen a ferry before,' Canio coaxed, tugging harder. Still the horse refused to budge, its front hoofs on the very edge of the planking. Canio swore. 'Give him a whack, will you Vindex.'

Vindex obliged with a hearty slap on Antares' rump. The horse gave a faint whinny and put one hesitant hoof into the boat. Vilbia watched as Canio increased the tension on the reins to maintain his forward momentum, and moments later Antares had stumbled stiff-legged down into the ferry, where he stood nervously tossing his head.

Vindex untied the mooring rope from the bollard and Vilbia stepped quickly aboard. As the ferry swung out into the current, Vindex dropped the rope and snatched up a large paddle. With quick, deft strokes he drove the boat across the river as Canio held Antares by the bridle, stroking his muzzle.

As soon as they bumped against the posts supporting the jetty on the far bank, Vindex released the paddle and grabbed the upstream post. With Vilbia's help he tied the ferry to the post, then stood back and let Canio persuade Antares to step out onto the jetty. Once the horse was safely on the planking, Canio dug into his belt pouch and pulled out a handful of small copper *centenionales*. 'Here, you pay the man,' he said to her. 'Two for you, two for me and four for master Antares.'

As she did so, counting the eight coins one by one into Vindex's eager cupped palm, she asked him a question that had been puzzling her. 'Are there any proper roads leading south from here?'

Vindex shrugged. 'There's a few decent tracks here and there, especially close to the big villas, but nothing anywhere near as long or as good as the Fosse Way. Where are you and old Canio heading for?'

But before Vilbia could reply, Canio shouted from above the belt of reeds through which he had already led Antares, 'Come on, stop sweet-talking old Charon. It won't do you any good anyway – he likes his women big and plump, don't you, Charon, you old ram?'

'Damn your eyes, Canio – I've told you before never to call me by that name!' Vindex yelled angrily back. He fished out from the front of his tunic a tiny wooden figurine of the goddess Fortuna and hurriedly kissed it. 'He knows I hate that name – it's terrible bad luck to speak it,' he muttered to Vilbia by way of explanation.

She waited for him to say more, but he did not. Hurriedly untying the rope he let the ferry drift out into the current, and she watched him begin paddling back towards the north bank. She waved to his unseeing back, then walked up through the reeds.

Side by side, she and Canio trudged along the stoned track which led up from the Abona to the skyline of a low ridge a quarter of a mile beyond. As they walked, Canio leading Antares, she asked why Vindex had so objected to being called Charon, adding, 'It must be a common enough nickname for a ferryman.'

'It's nothing. Don't worry your head about it,' Canio replied casually.

'But he must have had a reason,' she persisted. 'Why won't you tell me?'

Canio sighed. 'Well, if you must know, it goes back to the early days of the *Conspiratio* – the days when dozens and dozens of soldiers were crossing the Abona in that boat of his every day, before heading south-west down to the lower Sabrina

Estuary. A good few of those men never came back – not to Abona or to anywhere else, if you take my meaning. At that time his ferry was going backwards and forwards at all hours of the day and night, whatever the state of the tide, with Vindex and another man working it in shifts.'

'So?'

'So, someone claimed that it was mostly the men who Vindex himself carried over the river who went on to get themselves killed. I've no idea whether that was true or not, but that's how the whispers started.'

'Whispers that he brought bad luck?'

'Exactly – which is why the soldiers started calling him Charon. Some were joking, but some weren't. I heard he got really scared that one of them was going to stick a knife into him to kill the bad luck. Soldiers can be superstitious bastards.'

'You're not superstitious about things like that though, are you?' She was aware that Canio was looking sideways at her, but she kept her face expressionless.

'No I'm not … I just take sensible precautions, that's all. Vindex though, they say he came to half-believe that he had the evil eye and had become a chooser of the slain.'

'And once those chosen were on the other side of the River Styx, then they could never return, could they? Unless of course Hecate herself guided their ghosts back to this world.' She watched Canio's face as she spoke.

'So the old story goes,' he replied, apparently carelessly. 'Come on, you can ride for the first mile.' He crouched down and interlaced his fingers to form a step for her to mount.

'I can manage, thank you,' she said, and with easy grace took hold of one of the leather-covered horns at the front of the saddle and sprang up, twisting lithely in mid-air so that she sat side-saddle, demurely facing Canio.

'Don't you trust me?' he asked.

'Do I have any reason not to, Primicerius?'

'None whatsoever.' She gave him what she hoped was a

sceptical look and he added, 'Listen, I was a bit drunk last night. It won't happen again: you have my word on it.'

'In that case, then I'm sure it won't,' she said, flicking the reins and starting Antares into a brisk trot that left Canio having to jog to keep up.

***

It was late morning when they came across the ruined villa. Canio had left the stoned track after a mile. He didn't say why, and Vilbia didn't ask: she assumed he had a route planned. For an hour afterwards they travelled south-westwards, avoiding the thickly wooded rising ground away to the east and holding only brief conversations with the few people that they chanced to meet, mostly *pagani* working in the fields. Some time after the last of these encounters they passed through a narrow belt of trees and suddenly she saw the villa, standing before her in a sea of tall grasses that only a year before must have been meticulously scythed lawns.

It had not been large, but it had been beautiful; there was enough left standing for her to realise that. Burnt and deserted though it was, the place possessed a haunting, elegiac quality; a lingering echo of something wonderful that was all but gone.

After Canio had tethered Antares they both began looking around. The roofs had gone, most of the upper storey too, destroyed by the fire that had roared through the villa after the barbarians had torched it. Inside one suite of rooms, as she carefully picked her way over and between the blackened timbers and shattered roof tiles, she gazed at smoke and rain-stained frescoes on walls that now stood stark and open to the sky.

Most frescoes were damaged beyond recognition, but one remaining fragment caught her eye. It depicted an exotic garden with, in its centre, a circular fountain from which sprays of blue water rose and fell. Small brightly-coloured birds hopped and flew among the leaves and flowers of the garden, or perched around the rim of the fountain. As she looked at them she heard the chirruping of unseen birds outside the villa walls, and for a moment the painted birds came alive.

As she stood in front of that fresco she wondered who they had been, those people for whom it must have been an everyday sight when it was enclosed within the heart of the villa, its rich colours subdued in the shadows or glowing in the evening lamplight. Both logic and intuition told her that they must be dead; that they would never return to rebuild the villa and make it a magic place again.

Walking across the paved inner courtyard to find Canio, her eye was caught by a scrap of iridescent colour among the debris that littered it. It was a peacock's feather, bedraggled and faded by weather and sun. She picked it up and teased its separated filaments back together until its eyes were complete again. Despite the strong sunlight which gave life to its muted colours, she realised that it was only the wan ghost of what it once had been.

She found Canio inside the remains of the bath suite, closely examining a small semicircular cold plunge bath, the internal surfaces of which had been waterproofed with a thick coat of pinkish plaster, now greening with algae.

When she gave him a questioning look he explained that, 'I once heard tell of a man who kept a purse of gold coins hidden in the overflow pipe of a bath like this. Pretty good hiding place, don't you think? Nobody would have lingered long enough in the cold water to look up the pipe.'

'But not good enough, or you would never have heard of it,' she pointed out.

'True,' he conceded, 'but better than most. What's that you've got?' She held up the peacock feather for his inspection. 'Ah. No sign of the bird itself I suppose?'

'No, just this one feather to show that it ever lived.'

'Pity. It would have made a good dinner.'

'I suspect that someone else thought the same, a year or so ago.'

Canio, having given up on the cold plunge, was now outside the bath suite. He sat on the low wall that surrounded its sunken hypocaust stokehole and began poking around in the debris below with the end of a charred spar.

'Don't deserted buildings make you sad?' she asked.

'Sometimes; when I think of the pretty, laughing women who might once have lived in them and now are gone, maybe into the earth for ever ... Mercury! is that what I think it is?' In an instant Canio had dropped the spar, swung his legs over the low stone wall and was crouching down among the caked ashes. 'It is – it's a solidus!' he announced triumphantly, holding up the small gold coin for Vilbia's inspection. 'How in sweet Venus's name did it get there?'

Grabbing the spar again he started stirring vigorously through the ashes and dark, decayed fragments of brushwood. 'Well I'll be damned, there's another!' he whooped a few moments later, picking a second solidus out of the debris under the arched stokehole and rubbing it on his sleeve.

'Looks like it's one of old Constantine's.' He held the coin between finger and thumb and inspected it as it caught the sunlight. 'It must be well over thirty years since you saw the inside of a mint, but you're as fresh as the day the hammer came down, bless you.' He kissed the coin, and carefully placed them both deep inside his belt pouch.

'Hey, do you know what I'm thinking?' The question was rhetorical. 'I'm thinking that when he heard the Hibernians were coming, the man who owned this place hid his store of gold in there,' – Canio pointed into the darkness of the hypocaust – 'reckoning to come back for it later, of course.'

'But he never did come back, did he,' Vilbia sighed. 'Nobody came back.' She gazed at the weed-grown courtyard and the devastated buildings, and tried to suppress a shudder as she lived in her imagination the terror-stricken final moments of those men and women and children when the cruel blades slashed and stabbed and hacked. She could almost hear the screams.

But Canio did not reply. He was too busy climbing out of the stokehole pit and hurriedly gathering handfuls of last year's dead grasses, pale and desiccated, from among the fresh green stems. With his dagger he cut a short length off the end of a coil of rope fetched from his saddlebag, then unpicked the braided strands and used them to deftly bind a great wad of grass tightly around the end of his charred stick. When this crude torch was complete he lit it with flint and steel, blowing the smouldering grass until it was burning satisfactorily, then returned to the stokehole.

'Look after this for me.' He unbuckled his broad leather sword belt and handed it to her. Then, with the torch in his right hand held out in front of him, he crawled through the small archway into the hypocaust.

Vilbia sat on the grass and watched as the thick leather soles of his boots disappeared into the darkness. Then she glanced down at the belt and at the patterns of polished copper studs with which it was decorated. She lay the sheathed *spatha* on the grass beside her and looked more closely at the large belt buckle. It was cast in the form of the curved bodies of two dolphins, their wide mouths touching at the point where the pin rested, and from the head of each dolphin sprang a flattened horse's head facing outwards. All the flat surfaces of the buckle were covered with swirling patterns of tiny punched C's. She had to smile.

As he wriggled through the stokehole, Canio found that the hypocaust was some two feet high, its stone floor covered by a grid of short *pilae* – columns formed of stacks of square tiles which supported the stone slabs of the floor above. The *pilae* were spaced some twenty inches apart, and the rough edges of the fired clay scraped meanly against his body as he wormed his way between them. The air was dank and lifeless, and despite him waving the torch from side to side it soon dimmed to a smouldering glow that shed little light as he crawled deeper and deeper into the hypocaust.

As he advanced he scrabbled his fingers out over the rough stone floor, searching but finding nothing except the carbonised debris of long-dead fires. He had never before been aware of suffering from claustrophobia, but being trapped between those *pilae*, which restricted his every movement, made him think that this was what being buried alive must be like. He suddenly thought of Orgillus. Then he became aware of an odd, sour-milk sort of odour. As he inched forwards the smell grew steadily stronger and he had to force himself to concentrate on that bulging *follis* of gold coins that might now be only a finger's length away.

Feeling a faint movement of air on his face he began moving towards it, discovering that it was coming from one of the box tiles built into the thickness of the walls to act as flues, but now acting in reverse as the summer breeze blew over the roofless walls above. As he pushed the sullenly smouldering torch past the box tile's opening the downdraught of fresh air made it flare into sudden life. And there, caught in its lurid orange light, no more than a foot in front of his own, was a face out of nightmare.

For a long moment he stared at it, horribly fascinated, then cursed obscenely, dropped the torch and began scrambling wildly backwards, scarcely conscious of the pain as his elbows struck against the *pilae* tiles. He had only seen her for that moment, but it had been long enough to etch into his mind the image of the woman as she lay in the endless night of the hypocaust, where she must have taken refuge and then suffocated when the building above was fired. A woman with long dark hair and black parchment skin drawn so tightly over her face-skull that her mouth gaped open in a perfect 'O'.

The violent scrabbling alarmed Vilbia. 'Primicerius! Primicerius – what's the matter?' she cried, peering down into the dark stokehole.

There was no reply, only the sounds of something rapidly coming closer out of the darkness.

Leucesca protect me from the demons of the dark!

Thoroughly frightened now, she edged backwards and looked wildly around for a weapon. Canio's sword lay six feet away on the grass, but at her feet was an almost intact *tegula* clay roof tile. She grabbed the heavy tile and raised it above her head with both hands, ready to hurl it at whatever might emerge.

But to her relief it was only Canio's sweat-streaked face that she saw emerge blinking into the bright sunlight. Somehow he had managed to turn around inside the hypocaust. He scrambled to his feet, vaulted over the low wall and ran twenty yards before flopping down into the long grass.

He lay there for some time, absolutely still, his eyes closed, ignoring all her questions. Then he began cursing, slowly at first, then violently, shockingly.

Vilbia waited nervously until the storm had passed and he appeared calm again. 'What happened in there, Primicerius?' she asked. 'What did you see?'

'A ghost,' he muttered. 'I saw a ghost ... her ghost.'

'Whose ghost?'

Canio did not reply immediately. He sat with his head cradled between his hands until Vilbia asked again. Then he said, 'Nobody's ghost. I imagined it. I just dropped the torch, hit my head on the floor above and imagined it all.' He stood up and started vigorously brushing the already-drying ashes from his clothes, trying and failing to remove every trace. 'Here, you can have these.' He dug into his belt pouch and tossed the two solidi to her. 'If by some chance we should get separated then at least you'll be able to buy your own dinner,' he added with what she thought was an attempt at humour.

'I can buy my own dinner, thank you Primicerius.' But she did not return the coins, realising that he wanted to be rid of them and their association with whatever it was that he had encountered in the hypocaust.

'Come on, let's be away from this damned place.' Canio whistled to Antares, who pricked up his ears and neighed softly.

He strapped on his sword belt, helped Vilbia up into the saddle and then, when he must have thought she wasn't looking, gave one of the saddlebags a vicious punch.

A mile further on they came to a stream winding its way through the flatlands. There Canio disappeared behind a clump of willows in an apparent attempt to wash from his body and clothes all visible traces of the hypocaust. A modest distance away Vilbia waited patiently, eating some of the bread and cheese which Canio had bought at Abona.

'Your clothes are sopping wet, Primicerius,' she observed when he rejoined her.

He shrugged. 'It doesn't matter: the sun and the wind will dry me. And anyway, I learnt long ago that neither the world nor the gods care whether I'm wet or dry, cold or warm.'

CHAPTER NINE

At Canio's insistence she continued riding. He said that the exercise of walking would stop him feeling cold as his wet clothes dried. After that he said almost nothing and when, after several miles, she asked if he wanted to change places, he did not even turn to face her but simply muttered, 'No, I'm fine as I am,' and continued trudging on, reins in hand.

The sun was hot that afternoon, as Antares ambled along a green lane that wound south-westwards between overgrown hedges. Here and there wild rose briars had grown up through those hedges and smothered them with pink flowers, their perfume strong in the almost windless heat. Perched up on the gently swaying saddle, Vilbia stared uneasily at them as she passed, those un-needed reminders of the old cemetery near the Sabrina and the Caelofernus tombstone which stood there.

But neither could she forget the sacked villa, or cease wondering just what it was that Canio had encountered in the hypocaust. 'Perhaps he really did see a ghost,' she mused, deliberately loud enough for Canio to hear. When there was no response she added, 'Although it's more likely to have been an old badger who'd decided to make his home in there. Who would have thought that a big brave soldier would have been frightened by an old badger?'

But Canio still gave no sign of having heard her. He continued walking on at his own measured pace, sunk deep in thought and seemingly oblivious to her presence, or to anything else.

And so it was she who first heard the voices. They seemed to be coming from a long way ahead, and it was some time before she was even certain that they were voices, so slowly did they increase in volume.

Time passed without a meeting, and she realised that the unseen travellers must be moving ahead of them at almost exactly their own pace. But at last the voices grew loud enough for her to recognise that one belonged to a woman – a frightened woman. Although she could not yet make out a single word of what was passing between the woman and her male companions – for now she was almost sure that there were two male voices – Vilbia could hear plainly enough that the woman's voice was high and tearful. And all the while Canio trudged on, as if hearing nothing.

Then the woman screamed, a shrill scream of fear and pain which ended so abruptly that Vilbia almost felt the blow. It even roused Canio, who stopped and looked up, turning his head slightly to one side as one who, waking suddenly from sleep, is uncertain of what it was that has woken him. But still he said nothing, and after a brief pause walked on. Then the voices started again, male voices, angry and jeering, and much closer now.

Ahead was a great clump of brambles which was spreading, rampant in its summer growth, halfway across the track. As Antares rounded it Vilbia saw two big men, each wearing identical tunics striped in brown and black vertical bands. One had black hair, the other fair swept straight back from his forehead. Curled up on the ground lay a scrawny young woman in a plain dress of undyed wool. The fair-haired man was standing. The other was squatting on his haunches, his left hand grasping the young woman's hair, dragging her face up to meet the slap which his right palm was about to deliver. Her face was swollen and bruised, one eye half-closed.

There was a frozen moment during which the two parties stared at each other. Then the black-haired man released his hold on the young woman and stood up. 'What are you looking at, soldier boy? This is private business – a runaway – no concern of yours. Go lose yourself.'

'What did you say?' Vilbia could not see Canio's face, but she heard the cold anger in his voice.

'I said –'

'What did you say?' Canio repeated.

The black-haired man shot a quick glance at his companion. 'Are you deaf or just stupid, soldier boy. I said –'

'What did you say?' Canio asked again.

'For the last time,' the black-haired man shouted, his face reddening, 'I said –'

'Can you count up to ten?' Canio interrupted.

'What?'

'Can you count up to ten?'

'Of course I damned well can. What –?'

'I can count up to ten.'

'Why in the name of the Evil One should I care if you –?'

'Because it might save your life.'

'Are you mad? How could –?'

'Time.'

'Huh?'

'Time. If I count up to ten it might give you enough time to run far enough away.'

'Now why would we want to do that?'

Vilbia suspected that the black-haired man meant it to sound like a sneer, but there was uncertainty in his voice now.

'Because if I can't catch you, then I won't be able to kill you. And I want to kill you.'

There was complete silence, then the fair-haired man pointed to his chest and said, 'You do recognise these colours, don't you?' His voice mingled bafflement and anger in equal proportions.

'No,' Canio said blankly. 'I think I'll start counting now.'

The fair-haired man's face twisted in anger. 'This, you cretin, is the livery of Quintus Julius Muranus.'

'One.'

'Don't pretend you don't know who he is,' said the black-haired man.

'Two.'

'For your information, you ignorant bastard, he's –'

'You look just like they did.'

'What! Like who did?'

'You bastards look just like they did as they dragged her towards the stake.'

'You're insane, soldier boy – and I'll be damned if I'm going to take any more of your nonsense.' The black-haired man drew his sword from its scabbard, snatched a glance over his shoulder and called to the fair-haired man, 'Come on, let's teach this clown a lesson he won't forget.' Then he rushed at Canio.

It was, Vilbia realised afterwards, exactly what Canio had wanted him to do. Quicksilver fast, he dropped Antares' reins, drew his *spatha*, took one pace forwards and, as the black-haired man took a vicious swipe at his head, brought the blade up two-handed with such force that it smashed the sword out of the man's hand in a shower of sparks and sent it spinning away into the undergrowth.

The man screamed in pain and shock, his right wrist snapped like a twig by the savage power of the blow.

By then the fair-haired man had also drawn his sword and taken several steps towards Canio. Now he stood hesitating, pride struggling with survival instinct.

'Well, come on, my brave lad,' Canio sneered. 'You're not afraid of me, are you?' Vilbia saw fear in the man's eyes. Canio must have seen it too, and it seemed to act on him like the smell of blood to a wolf. With a savage howl he made as if to charge at the man, his *spatha* held high above his head like an executioner.

'No!' the man shouted, throwing down his sword and backing away, his hands rising in panic.

'No!' Vilbia's scream was instinctive, horrified by what she thought she was about to witness.

But it stopped Canio. Breathing heavily, he lowered his *spatha*, then without turning said, 'Get the rope from the saddlebag, will you.'

She slipped down out of the saddle and did as he requested. Warily she handed him the coil of rope. 'You're only going to tie them up, aren't you?' she asked.

Canio did not reply. He threw the rope hard at the fair-haired man, who grunted as he caught it against his chest. 'Tie his legs together,' he ordered, pointing to the black-haired man who knelt on the grass cradling his broken wrist, his face white with pain.

Nervously, the fair-haired man crouched down and did as instructed, while Canio stood over them both, ensuring that the knots were pulled tight.

'Well done, my hero – I can see you've had plenty of practice in the noble art of trussing up people like chickens for slaughter.' And before the man could reply, or even straighten up, Canio had chopped the pommel of his *spatha* down on the nape of the man's neck, dropping him like a pole-axed ox. Sheathing the sword he swiftly tied the man's hands and feet, then turned to the young woman.

She had been staring at the roughing-up of her persecutors, a look of savage excitement on her face. Looking closely at her for the first time, Vilbia realised that the woman was even younger than she had first thought, perhaps no more than her own age, although the weals and bruises on her cheeks had made her look older.

'What's your name, girl?' Canio asked.

'Litoria. What's yours?' she answered boldly.

'Best you don't know. Do you hate them?' Vilbia saw that the black-haired man's eyes were on Canio now, as if trying to guess what was coming.

'Of course I hate them! Wouldn't you? They treat us like dogs. Or worse than dogs, because dogs will bite if you hurt them, and we have nothing to bite them with. They're always looking for some excuse to beat us, and even when they can't find one they do it anyway. And they do other things to us women too,' she said, looking down at the grass. 'Like they would have done to me if you hadn't come along.'

Vilbia watched with increasing apprehension as Canio studied the girl's battered face, then picked the fair-haired man's sword out of the grass and held it out to her, hilt first. 'Go on, take it,' he said quietly. 'And then do whatever you like to them – anything at all. It's your chance to get even with the bastards.'

Litoria, still sitting on the ground, took the sword. She took it wonderingly, staring down its cruel, glittering length. The black-haired man watched in wide-eyed horror, like a vole cornered by a stoat. His mouth opened, but he seemed to have lost the power of speech.

Vilbia clutched Canio's sleeve. 'You can't let her do it!'

'Why not?' Litoria cried. 'The gods themselves know how much they deserve it!' She sprang to her feet and jabbed the point of the sword towards the black-haired man's face. He twisted violently backwards, yelping with pain as he rolled onto his broken wrist.

'Stop her! For pity's sake stop her!' Vilbia shouted at Canio.

But Canio ignored her, his eyes fixed on Litoria. 'Have they ever killed any of your people?'

Litoria nodded.

'Yes, I thought they had the look of executioners,' he murmured. 'Well, now they're yours to kill. As quickly or as slowly as you choose.'

Litoria turned and let the point of the heavy sword rest on the throat of the unconscious fair-haired man. She watched, apparently fascinated, as a trickle of bright blood appeared as if by magic around the point.

Vilbia saw the muscles of the girl's thin, bare arms tense as she lifted the sword six inches above the man's throat, as if about to let it drop to see how deeply it would penetrate. How far would it? An inch? Perhaps more. In her mind's eye, Vilbia saw the trickle of blood suddenly transformed into a jet which spurted out with every beat of his heart.

'Listen to me, Litoria – listen!' she pushed herself between the girl and the fair-haired man. 'Maybe they do deserve to die, but do you deserve to be their killer? Remember, their master sent them to find you, so he'll know that you played a part in their deaths. And he will hunt you down for it – not because he cares whether these two live or die, but because he'd be terrified that if you got away with killing them, then you and your people will no longer fear him, no longer obey him. He'll have to destroy you, or never sleep easily in his bed again. And revenge is sweet for a moment, but when it's over then there's nothing left – except the guilt and the ghosts. And those ghosts will pursue you for ever, Litoria. Like their master, they too will hunt you down, even in your dreams where you can never escape from them. Waking or sleeping, someone or something will always be pursuing you.'

Litoria hesitated. She turned and looked at Canio, who stood still as a statue, looking straight into her eyes but saying nothing.

'He's using you, Litoria: don't you see that? For some reason – I don't know what – he hates them and wants them dead, but he wants you to bear the burden of his guilt. And you will, for the rest of your life.'

Litoria looked again at Canio. 'Tell me what I should do?' she pleaded. 'I hate them too, I *hate* them, but ...'

'But what? They beat you, and you say they've killed your people. And men just like them dragged her to the stake.' Canio's voice seemed strangely distant.

'Dragged who?' Litoria looked bewildered. She turned to Vilbia, who mouthed, 'No.' Litoria stared again at Canio, who stared back at her and showed his teeth in a mirthless grin before drawing the index finger of his right hand across his throat.

Suddenly it was all too much for the girl. With a wailing cry she dropped the sword and fled away down the track, running like a hare.

Vilbia watched her go, and as she did so breathed a prayer of thanks to her goddess, Leucesca. Then she turned to Canio. 'Why?' she asked.

'Why what?'

'You know full well what I mean,' she replied, letting her anger show. His behaviour had left her bewildered and more than a little frightened.

He shrugged. 'They put me in mind of men I wanted to kill, a long time ago.'

'What men? Those who – ?'

'It doesn't matter, not now.'

And before Vilbia could question him further she heard moaning and incoherent speech from the fair-haired man as he began to regain consciousness.

'Seems it's time to say our farewells,' Canio murmured. He casually picked up the dropped sword, and for a stomach-lurching moment she thought that he was going to do what Litoria had refused. He must have read the thought in her face, because he gave her a bleak smile and shook his head. Squatting, he stabbed the sword two-handed into the earth almost up to the hilt, then walked over to the bound men.

'Look at me,' he said. 'Look at me, damn you!' He crouched down and grabbed the black-haired man by the jaw, forcibly turning his face towards his own. 'What happened here today never happened, do you understand? When people ask, tell them that you broke your wrist when you tripped over your tongue. Oh, and one other thing: I don't really think you'd be so stupid as to try coming after me with a few of your friends, but as an act of kindness to dumb animals I'm going to let you into a secret that might save your life. Are you ready for this? It's that I'm not really a soldier at all. Can you guess what I really am?'

Canio's hand, still gripping the black-haired man's jaw, shook his head slowly from side to side.

'No? Well I'll tell you then: I'm a magician. Do you believe me?'

This time he wagged the head up and down.

'That's good. Now, when me and my fellow magicians – who all go around disguised as soldiers, just like me – take it into our heads that somebody doesn't like us, do you know what we do? We use our magic powers to make that somebody disappear. One moment he's here, next moment he's gone – vanished clean off the face of the earth. Trouble is though, we're not very good magicians. We can make people disappear easily enough, but we can never manage to make them re-appear. Not alive anyway. Sad that ... Do you understand what I'm saying?'

He released the jaw and the black-haired man nodded all by himself.

Vilbia knelt beside him and hissed as menacingly as she knew how, 'And if anything happens to that girl, then long before you vanish you'll wish that you were already dead. Won't he?' she said, looking at Canio.

'Oh you will, and that's a promise. You see, I'll get each of my fellow magicians to demonstrate on you his own special trick for making a man disappear. You'll get to see them all, every single one – unless of course you're so ungrateful as to die before they've finished. Which does sometimes happen,' he added sadly.

***

After half a mile Canio abruptly turned off the track and began heading due east, towards a long, wooded ridge, hazy blue in the distance.

'Do you really think they might come after us?' Vilbia asked. 'Even after what you threatened to do to that man?'

'It's possible. Wise men wouldn't, but did they strike you as wise men?'

Vilbia shook her head. 'No, I think they are arrogant men, full of pride. Men like that are never wise.' She waited until they had gone another fifty yards, then said, 'Primicerius Canio, what did you mean when you said that those two men looked just like they did as they dragged her towards the stake? Who was she?'

There was a long pause. 'I don't recall saying that.'

'But you did. You said it when –'

'I'm sure I didn't. You must have misheard.'

She heard the warning in his voice and decided against replying, letting her silence and reproachful glance contradict him.

They travelled on until well into the evening, Canio changing direction several times so as to pass through those areas that appeared to be the wildest and most empty of people. If they glimpsed distant figures working in the fields or tending flocks of sheep or herding long-horned cattle, then she noticed that he veered right or left to avoid them by as wide a margin as possible.

As sunset approached, banks of grey clouds began to roll in from the south-west, threatening a rain that never actually came. Instinctively they began looking for shelter, heading deeper into a broad expanse of woodland. And there, as the light was fading, they came across a small building with a thatched roof and a circular wall constructed of thin slabs of grey stone, neatly cut and bedded without mortar.

It was windowless, with a wide arched entrance through which Vilbia, peering into the gloom, could see a stone altar about four feet high. Canio dropped Antares' reins and went inside. She dismounted and followed him into the shrine, seeing that behind the altar there stood an outcrop of living rock, the top of which had been crudely carved to resemble the head and trunk of a man.

'We'd best spend the night here,' Canio said. 'That thatch looks pretty old, but it'll be better than nothing if it rains.'

Vilbia looked at the altar, which was little more than a block of the grey local stone, roughly squared and hollowed on the top surface to form a focus where offerings could be burnt. She noticed that two sprigs of honeysuckle had been laid upon it, their slim yellow and white trumpets scarcely withered, their scent still alive and fragrant.

'Not pretty, is he?' Canio remarked.

She followed his gaze back towards the cult statue. To her it seemed that the rustic sculptor's chisel had done no more than accentuate features that had been present on the natural rock since the dawn of time. Beneath an overhanging brow, deepset eyes and a flattened nose, the mouth – itself little more than an enlargement of a natural fissure in the rock – had a faint upwards tilt at the corners that gave the whole face an air of malicious glee. The mouth was slightly open, as if the head were about to speak.

As she looked at it there crept over her the unsettling suspicion that the rock was pregnant with evil. That, long ago, something had been halted in the very act of emerging from it. And worse, that at any moment the spell might be broken and the demonic nativity resume.

She shivered. 'I really don't think we ought to stay the night here. We could go on for another mile or so before it gets really dark.'

Canio must have been watching her looking at the statue. 'Don't tell me that you're afraid of that thing,' he mocked.

'Aren't you? You can see what I can see.'

'All I can see is a lump of rock that somebody has hacked about with as much skill as a one-eyed donkey,' he replied dismissively. 'It's been a long day, we both need a good sleep, and I'm not about to let old arse-face over there stop us from getting it.' And with that he began unsaddling Antares.

He fashioned a halter out of one end of his rope and tied the other to a roof spar that projected from the eaves, so that the horse could move freely over a limited area. Then he carried the saddle into the shrine.

Suppressing her resentment at his apparent inability to sense what, to her, was so obvious, Vilbia began gathering armfuls of last year's dry and withered bracken from the open glade around the shrine. She carried it inside to serve as bedding, dropping it in two piles, one on either side of the altar.

Meanwhile she noticed that Canio was trying to start a fire in the focus of the altar. She gave him an apprehensive glance, but he only shrugged and muttered, 'No use lighting a fire outside if it's going to rain.'

A small hole had been left in the thatch near the apex of the roof, and as Vilbia was gathering the last of the bracken she saw a curl of grey smoke emerge from it and disperse lazily into the darkening evening sky. Over the fire Canio heated in his mess tin some of the wine he had brought from Corinium and topped up at Abona. With the air of a conjurer he produced two small pewter cups from out of one of his saddlebags, held them up for her inspection, then filled both with warm wine.

'Drink up, my pretty one,' he said, offering her one. 'I always find that a few drops of grape juice cheers me at the end of the day.' He downed the wine at a single swallow and poured himself another cupful.

Vilbia drank her wine slowly, looking down into the cup between swallows. 'I'm nobody's pretty one, Primicerius. Why don't you call me by my given name?'

They looked at each other in the twilight. 'If that's what you want. I'll call you Vilbia, if you'll stop calling me Primicerius. Agreed?'

'Agreed.' In the silence that followed she considered asking him what he had really seen in the hypocaust of the sacked villa. But remembering his reaction to her previous questioning she decided against it: he would either tell her in his own time or not at all. Either way, she was beginning to suspect that Canio was a more complex man than the near-buffoon described to her by Eutherius. 'What route are we taking tomorrow?'

'We'll head south-west until we reach the Lead Hills, then we'll follow the Hills down to the sea. After that, I'm not sure. Somebody once told me that from the end of the hills you can travel south down the seashore all the way to the far side of the Great Marshes. If that's true, it'll be a good straight route.'

'And a lonely one, I suspect,' she observed.

'Routes can't be lonely. Only people can feel loneliness.'

'People like yourself?' she asked.

'No, not people like myself.'

They ate some of Canio's cheese and hard-boiled eggs, which Vilbia had wrapped up in large, moist burdock leaves after crossing the Abona, and then, in the twilight, they settled themselves down to sleep on the bracken. She was at first apprehensive that Canio might attempt some sort of seduction, as he had on the previous evening at Abona, but before long the sound of steady breathing from the other side of the altar brought a measure of reassurance. Nevertheless, for her sleep came slowly.

But in the depths of the night it was Canio who woke. Lying quite still he listened to the rising wind moaning through the treetops of the wood outside. And as he listened he began to fancy he could hear another sound mixed in with the wind, a sound not unlike that of a great crowd heard from far away. At first he tried to ignore it, but then Antares whinnied and started restlessly shifting his hooves. He swore softly, drew his *spatha* and laid it beside him, pulled on and laced his boots and crept to the entrance of the shrine. Outside he saw that the clearing was bathed in moonlight and full of swaying moonshadows as the boisterous wind rocked the trees.

As he waited, sword in hand, he became increasingly certain that those noises he could hear above the wind were indeed voices. Given the devious route that had led them to this place, he was fairly certain that they were not connected with the bailiffs he had roughed up. Rationalising, he decided that they might be a bunch of the local *pagani*, affronted that he was using the shrine of their very own godling as a *mansio*.

In which case … 'Bugger off you bastards, or I'll give you a taste of this sword!' he roared in British Celtic as he strode out into the middle of the clearing.

But to his annoyance the almost-voices did not diminish. If anything, they seemed to grow louder. Antares whinnied again, and he glanced over his shoulder to see the horse tossing his head as if trying to break free. Caution was overcoming anger now and he kept well away from the trees and whatever might be hiding amongst them.

'If I come after you with this sword you'll regret it!' he shouted, holding the long blade of the *spatha* out in front of him so that it caught the moonlight. 'A slash across the ribs with this is something you won't forget for many a long day.'

This last bellowed threat woke Vilbia. Confused, she heard the strange noise made by the wind and peered cautiously out of the doorway, where she saw Canio standing in the middle of the clearing, his back to her. She watched him briefly, curious to know what he was doing, before realising that this presented an opportunity to do what she should have done when he was in the hypocaust of the sacked villa. Quickly drawing back into the gloom of the shrine she located his saddlebags, more by touch than sight, and began hurriedly searching through them.

At the bottom of one she found the Hecate figurine. Feverishly unwrapping it she ran her fingertips lightly over the face, the torch, the sword, then held it to one ear and gently shook it. She was unable to stifle a gasp of astonishment at what she heard. To view it better she edged over to the doorway and held the figurine out into the moonlight, the slightly bluish light bathing both it and herself. As she raised the figurine higher, to clear the moving moon shadows, she became aware that the odd wind noise was changing.

Sounding like a great swarm of bees taking flight it rapidly swelled to a crescendo, then slowly diminished until it had gone completely, leaving nothing but the gentle sighing of the wind in the trees. And as she held the figurine she became conscious of a

111

feeling of serenity creeping over her, all fears of the demons of the dark fading away. A slight sound made her look up, to see Canio starting to walk back towards the shrine. Flustered, she realised that there was no time to replace the figurine in his saddlebag, so in the darkness she hurriedly lay down on her bed of bracken and pretended to wake just as he came back into the shrine.

'Is something the matter, Primi ... Canio?'

'Yes ... No ... I thought I heard something in the wind ... didn't you hear it?'

'Hear what?'

'Voices: it sounded like voices.'

'And was it?'

Canio hesitated, then said, 'No, it was only my imagination – nothing but the wind through the treetops. We'd better get some more sleep if we're to set off again at first light.' He said nothing more, and stretching out on his own bed of bracken he spent some time pummelling and cursing it, apparently because he could not get comfortable again.

Lying silent and watchful in the darkness, Vilbia waited for Canio to sleep, the Hecate figurine clutched against her body. Through the doorway she could see a little patch of night sky and a few stars. It was the last thing she remembered before she herself fell asleep. But as she slept she saw again that night sky, not just a tiny fragment but now the whole vast sweep from horizon to horizon, glittering with a myriad of stars. Then, in the way things do in dreams, the sky metamorphosed into a great meadow starred with flowers.

Away in the middle distance she saw a small group of young women and girls walking towards her, chattering and laughing and picking a flower here and there which they added to the baskets they carried. Soon they would be close enough for her to see their faces clearly, and to call out to them, and they to her. Yet, as they approached, there came to her a creeping sense of foreboding and unease, a sense that something terrible was about to happen.

The thunder woke her, an isolated clap almost directly overhead, product of the summer lightning rolling around the night sky. Startled, she lay motionless, at first confused, then wondering. Suddenly conscious that her fingers were still curled around the figurine she quickly rose and slipped it back into Canio's saddlebag. But before doing so she could not resist holding it close to her ear and giving it one last gentle confirmatory shake.

Although she had wanted to leave at dawn, the sun was already some way above the treetops when at last she woke. Canio himself was still sleeping. When he did eventually wake he blamed the Abona wine for his oversleeping and hinted too that it must have been responsible for him imagining the voices in the night. However, before they left she noticed that he took care to remove from the shrine all the bracken and other signs that they had spent the night there, scattering them in the surrounding woodland.

'Just a precaution, in case anyone's following us,' he told Vilbia.

'I think that's wise,' she replied diplomatically. 'It's best that no one knows we were ever here.'

CHAPTER TEN

They started off again, heading south-west through woodland that was forever changing. Broad glades, in which great spreading ashes and oaks drank up the sunlight, alternated haphazardly with places where the trees appeared to have been felled several years before. There the re-growth was so dense that they could find no way through and had to detour around. Canio led Antares while Vilbia walked either beside or behind him, over the leaf litter of curled and desiccated dark brown ghosts that rustled at the slightest touch, whispering to her that all summers die.

By and by she drew Canio's attention to a drift of smoke hanging over the trees some way ahead, thinking that he would want to change direction again. But to her mild surprise he muttered, 'It's only charcoal burners – can't you tell by the smell?' and carried on walking until they emerged into a large clearing where all but a few of the trees had been felled.

She saw that the source of the smoke was a large, circular mound, the upper half of which was wreathed in lazily-curling greyish-white vapour. Scattered around the clearing were several other mounds in various stages of construction, and two huge stacks of short, split logs and thick sticks. There was not a soul in sight: the charcoal burners seemed to have vanished into the earth. But as she waited beside Canio at the edge of the clearing she saw figures begin to emerge from behind the mounds and the timber stacks and from out of several of the small, conical huts whose patchwork of turf coverings blended them wonderfully well into the background.

Eventually there were at least a dozen people visible; men, women and children too, peeping from behind their mothers' skirts.

'Welcome to you, soldier,' said a short, muscular man wearing a ragged tunic and whose face and arms and hands were pickled to the colour of centuries-old oak. 'Would you be lost?' he asked. 'A man can easily lose his way in these woods. But if you're looking for a proper road then I'm afraid there's none hereabouts, though I can set you off in the right direction to find one.'

Vilbia thought he seemed not unfriendly, but distinctly wary.

'We're not looking for a road, thanks all the same,' Canio replied casually. 'We're on our way to Aquae Sulis, travelling at our own pace and seeing the country as we go.'

'Well, it's a good day for travelling, for those that are free to do so.'

'That it is,' Canio replied. 'And a good day for a burn too. Hardly a breath of wind.'

'Aye, we'll not need the windbreak hurdles today.' As he was speaking another man, younger than the first, picked up a sharpened pole and looked towards the speaker.

Vilbia saw Canio's right hand slide towards the hilt of the *spatha* hanging at his left hip. The older man abruptly stopped speaking, and for several moments she could almost feel the tension in the air.

The younger man halted, uncertain. 'I only – ' he began.

'Yes, go ahead,' said the older man, nodding assent to the younger, who hurried across to the smoking mound and began jabbing a ring of holes into its earth covering, some two feet below the point from which the smoke was issuing. At each location he worked the pole around with a vigorous circular motion to enlarge and deepen the hole, and well before he had completed a circuit of the mound vapour began curling up from these new vents.

Turning from watching the hole-maker, the older man

remarked, 'Good weather it may be, soldier, but that stack's got a long way to go yet. I reckon it'll still be burning at dawn tomorrow.'

Vilbia still detected a cool wariness in the man's voice. She was not surprised: she realised that he must regard Canio as an enforcer of a system that took far more from his people than it gave back.

While the man was talking to Canio, one of the women walked over to another, who carried a swaddled baby in her arms, and whispered something in her ear. This whispered conversation went back and forth for a little while and then, seemingly at the prompting of the other, the woman with the baby went up to Canio and asked, 'Are you the one who rescued Litoria from Muranus's dogs?'

Canio said nothing. He just looked at the woman and then, briefly, at Vilbia.

'Don't look so surprised,' said the woman. 'Good news travels faster than bad around these parts. It can travel light because there's so little of it.'

'Is she here?' Canio asked.

'She was, but she's gone now,' the older man replied. 'Tell me, after she'd left you, did you kill those bastards?'

'No, I didn't kill them: just left them trussed up like a couple of hogs. You say she's gone?' Vilbia thought Canio sounded slightly angry.

'Left at dawn. She'll be all right though – she has kin around the Lead Hills.'

Vilbia noticed that the man's wariness was completely gone now.

By then the first woman had come to join them. 'Did you really give Litoria the chance to cut their heads off?' she asked excitedly.

'I did,' said Canio. 'With one of their own swords too.'

The man spat in exasperation. 'Mother Goddesses! I swear that if someone had offered me that chance then I damned well wouldn't have turned it down. I've a few scores of my own to settle with those greedy vermin.'

He would have done so too: Vilbia was fairly sure of that. 'Are we still on Muranus's land, even here?'

The woman with the baby laughed bitterly. 'Here, there, everywhere! They say that if you stand up on top of the Lead Hills and look north, then at least half of everything you can see belongs to him. The place where you ran into his dogs is near the northern boundary of his land: Litoria had almost got clear when they caught her.'

'And he owns everybody on it too, or behaves as though he does,' the man added, and spat again. 'Even us, who won't admit to being owned by anyone. I can see you don't come from these parts,' he added.

'No, we've come from –' Vilbia began.

'A little place not far from Londinium Augusta,' Canio broke in quickly. 'And that's where we're heading back to now, after we've visited Aquae Sulis.'

'Will you stay and take a meal with us?' the woman with the baby asked. 'The stew pot's bubbling.'

Although hungry, Vilbia looked questioningly at Canio, but he seemed to have no misgivings and readily accepted the offer.

'My name's Bacula,' the woman with the baby said. 'This is Moricamulus, my man, and that's Quinta, my half-sister,' she added, pointing to the first woman with her free hand.

'I'm Italicus and this lady is my wife, Claudia,' said Canio.

They sat on a pile of logs beside the doorway of Bacula's hut while she stirred the contents of a large bronze pot, blackened and dented, that simmered over a slow fire suspended by a hook and chain from a tripod of poles. Quinta disappeared into the interior of the hut and emerged with five bowls of turned wood and a bundle of spoons carved out of bone. Vilbia noticed that the smell of wood smoke went with her everywhere, as it did with them all. It had permeated her clothes, her hair: even, it seemed, her very skin.

The stew smelled delicious as Bacula ladled it out into the bowls; a rich, meaty smell that reminded Vilbia that she had not eaten a proper meal since leaving Abona. It tasted good too; venison flavoured with chives and bulked out with barley grains.

'Well, at least Muranus feeds you well, whether he knows it or not,' Canio remarked drily.

'He lets us help ourselves to anything we can find in the woods. But there's one condition though,' Moricamulus replied.

'Oh, and what's that?' Canio asked.

'That we mustn't tell anyone how generous he is.'

'Hate that, would he?'

'Too right he would. Apparently he's frightened stiff that if word ever got out of how he stocks his forests with deer especially for us, then people might think he'd gone soft and start taking advantage of him.'

'So taking them secretly is the least you can do to express your gratitude?'

'Exactly,' Moricamulus replied. 'Just to please him we go hunting in the middle of the night, even though it would be much easier by daylight.'

'I'm sure that if only he knew the sacrifices you make for him, then it would bring the tears to his eyes,' said Canio, and the two women laughed. He fetched his goatskin of wine and the pewter cups and passed the skin round to his hosts. He also gave a swallow to those other burners who came across to introduce themselves, singly or in pairs, as word of what he had done spread around the campsite.

As she sat in the sunlight finishing her wine, Vilbia watched another kiln being built some distance away across the clearing. Three tall poles had been driven into the ground, and around them a man was binding hoops of thin withies at regular intervals.

'That's the flue he's making,' said Moricamulus. 'When he's done, we'll stack the char-wood all around it, cover it with a good thick layer of bracken, then heap earth over the whole thing.'

'Yes, I've seen it done several times,' she replied. 'And when it's finished you'll drop burning wood down the flue to start the burn, won't you?'

'Red-hot embers are what we use for choice, the sort you only get when a big fire has been going for a long time. A few shovelfuls of those have got so much heat trapped inside them that they can make even damp wood burn.'

Canio took another swallow of wine and handed the goatskin to Moricamulus. 'Still a good demand for charcoal, is there?' he asked. 'Even after all the things that have happened in this past year?'

'There's always a market for good charcoal. Always was, always will be,' said Bacula, as though it were an article of faith. 'Even in the middle of the troubles people still needed to cook their bread and warm themselves. Those that could afford it, that is.'

'Didn't the barbarians ever trouble you?' Vilbia asked.

Quinta looked about to reply, but before she could do so Moricamulus said quickly, 'No, never. We always knew when they were near – and if we don't want to be found then there's few that can find us, not in these woods.'

'Besides,' said Quinta, 'we had nothing worth stealing, but we could tell them where –'

'And the army would have taken every last crumb of charcoal we could make, and more besides,' Bacula hastily interrupted. 'Muranus was sending three wagon loads a week down to Venta Belgarum, where they had a big armoury set up. They say the forges there were going day and night for weeks on end, and in the dark you could see their glow from miles away.'

'Yes, that dog-turd did well out of the misery,' Moricamulus said bitterly. 'Sold the army mutton at a damned good price too. That's why he can afford to keep that private army of his, may the Infernal Gods fly away with them and him both!'

'You really love the man, don't you,' Canio observed.

'I'd love him to death if I got half the chance,' Moricamulus said darkly.

'But there'd always be another to follow him,' Bacula sighed. 'Muranus and his kind are like fleas: even if you could manage to kill one, before you could turn around two more would have hopped onto you to take its place. You once said as much yourself.'

Canio retrieved the goatskin and stoppered it with an air of finality. 'It's time to go. If we're to reach Londinium by the moon's last quarter, then we'd better put some more miles behind us by the end of the day. Do you think we could get as far as Aquae Sulis by nightfall?'

'Oh, I doubt it,' said Bacula. 'It must be all of fifteen long and hilly miles away. Not that I've been there myself for many a year,' she added wistfully.

'Well, we can always try. If we can make it then we won't have to spend another night under the stars, eh Claudia?'

Canio stowed the goatskin and gathered up the reins. Vilbia thanked the charcoal burners, then followed Canio as he led Antares towards the eastern edge of the clearing, where they both turned and waved before walking into the denser woodland.

They continued on eastwards for at least two miles. Several times Canio signalled Vilbia to stop, while he listened intently for the sound of stealthy footsteps following behind them. She heard nothing, and after the last of these sudden halts Canio too seemed satisfied that they were not being followed. So they turned and started southwards again.

'Do you really think that any of those charcoal burners would inform on us? They seemed to hate Muranus and his men.'

'They probably do,' said Canio, 'but why take the chance? If there's one thing that life has taught me it's this: that in any squad of men there's always at least one bastard who'd sell his own grandmother to the galleys for a bent siliqua. Besides, there's other reasons to betray besides money.'

'Such as?'

'Didn't old Eutherius tell you?'

'No, why should he?'

'I thought he was the man in your life, now that Gulioepius is gone.'

'What have you got against him?'

120

'Who?'

'Eutherius, of course.'

'They say he can see in the dark. Hey, I've just thought – that must come in useful when he's pleasuring goddesses in the middle of the night.'

Vilbia shook her head in exasperation. 'Tell me the other reasons why men betray.'

'Ambition. Give your persecutor something you think he wants and maybe he'll let you become a persecutor too. That's the way to power and wealth. And then of course there's fear.'

'Fear of the persecutor?'

'That too, but also fear that someone you know will do the betraying. If that happens then the persecutor might think that you must have known the secret too, and want to know why you kept quiet.'

'Guilt by silence, you mean?'

'Correct. That's why fear leads people to betray even when they don't want to, just to save themselves.'

'Money, ambition and fear – so many reasons to betray and be betrayed,' Vilbia sighed.

'And the greatest of these is fear.'

'Why?'

'Because you can decide that you don't want money or power, but you can never decide not to be afraid. Fear comes whether you want it or not. Didn't Eutherius teach you that?'

'He didn't need to.' And Vilbia thought of the things she feared, and then of her goddess, Leucesca, and then of Saturninus – who might, or might not, be at the lake which was still so far away.

***

Throughout that long afternoon they walked southwards through hilly woodland. They forded a little river, she riding Antares and Canio jumping between the flat rocks that men, centuries before, had dragged into the water to act as stepping stones. A little later she noticed the many-sided tower of a temple, on a hilltop a mile or so away to the west. Perched on Antares' gently swaying back she watched it for some time through successive gaps in the trees, but saw no people moving in its vicinity and wondered if it had been sacked during the *Conspiratio.*

She asked Canio, who shrugged and said, 'Could have been – but I'm certainly not going all the way up there to find out.' She got the impression that his mind had been on other things.

From time to time, through breaks in the trees, she glimpsed the still-distant Lead Hills rising up in front of them, their undulating bulk filling the southern skyline.

'Two days it's taken us to get from Abona to those damned hills,' Canio grumbled. 'It should have taken less than a day – and we're still much too far to the east.'

And then, as on the previous day, the sunshine gradually became intermittent and finally died as banks of dark clouds began rolling in from the sea far away to the west. But this time they did bring the rain: occasional drops at first, which gradually turned into a steady drizzle. At first the trees shielded them, but soon the rain began dripping down through the branches, the heavy drops splashing onto their heads and arms. It was time to seek shelter.

In a clearing they came upon a charcoal burners' abandoned campsite. Although the main bothy was at least a year old it had lasted well, probably because the mossy turf that clothed it had retained sufficient water to keep the grass alive. It was a conical structure about ten feet in diameter, the interior dry and still containing two beds, though they were little more than springy piles of interwoven hazel poles packed out with brushwood.

Canio tethered Antares, then carried his saddle and saddlebags inside. Vilbia hunted for bedding and brought back several armfuls of dead bracken, now damp from the rain.

'Never mind, it'll dry once I've got a fire going,' Canio assured her, as with a flint and the blade of his dagger he sent showers of sparks down onto a handful of the dry grass that he had found tucked under one of the beds. When the grass caught fire he fed the flames first with twigs broken off the beds, then larger sticks until a small fire was burning brightly. The smoke rose vertically and found its way out through a small hole near the apex of the roof.

As they ate some more of the food which Canio had bought at Abona, Vilbia pointed out to him that there wasn't a great deal left.

'Not to worry. Once we're clear of these woods we're bound to run across a farmstead where we can buy more.' Canio spread his hands over the fire and rubbed them together. 'Mercury's bones, this damned rain's chilled the air. Don't you feel cold?'

The question surprised Vilbia. 'No, I'm not cold at all. I thought the air outside was pleasantly cool now.' She raked her fingers through the pile of dead bracken heaped up beside the flames. 'It's quite dry now. If we sleep early then we'll be fresh to set off again at dawn.' She hesitated, then asked, 'How long now before we reach that lake where Saturninus was seen?'

'Oh, only about a couple of days I should think,' Canio replied, looking not at her but down at the fire. 'Of course, he may have moved on by now, but he could still be there. And even if he isn't, maybe there'll be people around who'll know where he's gone.'

'Yes, I remember you saying as much on the edge of the Hills near Ovilregis, but I hope he is still there. Sometimes I imagine myself sitting and listening to him telling how he and Pascentia met that night at Ovilregis, and where they've both been this past long year. It's such a romantic story, don't you think?' She looked him in the face as she spoke.

But Canio was still gazing down at the fire, seemingly fascinated by the tiny shape-shifting flames. 'Yes, it must be quite a story. Which bed do you want?'

'Either will do for me. You choose,' she said quietly.

Canio scooped up an armful of bracken and scattered it over

the left hand bed, pushing it down into the larger voids between the brushwood. 'I think you're right: an early night wouldn't come amiss, particularly as I'm feeling a bit rough. Maybe it was something in that stew the charcoal burners gave us?'

He didn't wait for her to reply but went out into the rain and returned shortly afterwards with another armful of sticks. Squatting down he extracted his regulation blanket from one of the saddlebags. 'Aren't you cold? There doesn't look to be much warmth in that cloak of yours.'

'It's not cold, Canio, and even if it was there's always the fire.' It was the second time he had mentioned the cold that she did not feel. She made up her own bed with the remaining bracken, unlaced her soft leather shoes and kicked them off before wrapping herself in her cloak and laying down. But sleep did not come quickly to her, and it was not until the time of deep twilight that she finally drifted into oblivion.

***

As she usually did in midsummer, Vilbia woke in the spectral pre-sunrise light and lay listening to the birdsong that was all around. She looked over to Canio and made out his shape huddled up under the blanket, then eased her legs off the bed and wriggled her feet into her shoes. Taking a stick from the pile she stirred through the ashes of the fire. They were lifeless and cold.

Outside it had long stopped raining, and in the fresh cool of the morning Antares was cropping the grass. He neighed softly when he saw Vilbia, and she walked through the dew and stroked his muzzle before turning back to the bothy. Canio was still hunched under his blanket. She hesitated, then pushed him gently on the shoulder. At first there was no response, so she pushed again, harder this time.

'Canio – Primicerius Canio. Wake up: it's time we were leaving.'

Canio grunted and twitched awake. 'Who's that?' he muttered, turning so that even in the gloom she could see that his face and hair were soaked in sweat.

Startled, she repeated that it was time they were going.

'Going? ... Going where?' There was a long pause. 'Oh, the lake. Yes. Got to get to the lake.'

At first she thought he was drunk, until she remembered him remarking wryly on the previous evening that the goatskin was almost empty and that he'd better save a swallow or two for the morning. Impulsively she reached out and felt his forehead. It was burning hot.

He shook her hand away. 'Don't fuss, girl; it's only a touch of fever. I'll be all right as soon as I'm up and about.' He threw off the blanket and tried to stand, but immediately his legs buckled and he sat back down heavily on the bed, some of the dead twigs cracking noisily beneath him. 'Damn! Worse than I thought,' he mumbled. 'By the Mothers, I could drink a river dry.'

'We'd better stay here for a little while, at least until you're feeling better,' Vilbia said anxiously. She unstoppered the goatskin and held it out to him, together with one of the pewter cups.

Ignoring the cup, Canio clutched the skin and gulped the wine straight down, then lay back and closed his eyes. 'See to Antares, will you. Expect he needs a drink too. Must be a stream somewhere around here. Just give him his head and he'll find it for you.'

'Are you sure you'll be all right?'

'Of course I will,' he replied irritably. 'I'll be up before you get back.'

So with some trepidation she went back outside, stroked Antares' muzzle again and untied his tethering rope. Antares remained stationary all the while, like the well-trained cavalry horse he was.

'Come on boy,' she said encouragingly. 'We'll go and find

you some water.' She pulled gently on the rope and the horse started ambling towards her. Trying to let him find his own way, she walked southwards, seeing the grassy upper slopes of the Lead Hills above the treetops. Twice she stopped to let him snuffle the air, and at the third halt Antares seemed to get the scent of something and began moving off without being urged to do so. She let him go, walking quietly behind him but still holding on to the rope.

After another fifty yards the horse neighed softly and veered off to the left, leading her through a patch of dense woodland and then down a steep slope thick with the yellowing leaves of bluebells. At the bottom of the slope she saw a little stream, no more than three feet wide, winding between the trees and bubbling over miniature waterfalls formed by the dark tree roots which crossed it.

The water was cool and clear, flowing over the sandy stream bed that had been sculpted into ripples by the current. She tethered Antares to the low branch of a hazel bush which overhung the stream, making sure that he could drink unimpeded, before walking a few yards upstream. There she crouched, cupped the water to her lips and drank. Then, after looking all around, she impulsively kicked off her shoes, unbuckled the belt from around her waist, unlaced and slipped the dress over her head and stepped naked into the stream.

Crouching down, she quickly splashed the water over her body, gasping at its early-morning coldness but revelling in the delicious feeling of renewal as she washed off the dirt and perspiration of the last days. Reaching up she untied the ribbon that secured her abundant dark-copper hair in a tight bun on the top of her head and shook it free. Kneeling on the soft sand she dipped her head into the stream, letting the current spread out her hair before running her fingers through it to expose every strand to the cleansing water.

Afterwards, she patted herself reasonably dry with the dress before putting it back on. Then she quickly put on her belt and shoes, coiled up her still-damp hair and secured it with the ribbon, before untying the rope and leading Antares back to the bothy.

To her dismay, Canio was still lying on the bed, his face even paler than before and contrasting starkly with the blackness of his hair and beard.

'Who's that?' he asked hoarsely, making an effort to sit up but only succeeding briefly before flopping back down onto the bracken.

'It's only me, Canio. I've watered Antares.' She was alarmed to see just how much his condition had deteriorated in the short time she had been away.

'Good. Always look after your horse and he'll look after you. Perhaps I should ask the old bugger for a drink,' he cackled weakly.

She took the hint and helped him to sit up, then supported the goatskin while he took several gulps of the last of the wine. Some of it dribbled out of the corner of his mouth into the short, dense hairs of his beard. 'Is there anything else I can do?' she asked, distinctly worried now.

Canio moved his head slowly from side to side. 'Be fine after a little sleep. Had this sort of thing before. Just need a good sleep.' Her face must have betrayed her anxiety, because he added, 'For sweet Venus's sake, stop fussing. They breed us tough in the army; I've shrugged off far worse than this.'

Vilbia felt his forehead again: it was even hotter than before. 'I'm just going for water. I won't be long.' He did not reply. Taking the now-empty goatskin she hurried back to the stream and filled it with the cool water.

It was a long day. Noon slowly came and went, and then the afternoon dragged into evening. From time to time Canio would mumble incoherently that he would soon be fit to travel and again attempt to stand, and again have to flop back onto the bed as his legs refused to support him.

Vilbia searched through his saddlebags and took one of the cloths in which the cups had been wrapped, soaked it with the fresh water and repeatedly bathed his face and neck. At first he tried to push her hand away, protesting that there was nothing wrong with him that a short rest wouldn't cure. Later, he ceased to object, and later still he even murmured his thanks as she wiped his face and laid the cool folded linen on his forehead.

In the evening he fell into a fitful sleep that lasted well into the following day. Vilbia also slept poorly, frequently waking and listening in the dark to his noisy, uneven breathing and occasional jerky movement.

At around noon she saw him suddenly wake, muttering and turning his head restlessly from side to side before sinking back into unconsciousness. She bathed his face again and was alarmed by how hot it still felt to her touch. Gently shaking his arm she tried to rouse him. 'Canio … Canio, can you hear me?' she asked several times, but he did not respond.

Throughout that day the fever steadily increased its hold over him. Sometimes she heard him speak rambling, disconnected words, his eyes unfocussed, apparently oblivious of her presence. Most of the time he lay quite still, his breathing shallow and rapid. And all the time she watched over him and bathed him and spoke to him and squeezed his hand to let him know, if he were capable of knowing, that she was still there.

Several times she contemplated going for help. But this was unknown country to her and the only place where she was certain of finding it was the charcoal burners' camp, the better part of a day's walk away, there and back, even if she could find it again. Much too long to leave Canio alone. Also, she remembered his fear of betrayal.

As the evening light was beginning to fade she came to a decision. Delving into one of the saddlebags she unwrapped the Hecate figurine and, sitting in the doorway, examined it for the first time in daylight. The lady's face was glacially beautiful, but seemed unanimated by any passion or human warmth. It was not smiling now, and Vilbia was more uncertain than ever that she really had seen it smile back in Corinium. Holding the figurine to her ear she shook it gently, listening to the soft rustle within before replacing it, very carefully, into the saddlebag.

After bathing Canio she trotted back to the stream, where she once again filled the goatskin with fresh water. When she returned it was almost dark. There was no apparent change in his condition, so she took one of his hands, broad enough to make two of her own, and gave it a final squeeze before stretching out on her own bed and attempting to snatch a few hours sleep.

During that night the rain returned. Awake again, she heard it come, a gentle sighing so stealthy that at first she mistook it for the night breeze lisping across the bothy. But gradually the intensity increased and soon water began dripping steadily down from the head of the doorway, the row of drops outlined against the night sky. Lying back on the bracken with her hands cupped behind her head, she watched each drop as it swelled almost imperceptibly larger until, tear-shaped and trembling, its own weight tore it away and it fell and was lost in the dark void below. 'And so we go,' she murmured, and turned on her side to face Canio.

He seemed to be sleeping peacefully, so she closed her eyes and willed sleep to return. At first it would not and she lay listening to the patter of the rain on the bothy sides and its hiss on the grass outside. Occasionally there was a long splash from the depths of the surrounding wood as the wind sighed and a thousand raindrops that had been beading on the high leaves coalesced and cascaded to the ground.

CHAPTER ELEVEN

Again Canio sees himself standing on that bleak plain in front of the city walls which rise up tall beside the bank of the wide, black river. The air is chill, an icy breeze lisping across from the river. But Canio is sweating, the thoughts racing through his brain creating their own unwelcome heat. On the plain is the remembered great crowd of people; men, women and a few children. They are both beside and behind him, although when he turns to look at them he sees only ranks of translucent ghosts. But his eyes keep returning to the tall stake, and to the chains and coils of thick rope looped over its top, and the great bundles of brushwood piled around and beside it.

Now he is dimly aware that the crowd is again talking animatedly, although the voices sound strangely far away. Suddenly the babel swells louder and higher in pitch, and there is a cruel excitement in it. Canio flinches. Even without looking he knows what is happening. Reluctantly his eyes follow the eyes of the crowd and he stares towards the wide gateway in the city walls, through which a squad of soldiers has just emerged. In their midst a woman is being half led, half dragged by several men in brown and black tunics towards the stake and the baying crowd.

'Don't look at me, Marcia. Please, please, please don't look at me!'

And now she is nearer, so near that he can see her ravaged face, see clearly the terror in her eyes as they dart along the lines of the crowd. He knows those eyes are searching for him, knows with utter certainty that they will find him, that he cannot escape them. That he will never escape them.

'Stop staring at me, Marcia. Please, please stop staring at me! I can't save you ... I can't ... I can't!'

His screams wake Vilbia and she scrambles to his side. 'What is it, Canio? I was asleep ...'

But her voice, dimly perceived, make the pictures in his brain vanish and he sinks back into shallow, dreamless sleep. And after a while Vilbia herself lies down again and closes her eyes as the rain patters against the bothy sides.

Time passes, and then the cruel fire is raging. He can feel its heat on his face and he thrashes his head from side to side, trying to escape from its searing intensity and the crackle of burning wood. But he cannot escape – the heat and the smell of wood smoke are inside his head and, try as he might, he cannot stop himself from opening his eyes, dreading what he will see. At first he can see nothing but a great tower of flames in front of him, roaring and convulsing like a chained beast.

Then, as if a curtain has been torn aside, he can see deep into the very heart of the flames, where a black figure writhes and twists. Its head is thrown back and its mouth gapes open, screaming in agony.

'Marcia! ... Marcia! ... Save her, Hecate, save her, save her!'

His terrifying howl echoed through Vilbia's brain, jerking her out of sleep again, her heart thumping like a drum. By the hazy moonlight filtering through the doorway she saw that Canio's whole body was twisting and contorting, his blanket thrown to the ground. She sat there for a few moments, breathing heavily and gathering her scattered wits. Then she stood quickly, hunted for the goatskin and bathed Canio's face as best she could, while he babbled and called out again and again that name, "Marcia".

There was a short period of calm, during which she repeatedly bathed his face. Then Canio began muttering, sometimes incoherently, sometimes saying things which she did not understand, sometimes saying things which she did.

'Hush, Primicerius, hush,' she whispered at last, pressing the damp cloth against his forehead.

At the sound of her voice he shot out a hand and grabbed her wrist, holding it so tightly that she cried out in pain.

'Marcia! Marcia, is that you? You told me she'd send you back, but I never believed she would ... I never believed ... never believed.'

'Canio – Canio! It's me, Vilbia! Don't you recognise me?' The fever had weakened him and his hand was slippery with sweat, but even so it took all her strength to wrench her arm away. She jumped up, trembling at the violence of his delirium.

But Canio said nothing more. She watched him as he lay, his eyes closed and his breathing rapid and shallow again. And gradually she came to realise that the storm was finally passing, leaving only exhaustion. She bathed his face once more, spread the blanket back over him, then sat on the edge of her own bed, from where she reached across the space between and held his left hand until at last he appeared to be sleeping peacefully.

***

At dawn she was almost certain that his fever was past its worst. Nevertheless, she stayed close to him all day, frequently bathing his hands and face and noting with relief that, as the day passed, his skin became less hot to her touch. He did not mention the name Marcia again, and in the evening, more tired than she knew, she fell into a deep sleep.

She woke in the grey light of the next day's dawn, which was by her reckoning the eighth before the kalends of July. Instinctively she looked across at Canio and saw that he was breathing normally again and sleeping almost peacefully, only an occasional slight twitch of the head betraying that the effects of the fever still lingered. Reaching out and laying her hand on his brow she found that it was almost as cool as her own.

Leaving him asleep, she led Antares back to the stream and

let him drink while she refilled the goatskin yet again. Returning, she found Canio awake, although still slightly confused and disorientated. But at least he recognised her, and gratefully accepted several mouthfuls of the fresh water. As she helped him to struggle up into a sitting position to drink more easily, she realised just how much the fever had drained his strength. He was far too weak to travel.

But, as first that day and then the next slowly passed, so Canio's vitality began to return. Leaning heavily on her slim shoulder, he several times managed to stagger out of the doorway to the nearest tree and lean against it while he urinated, she modestly retiring while he did so. When, on the final occasion, he asked with a weak grin if she would mind holding his member for a moment while he scratched a furiously itching ear, she knew that he was well on the way to recovery. She gave him a look which, she hoped, conveyed horror at the very thought and primly declined to comply with his request.

With increasing frequency she found herself reflecting how strange it was that, in the five days they had been at the bothy, she had seen nobody: no hunter or charcoal burner, not even a solitary *paganus* collecting firewood. And with those reflections there came the uneasy thought that, even if she had seen nobody, it did not necessarily follow that nobody had seen her.

That evening, for the first time since the onset of the fever, Canio managed to eat some cheese. It was the last of the food that he had brought from Abona, food which she had been eking out by restricting herself to little more than enough to keep a sparrow alive. Unsurprisingly, by dawn next day she was extremely hungry.

'Canio – Canio, wake up.' She knelt so that their eyes were at the same level.

'Huh?'

'I've got to go and get food. We've absolutely nothing left. I'll be as quick as I can ... will you be all right while I'm away?' Even as she spoke she knew that it was a pointless question.

'Of course I will,' he replied impatiently. 'I've just had a touch of fever. Everyone gets it from time to time.' There was a pause, and then he asked, slightly awkwardly, 'Did I say anything silly when the fever was on me?'

The temptation to ask questions about Marcia was almost irresistible. But instinct, born of the incident with the bailiffs, whispered that it might be unwise. Delphically, she replied, 'I didn't hear you say anything that I would call silly.'

'Good. That's good,' was all he said, but she thought he sounded relieved.

'I'll be as quick as I can,' she repeated.

'Wait – you'll need money.' Canio scrabbled at his belt pouch and held out a handful of coins. 'Go on, take as much as you want.'

Vilbia hesitated. She had money in her own belt purse, including the two solidi that Canio had found at the sacked villa, but who could say when they might come in useful? Picking the coins off his open palm she said, 'I'll take these two siliquae and fifteen *centenionales*. I shouldn't need more.'

'Take the horse as well. Antares will be no trouble – I think he likes you. Just say "walk" and he'll walk.'

Vilbia hesitated, tempted but uncertain, conscious that if a horse as powerful as Antares took it into his head to break into a gallop she would never be able to stop him. Another thought decided her.

'Is that wise? If I were to meet an army patrol they might want to know why I was riding an army horse.' And then, just to see how he would react, she added artlessly, 'Although, if I did, I suppose I could bring them back here to help you.'

'No ... Stay well away from the army – there are too many evil bastards in it these days.' Canio lay back on the bed and closed his eyes. 'Perhaps it wouldn't be such a good idea to take Antares.'

'I think you're right. If I head east perhaps I'll find a farmstead, or maybe even a village. Whatever happens, I'll be back by noon at the very latest.' She helped him to take a final drink and left the goatskin propped against the bed.

On the point of leaving she hesitated. Looking at Canio, for a moment she thought of demanding that he tell her the truth about Saturninus. Then it came to her that perhaps she did not want to know the truth, not then anyway. 'Back by noon,' she repeated softly.

Canio briefly opened his eyes, just in time to see the slim ankles below the swinging hem of her dress disappearing through the doorway. Then his leaden eyelids slid down again and he drifted back into sleep.

***

Throughout that morning, the ninth since leaving Ovilregis, Canio slipped in and out of consciousness, with little or no sense of the passing of time. Twice during the morning he woke with a raging thirst and groped for the goatskin, holding it up to his mouth with slightly shaking arms. Shortly after midday, at the insistence of his bursting bladder, he staggered out of the doorway to relieve himself, then slumped back onto the bed and fell asleep again.

It was late afternoon when he next woke, roused by the neighing of the thirsty Antares. Cautiously he sat upright, feeling considerably better now, the fever gone but the weakness in his limbs remaining. Antares neighed again and Canio clambered to his feet and slowly walked outside.

He patted the horse roughly on the muzzle. 'All right, I get the message: you want a drink. You and me both,' he muttered.

Returning to the bothy, he sat for a little while on the edge of the bed drinking the now stale water in the goatskin, then went and untethered Antares, keeping hold of the free end of the rope.

'Right my boy, now you can show me where the water in this skin came from,' and he slapped the flaccid goatskin against the horse's rump.

But Antares needed no urging, and it was as much as Canio could do to restrain him, by a combination of tugging the rope and bad language, as the horse trotted off to the now-familiar stream.

Back at the bothy he found that Vilbia had still not returned. At first he rationalised, told himself that she had had to go further than anticipated to find a farmstead, or at least one willing to sell her food. Or perhaps she had simply lost her way in unfamiliar country. But then he looked up at the sun and saw by its position in the north-west sky that evening was now not far away: she should have been back long ago. A wave of fatigue forced him to sit down on the bed. Not for the first time since he had fallen ill he wondered if the malign influence of that damned Hecate figurine was somehow responsible for his misfortunes. Suddenly the two streams of thought ran together. 'Merda! Has she …?' He groped frantically inside the saddlebag where he had hidden it. The figurine was still there, neatly wrapped in the scrap of cloth.

Feeling a little ashamed for having doubted her, as he leant back against the bothy wall the nagging suspicion that something must be preventing her return hardened into a near-certainty. Wondering what he should do, he peeled away the cloth again and gazed at Hecate's unsmiling face. Hecate stared back. Was it, he wondered, just his imagination that made him see contempt in that stare?

With some difficulty he saddled Antares, packed his blanket and the goatskin, struggled up onto the horse's back, turned eastwards and urged the horse into gentle motion. He told himself that he still needed Vilbia to placate whatever malignant powers might reside in that figurine. But even as he did so he was remembering the hand that had gently squeezed his own in the darkness when the fever was burning him.

Even riding at walking pace he managed to break clear of the woods by early evening, and by then he could feel some of the old energy beginning to flow back into his body. Before him stretched a pleasant, undulating countryside; a patchwork of small fields and scattered spinneys. At the first farmstead he came across he learnt that Vilbia had been there early that morning and had bought one small loaf, which was all they had until they baked again.

'I've just taken four fresh out of the oven. I can sell you a couple if you want them?' said the farmer's wife hopefully.

'I'll take them,' said Canio, noticing that, despite the two small children he had seen playing in the yard outside, she was not unattractive. 'One *centenionalis* each?'

'Two,' said the woman firmly.

'Throw in a kiss and two it is.' He wanted to banish the memories of those dreams of Marcia.

'Just a kiss?' she said archly.

'Of course,' said Canio with mock rectitude. 'Do I look like the sort of man who'd take advantage of a married woman?' He was feeling much better now.

Whatever his intentions, at that moment they heard her husband returning from the fields. From him, Canio learnt that Vilbia had headed eastwards when she left that morning, but neither husband or wife had seen her since. As he rode off, gnawing one of the loaves, he remembered that he had not even asked if they had any barley beer for sale. He regretted the omission, but did not even consider turning back.

He rode on through the long summer dusk, noticing bats flitting noiselessly overhead as they quartered the darkening sky, much as his eyes were quartering the darkening land. At last, when it was truly night and he was so bone-weary that he simply could go no further, he decided to make camp on the short, sheep-nibbled turf of a ridge top, under the canopy of a great oak. There he wrapped himself in his blanket and almost immediately fell into the deep sleep that comes with bodily exhaustion.

***

He woke at around midnight and stared up at the sky. The night was dark and still, clouds hiding most stars, the waning moon not yet risen. Sitting up, he immediately noticed a single sparkling point of yellow light far away in the darkness. It appeared to be located on the low ground to the north. Fascinated, he watched the light, and as he did so realised that every so often it dimmed for a few moments as a dark shape moved across it.

Then he thought of Vilbia. Determined to resume his search for her at first light, he lay down, shut his eyes and waited for sleep to return. He dozed, then seemed to wake again. Opening his eyes he saw that the intriguing light was still there, if anything brighter than before. Feeling strangely exhilarated, with all fatigue now gone, he pulled on his boots, rolled upright and began walking down the dark slope of the ridge towards the light, picking his way between small trees and the occasional sprawling bush of dog roses, their pale flowers scentless in the cool night.

As he descended, so the light grew steadily larger, until he realised that it was framed by the rectangular outline of a window. Then he saw the dark shape move across it again in the still-distant room. He only saw the shape for a moment before a leafy branch obscured his vision, but he was almost certain that it was the figure of a woman. He ducked under the branch and looked again: the light still radiated brightly, but the woman had vanished. Her image, however, lingered in his mind and hurried him on.

Towards the bottom of the ridge a line of bushes loomed black in front of him, abruptly blocking his view of the window. Impatiently he thrust his way into the blackness, the rank smell of new green elder growth closing in around him. He trod slowly and carefully now, fearful lest he break the silence of the night as he moved forwards in the almost total darkness. With arms outstretched he eased aside sprays of elder more sensed than seen, a swimmer through a sea of leaves.

The bushes suddenly ended and he found himself standing on the bank of a small stream meandering along the bottom of the valley. Startlingly close now, no more than twenty paces away on the rising ground beyond the stream, was the window. He stared into it as the yellow light from a tall stand hung with several oil lamps streamed out into the night, its brightness paradoxically making the rest of the building all but invisible, no more than a vague outline against the bulk of the rising ground behind.

The woman appeared to be sitting on the edge of a bed beside the lamp stand, but even as Canio watched she rose up and began walking towards him. Framed in near-silhouette she stood at the window, looking up and down the path that he could just make out running beneath it. She seemed to be awaiting the coming of someone or something.

The light behind her made the loose robe she wore translucent, outlining the taut curves of her slim body. Her dark hair was coiled up high onto her head, and although her face was in shadow Canio knew that she was beautiful: it was impossible that she could be otherwise. Suddenly he realised that she was staring out into the night directly at him. Instinctively he crouched down, hearing the muted lisp and gurgle of the dark waters flowing past just inches away.

As he straightened up he glimpsed movement and a column of darkness way back in the room, as a door seemed to open and close and another figure entered. The woman turned quickly away from the window, momentarily outlining her profile against the light. Canio's eyes lingered on her – lingered too long to get anything more than the most fleeting sense that there was something strange about this newcomer, this man – for he was sure that it was a man, although her body largely hid his. And before he could even begin to work out just what the strangeness was, the light dimmed slightly, then dimmed more, and with a sting of disappointment he realised that the man was snuffing out the lamps, one by one.

But he did not extinguish the last lamp, and by its feeble light Canio saw the man and the woman embrace and kiss, slowly and sensuously. Two dark hands reached behind the woman's head, pulling out and carelessly tossing aside the long pins that secured her coiled hair, then teasing it out and letting it cascade down over her shoulders. They kissed again, the man's hands stroking unhurriedly up and down her back through the thin material of the robe. Briefly they separated, and in that eternal moment Canio glimpsed, below the man's swept-back mane of hair, a face out of nightmare.

It was a broad, flattened face; a face where elements of the human and the feline mingled and the latter just predominated, especially in the large yellow eyes and the wickedly pointed teeth. For a few moments Canio's brain raced wildly as he tried to remember where he had seen such a face before. And then he remembered: it was the face of a statuette of Ahriman, the Mithraic lord of darkness and chaos, that he had seen, long ago, at a remote fort on the Rhine frontier.

Now every instinct whispered frantically that he should get away, that he should creep noiselessly back into the cloaking night, then start running, and keep running until he was far away from this unearthly place. Every instinct except one. For now the couple were coming together again, the man's hands moving silently, first below the woman's throat, then outwards, spreading the neckline of her robe to the full extent that its untied drawstring permitted. The woman flexed her shoulders and the robe slid to the ground. She wrapped her arms around the man's neck as his hands resumed their stroking of her now-naked back, moving from the nape of her neck to the smooth curve of her hips as she undulated her body against his.

His heart thumping, Canio stood upright, his eyes not for one moment leaving the couple in the room. Then the night breeze sighed, drifting a hanging frond of willow leaves across his line of vision. Impatiently he snatched it aside and tugged hard, but the tough, flexible shoot refused to break. Without thinking he pulled harder, two-handed now. There was a loud crack and the whole branch came crashing down into the water.

A little way downstream a pair of ducks on the far bank,

apparently startled from sleep, took flight, filling the air with their raucous quacking and shattering the stillness of the night. Canio stared wildly towards them, and when he looked back the light had vanished. Where it had so recently been there was now nothing but an ink-black darkness. And from out of that darkness there came a roar like that of an enraged animal.

For a fleeting moment pride fought with fear, before fear won and Canio turned and started running blindly back though the bushes, spurred on by the dread of what might be just behind him in the darkness, the sounds of its racing feet masked by his own.

Once clear of the elder thicket he kept on scrambling up the ridge, his chest heaving and the blood pounding in his ears. Only when he reached his campsite did he risk looking back, seeing nothing there except the dark and silent countryside, dotted with the shapes of trees and bushes trembling in the thin night breeze. Now dizzy with fatigue, he drew his *spatha* and lay down on the blanket to rest for a few moments: he would decide what to do next when his head had stopped spinning.

The next he knew he was waking at dawn, stiff and chilled, a white fur of dew on the blanket. As he lay there, shivering slightly, memories of the night swiftly returned, but they were no more substantial than the remembrance of a dream. Indeed, the more he thought about it, the more certain he became that it must have been a dream. That it could only have been a dream.

Nevertheless, as he hurriedly packed the blanket and saddled Antares he carefully avoided looking northwards until the very last moment. Then, as he rode off, he could not resist snatching a glance in that direction. In the little valley below, his eyes drawn irresistibly to them, he saw a winding stream and, beside it, the roofless shell of a small villa. Even at that distance he could make out the row of blank windows and, above each one, the flare of black left by the smoke and flames that had once billowed from it. He urged Antares into a canter and rode quickly away, forcing himself not to look back again.

CHAPTER TWELVE

At the first farmstead Canio came across that morning he asked if anyone there had seen Vilbia, but it seemed that nobody had. Telling himself that he had to get his strength back, he wolfed down the entire contents of their simmering cooking pot, which, for half a silver siliqua, both sides considered a bargain. For the other half of the siliqua, plus a few extra *centenionales*, he got his goatskin filled to rotundity with barley beer. After taking a few hearty gulps he felt almost back to normal, though irritably conscious that his arms were trembling slightly as he held up the goatskin.

As he was about to leave, the farmer, one of Muranus's unfree tenants, remarked that, 'Besides yourself, the only strangers I've seen around here for days now were a pair of the master's mounted slave bailiffs. Those vermin passed by at around this time yesterday, leading three men in chains. Runaways, so they said.'

'And were they?'

The man shrugged. 'Who can say? If they were, then they hadn't run fast enough.'

That set Canio wondering. 'Which way were they heading?'

'North. Back to Muranus's main villa I suppose, unless the earth opens up and swallows them before they get there – which I'd willingly vow a whole sack of wheat meal to the Cucullati if I thought it would persuade them to make that happen.'

In mid-morning, when the sun was already high and hot in an almost cloudless sky, Canio came upon a gang of mowers working its way across a large hay meadow. Each man was stripped to the waist, some wearing wide-brimmed hats of woven straw to keep the sun off their heads as they rhythmically swished their scythes backwards and forwards, the long, curved blades slashing through the still-sappy stems of the grasses.

They looked up as he approached, studied him briefly, then continued mowing, their tempo unbroken. Behind the men a gaggle of children of both sexes and various sizes were turning and spreading the cut grass with rakes. With faint amusement he noticed that the widths of the rakes' wooden-toothed heads frequently exceeded the heights of their smallest users.

In the shade of a tree at the edge of the field an old man sat, watching the mowers with a critical eye.

'*Salve*, Grandfather,' he greeted him.

'I've no grandsons as are soldiers, thanks-be to Mercury,' the old man replied.

'Well don't give up hope yet, Grandfather. After the troubles of the past year the army will take even a one-eyed sheep, provided it can hold a spear and baa when a centurion barks at it.'

The old man looked shrewdly at him, and Canio thought he might be contemplating asking him how well he baa'ed. He fixed him with a cold eye, whereupon the old man said simply, 'Just passing by are you, soldier?'

'I'm looking for a woman –'

'Most soldiers are ... Usually somebody else's,' the old man added reflectively.

'The one I'm after is a young redhead. Have you seen her?'

Canio could tell that the old man was thinking by the way his nose wrinkled upwards. 'She wouldn't have been wearing a pale-coloured dress, would she? Quite long, almost down to her ankles?'

'You've seen her?'

'Maybe. Early this morning that bastard Victorinus rode past, heading north with three men and a young woman, all chained together. Could be she was the one you're after.'

'How long ago was this?'

'Not long after they'd started.' The old man pointed towards the line of mowers with the feathery end of a long grass, whose sweet and juicy stem he had been chewing.

Canio looked at the field. Only about a third had been cut, but it was a large field. 'Was he on his own, this Victorinus?'

The old man looked at him derisively. 'He never goes anywhere alone does Victorinus. Always has somebody with him to watch his back, just in case someone might try sticking a knife into it.'

'So who was this somebody?'

'A big man with a look on him as mean as Victorinus's. Don't know his name though: don't want to neither.'

Canio was already moving off when the old man called out, 'And they had a big hound with them too. Vicious-looking brute it was, with a spiked brass collar. Dare say he'd have your throat out just like that,' he said, snapping his fingers.

'Thanks, Grandfather; I'm glad you told me that.'

Canio rode fast now, wherever possible keeping to the high ground, from where he could scour the landscapes on both sides as he went. After a long summer hour had passed he began wondering whether the slave bailiffs had changed course, or if he had simply missed them by being on the wrong side of a hill or a wood. More than once he contemplated turning back, increasingly certain that he had overshot his quarry. But then, shortly after midday, he spotted them.

Just as the old man had said, there were two men on horseback, four prisoners in manacles linked together by a chain, and a large hound that trotted beside the leading horseman. Even from a distance he knew that the woman was Vilbia. As he watched her walking calmly, looking straight ahead, her wrists weighed down by the heavy chain and the iron manacles, he felt an odd little sense of loss, almost like pain, followed by a surge of anger.

Keeping out of sight, he cantered along the ridge until he was a little way ahead of them. Then, hidden among the trees, he considered what to do next. His first instinct was to draw his *spatha* and charge at them. Then his brain started working. The fever had left him weak, but his strength was rapidly returning and in another day ... but he did not have another day.

He could see that both slave bailiffs also carried long swords, the scabbards jogging at their left hips. If he charged, then maybe he could cut down the rearmost of the two before the other could draw his sword, but what then? And then there was the dog. It looked huge, part staghound, a beast fully capable of pulling a man off his horse.

Maybe he could bluff them: claim that Vilbia was his wife or sister or daughter, and demand that they release her. But perhaps she had already told them some other tale? In any case, he doubted that it would work, and then what would he do?

Bribe them to release her? But a young female slave might fetch twenty gold solidi at auction, perhaps even as much as thirty if the buyer wanted her for his bed. He had only three. The bailiffs and their captives were drawing ahead again. Still undecided, he flicked the reins and began following them.

He still kept to high ground and the cover of trees; anywhere from which he could observe without being seen. He had no plan, other than a vague idea of waiting until nightfall and then taking whatever opportunity the darkness might offer.

As it happened, he did not have to wait very long. After no more than half a mile the bailiffs halted. The one in front – Victorinus, Canio assumed – then trotted back and spoke with his colleague. Canio was much too far away to hear what was being said, but it seemed from their gestures that they were arguing about something. It was a short argument: the second man spread his hands in a gesture of resignation and then both dismounted and tied their horses to nearby trees. Canio saw Victorinus take something from his belt pouch and walk over to Vilbia. He stooped over the manacles and Canio realised that the something must be a key.

Pulling open the manacles and disengaging them from the chain that linked all four prisoners, Victorinus grabbed Vilbia by the arm and began dragging her, struggling, towards a grove of trees some thirty yards away. Meanwhile, the other guard looped the chain around the trunk of a great oak and pushed what Canio guessed was the plunger of a cylinder padlock through the links at both ends. Then he called the hound to heel and set him to guard the remaining prisoners before hurriedly following Victorinus towards the grove.

Canio realised only too well what was about to happen. 'Damn you!' he snarled. 'Damn your eyes and livers and guts!' He kicked his heels into Antares' flanks and rode wildly down the hillside. But the route from his vantage point to the grove was not straight because he had to swerve around bushes and trees, and by the time he reached the level ground he could see neither Vilbia nor the bailiffs.

Grim and furious now, he lashed the horse and charged straight towards the grove. But well before he reached it the hound spotted him and came bounding towards Antares, barking furiously. It launched itself at Canio, who snatched out his *spatha* and took an almighty swipe which should have cut the beast in half.

But both man and dog misjudged their aims and connected with nothing but air. The momentum of the missed blow almost unseated Canio, and before he could recover the hound had turned and was snapping at Antares' forelegs. The horse reared up, trying to catch his tormentor with his hooves. Weak and one-handed, Canio could not hold on and he slid sideways out of the saddle and landed clumsily but feet-first on the grass. And all the while the hound, intimidated by Antares' flailing hooves, was prancing from side to side and barking loudly enough to wake the dead, saliva dripping from its jaws.

Recovering his balance, and dodging round Antares, Canio gave a fair imitation of a Hibernian's blood-curdling battle cry, a cry he had heard several times too many over the past year.

Then he rushed at the hound, his *spatha* gripped two-handed, intending to split its snarling head in two, right down to its spiked brass collar. But before he could get close enough to land a blow, the hound suddenly stopped as if frozen, turned momentarily towards the grove, gave a shrill yelp and fled. One moment it was there, the next it was gone. Confused, Canio watched it go, its tail between its legs and running like a hare.

Then Antares began backing nervously, whinnying as he did so. Canio grabbed the reins and pulled the horse's head down to steady him, but it took all the strength he could muster to stop him from bolting, and from that point on he had only a hazy impression of what was going on around him. Out of the corner of his eye he saw both the bailiffs' horses rearing and plunging wildly, until either their reins or the branches to which they were tethered gave way and the terrified beasts galloped off.

Immediately afterwards he had a momentary image of the two bailiffs themselves running past him, heedless of anyone or anything in their wild-eyed flight. Then they were past him and gone and Antares was trying to break free from his grip on the reins. Attempting to watch the two bailiffs, still running like men possessed as they rapidly dwindled into the distance, he struggled to hold the frantic horse. The reins were biting cruelly into his hands and he was on the point of giving up the unequal struggle and letting go, when Antares suddenly calmed and stood quite still, his nostrils flaring as he snorted softly.

Exhausted, Canio dropped the reins, picked up and sheathed his *spatha*, and stumbled over to the grove. As he entered it he thought he glimpsed something big and black disappearing like a shadow into the trees on the far side. It had barely registered on his consciousness before he saw Vilbia sprawled on the ground, her face tight with pain as she fingered the back of her neck.

For a long moment they stared into each other's eyes. Then he walked quickly over and crouched down beside her. 'Are you all right?' he asked anxiously. 'Have those bastards hurt you?'

'I'm fine … more or less,' she said slowly. 'One of them rabbit punched me and knocked me down. I don't remember much after that,' she added, gingerly rubbing her neck.

She sat up and Canio rocked back on his haunches. 'Here, let me look.' As she bent her head forwards he eased away her hair and the neckline of her dress as gently as he knew how and examined the nape of her neck. 'Well, the skin's not broken, but you've got quite a bruise coming.'

'Ah well, bruises come and go. Could you help me up, please; I want to get out from under these trees.'

Canio took both her hands and helped her to stand, noticing as he did so that she was trembling slightly and that her wrists were reddened where the iron manacles had chafed her skin. He wrapped one long arm around her waist and supported her as she walked unsteadily out of the grove. 'What happened in there?' he asked quietly. When she didn't reply, he added, 'Those bastards came running out like a couple of foxes with their tails on fire.'

'I … don't know.' She looked him in the face and must have seen his eyebrows rise in disbelief. 'As I said, when they knocked me down I passed out. I think I heard a great roar, but perhaps it was only inside my head.' She gave a wan smile. 'But how are you feeling now, Canio? You look pale and thin.'

'I always do: it's why women find me so irresistible.' He saw the smile flicker on her face again. 'Seriously, I'm fit as a flea. You have to be tough to survive in the Rhineland *limitanei*.'

Antares came ambling up to them and she stroked the horse's muzzle. 'Hullo, my hero; did you come racing to my rescue?'

Before Canio could protest that they had both come racing to her rescue, he became aware that the nearest of the three male prisoners chained to the oak was gibbering manically. Canio ignored him. 'How did they manage to catch you?'

Vilbia glanced anxiously towards the gibbering man. 'By bad luck,' she replied distractedly. 'I saw them coming and hid, but that great dog got my scent and they found me anyway.'

'Did it bite you?'

'No, it didn't touch me. But they had horses, and once they knew where I was hiding I couldn't escape.'

'Did they …?'

'Did they what?' she asked sharply.

'You know what I mean. Did they … molest you?' he asked awkwardly.

'No,' she said quietly, and began walking towards the gibbering man.

✻

Canio tugged Antares' reins and followed her. As they approached the prisoners, two of them, one young, one considerably older, began rattling the heavy chain that bound them all around the trunk of the great oak.

'Gargilius,' Vilbia indicated the older man, 'and Togodumnus, this is … what did you say your name was, soldier?'

'Flavian,' Canio said promptly. 'Who's your friend?' he asked, nodding towards the third captive, a young man who was still babbling and hiding his face with both manacled hands.

'Avidus,' replied Gargilius. 'But don't worry about him. Can you get these damned manacles off us?'

'Not without the key I can't, and Victorinus and his little friend must have taken it with them.'

'But I'm sure that a soldier like Flavian knows ways to pick a lock, don't you?' Vilbia said encouragingly. 'Help them, please,' she murmured to Canio, adding, 'But be quick: I want to be far away from this place.'

Canio heard the anxiety in her voice. 'I'll think of something,' he assured her, and winked.

Taking hold of one of the rigid iron manacles he looked at it critically. It had a hinge on one side and a spring-steel barbed plunger and box-like lock on the other, opening, side. Before he had snapped each manacle shut, Victorinus had threaded its plunger through one of the links of the heavy iron chain which was now wrapped around the oak.

'Don't go away,' he said to Gargilius. 'I won't be long.' Handing Antares' reins to Vilbia he walked a few yards to a small elder tree, selected a straight length of slim branch, snapped it off and returned, cutting it down to size with his dagger as he did so. First he offered up the end to the hole in the bottom of one of the locks, whittled the wood to fit, then burrowed out the soft pith with the dagger point to produce a tube.

Inserting the tube into the keyhole he pushed cautiously until it met resistance, then pushed harder, so that the tube slid over and compressed the spring-steel barbs inside. When the stick was in as far as it would go, he tugged at the manacles – and the barbed end of the plunger popped out of the other end of the lock. With the air of a conjuror he held out the open manacles for Vilbia's inspection.

'Easy,' he said, and proceeded to repeat the operation to free the other two captives.

'That's a trick worth remembering,' Gargilius muttered as he licked the raw flesh of his wrist where the iron had rubbed.

'It certainly is. But if I were you I'd get out of here fast, before your friend Victorinus thinks about returning. Here, you can keep this as a souvenir,' Canio added, tossing the makeshift key to Gargilius.

'I did see it! They don't believe me, but I did see it.'

Canio turned, to see Avidus peeping between his spread fingers towards the grove. 'Saw what?' he demanded.

'The beast of course – the huge beast. It must still be in there, or somewhere close by. Hide me – don't let it see me!'

'It's gone. The damned thing ran away with Victorinus and the other bastard.'

'No, not that one!' Avidus protested. 'The other one.'

'What other one?'

'The one that was in those trees over there!' Avidus sobbed, pointing to the grove with one hand while still attempting to hide his face behind the other. 'Huge it was – big as the biggest ox I've ever seen. And it was black as jet, with eyes that glowed like hot embers and teeth like sickle blades.'

'Don't take any notice of him,' Togodumnus broke in impatiently. 'He's brainsick – has been since the day he was born.'

'He sounds it,' Canio grunted.

'I saw it, I saw it!' Avidus howled. 'You didn't see it because you were round the other side of the tree.'

'I didn't see it because it was never there.' Togodumnus looked at Canio and tapped his temple with one finger.

'Flavian, I really think we ought to get away from here. As you said, Victorinus might be coming back.'

Canio inclined his head to Vilbia. 'The lady's right. Time we weren't here.' He gathered up Antares' reins and he and Vilbia started walking away.

'I'm not going anywhere until I've smashed these damned things,' Gargilius declared grimly, as he began hammering against the hard bark of the oak the lock of the manacle that had so recently been biting into his wrists.

'Suit yourself,' said Canio, and shrugged to Vilbia.

They set off southwards, Vilbia setting the pace. When they were out of earshot, Canio glanced back and muttered, 'Silly buggers: Victorinus and his like will never run out of iron bracelets.'

'Wouldn't you feel like that, if you'd been shackled in those things?'

'No. I'd feel like killing the man who put them on me.'

'And would you?'

But before Canio could reply he noticed something interesting. 'Hey, what's that?' It was a saddlebag from one of the bailiffs' horses, lying on the grass beside the multiple trunks of a coppiced ash. He guessed that, in its headlong flight, the horse had blundered close enough to the tree for the out-flying saddlebag to wedge momentarily between two trunks and tear free.

He pounced on it and delved inside. 'Oh, look what we have here: bread … cheeses … and a couple of bags of shelled hazelnuts,' he announced gleefully as he ferreted around and drew them out, one by one. 'And what's this little darling?' He pulled out a wineskin, unstoppered it and sniffed. 'Southern Gaulish, I do believe.' He took a hearty swig. 'Yes, definitely from the Burdigala region, I'd say. What do you think?'

Vilbia took a small drink from the proffered skin. 'I think that we should be taking your own advice and getting away from this place before Victorinus decides to come back. I'd like one of those cheeses though: I haven't eaten for almost a day.'

'This one?' Vilbia nodded and Canio picked up a cheese and lobbed it over to her. Then he quickly scooped the rest of the food back into the saddlebag and hung it over Antares' saddle. 'Hop up. We can make a dozen miles or more before evening.'

'You ride first. Your face still looks as though you haven't slept for a week.'

'I told you, I'm fine now.'

'Ride anyway. I just want to walk free.'

'As you wish,' he replied. 'If you change your mind, just say.'

Over the first mile, some of the contents of the bailiffs' wineskin disappeared down Canio's throat, and thence to his bladder. He dismounted and went behind a tree to relieve himself. When he returned Vilbia again declined his offer to ride, and as time passed the lulls between their conversations grew longer. There was something he wanted to ask her, but couldn't find the right words to begin. It occurred to him that perhaps she had the same problem.

However, it was Vilbia who first broke the silence. 'Tell me something … why didn't you seem bothered by what Avidus claimed he'd seen back there under the trees?'

'Why? Because Avidus is a jackass, that's why. You heard what the others said.'

'But surely there must have been *something* in that grove, something that frightened Victorinus out of his wits?'

'There was something, and I'm pretty certain I know what it was.'

'What?' He thought she sounded tense.

'A bull of course – a big black bull.'

'A bull? Did you see it?'

'Yes ... more or less. Listen, back at Abona, when I was in The Guiding Star, I remember overhearing someone say that half a dozen fighting bulls had escaped from a place just south of Aquae Sulis. Apparently some retired governor of one of the Hispaniae provinces breeds them there on his estate.'

Vilbia shook her head. 'But Victorinus wouldn't have been that scared just by a bull – would he?'

'Well, maybe he didn't realise what it was and his imagination got the better of him – or maybe there were more than one. Maybe all six came crashing out of the wood together, pawing the ground and looking as though they'd been waiting all their lives to skewer him with their big sharp horns. And those fighting bulls are enormous beasts – they would certainly have scared me.'

Vilbia said nothing. He took her silence for dissent. 'Well, can you think of anything else it could have been?'

'No ... no I can't. I'm sure you're right.'

'You don't sound very sure.' Canio reined Antares to a halt and looked quizzically down at her. After the experience of the previous night, he was determined to find a rational explanation for everything, and that included whatever it was that had frightened Victorinus.

'I admit it's the only explanation that makes sense.'

'But?'

'But nothing, Canio. Let's keep moving. When night comes I want to be far away from that place.'

'And the nasty big black bulls?'

'And the nasty big black bulls – or whatever it was that I never saw.'

Canio let Vilbia stride on ahead for a while, then slowly rode up beside her. For a while neither spoke. Wondering why she seemed so calm, he rationalised that she must only be pretending that what had happened over the last day had not affected her.

But before he could say as much, she said simply, 'Thank you for rescuing me.'

'I didn't rescue you: the bulls did.'

She smiled. 'Of course; I forgot. But you did risk your life trying, and while you were still weak from the fever too.'

'Didn't you think I would come looking for you?'

'I ... wasn't sure.'

'Saturninus would have. Do you think I'm a lesser man than him?'

'I don't know, Canio – do you? Back in Corinium I heard someone say that you had, well ... certain character flaws.'

Eutherius, damn him, Canio thought. 'And did you believe that someone?'

'At the time I had no reason not to.'

'And now?'

'Now? Now I think that you are a different man from the one who was described to me in Corinium.'

'Different in what way?' he persisted.

'Just different.'

'Better different or worse different?' He had suddenly realised how much knowing mattered.

There was a pause. Then, 'Not worse,' she said quietly. 'At least, not in most ways.'

***

By evening they were many miles away, travelling west along a narrow trackway which wound between the trees on the lower slopes of the north side of the Lead Hills. By then Canio was very tired, and with fatigue had come an acute consciousness that, if they were to encounter any more of Muranus's men, he would be unable to fight them off. Even in the woodland he was unable to relax, his eyes forever seeing dark, amorphous shapes lying in wait behind the encircling trees.

But Vilbia appeared quite untroubled by such fears. 'Why don't we climb the high slopes above the trees? We might be able to catch sight of the sea from up there.'

'And let the whole world catch sight of us too?' he objected. 'Best we keep under cover.'

Vilbia sighed. 'Perhaps you're right. I've never seen it though.'

'What, the sea?'

'No, I've never seen it. I suppose that must seem strange to you, but I never have.'

'You'll see it tomorrow, I promise.'

They spent the night under the trees, looking up through the leaves and seeing pale grey clouds drifting away northwards and hazy stars begin winking down. In the cool dawn, before they set off again, Canio noticed Vilbia wincing as she twisted and massaged her neck where Victorinus had punched it.

As they journeyed on towards the sea they came across two small villas, both some distance away to the north. At the first, Canio could make out only a solitary old *paganus* carefully whittling a handle to fit the iron socket of a hoe. The second villa, a mile or so nearer the coast, appeared completely deserted.

At around mid-morning they at last reached the western end of the hills, and there he reluctantly decided to climb to the top to look out over the land ahead.

With Vilbia standing beside him he gazed westwards and saw, in the distance, the sea, a vast sparkling patchwork of rippling blues and browns. Between land and sea was the wide sandy beach he remembered, but behind the beach was a great expanse of smooth grey mud, featureless at first, but further inland becoming dotted with patches of dull green vegetation. North of the hills the mud seemed to be encroaching onto what had once been pasture land. South, the band of mud was even wider, only ending when it came up against a great sea of reeds that stretched back inland for as far as he could see.

'Sweet Venus! ... I'd heard rumours that the sea had flooded some of the land down here and was turning it back into marsh, but I didn't realise it had got this far north.'

'Wasn't it always like this?' Vilbia asked anxiously.

He shook his head. 'No. Further south it was – that's why it's called the Great Marshes, but when I was last here there were herds of beef cattle grazing. There's precious little for them to graze on now,' he added, eyeing the half mile or so of scrubby grassland that separated the lower southern slopes of the hills from the encroaching mud and reeds.

'How long ago was that?'

'Since I was last here? Maybe six or seven years.'

'And it's changed that much in so short a time?'

'So it seems. We live in a changing world, Vilbia.'

'And these days it seems never to change for the better,' she sighed.

'It does if you make it.' He waited for her to ask what he meant by that, but when she didn't he realised that she was staring in fascination at the horizon-filling expanse of the distant sea.

'It's so big,' she murmured. 'I'd heard people talk of it, but when you actually see it for yourself ...'

'And that's just a tiny little bit of it. It's only when you've sailed out on it, like I have, that you begin to realise just how immense it really is.'

'When did you sail on it?'

'Oh, when I was younger. I had to sail across the Fretum Gallicum several times on my way from and to Gaul and the Rhineland.'

'It looks so bright and happy, with the sun dancing on the waves.'

'You wouldn't say that if you saw it in a storm, winter or summer. It's a dark and fearsome thing then.'

'Yes, I remember what Saturninus said about ...' She stopped abruptly, then pointed to something in the distance. 'What's that?'

'What?'

'That great promontory of land sticking way out into the sea. It looks like these Lead Hills starting up again.'

'Ah, that. That's Moriduno. It marks the northern end of the long beach that runs for miles southwards. Come on, let's see if we can reach it without getting our feet wet.'

Leading Antares, he picked his way down a narrow sheep track to the foot of the hills, the sea dropping jerkily out of sight with every step. Together they walked through the scrubby grassland until they reached a sluggish, winding river with banks of steep grey mud. It looked treacherous, and it also blocked their way to the sea.

He scrutinised it doubtfully. 'The tide's still going out, but I don't fancy trying to cross here. Get stuck in that mud and we'll need a few of those big black bulls to pull us out again.'

'And you can't always rely on them turning up when you need them.'

He looked at her, but she was practising her trick of keeping her face completely expressionless. 'Quite. Anyway, let's follow the river upstream for a bit; maybe it'll narrow down.'

'I suppose you don't know its name?' Vilbia asked. He had noticed that she seemed ever curious to learn new things.

'No, but I can think of one or two,' he muttered, surveying the dismal grey mud. Relenting, he added, 'I seem to remember someone once telling me it's called the Iscalis – or maybe that was one of the rivers further south?'

Whatever its name, he followed the twisting river, first south, then east, as it slowly narrowed, seeing along both banks the eroded remains of clay levees that, on his last visit, had prevented the incoming tides from flooding over the land. Eventually he came to a point where the levees on both sides had virtually disappeared.

'Might as well cross here,' he told her. 'Looks as though it's not going to get any better.'

Even with Vilbia perched up on Antares' back behind Canio, the horse had no difficulty in fording the little river, although his hooves sank six inches into the silty bed so that for some time afterwards, as Vilbia commented, he appeared to be wearing two pairs of boots, dark grey at first, then light grey as the silt dried.

Once on the other side, Vilbia slid down from Antares' back and stood gazing at the mass of ankle-high plants that spread across the grey mud of the salt marsh – strange plants, with fleshy, upward-pointing branching stems. 'So now we follow the river back to the beach?' she asked.

'Unless you fancy walking through the mud, or finding your way through that lot,' Canio replied, glancing at the reeds behind them.

So they walked back along the south bank of the Iscalis, watching the promontory of Moriduno loom ever larger. The curve of the estuary led them inexorably towards it as it rose up out of the desolate land, an enormous hump of rock well over a mile long which ran far out into the sea.

'Do you think that anybody lives up there?' Vilbia asked, after she had hopped over one of the narrow rivulets which trickled out of the marsh and meandered down the beach.

'Shouldn't think so,' he replied. 'It can't be an easy place to get to.'

'But that is a building up there, isn't it?'

He followed her pointing arm and saw what appeared to be a red tiled roof a little less than halfway along the promontory. 'So it is. Come to think of it, I remember noticing it myself last time I was here. Can't say I'd fancy living up there though, especially in winter.'

At last, after several minor diversions to avoid the softest of the mud, they reached the beach on the south side of Moriduno, quitting the estuary of the Iscalis as it disappeared around the north side of the promontory. As they walked down the beach Moriduno's massive cliffs towered above them, dwarfing them like ants against its split and weathered rock faces.

Vilbia knelt and scooped up a handful of the dark yellow-brown sand and held it up for Canio's inspection. It was warm and fine-grained and smelt faintly of the sea. 'How certain are you that this beach goes all the way down to the far side of the Great Marshes?' she asked, apparently casually.

'Not so sure as I was – not with all the changes that have happened since I was last here. Years ago a man told me that it went all the way, but I never used the route myself.'

'So it could be a long, wasted journey if we find it leads nowhere.' Before he could reply, Vilbia continued, 'From the top, though, we might be able to see where the beach leads?' She shaded her eyes with both hands against the brightness of the sky and stared up at the towering cliffs. 'And back there I noticed a path leading up to the top.' And she pointed to a small gully some two hundred yards back towards the landward end of Moriduno, a gully which zig-zagged up the side of the promontory where it was lower and the slope less vertiginous.

Canio sighed. 'All right, if it'll make you happy, we'll take a look from up there. If nothing else, you'll get a good view of the sea,' he added, just to let her know that he had guessed her real reason for wanting to go up there.

CHAPTER THIRTEEN

So they walked back up the beach and began climbing the gully that led to the top of Moriduno, Vilbia in front, Canio leading a distinctly reluctant Antares by his reins. The path was quite narrow, but in places the passage of many feet had cut through the turf and polished the rock below.

This puzzled Vilbia. 'Who do you think uses this path? I mean, we haven't seen any other people since early morning, and those we did see were in the fields on the north side of the Lead Hills.'

The same thought must have been going through Canio's mind. 'I suspect it hasn't been much used by anybody for quite a while.' Pointing to the path immediately in front, he said, 'Look at the way moss is growing back across that patch of rock there.'

Reaching the top of the promontory she found that the wind blowing into her face from the south-west was surprisingly strong and cool, almost cold, even on that hot June day. Narrowing her eyes against it she saw the broad, grassy top of Moriduno stretching out in front of her, undulating towards a rounded peak more than half a mile seawards.

'It looks like a temple.' Canio's words were battered by the blustering wind, but by then Vilbia had already seen and was walking excitedly towards the stone building with the weathered-orange tiled roof. Outlined against the sky it had appeared huge, but as she got closer it seemed to shrink down and down until, standing beside it, she realised that the main building was no more than fifteen long strides square, with a high cella tower rising up through its centre.

On the landward side of the temple was an iron-studded door, sheltered by a portico with a tiled roof supported by two lathe-turned stone columns. Handing Antares' reins to her, Canio lifted the rusty iron latch and pushed. It didn't move. He pushed again, but the door wouldn't budge.

'Damned thing must be locked. Either that or it's bolted from the inside.' Hammering against the door with the side of his fist he shouted, 'Hey, wake up in there – you've got visitors!' Silence. 'Come on, we know you're in there.' Still silence. He tried once more, then turned to her and shrugged. 'It seems that there's nobody at home today. Let's go over to the edge of the cliffs and look down the beach.'

'I wonder which god or goddess it's dedicated to?' Vilbia murmured to herself as, following Canio, she wandered among carpets of white-petalled flowers. And in the dips and hollows, where the grass was longer, she noticed several bluebells, those flowers of the woodland spring, still fresh and unwithered even now in midsummer.

'Are you coming or what?' she heard Canio shout.

Startled, she looked up and saw that he and Antares were already some forty yards away, standing in a large bed of knee-high bracken at the edge of the high cliffs. She hurried to join him and they stood together, shading their eyes against the sun as they looked southwards out over the beach far below.

She sighed. 'I hate to admit it, Canio, but with this sun in my face I can't see much further than I could down on the beach.'

'I was thinking the very same thing myself. Back down to the sands then?'

But Moriduno held a fascination for Vilbia that she couldn't properly explain. 'No, let's go right to the end. From there we'll be looking more sideways-on to the beach, so the sun won't be glaring straight into our eyes.'

'But that must be the better part of a mile,' Canio objected. 'Two miles, there and back, and we've a long journey ahead of us down that beach. Don't you want to get started?'

Vilbia was torn. She did, and yet …

It seemed that Canio mistook her silence for dissent. He gave an exaggerated sigh. 'All right, we'll go to the far end – and have another look at the sea.'

As they walked together along the undulating crest of the promontory she noticed that the colour of the sea was forever changing: first blue in the sunlight, then dull brown when the sun was hidden by the white fluffy clouds, then blue again as the clouds raced on by. She heard the lonely song of the wind, the crash of the waves breaking against the rocks far below and the cries of the gulls as they glided past at eye level out over the sea.

Halting at the highest point of Moriduno she saw that the beach appeared to run all the way southwards until it merged with the misty horizon. Cheered by this they walked on, right to the western end of the promontory, where it sloped down one last time before finally vanishing into the wave-rippled sea in a mass of tumbled rocks. Sitting beside Canio, in a grassy hollow sheltered from the wind, she first gazed out over the ever-changing sea, then lay back on the sun-warmed turf and watched a quartet of small, bright-blue butterflies gyrating low over the grass on the slope in front of her. She was already half-asleep when she felt a nudge in the ribs, and sat up to see Canio pointing to an object far out to sea, a little to the south of a small, steep-sided island in the middle distance.

'Looks like there's a ship coming this way.'

She shaded her eyes and watched as the ship steadily drew nearer, until at last it was no more than a quarter of a mile distant. By then she could see its twenty or so oars on each side, drawn half inboard and sticking out horizontally above the sea, as it flew before the wind that filled its large single sail which, like the rigging and even the tunics of the crew, was dyed a bluish-green.

But, to her disappointment, that was the closest it was to come to Moriduno. Even as she watched she saw two tiny figures throw themselves against the great steering oar at the stern of the vessel, and almost immediately it began to slowly change direction and start heading north-eastwards up the coast towards the Sabrina Estuary.

That sea-green coloration awoke a memory of something Gulioepius had once told her. 'Is that a war galley? I've heard of them, but never seen one.'

'One of the Classis Britannica's finest. They don't usually go further up the Sabrina than Abona. Occasionally one goes all the way up to Glevum, but that's only to reassure old Governor Laeto when he's visiting the city – and wetting his ceremonial toga with fright at the thought that the Hibernians might be coming sailing up the river again.'

'How far westwards do those galleys go?'

'Oh, all the way along the southern coast of Cambria, I think. Maybe further – I don't really know.'

Vilbia was silent for a while, gazing at the galley as it slowly dwindled and merged into the blue distance, like some mysterious bird of passage, glimpsed once but never to be seen again. 'In the *Conspiratio*, did those galleys ever fight the Hibernians out on the sea?'

'Not that I know of. They spent most of their time chasing the Saxons and Franks on both sides of the Oceanus Britannicus, and then helping themselves to whatever those bastards had plundered, if what I heard was true. By the time they'd finished doing that, most of the vermin that had caused the mischief around these parts were either dead or back on the other side of the Oceanus Hibernicus. Mind you, if I was in a sticks and leather curragh I wouldn't want one of those galleys coming after me. Their crews are really evil bastards. Most of them are either captured pirates, or army men who've stuck a knife into someone they shouldn't and been given a simple choice: either start pulling on the oars or kiss goodbye to this world. One good thing about their sea-green uniforms, you can usually spot them for what they are, even if they've got their anchors covered up.'

'What anchors?'

'The anchors branded on their left forearms,' Canio explained casually. 'Done with a red-hot iron when they're first drafted into the galleys so they'll be recognised if they desert.'

Vilbia shuddered. 'Perhaps we should go back to the beach now. As you said, we've still got a long way to go today.'

So she strolled back the mile or so to the temple, treading the thin grass which grew along the centre of the promontory, and noticing again how the stunted hawthorn bushes on both sides seemed to have been permanently bent towards the north-east by the incessant wind.

As they walked, Canio said, 'Seeing that galley reminded me of a good joke I once heard. Want to hear it?'

She looked at him doubtfully. 'It's not filthy, is it?'

'No, of course not. It's funny. It's about priests trying to foretell the future – your bag of tricks.'

'All right then, tell me.'

'Hundreds of years ago there was this Roman general. He was on his galley sailing across the sea to fight someone – I can't remember who – and he wanted to find out whether or not he was going to win the battle ahead. There were a couple of priests and a crateful of chickens on board, and the priests said, "Watch how the sacred chickens eat." Apparently the priests were supposed to be able to foretell the future by studying the way the chickens ate corn. Have you ever come across that?'

'I've heard of it, but I've never seen it done.'

'No: somehow I don't imagine that many people have. Anyway, they scattered some corn in front of the chickens, then sat back to watch them. But the stupid birds wouldn't eat. No matter what those priests tried, they couldn't make them eat so much as a single grain. In the end the general got so angry that he said, "Right, if they won't eat then they can damned well drink instead." And he promptly grabbed them by their necks and threw them overboard into the sea.'

'What – the priests?' she asked slyly.

'No, the chick ... Oh, very funny.'

'It was a silly thing to do though. You wouldn't do a thing like that, would you Canio?'

'No, of course not: I'd have eaten them, roasted slowly over a charcoal fire.'

'The sacred chickens?'

'No, the priests of course. They're delicious with the right herbs and seasoning.'

She pulled a wry face. 'You must let me have the recipe.'

***

As they re-passed the temple, Vilbia happened to glance back. She halted for a few moments, then ran to catch up Canio and wordlessly tugged his sleeve.

'What's the matter?' he asked, turning.

She pointed to the temple. Inside the portico he saw that the door now stood wide open. He looked questioningly at her, then handed over Antares' reins and walked back to the doorway. It was almost as dark as night inside the ambulatory, the contrast accentuated by the brightness outside.

'Is anyone in there?' There was no reply, so he added, 'Don't be shy, we won't hurt you.' Suddenly realising that being silhouetted in the doorway made him vulnerable, he quickly took one step inside and then another to his left so that the same darkness hid him. By the shaft of sunlight that now streamed in from the doorway and the dim light that filtered down from the narrow windows in the high cella tower, his eyes began to make out the shape of a figure standing in the middle of the cella, the heart of the temple.

'I bid you welcome, stranger,' came a woman's voice, thin and reedy.

'Welcome to where?' he asked.

'Why, to the temple of the Goddess of the Winds, of course. Have you never been here before?'

'No, never.' He peered into the gloom, but still could make out nothing but a black shape, like a shadow formed without light. 'Is there anyone else besides you in here?'

'No, I am quite alone, as are we all. Does that journey into self-knowledge still lie ahead of you?'

'No; I made that journey long ago. Who are you?'

'My name is Sotera, priestess and guardian of this holy place.' The shadow shortened slightly and then rose again, as if the woman were bowing.

He saw movement out of the corner of his eye as Vilbia slipped into the temple and stood on the other side of the doorway.

'So you have a companion. Welcome to you too, young woman.'

'Thank you. Tell me, Sotera, does the Goddess of the Winds have a name?'

'None that mortals know. You too must be a stranger to these parts not to know that?'

'I am indeed a stranger here,' Vilbia acknowledged. 'And I've never before heard of a temple dedicated to the Goddess of the Winds.'

'Ah, they are not common hereabouts. But there is another reason, besides the ever-present wind, for it being here on Moriduno. Do you wish to know what that reason is?'

'Yes, if you are willing to tell us,' Vilbia replied.

'Then tell you I shall. Perhaps the third member of your party would also care to hear?'

Vilbia saw Canio shoot her a puzzled glance. Then he said, with more than a trace of irony, 'My horse? No, I don't think so: I've never known him to show much interest in theological matters. Mind you, I don't really know what he does get up to in his own time. I've always imagined him standing in his stable just discussing the finer points of mares and oats with his mates, but these days you never can tell. For all I know he might even be a Christian on the sly, though if he is he's never tried to convert me.'

'Perhaps he thinks you're not worth the effort,' Vilbia hissed. There was something about Sotera that made her feel nervous and uneasy, and Canio appearing not to notice it too made her feel isolated and vulnerable.

'Only a horse?' said Sotera. 'Strange – I seemed to sense the presence of another woman? No matter: twenty-six years ago a man called Metellius, a merchant from Londinium who traded in wheat and barley – a very rich man – was sailing back from Gaul when a great storm arose out there on the sea. So fierce it was, so dark the air, so mountainous the waves and so howling the north wind, that all on board were despairing for their lives.

'When all seemed lost, Metellius called upon both Lord Mercury, protector of merchants and travellers, and Lord Neptune, the ruler of the Ocean, to save him. But still the storm raged on. Then one of his crew cried out to his own protector, the Goddess of the Winds, to take pity upon them. And immediately the wind began to slacken. So Metellius vowed that, if he should make landfall safely, then, wherever that landfall chanced to be, there he would build a temple dedicated to the Goddess of the Winds.

'He had hardly finished uttering those words before the wind veered around from the north, and like a great hand it steered his ship away from the cruel rocks around the foot of Moriduno and pushed it gently onto the sands below. So Metellius and all his crew, still shaking with the terror of the storm, were able to climb down onto the blessedly unmoving land. Which is why he built this temple here, overlooking the spot where his ship was beached, in a place where the winds scarcely ever cease to blow.'

'Is Metellius still living?' Vilbia asked. 'Does he ever come back to this place?'

'He used to return once every year, on the day of his deliverance. But in the spring of last year I heard that he had died. And a month later the Hibernians came.'

'They came here?' *And why,* Vilbia wondered, *in this temple of a goddess, do I feel so ill at ease?*

'Oh yes, they came. But the goddess made me watchful and I saw them approaching, although not until their skin boats were less than a mile away out on the sea.'

'And then what?' Canio asked.

'And then, soldier, I hid my regalia and sceptre and all the precious gifts that Metellius and other worshippers had given over the years. And finally I myself hid, to wait until they had gone.'

'Are they here now, Metellius's gifts and the rest? Could we see them?' Vilbia suspected that Canio's interest was not entirely due to their possible artistic merits.

'Alas no, soldier. When I returned every last one had gone. The barbarians must have found them and carried them away.'

'But where did you hide yourself?' Vilbia could not recall noticing any obvious hiding places on the top of Moriduno. 'In the reed marshes?'

'Oh no, young lady – there wasn't time to reach them. The barbarians were too close and the tide was sweeping them fast towards the shore. Have you been on the beach below?'

'Briefly. Why?'

'Did you see a great cleft in the rock face there?'

'Yes, I saw it,' Vilbia confirmed. 'You hid in there?'

'I ran down the beach and reached it just as the first of the curraghs came around the tip of Moriduno. I was terrified that they might have seen me, but by then it was too late to go back. So I scrambled over the great slabs of rock on the floor of the cleft and hid behind them: there was nothing else I could do. And then, trembling with fear, I crouched there in the half-light, listening to their harsh, cruel voices, faint at first, then growing louder and louder, while in my mind's eye I could actually see them coming closer ... ever closer.' Sotera's thin voice trailed away into silence.

'And did they find you?' *What on earth prompted me to ask*

that? Vilbia wondered, but she ignored the searching look that Canio gave her.

'No one found me. I believe that the merciful goddess herself must have thrown over me a great cloak of sleep, for the next thing I knew it was night and the tide had come and gone, and the only sounds remaining were those of the waves breaking far away. But the terror I felt that day has never left me, and since then I have avoided the bright day whenever possible and live in this sheltering twilight.'

'Do people still come here, to the temple?'

'Sometimes, young lady. Not many though, not since the *Conspiratio.* And of course the restless sea still continues to invade the land, especially when the moon is new or full and the tides are at their highest, driving men away.'

Vilbia's unease had not lessened. She wanted to be gone from this place, from Sotera, although she could not have explained exactly why. 'Tell me, if we walk southwards down the beach will we come to the far side of the Great Marshes?'

The shadow that was Sotera shook its head. 'Some say you will, some say you won't. Over these last years I have seen people walk that way. Some have returned, but some have not – so they must have reached the far side. But the sea and the sand and the marshes are fighting an endless war, and who can say which of them is winning now?' Sotera paused, then asked, 'Are you quite sure that there is not someone else outside, someone waiting and watching just beyond the threshold of the temple?'

Vilbia turned, frowned at Canio, then stuck her head out into the sunlight and looked around. There was no living creature in sight except Antares, who was biting leisurely mouthfuls of grass off the tussocks that grew near the edge of the bracken. She resumed her position at one side of the doorway. 'There's still nobody there except our horse, Sotera ... They do say that spending too much time alone, especially in the darkness, can make people imagine things that aren't there. Isn't that so, Marcus?'

Canio nodded. 'Yes Claudia, that is very true.'

'But we really must be going now, if we're to reach our destination by nightfall,' Vilbia said, easing herself around and out of the doorway. 'Farewell, Sotera – and may your goddess grant you peace.'

'Farewell to you, Claudia. Perhaps we will meet again one day.'

'Perhaps,' Vilbia called back. 'Who can say?'

As she walked rapidly eastwards, back towards the path that led down to the beach, she was aware of Canio strolling after her, leading Antares. But he made no attempt to catch up, and at the top of the path she halted and turned to him.

'You look as though you've seen a ghost,' he remarked mischievously.

'So you thought she was too!'

'No, she was no ghost. Just an old woman sent a bit weird by fear as she hid all alone, thinking that at any moment the goat-shaggers were going to find her and butcher her. Remember Necalames?'

'But she was so *strange*. I know the light was poor inside that temple, but however hard I looked I could never really see her face, only a sort of blur of lighter darkness. And why did she twice ask if there was someone else with us? It was as if she had sensed that ...'

'Sensed what?' Canio asked – warily, she thought.

Don't tell him you know about the figurine! a voice inside her head urgently whispered. 'Oh, nothing. I suppose you're right – she's just a fey old woman.'

He gave her a curious look, but said nothing more before starting down the path to the beach.

Once there, as if reading each other's thoughts, they walked in silence down the beach, beneath the massive weathered faces of the cliffs, until they came to the cleft. It was wide at the base, then narrowed lopsidedly as it curved upwards to its apex some thirty feet or more above the sands.

'I suppose that must be where Sotera hid when the Hibernians came,' Canio remarked.

'Yes.' She hesitated, then couldn't stop herself from saying, 'But suppose they *did* see her go in? She'd have been trapped there behind those rocks, helpless; and then they'd have caught her and –'

'But they didn't catch her,' Canio interrupted. 'She's still alive. We saw her, we spoke to her.'

'Yes, we saw her, but … Don't you believe in ghosts?'

'I believe that the dead stay dead forever,' he replied, staring out at the restless sea. 'And I intend to keep on believing that until any of the dead I've known come back and tell me otherwise.'

CHAPTER FOURTEEN

The sand of Moriduno beach felt hard and smooth under Vilbia's feet, its fine grains compacted down by the waters of the innumerable tides that must have washed over and drained through them. As they trudged along she noticed how Antares' hooves made shallow depressions and the occasional scuffed flurry in its surface, the nailed soles of Canio's boots made faint indentations, but her own soft shoes left no marks, no record at all of her passing.

As if I were not here at all. Strange thought.

The noon sun was high in the southern sky, its diffuse brightness so painful to her eyes that for much of the time she walked with head down, seeing the small dead crabs and tiny circular shells, both white, and fragments of bladderwrack which littered the beach. Canio stamped on a large olive-green bladder and it burst with a satisfying pop. She tried the next frond she came across, without success, its bladders being black and shrivelled. Canio pounced on the next and made two almost simultaneous pops.

'Three nil,' he grinned.

She noted that he was growing more cheerful as his strength returned. Perhaps now was the time to ask? Altering direction slightly she moved towards the muted roar of the breakers of the incoming tide, several hundred yards away down the wide beach. When Canio caught up with her she took a deep breath and said softly, 'Who was Marcia?'

There was no immediate reply and she began to think that the strong, cool wind off the sea had carried her words away unheard.

172

Then: 'You told me that I didn't say anything silly when the fever was on me.'

She heard the accusation in his voice. Perhaps repressed anger too? 'I said that you didn't say anything that *I* would call silly,' she reminded him.

They must have walked on in silence for a quarter of a mile before Canio suddenly seemed to come to a decision and asked, 'So what did I say about her? Tell me.'

'You said enough for me to understand that she died by fire, and that her death caused you terrible pain.'

'Terrible pain,' Canio repeated. 'But not nearly as much as it caused her. Death by burning is a horrible way to die. And I watched her die, Vilbia – watched her die and did nothing. She saw me; even though I was hidden in the crowd her eyes still found me. And she must have died despising me.'

'Were you very close?'

He nodded. 'She was the nearest thing to a mother that I ever knew, in the cold city beside the Rhine where I was born. I wasn't yet five years old when my real mother died, and I've only the vaguest memory of her. I never knew who my father was: from what I heard later, I don't think she did either. Probably just another soldier passing through the city. Marcia was her half-sister. She must have been about eighteen then, and she took me in.'

They were now in the zone of worm casts. Vilbia gazed down at the countless squiggles of voided mud and the adjacent small, circular depressions, many with holes at the bottom formed as neatly as if drilled by a carpenter's auger.

'What was she like?' She found herself wanting to know more about this woman who it seemed had once meant so much to Canio.

'Marcia? She had hair the soft black of a summer night, and green eyes that I swear could see in the dark ... I suppose you won't be satisfied now until you know the full story?'

'Only if you want to tell me.' Even as she spoke she was conscious of the lie: she was eager to know.

173

'I don't want to, but I'll tell you anyway. It'll be an education in human nature.'

So he told her, as they walked isolated together on that lonely beach between sea and marsh, where Vilbia could imagine that they were the only people in the whole world and where, she guessed, the fiery sun in Canio's face was an inescapable reminder of that other fire.

'She made a living as a wise woman; a healer, a maker of ointments, of wound salves, burn salves and such like. Skills she had learned from her own mother, my grandmother. But she also did other things, things that she tried to keep secret from me.'

'What sort of things?'

'Selling love potions, telling fortunes, pretending to cast spells on the enemies of those fools who were stupid enough to believe that they'd have any effect.'

'That can be a dangerous thing to do. Is that what led to her death?' Vilbia wondered aloud.

'In a way. She had a lover, a junior officer from one of the army units stationed in the city. He was married, but it wasn't what you could call a happy marriage. His wife was no longer young and he'd fallen out of love with her, if he'd ever been in it. She knew he had a mistress, but not who she was. So she went to Marcia for one of her love charms, to try and win him back. Funny, eh? And the really ironic thing was, Marcia didn't know who she was either.'

'Didn't the charm work?' She thought she ought to ask, although she was almost certain what the answer would be.

Canio gave a sardonic grunt. 'Do they ever? But that didn't stop her trying it one night. That and all the rest, like putting magical signs written on scraps of parchment under all four legs of the bed, and stuffing enough different sorts of dried herbs under the mattress to stock an emperor's kitchen. But her husband just laughed at her; told her she was pathetic.

'And somewhere, in all the shouting and screaming that followed, it came out that Marcia was his mistress, and that pushed the damned woman over the edge. After that, all she wanted was vengeance at any cost – to herself or to anyone else. Without her husband she was nothing – she knew that as a stone cold certainty. But the raging lust for revenge was just too strong for her to resist.'

'And Marcia didn't know that she'd found out?'

'No, not until it was too late. This all happened in the autumn and winter of 351, in the months that followed Magnentius's defeat at Mursa.' He paused. 'You've heard of Mursa, haven't you?'

She nodded, remembering Saturninus and that warm May night they had spent talking together beside her own little temple in the greenwood on the edge of the Long Limestone Hills.

'It was a time of fear and suspicion. Magnentius had gone to earth somewhere in Northern Italy to lick his wounds, and in that city beside the Rhine people were going about whispering that at any moment Constantius was going to return from the East and invade Gaul and Germania. Magnentius had left his brother, Decentius, in charge of all the provinces north of the Alps, and the man was panicking like a headless chicken because the air was full of rumours. One of those rumours was that Constantius had bribed some of the German tribes who lived in the endless forests east of the Rhine to cross the river and make trouble. So in the city men crept around in the darkness of the endless winter nights, wondering if it would be the barbarians or Constantius who would be the first to arrive and slaughter them.

'And in that time of fear the officer's fool of a wife went to the city prefect and told him that Marcia had practised witchcraft and sorcery to seduce her husband. Not only that, she said that together they'd been casting the horoscopes of both Magnentius and brother Decentius to discover the dates of their deaths. And that was a far worse crime – I'm sure you can guess why.'

'Because if he discovered that the brothers were fated to die soon, then that officer could have gone over to Constantius and been on the winning side in any coming battle – right?'

'Right.'

'And the prefect believed her?'

'He didn't dare not believe her. Brother Decentius had got to hear about the accusation and his eyes were out on stalks, looking to stamp on the first signs of defections. He knew well enough that sometimes it takes only one loose pebble to start an avalanche. And it didn't help that, when they searched Marcia's room, they found a little shrine to Hecate, goddess of witches and ghosts – or so some fools believe ... I take it you've heard of her too?'

'Yes, I've heard of her,' Vilbia answered simply, aware that Canio was looking hard at her.

'Yes. Anyway, Marcia believed that Hecate was her protector, and she used to place a little offering on that shrine every single night that I knew her. Several times over the years she told me that if anything were to happen to her, even if she were to die, then Hecate would one day send her back to me again. It was nonsense of course: just words to comfort a child.'

She noticed that their meandering path had brought them back to a ragged line of blackened bladderwrack at the top of the beach.

'They put Marcia on trial for sorcery, though the trial turned out to be little more than an excuse for half the lying bastards in the city to parade his or her undying loyalty to Decentius. Then they dragged her out, tied her to a stake on a patch of waste ground outside the city walls, and burnt her. And when it was over they shovelled up what was left of her and threw it into the dark, cold river Rhine. Like a dead dog. And I just stood there and watched, and did nothing.'

'But surely there was nothing that you could have done?' She guessed it was what he wanted her to say, but she would have said it anyway, because it seemed no more than the truth.

'Wasn't there? If I'd loved her enough and been brave enough, then I would have thought of something. But I didn't and I wasn't. Believe me, whatever sins you may have heard I've committed, they don't even begin to compare with being too much of a coward to risk my own life to try to save the woman who took me in and raised me, when otherwise I would have starved or frozen to death.

'And her eyes seemed to find me. Even hidden in the crowd they found me. I saw them staring at me, wide with the terror of death, and I knew she was begging me to save her, to do something, anything. But even then I just stood and watched, even when she was screaming and writhing in the flames. I wonder if somehow she knew?'

'Knew what? That you were there?'

'No: knew that after she was arrested I had taken her little three-headed figurine of Hecate from her room. I held it tight in my hand, and again and again I begged it to save her, even when I was watching her being dragged to the stake. But nothing happened. Nothing at all.'

Vilbia noticed that he was looking ahead and upwards, straight into the fire of the sun. She looked at his face and that sun and shuddered, guessing what pictures were passing through his mind. She began to imagine those pictures too, and to drive them away she asked quickly, 'What happened to the officer?' Canio did not reply so she repeated the question, adding, 'And to his wife?'

'They chopped off his head. His wife's too. Oh yes, he made damned sure that she went with him on that dark journey to the Styx. He told them that she was the one who persuaded him to seek those horoscopes, because she was desperate for him to get promotion. That was a marriage of equals if ever there was one. She denied it of course, but then someone remembered seeing her go into Marcia's house for that love potion.' Canio chuckled. Humourlessly, she thought.

She stroked Antares' neck. 'How old were you when this happened?'

'Twelve. Old enough to have done something, if I'd been brave enough.' She wondered if it was to stop her replying that he swiftly added, 'At nightfall I went to the banks of that wide black river, still clutching her three-headed figurine, and begged Hecate to send Marcia back to me, as Marcia had promised she would. And then I waited. I remember that by then it was snowing quite heavily, the snow drifting silently down onto the dark water and vanishing the moment it touched.

'I waited long into the night, in that bitter cold black and white world, but Marcia never returned. And then I cursed Hecate. I screamed curses out into the darkness, calling her the foulest names I knew, and I knew plenty. But still nothing happened. So I shouted that she didn't exist, had never existed, her and all the other gods and goddesses. That it was all a pack of damned lies. Then I threw the figurine far out into the river and walked away from that city and never returned.

'Somehow I survived the winter, and for the next three years I fended for myself here and there in Germania and Gaul. A little thievery, a little trickery, even a little hard labour; and then, when I was fifteen, I joined the army. They didn't ask my age and I didn't tell them.'

She waited, and then Canio said, almost apologetically, 'Well, you wanted to know, and now you do.'

'And all this happened in the first winter after that terrible battle of Mursa?' she murmured.

'In the December of that year. Long ago. Before you even came into the world, I suppose.'

'December 351? No, that was the month I was born. Or at least, that's what my mother once told me, though she never said the exact date.'

Canio halted and gave her a strange look. She thought he was about to say something, but then he seemed to change his mind, and after a few moments walked on, saying nothing more.

The tide had turned and was advancing steadily up the beach. They continued on in silence until, squinting anxiously ahead, she saw that in the distance the sand appeared to come to an end.

She pointed this out to Canio, who simply shrugged and said, 'Maybe it's just the high tide.'

But he was wrong. After a quarter of a mile they found their way forwards completely blocked by a wide, slimy-banked river estuary, where some of the sluggish waters of the marshes at last oozed out into the sea. Canio glared at it and swore venomously, as though it were a living thing.

But she scarcely heard him. In horrified fascination she found herself staring at the stack of near-skeletal human bodies that stood at the edge of the salt marsh. In all there were perhaps thirty, or forty, or fifty: she did not attempt to count them. There was little flesh remaining on the stained, dirty-white bones, just scraps of black skin and sufficient sinews in the joints to hold the bones more or less together.

All the bodies were headless. Those in each layer had been placed the opposite way to the ones above and below, rows of bony feet alternating with rows of flattened rib cages, giving a grotesque symmetry to the six feet high stack. The wind was still blowing off the sea, but as it eddied round the stack it carried the sour smell of old death to her nostrils. She had to fight back the urge to be violently sick.

The heads themselves, all facing outwards, appeared to have once been placed evenly on the top of the stack. Now she saw only a jumble of whitish, blank-eyed skulls, undulating and tipped askew by the decay of the bodies below. Several skulls had fallen and lay on the mud. The lower jaw of one had remained attached and now gaped wide, as if it were laughing at some tremendous joke that she prayed she would never hear.

She did not want to look at them, anywhere but at them, but found she could not look away. 'Who were they?' she whispered at last.

'Hibernians probably,' Canio replied. 'Looks like I was wrong about the Classis Britannica galleys not fighting them out at sea. At a guess, I'd say that these jolly fellows were stragglers who lingered a little too long and got captured by the anchor men. They must have brought them ashore here for a spot of sword practice. As I recall, the rule of the game is that anyone who doesn't manage to take a head off with only one stroke has to buy the drinks next time they're in harbour.'

'You mean, they make a sport of it? That's ...' She stopped abruptly as a spasm of revulsion shivered through her body.

'Barbaric?' Canio suggested. 'But that's the way the world is. The way it's always been.'

'But when did they do it? Last winter?'

'Maybe. Or perhaps no more than a couple of months ago. I've known men's bodies to rot away to little more than bones in a month of wet weather. The rain makes them swell up and burst, and then ...' He must have seen the disgust on her face, because he looked towards the stack and said, 'Don't waste your tears on them. Given half a chance they'd have raped you and cut your throat, though not necessarily in that order. Come on, let's see if we can find a way across.'

But there was no way across the estuary. And it seemed that Antares had already sensed it, reluctantly advancing at Canio's urging until his forefeet sank deep into the grey mud. Canio, who had climbed up into the saddle to get a better view of what lay ahead, instantly dismounted, but even so the horse had some difficulty in extricating himself from the viscous ooze.

Vilbia shielded her eyes against the glare and gazed inland. 'Is there any chance of getting around the river? Or could we find a way through the marshes, perhaps?' She thought she had to ask.

'No. No chance. Or not a chance I'd care to take. It looks as if the salt marsh just merges into the river, and I wouldn't want to find out which of the two is the more treacherous.' He looked down at his muddy boots. 'I'm sorry: I should have worked out for myself that there had to be at least one major river like this at some point along the beach. The water trapped in those marshes has to find its way out to the sea somewhere.'

She forced a smile. 'It's not your fault. Perhaps the river is fordable at some times of the year, or when the tides are lower?'

Canio sighed. 'But when will that be? Not tomorrow, that's for sure, and maybe never. No, we'll have to go back the way we came, then try working our way along the southern edge of the Lead Hills until we find a track heading south. There must be one somewhere.'

'You think so?' She tried hard not to let her doubts show.

'Yes, bound to be.'

As they re-passed that stack of things which, such a short time ago, had been living men, Vilbia looked away, out towards the eternal, unquiet sea. But Canio's eyes were morbidly drawn to it, even as he fought against seeing both it, and the ending of the beach, as omens. Omens that whispered to him that there would always be some obstacle to stop him finding that lake and the longed-for gold. And the fallen skull was still laughing. Laughing at him. Laughing at the futility of all human life and hopes and striving. In a flash of defiant anger he dropped Antares' reins and gave it a savage kick that sent it spinning way out into the surf.

***

It was early evening when they arrived back at the western end of the Lead Hills. They re-crossed the river – the river that a tired Vilbia remembered might, or might not, have been called the Iscalis – and walked along its northern bank until they came to a spot where a great clump of common mallows grew chest-high.

'Good for toothache those,' Canio remarked, pointing to the deep pink, purple-veined flowers.

'So I've heard. Sore eyes too – or was that the leaves?' Her thoughts had been far away.

'Ask Eutherius next time you see him.'

'Perhaps I will,' she said quietly, thinking how strange it was that he should have spoken of the very person who was at that moment occupying her thoughts.

As she walked through the scrubby grassland which separated the Lead Hills from the reeds she noticed how the low sun was bathing the southern slopes of the hills in a golden glow, picking out the narrow sheep tracks that wound diagonally across them.

Canio began edging towards the higher ground, and eventually they came across and began following a well-worn path which undulated eastwards along the lower slopes of the hills. Tall briars scattered with sweet-smelling dog roses grew beside the path in the sunnier spots, while in the green twilight under the trees long tendrils of wild clematis trailed down and brushed her face as she passed.

Towards sunset, Canio pointed to a sheep track which branched off their path and headed uphill. 'Before the light goes I'm going to climb up as high as I can. Should be able to get a good look south over those reeds from up there.'

'Do you think you might spot a path through them?'

'It's possible – more than possible. Paths certainly existed further south, or so I was told.'

'And if you can't find one?' She couldn't help wondering if he'd heard about the paths through the reeds from the same person who'd told him of the route along the beach.

Canio shrugged. 'Then we keep going east.' She realised that he must have seen the less than enthusiastic expression on her face, because he added, 'Cheer up: the damned things must come to an end eventually.'

'Everything comes to an end eventually ... or sometimes sooner,' she murmured. Her mind's eye couldn't stop staring at that pile of hideous things which, such a short time ago, had eyes that could have seen the beauty of this summer evening as she was seeing it now. Life was so brief, so fragile. Canio had appeared untroubled by those things that had once been men: she couldn't decide whether she envied or pitied him for that.

As they climbed higher, so the soil grew thinner. Flakes and tiny outcrops of whitey-grey stone began showing through the short grass, already browned in places by the fierce June sun. She noticed how the flowers changed, as gradually the scrambling mauve vetch and etiolated herb Robert which grew on the richer, moister soils below gave way to carpets of yellow rockroses, which quivered on their short stems as the evening breeze blew across them. At the top, several hundred feet above the marshes, Canio halted and turned to survey the scene below. Vilbia sank gratefully down onto the warm, sheep-cropped turf and interlaced her fingers around her drawn-up knees.

Way below her she saw the reeds stretching all the way southwards to the misty blue horizon, a green sea on whose surface the breeze was making transient patterns of light and shade as it sighed across it. In the far distance she could make out trees – willows, she assumed, tiny in the distance – and the evening sun glinting gold on watercourses snaking between the reeds.

She savoured that cooling breeze as it bathed her and carried away some of the fatigue of that long, hot day. Looking across at Canio she asked. 'Can you see a way through them?'

'No, not from here,' he admitted. 'But the reeds are so high that I don't think you could see any path unless you were directly in front of it.'

'Perhaps we'll find one tomorrow.' Resting in the cool breeze she felt relaxed and more optimistic.

'We will, I'm sure. There must be paths. I was told years ago that people live in the marshes further south. Chances are they've moved north as the reeds spread, so there's got to be ways through them.'

A large damselfly, its body bright bronze-gold, settled on her knee and folded its wings along its back. It stayed only for the time of a single breath, and then it was gone: a chance intersection of two lives that would never meet again. *Like my own and Saturninus's?* she wondered.

'Canio ... that soldier from the *Jovii* ... back near Ovilregis you said it was just possible that he was mistaken about seeing Saturninus at that lake. Do you still think that?' It was a simple question, but she had spent a long time wondering exactly how to phrase it. 'I mean, you said yourself that he'd only seen him once before.' She was trying to make it easy for him.

'Well, that's so, I must admit,' Canio replied slowly. 'And the chances are that even if Saturninus was there once, he won't be there now – not with all the time we lost when that damned fever was on me. It's possible that we might have come a long way for nothing.' As he spoke she noticed that he was looking out over the marshes, away from her, perhaps deliberately so she couldn't read his face.

'Yes, there's always that possibility. But on the other hand, maybe he wasn't mistaken. Maybe Saturninus was there. And maybe he's still there. Anything's possible, isn't it?' Canio turned to look at her then, and his eyes seemed to say, '*You know, don't you?*' But perhaps, she reflected, it was only her imagination that made her think that.

What he actually said at last was, 'Yes, anything's possible.'

She waited for him to say more. He did not. Saddened, she gazed over the slopes below them. 'One of those patches of grass down there between the trees would make a good campsite for the night.'

'I was just thinking that myself,' Canio replied, and snatching up Antares' reins he led the way down. She thought he sounded relieved to end the conversation.

CHAPTER FIFTEEN

They made camp just off the path, where the earth between the grass stalks was dry and Vilbia could still feel on its crumbly surface the trapped warmth of the sun. There were other questions which she had wanted to ask Canio, but she doubted now that she would receive truthful answers. So she wrapped herself in her cloak, lay down and presently fell asleep.

Later, thinking back, she suspected that it had been Antares, restlessly snuffling at what he had scented or perhaps heard, that had woken her. Whatever the reason, she lay looking up into the moonless sky and seeing scatters of fuzzy stars set in a velvet firmament. Being midsummer it was far from pitch dark, more a deep twilight in which she could still make out individual flower-smothered gorse bushes growing on the slopes several hundred feet above.

She looked at Canio, sleeping peacefully stretched out on the ground under his blanket, his back towards her, using one of the saddlebags as a pillow. She was almost certain now that he had lied to her about the sighting of Saturninus: almost, but not quite. Hope still lingered. But if he had lied, and was still lying, then even now she did not really understand why. Whatever his motive, it seemed that it was not the obvious one that his reputation as a womaniser had at first suggested. And of course, he had risked his life to rescue her from the slave bailiffs.

Watching the minute risings and subsidings of his blanket as he breathed, she surprised herself by feeling something very close to affection for the man. Slightly disconcerted, she turned over to face away from him and willed sleep to return, but it

185

would not, and she lay gazing up at the stars and the occasional puffs of pale cloud that slowly drifted across the almost windless sky.

And then she caught the first faint breath of it – of a perfume like incense. Sitting up she sniffed the air. It seemed to be coming from the east, from somewhere further along the as yet unexplored path. Intrigued, she debated with herself what to do. Curiosity won. Deciding against waking Canio, she impulsively pulled on and laced her shoes, then set off to find the origin of the incense.

After a while the path grew darker, as it came to be flanked on both sides by black trees. But by then the wafts of incense were becoming stronger, enticing her on.

Suddenly she heard voices, and at that same moment saw first one, then two, orange glows away to her left. Instinctively she crouched down and froze, seeing nothing in that direction now except the silhouette of a ragged screen of low bushes. She paused briefly, then began inching forward on all fours, intending to crawl through those bushes. But as she did so her outstretched hand encountered only empty air, momentarily throwing her off balance. She recoiled back, only then realising that the bushes were growing along the rim of a small cliff at the side of a coombe which cut back into the hills.

Recovering from her fright, she cautiously parted the bushes with both hands and peered between them. As far as she could tell in the deep twilight the cliff was some thirty feet high, and below it was a clearing flanked by trees. The heavy incense drifted into her nostrils again, much stronger now. *Burning pine cones!* She was annoyed with herself for not having recognised it sooner. It seemed to be coming from the base of the cliff, immediately below her.

Peeping down, the first thing she noticed were four men, two on each side of the clearing. One of each pair carried a burning torch held upright, the other an unlit torch pointed downwards. And all four wore close-fitting hood-like caps, the tops of which were bent forwards in a roll. In the centre of the clearing, darkly illuminated by the flaring orange light of the torches, a row of nine men stood facing the cliff. By their helmets she realised that six of them were soldiers, but with a little thrill of fear she saw that the other three, one at each end and one in the centre of the row, had their heads and shoulders hidden by hoods fashioned to resemble the heads of dark, heavy-beaked birds.

Like crows ... or ravens?

Those raven-hoods awoke a faint memory of something that old Gulioepius had once told her. But before she could remember his words she realised that all nine men in the row had suddenly become utterly silent, utterly still, and for a heart-stopping moment thought they had detected her presence. She waited, scarcely daring to breath, until she heard movement below her and, from where he must have been hidden below the cliff, she saw another man stride into view. He too wore a hood-mask, although in those first moments she couldn't see what it represented.

Then he turned, and Vilbia saw that his was the head of a lion. Its mane flowed down to his chest and its mouth was slightly open, revealing cruel, pointed teeth. In one hand he held a large goblet, in the other a small, circular box that reflected a metallic lustre in the torchlight.

Facing the cliff, the lion-headed man stretched out both arms and boomed in a deep, slow voice, 'O God, you who slew the great bull that Lord Ahura-Mazda created when time itself began ... You, who by the shedding of its blood created all the benign creatures and herbs that are now upon the earth ... Now that you have bestowed your blessing on this bread and this wine that are soon to become a part of our mortal bodies, let your light shine out upon us now ...'

As he spoke, lion-head seemed to be looking up towards one side of the cliff, the side from which he had emerged. He turned again, back towards the nine, and Vilbia, staring down through the bushes, saw that there was now a glow coming from the face of the rock on that side.

'Are you all ready – ready to receive the bread and the wine that The God has blessed?' intoned lion-head.

'We are ready!' shouted the nine. 'Blessed be he who slew the bull that Lord Ahura-Mazda created when the first aeon of time began!'

That name again. And now I remember what Gulioepius said – and who those men must be. She felt a little thrill of fear run through her body.

'Then eat and drink, my brothers!' cried lion-head, and began moving down the row, placing in each man's mouth something from the circular box – she couldn't see what – and allowing each man to drink from the goblet. Slits, hitherto unnoticed by her, enabled the three men in the raven masks to eat and drink without removing them.

As each man received this sacrament there seemed to be a whispered catechism between giver and receiver, a catechism which she could not properly hear. But a stray word here and there convinced her that the same phrases were repeated every time. At the conclusion of each exchange of words the recipient gave a salute of a clenched fist laid over his heart. Driven by curiosity, both to catch the words of this strange communion and to discover the source of the light below her, Vilbia drew back from the cliff edge. She raised herself into a crouch, then crept stealthily past the cliff and into the woodland beyond, intent on reaching the trees on the right hand side of the clearing.

This is insane … go back! … go back! a voice inside her head screamed, even as she began easing down the slope and into the Stygian gloom under the trees. It took considerably longer than she had anticipated, since the nearer she came to her goal, so her instinct for self-preservation made her test each footfall to avoid snapping one of the dead twigs, unseen but felt, which littered the loamy soil.

As she drew closer to the edge of the clearing, guided by the pulses of torchlight glimpsed between the black trunks and leaves, she realised to her disappointment that the catechisms had ceased. She stopped and listened intently, fearful now that it had been some noise made by herself that had caused them to end prematurely. Then a voice that sounded like lion-head's started speaking again, seemingly from some distance away.

Thinking that perhaps the soldiers were about to leave, and anxious for a last glimpse of them, she began to move forward more quickly – so quickly that before she knew it she had almost blundered out beyond the sheltering darkness of the trees and into one of the bearers of the unlit torches. She shrank back, scarcely daring to breath, her heart thumping like a drum. Then, to her intense relief, she realised that all four torch-bearers and the nine soldiers in the now-silent row were looking away from her, gazing towards the back of the clearing and at the two figures that were coming towards them out of the deep twilight.

One was lion-head, the other a young man dressed as a soldier but bare-headed. As they passed the nine she heard lion-head say crisply, 'Ravens, to me!' and the two outermost men in bird masks each left his end of the line and swung in behind them as they walked slowly to a point mid-way between the cliff and the remaining soldiers. It was only then that she realised that the glow she had seen coming from the face of the cliff when she was hiding above it was no longer there.

Now the young man had halted and was standing absolutely still with both hands held out in front of him at waist height, palms upwards. From out of the grass one of the ravens lifted a small flagon and slowly poured its contents over the outstretched hands of the young man, who then went through the ritual of washing them with slow, exaggerated movements. After shaking off the remaining droplets, the young man then carefully drew his sword, reversed it, and proffered the hilt to lion-head, who took it, raised the blade as if in salute, then lowered it until it was pointing at the young man's heart.

Watching the young soldier, Vilbia had barely noticed the

second raven slipping away into the shadows. Now he was returning, holding what appeared to be a garland woven of ivy leaves. At a nod from lion-head he carefully impaled this garland on the point of the sword, then stepped back two paces.

Everyone's eyes were now on lion-head.

Holding out the garland-tipped sword as far as his arm would reach, she heard him say in his loud, commanding voice, 'This, which I offer you, is the crown of worldly glory. Take it – take it now – and enjoy fame in the eyes of men!'

The young man remained absolutely still, absolutely silent.

Twice more she heard lion-head repeat those words, and all the while the young man said nothing, nor made the slightest attempt to take the proffered garland.

After the third offer had been ignored the first raven stepped forwards, pulled the garland off the sword point, and with both hands placed it on the young man's head.

Instantly, as if it were made of nettles and thorns, the young man snatched it off, flung it far away into the night, and cried out in a voice that echoed back from the rock face, 'The smile of The God is the only crown that a man should strive to win – for that, and that alone, is proof that he has done his duty in the eternal battle to drive back the encroaching darkness!'

No sooner had he finished speaking than a blaze of light suddenly streamed out from a point about a third of the way up the cliff face, and a voice like thunder from behind the light boomed out, 'Welcome new raven! The God is pleased to accept you into this, his company of brothers!'

Startled almost out of her skin, Vilbia stared up towards that radiant light and saw there the face of a man of greater than human size. It was illuminated by a ring of small flames and had eyes that glowed like red-hot embers. The flames cast rays of light and flickering shadows across the face, so that its expression seemed to be constantly changing. And all the while those glowing eyes glared out across the clearing, seeing everything, missing nothing, including herself.

A cold hand of paralysing terror gripped her heart, and had her legs not turned to water she would have fled. As it was, all she could do was shrink down against the earth and pray that this fearsome apparition would not see her or hear her pounding heart. In the blinking of an eye she had become again the terrified child who had hidden curled up in the night, making herself as small as possible, so that none of the prowling demons of the dark might find her.

Protect me, Leucesca – don't let him see me!

But, amidst the cries that the assembled soldiers raised in acclamation of the new initiate, it seemed that neither the apparition nor any one of them had noticed her. And then, as lion-head solemnly placed a raven hood over the young man's head and shoulders, all the soldiers began to chant a sort of hymn. With curiosity slowly overcoming terror, Vilbia tried to make out the words, but could not hear them distinctly above the cacophony now being raised by the original three ravens. For no sooner had the hymn begun than that trio had thrown back their heads and, with beaks pointing up at the night sky, started to emit a series of harsh croaks that parodied those of the birds whose masks they wore.

The only sequence of words that she was able to piece together was that of the refrain repeated at the end of every verse, which was, "Guide us, O Mithras, towards the light!"

❖❖❖

Possibly it was the unearthly cries of the ravens that unsettled them, or perhaps it was some other cause which she never knew. Whatever it was, in the darkness further up the coombe the soldiers' horses, picketed there unrealised by her until that moment, began to stir restlessly. She heard one whinny, then several more joined in. And then, from the west, she heard the neighing of another horse. Horrified, she realised at once that it must be Antares answering his fellows, and began praying feverishly to Leucesca that the soldiers wouldn't hear him. But it seemed that the soldiers did hear him. Even above the shrieks of the ravens they heard him, and the hymn stopped abruptly.

Suddenly the spell was broken and Vilbia, as if waking from a dream, stared at the dark figures illuminated by the waning torchlight, and for the first time fully realised the danger she was in. Self-preservation at last conquered curiosity and, silent as a cat, she drew back into the depths of the woodland and started creeping up the slope that led to the path above the cliff. Even as she did so she heard, coming from the clearing below, first the buzz of voices, low and urgent, then the voice of lion-head shouting something which she assumed were commands.

As she reached the path she could feel the blood pounding in her ears. She paused, listening for sounds of pursuit behind her. To her relief she heard none, and so began scurrying along the path, crouching low and scarcely daring to breath as she passed the cliff. Fifty paces further on, just as she was beginning to relax, there was a slight scuffling to her right. Instinctively she turned, only to see a great, dark shape rearing up from where it had been crouching among the trees beside the path. The next moment it had grabbed her around the throat with hands as strong as iron manacles, and she found herself staring up at a nightmare creature with two faces.

Above the bearded face of a man was the head of a great bird with a cruel, dagger-like beak. Instantly there flooded back into her mind all the terrors she had prayed would be left behind with childhood, memories of the things that were said to walk the world of night when the sun slept below the horizon. A choked scream welled up inside her, even as she realised that her assailant was one of the ravens, who must have run up through the trees from the other side of the clearing.

Those iron hands were flattening her windpipe, stopping her breath. Panicking, she tried to tear the raven's hands away, but his strength was many times her own. Swarms of tiny red spots began to dance before her eyes. Even as she began falling into the dark chasm of unconsciousness she was dimly aware of the raven's harsh voice above her shouting, 'Up here! Come and see what I've caught!'

The next thing she knew she was lying on the stony path, her breath rasping as her tortured throat sucked in the life-giving air. Then she was being dragged to her feet again. She tried to pull away and struck out blindly, her fists thudding against something solid.

'It's me, you damned fool,' came a gruff whisper.

It took several moments for the voice to register, then she wheezed, 'Canio?'

'No, it's Antares. I left Canio behind to guard the camp.'

Her brain was still not functioning properly. 'But where's he gone? ... The raven, where's he gone?'

'For both our sakes will you stop wittering!' Canio hissed. He grasped her wrist and pulled her into a stumbling run. Starting forwards she tripped over a large, dark shape lying motionless on the ground, and it was only Canio's strong grip that prevented her from sprawling headlong. With a grunt of exasperation he stooped and swung her over his shoulder like a sack of corn, before starting jogging back along the path that led to their camp.

Reaching it, he deposited her unceremoniously on the grass and began rapidly packing and saddling Antares. The horse was shuffling its hooves restlessly, as if itself sensing the imminent presence of danger. By the time Canio had finished, Vilbia, with the elasticity of youth, had almost fully recovered.

'That man, the raven, what did you –?'

'Quiet!' Canio's voice was low and urgent. 'I think I can hear horses coming this way. How many of them were there?'

'How many? ... About fifteen, I think.'

'Oh, merda! That's all I damned well need.' Canio swung up into the saddle, then reached down and held out one arm to Vilbia. 'Come on, climb up behind me.'

They clasped wrists and Canio heaved her vertically

upwards until she was able to scramble onto Antares' back.

'Ready?'

'Yes,' she gasped, her fingers scrabbling for and hooking behind his sword belt.

Canio kicked his heels into Antares' flanks and they started westwards, back along the way they had come the previous evening. The path was undulating and stony, and with two riders on his back Antares could not be urged into a pace faster than a brisk trot.

She turned her head to one side and listened intently, hearing above the rhythm of Antares' hooves first the drumming of other, rapidly approaching ones, and then brief squealed neighs, as if two of the pursuing horses had bumped together on the narrow path. 'They're getting closer!' she shouted.

'I hear them,' Canio called back, and almost immediately afterwards reined to a halt. Before she could ask why, Canio was saying, 'There's no chance of outrunning them on this path, so there's only one way to go.'

Without waiting for a reply he turned Antares' head and started forcing the reluctant horse down the slope towards a dark clump of trees at the foot of the hills.

They were almost there when Antares trod on a patch of loose scree. It was as treacherous as ice, and his hooves slipped and scrabbled noisily for a few heart-stopping moments as he fought to keep upright. In the deathly near-silence that followed she heard excited voices on the path above and made out a group of at least half a dozen horsemen milling there. Then one of them began to follow the route down the hillside that they had taken.

'Hades rot them!' Canio snarled and drove Antares forwards, past the pools of darkness under the trees which would have hidden them, and out onto the grassland that separated the hills from the reeds.

'I think they've seen us!'

'Of course the bastards have seen us! Hang on tight for

sweet Venus's sake, because now there's only one way to go.' Canio's voice was harsh, the anger and exasperation showing as he tried to kick Antares into a gallop.

To Vilbia, that mad dash across the half mile of tussocky grassland seemed to take forever. Several times she snatched a glance behind, and every time the pursuing soldiers were closer, so close that soon she could hear the snorted breath of their horses. Then Antares was splashing through the shallow waters of the meandering Iscalis and almost immediately afterwards plunging into the great sea of reeds, which grew taller around her with each jolting moment.

For the first hundred yards the ground was fairly firm, in that dry season of the year. After that it became wetter and the reeds ever taller and denser, so that when Canio hastily dismounted as Antares struggled in the first really boggy spot they encountered, the feathery heads of the reeds were almost a foot above his own. Vilbia, suddenly conscious that her own head was now the only thing showing above the reeds, scrambled down and joined Canio on the quaking ground.

No sooner had she done so than she heard the soldiers blundering through the marsh behind them. Canio muttered a savage oath and began thrusting through the dark reeds, tugging Antares behind him.

For several dreadful moments, with the sounds of the unseen riders surging ever closer behind her and the wall of reeds in front impeding flight, she felt the terror of the trapped and defenceless rising uncontrollably inside her, paralysing her body and will. Then survival instinct took over and she found herself stumbling after Antares as the horse pushed forwards, widening the gap through the reeds that Canio was making, his outstretched left arm furiously thrusting the tall stems aside.

She heard a high-pitched squeal from one of the pursuing horses, followed by a tremendous splash and men's voices screaming in anger and shock. Too terrified to look back, afterwards she reasoned that one of the horses must have stumbled and fallen and the others collided with it, unseating one or more of their riders.

But nothing stopped Canio: not the reeds, or the semi-liquid mud into which they occasionally sank up to their calves, or the dark, narrow watercourses that flowed almost silently between the reeds and into which they sometimes plunged before they even realised that they were there. And always she was acutely aware that, if the short summer night were to end before they had shaken off their pursuers, then they would stand no chance in the pitiless morning light.

It was only long after she had lost all sense of time and distance that Canio halted and listened intently. She did the same, but the endless sighing and lisping of the reeds as the night breeze rose and fell made it impossible to be sure that the soldiers were not still hunting them. That cruel uncertainty drove them on and on, until the streaks of cloud in the eastern sky had been stained pink by the dawn. Then at last they came across a small island which, although rising no more than a foot above the surrounding marsh, was quite dry and the reeds that grew there were sparser and no more than chest high.

By now utterly exhausted, she slumped down upon it and stretched out to allow her aching muscles to relax. With the coming of dawn the breeze had died, the reeds were still and she could hear no sounds at all, other than the occasional plop as an unseen water vole dived into a watercourse. After a while Canio got up and climbed wearily onto Antares' back. Kneeling in the saddle he was able to peer above the delicate pink and green feathery tops of the reeds, and she heard him murmur in surprise at how far away the Lead Hills now appeared in the misty light. He dismounted and said in response to her questioning gaze, 'Nothing: they're long gone.'

'Are you sure?' In her head she could still faintly hear the pursuing soldiers crashing through the reeds.

'Quite sure. Want to tell me about them?'

'They were Mithraists.'

'No, really? What makes you think that? Apart, of course, from the feathered gentleman whose chastity you were attempting to violate when I came along and saved him. So what happened?'

'I saw them carrying out some sort of initiation ceremony in a clearing below a cliff. I'm sure they didn't see me though,' she added quickly. 'I think they heard Antares neighing and went looking for him.' She was painfully aware that Canio must be blaming her for their current predicament.

Canio seemed to detect the defensiveness in her voice. At any rate, he dropped the sarcasm. 'I'm not surprised,' he said quietly. 'It was that old bugger's racket that woke me up and sent me off after you.'

Feeling mean for blaming Antares, she decided to turn the conversation back to the Mithraists. 'I didn't know that these days men still worshipped Mithras. Didn't Constantinus Maximus forbid it when he became a Christian more than fifty years ago?'

Canio grunted with what she thought was amusement. 'Some say he did, but even emperors can't destroy something as deep-rooted as the cult of Mithras was in the army.'

'So why did they try to ...?'

'To kill you? Oh, I can give you at least three reasons. First, you're a woman, and Mithraists don't allow women in their club. Second, they like to keep their rituals secret. Very secret. Nobody but initiates are supposed to attend them. And third, it wouldn't do their chances of promotion much good if their senior officers, pious Christians that most of them claim to be these days, got to know that they were practising Mithraists.'

'To whom it seems my life was worth so very little,' she sighed. 'Tell me, I saw them doing the sort of thing that the Christians are said to do – eating bread and drinking wine which they said their god had blessed. Is that why the Christians hate them, because their rituals are so like their own?'

'So I've heard.' Canio sounded less than interested.

But she wanted to know more. 'There were three of them who wore those raven masks. Another man though, the one who seemed to be in charge, he wore a mask like the head of a lion. Why was that?'

'Because that's the rank he holds in the Mithraic hierarchy, of course. Didn't old Gulioepius teach you that?'

'Yes, of course he did,' she exaggerated. 'But I can't remember everything he said. How many ranks are there?'

'Seven.' He said it so quickly that Vilbia, who had been staring up at the brightening sky, sat up and looked questioningly at him. He shrugged. 'I was in the army once myself.'

'Yes, of course. What are they all called?'

Canio blew out a long breath. 'Ravens.' He started counting them off on his fingers. 'Then there's bridegrooms, soldiers, lions, Persians, couriers of the sun and, highest of all, fathers – though I never heard of anybody making those last three grades.'

'So what rank were those men who weren't wearing masks?'

'How should I know? Bridegrooms or soldiers, probably: most get no higher than that. Anything else you want to know?'

'One more thing: on each side of the row of soldiers there were two men wearing strange headgear. One of them held up a lit torch, and the other –'

'Cautes and Cautopates.'

'What?'

'Old Mithras's little helpers. The men with the lit torches were pretending to be Cautes, who's supposed to represent light, life, good, etcetera, etcetera. The men with unlit torches pointing down were Cautopates – darkness, death, evil, and any other nasties you care to name.'

CHAPTER SIXTEEN

He realised that Vilbia was waiting for him to tell her more about the Mithraists, but when he did not she said, 'At the end of their ceremony I saw something that I'll never forget, not for as long as I live.'

'Oh yes – and what was that?' he asked neutrally. But he thought he knew what was coming.

'On the side of the cliff there appeared the face of Mithras himself. He had eyes that shone out into the darkness and his entire head was ringed with little flames. I saw him as clearly as I can see you now – and I heard him speak.'

Canio tried to suppress the snigger, but it came out anyway. 'Yes, it's a good trick when it's done well. Scared the life out of me the first time I saw it.'

'Oh dear, I was afraid you'd say that,' she said sadly. 'But if it was a trick, then how was it done?'

'Was there a cave in that cliff?'

'No ... at least, I didn't see one.'

Canio saw the comprehension beginning to dawn on her face. 'I'd bet you a month's pay there was one – those hills are said to be riddled with them. And they always sought out caves did the Mithraists. In places where there weren't any they used to build their temples half underground. Didn't Gulioepius or Eutherius tell you that either?' She said nothing, and he added, 'Mithras is supposed to have sacrificed the great bull in a cave.'

'Yes, I heard them speak of the bull that Ahura-Mazda created.'

'Ahura-Mazda, sometimes called Ormazd,' Canio said,

remembering. 'I once saw an altar-front made out of sheet copper sculpted into the face of Mithras, with holes for the eyes and mouth, and a ring of slits cut around the head. As I recall, there were a couple of large oil lamps burning inside the altar and a horse blanket hanging in front. Then, when the big moment came, someone whipped away the blanket, and look! – there's old Mithras, shining out into the darkness like *Sol Invictus* himself.'

'But I heard him speak ...' Vilbia began to protest, then stopped. 'I suppose that was just a man inside the cave.'

He chuckled. 'Don't tell me you really did think you'd seen a god? Never mind, perhaps you will one day.'

'It's a goddess that I'm seeking now,' she murmured, then, louder, 'By the way, what rank were you?'

He gave her a sideways look, hesitated, then decided not to lie. 'When I was stationed at a big fort in Germania they did once invite me to join the brotherhood.'

'And did you?'

He gave her a fierce grin. 'Can you really imagine me getting dressed up like an oversized rooster and running around the countryside making funny noises? Want to eat?' He nodded towards the saddlebags.

Vilbia must have realised that he wasn't going to tell her if he'd ever joined the Mithraists, because she shook her head and stood up. 'No. I'd rather put some more distance between us and those soldiers ... You're not thinking of going back the way we came, are you?'

He heard the anxiety in her voice. 'No. I don't think that would be a wise thing to do. My guess is that they came from the garrison guarding the lead-silver mines further along to the east, where the hills widen out. If we went back that way and they spotted us ...' He decided to let her imagination complete the picture.

Standing, she cautiously felt her bruised throat with her fingertips, then asked, 'That raven who caught me ... you didn't kill him, did you?'

'No, of course not. I just sang him a lullaby and he fell asleep in my arms.' Seeing the pained expression on her face he said quietly, 'Well what do you want – a comforting lie or the brutal truth?'

'I want the truth, Canio, just the truth.'

He stared back at her. He wanted to tell her the truth about everything now, but what if that truth were to destroy the bond which the incidents of the last eleven days seemed to be forging between them? The risk was too great. He turned away, stooped and snatched up Antares' reins. 'And the truth will make you free, as I once heard some jackass of a Christian say ... Aemilianus, I think it was,' he muttered.

She did not ask about the raven again.

They set off once more, their pace less hurried now that he was confident that their pursuers had abandoned the chase, in spite of Vilbia's lingering unease. And the bright daylight enabled him to see and hop over the watercourses and detect the boggiest areas of ground in time to detour around their margins.

On another small island they halted to wash most of the mud from their legs, clothes and footwear, then stretched out and snatched a few hours sleep before starting off again through the sea of reeds. Now the sun guided Canio southwards, just as the stars had guided him through the night. And always the tall reeds arched over them both.

'Strange, isn't it,' Vilbia remarked. 'How in the night these reeds seemed to be our enemies, forever in front of us, blocking our way when we were desperate to escape the Mithraists. But now they're our friends, our green fortress walls, miles thick, protecting us from the dangerous world outside.'

Canio grunted his agreement, although by then he had begun to realise that the nature of the marsh was slowly changing. The once-rare islands of slightly higher ground were becoming more frequent and larger, and on them grew willow and alder trees. Between these islands the myriad streams and streamlets of the reed beds occasionally flowed out into sheets of open water, whose surfaces were alternately flattened and rippled by the breeze. And between the islands and the pools the reeds marched on, like a great army whose power had been weakened but not destroyed.

At around noon they reached another willow-studded island. 'Well, I don't know about you,' he said, 'but I could do with some food.' He unpacked one of the cheeses which he had liberated from the slave bailiffs, sat on the lush grass and carved off a generous portion with his dagger.

He offered it to Vilbia, who thanked him and then remarked, 'Those willows have been pollarded.'

'So were the last ones we came across, and more than once by the look of them. Wine?' he asked, offering her the plundered goatskin. He was keeping the barley beer in reserve.

Vilbia swallowed a few drops of the strong wine. 'Do you think we're near the end of the marshes?'

'Perhaps.'

'You don't think we are?'

'I think we still have some way to go.'

'So who pollarded the willows?'

'Like I told you back on the Lead Hills, they say people live in these marshes.'

'Strange we haven't seen any of them.'

He shrugged. 'Perhaps they don't want to be seen.' Seeing her starting to walk towards the far side of the island, he called out, 'Hey, if you come across another big bird, sing out and I'll come and help you strangle him – then we'll cook him for dinner.'

She turned. 'How can you joke about it?' She seemed genuinely puzzled.

'How? Because it's over, done, finished. Life's like a river in flood and you can never swim back upstream. And if you try to carry all the worries of the dead past with you as you're swept along in that river, then they'll drag you down and drown you. That's what I always tell myself.'

'And do you always believe yourself?'

'Of course.'

She said nothing and walked away. Too late, he wondered if she was remembering what he had told her about Marcia?

Soon afterwards she came hurrying excitedly back. 'Come and see what I've found!'

He rose and followed her to the far side of the island, seeing there another area of boggy fen with reeds at least seven feet tall and a tunnel-like path leading into them. 'Who do you think could have made that?' she almost whispered.

'Water rats. They're enormous here: big as donkeys. Haven't you noticed them?' She gave him a sharp look. He sighed. 'Well, there's only one way to find out.' He went back, collected Antares, and stepped into the reed tunnel. To his surprise the surface felt solid underfoot. Squatting down he discovered that, just below the muddy surface, was a trackway formed of many small split logs. By prodding with the toe of his boot he also discovered long timbers laid lengthways along the edge of the track to support the ends of the shorter ones.

'Someone's gone to a lot of trouble to keep their feet fairly dry,' he remarked. After a while he realised that the trackway was following a zigzag course southwards, linking the scattered islands of willow and alder.

Crossing one of these islands he heard Vilbia say, 'Oh, look at that,' and turned to see her pointing to a curious wooden object stuck into the ground. About four feet high, it appeared to have once been the thrice-forked trunk of a sapling, two forks originally growing vertically, the other extending out horizontally. Now, inverted so that the twin forks formed legs, and with the top end crudely carved into a bearded male head, it was undoubtedly a rustic fertility god.

'*Priapus Agrestis*,' he remarked and winked at her.

'I can see what it is,' she replied coolly. 'The question is, who put it there?'

'I'll go and ask him if you like.' And Canio did just that,

then waited several moments with one hand cupped to an ear. 'No, he won't tell me. Just stands there as if he's made of wood.'

'You surprise me.' He thought she was trying to put on her prim expression, but noticed that she was unable to wholly suppress a smile.

'Don't worry, I'll get the truth out of him.' He pulled up both sleeves, flexed his fingers, stooped and grasped the "neck" of the wooden man. In doing so he brushed against the horizontal fork, which promptly snapped off. Feeling foolish he picked it up and examined it, seeing the tunnels made by wood-boring beetles under the flaking bark.

He heard what sounded like a smothered giggle, although when he looked up her face was composed and demure. 'Oh Canio, sometimes the gods send their warnings to us mortals in such strange ways.'

'Very funny,' he growled. He lobbed the broken stick over to her. 'Here, you keep it: as a professional virgin the chances are you'll never be offered a real one.'

'For which I thank my goddess,' she riposted, but the hurt showed in her voice.

Saturninus? He instantly regretted the jibe. 'I'm sorry: I don't know what in the House of Hades made me say that.' And he truly did not.

'Nothing to be sorry about. My choice,' she replied quietly.

But in the silence that followed he cursed himself for a cretin. Walking over to her he impulsively snatched up her right hand, kissed the backs of her fingers and then released it before she could even begin to protest. 'Friends again?'

Flustered, she replied, 'Yes ... but for how long, Canio? Until we reach that lake, perhaps?'

***

Thumb in mouth, the naked boy-child stood watching them from the entrance of another long, straight tunnel through the reeds. He stared, wide-eyed, until Canio was only yards away, then lost his nerve and fled, howling, back down the tunnel as fast as his short legs could carry him. They followed, and so came to the island village.

It was a small cluster of circular houses with wattle and daub walls and reed-thatched roofs that came down to within a couple of feet of the ground. Canio could see no sign of the boy or anyone else, but two half-finished wickerwork eel traps and a scatter of osier wands suggested that people had been working there until moments before their arrival. While Vilbia held Antares, he strolled around the low island, peering into the doorway of each house in turn until he came to one where a curl of smoke was emerging from the apex of the roof.

In the dim interior he made out a blackened metal pot suspended over a small fire, and beside the fire, slowly stirring the pot, there sat a shrivelled old woman in a long dress dyed in muted multi-colours and ragged at the hem.

'Hullo, Grandmother. Where is everybody?'

'Not here,' said the old woman, eyeing him incuriously.

'I can see that. When will they be coming back?'

'Not until you've gone,' the old woman replied bluntly, and continued stirring.

'Another of my countless admirers,' he muttered to himself as he walked back to Vilbia. She was perched on the stump of a willow used as a chopping block, its surface criss-crossed with innumerable cuts and surrounded by scores of osier rod offcuts. 'There's nobody here except one old woman,' he told her. 'Seems that the others ran off into the reeds when they heard us coming.'

'They can't be far away though. Shall we wait for them to return?' And before he could object, she added, 'They might be able to show us the easiest route south.'

'They won't be coming back, not until we've left – or so the old gorgon in that hovel over there tells me.' He extracted the wineskin from Antares' saddlebag and offered it to Vilbia.

She took a swallow of the wine, then went over to the house that Canio had indicated. He took a long drink himself, then stowed the skin and followed her.

'We mean you no harm,' he heard Vilbia say to the old woman in British Celtic. 'We've come from the north and we're lost. We were chased into the marshes last night by a gang of soldiers.'

The old woman scrutinised her closely, perhaps noticing the mud stains on her dress that her washing had failed to completely remove. 'But that man with you is a soldier himself. Why would they be chasing him?' she asked suspiciously.

'I'm civil guard, not army,' Canio butted in. 'Even here in this swamp you must know the difference.'

'I know the difference between a wasp and a hornet, and it's not much. The evil little buggers can both give you a nasty sting, just for their own amusement,' the old woman replied crisply.

'But we're nothing to do with the local civil guard or army,' Vilbia assured her. 'We've come on a long journey, trying to find a friend of ours who may be on the south side of these marshes.'

'What's this friend's name?'

'You wouldn't know him,' Canio said impatiently.

'His name's Saturninus. By the way, my name's Vilbia. What's yours?'

'Doccia. And I've never heard of your Saturninus. What's his name?' she asked, pointing at Canio.

'Italicus,' he said quickly. 'Why did all your friends and relations run away?'

'They didn't run. They just slipped away. It's the safest thing to do: the reeds taught us that long ago.'

'How do you mean?'

'I'm sure you know, don't you Vilbia? You look cleverer than him.'

'Yes, I think I know.'

'So which one of you ladies is going to enlighten me?' Canio asked, giving Doccia a hard stare, which she completely ignored.

'When the wind blows over the reeds, they simply bend

'their heads away from it,' the old woman explained patiently. 'The harder it blows, the further they bend. But when the wind dies, then they straighten up – just as if the wind had never blown at all.'

'And no matter how much they bend, they never break. And their roots never move,' Vilbia added. 'Didn't you ever hear the old fable about the oak and the reeds?'

'Not that I can recall. What's stewing away in that pot, Grandmother?'

'Eels and small pike mostly; barley too – the grains have swelled up nicely now. And herbs, of course. Want a taste?' She lifted the long wooden spoon out of the pot and offered the steaming end to Vilbia.

Canio intercepted it. He squatted down on his haunches and sniffed it cautiously, before steadying the end of the spoon with one hand and nibbling a morsel of fish. 'Hmm, I've eaten worse. I'll give you a couple of *centenionales* for the lot.' Delving into his belt pouch he extracted the two small coins and held them out to the old woman.

'Copper money?' she said, wrinkling her nose in distaste. 'That's not worth anything here in the marshes, especially not to me who's never been near a town for years and years.'

For a few moments he tried eyeing her threateningly. But he was very hungry and the fish had actually tasted delicious. 'What about a silver coin then?' he asked, fishing a siliqua out of his pouch.

Doccia regarded it contemptuously. 'That miserable little thing? I can barely see it.'

'In Corinium, Grandmother, that miserable little thing would buy twenty pots of stew – and all of them a damned sight tastier than yours.' He thought he did outraged well.

'Best go to Corinium then, if you're hungry,' the old woman murmured complacently, and went on stirring the pot.

Canio, conscious that Vilbia was trying not to let her amusement show as she watched this battle of wits, stifled his anger, stood up, stalked outside to where Antares was tied to a willow, then returned with one of the pewter cups he had acquired at Abona. He held it out for Doccia's inspection. 'That – for as much stew as the pair of us can eat,' he said with an air of finality.

Doccia carefully appraised the proffered cup with the air of a connoisseur.

'Your very own pewter cup,' he pointed out. 'Who else here has got one of those, eh?'

'Just the one?' she asked with a mix of indignation and disappointment.

'Just – the – one,' he replied, giving the words a quiet menace he was sure would not be lost on Doccia. He did menace well too.

'Oh, all right then,' she sighed. 'You drive a hard bargain,' she added pathetically, fondling the cup that Canio had dropped into her outstretched hand.

He gave her a flinty look. She smiled at Vilbia. Vilbia smiled back.

'Any chance of a couple of spoons?' he asked acidly, well aware of who had got the better of the bargain.

Doccia raised herself stiffly, wincing as her old joints creaked, and from the dim recesses of the house produced a pair of carved and polished wooden spoons. 'You'll have to make do with these – I only get the gold ones out when the emperor himself comes to dinner,' she cackled.

'Har, har, har,' he said, and started on the stew. Vilbia took the other spoon and joined him. By now he was ravenous, and never had a simple fish stew tasted so good. Having to wait and blow on each spoonful to cool it before it could be eaten forced him to eat slowly, and the aroma tantalised.

Part way through the stew he went outside and returned with his remaining pewter cup and the goatskin containing the barley beer he had bought at the farmstead two days before. Vilbia took the offered cupful, but before he could take his intended hearty swig, Doccia held out her new pewter cup. He hesitated, still smarting from being bested by the old woman, but catching Vilbia's wink he half filled it, although not without baring his teeth at Doccia when he thought Vilbia wasn't looking.

Doccia sat back, cradling the cup in both hands as she savoured its contents. In response to Vilbia's questions (and more beer, this time, at Vilbia's prompting, with the cup filled to the brim) she told them of the life of the marsh people. She told of the boats made of hollowed logs from which they fished the lakes with baited iron hooks, or hunted wildfowl with bow and arrow in winter. Of the eel spears with triple barbed points, like Neptune's trident, with which they waited patiently beside the narrow watercourses that flowed between the reeds. She showed them the long salmon traps that they made for the fishermen on the great Sabrina Estuary, and the baskets and eel traps, some woven of willow, some of the osiers that grew on the drier lands to the east, that they made for their own use and for trading with people who lived beyond the marshes.

And finally, she told of the fired-clay salt pans built along the tidal estuaries of the rivers further south, the pans that they heated with wood or charcoal to boil off the sea water and leave the salt behind.

'Salt? That always fetches a good price. You should be rich, not living in this hovel.'

His remark appeared to hit a raw nerve. 'Rich! We would be rich if we could keep the salt we make. But those bastards who live in their warm, dry villas over Lindinis way, they claim to own everything in these parts – even the fish in the rivers and the salt in the sea. There was a time though, when I was young, when they let us keep some of it for ourselves. Then we bartered it along all the length of the Lead Hills for grain or raw wool, or sometimes even for those bright blue glass beads and enamelled copper brooches I loved to wear when I was a girl.'

'That must have been a very long time ago. Tell me, did you

ever catch sight of Emperor Hadrian when he came over to build the Great North Wall?'

Doccia ignored him. 'But now that so much of their cattle pastures further north have turned back into marsh, their bully boys grab every last grain of salt before the boiling pans are even cool.'

Vilbia nodded. 'Yes, Italicus told me that some of the marsh we came through was once grassland.'

'A lot of it was, and until not so long ago too,' the old woman replied. And she went on to explain how the land immediately south of the Lead Hills had indeed once been rich pasture, with fat cattle grazing over it in summer, when the grass never browned and died no matter how fierce the sun. But then the level of the sea had begun to rise, turning the coastal lands into salt marsh and blocking the flow of the rivers, which burst their banks and flooded the fields further inland with fresh water, turning them back into reed marsh.

'You see, long, long, long ago – before even his lot came,' she said, pointing a horny finger at Canio, 'they say this land was all a reed marsh, one even bigger and wilder than it is today. Then his lot built great clay banks along the estuaries to stop the tides from flooding over the land. They dug out the rivers too, so they flowed faster, and the old marshes dried out and turned to dry land. But the gods aren't mocked forever, oh no, and now the sea gods are driving the salt waters inland again. And soon it will be all as it once was, hundreds of years ago.'

Canio was now impatient to be off, and decided to signal it by a couple of exaggerated yawns. He guessed that Vilbia wanted to stay longer, but she seemed to take the hint, asking Doccia how far it was to the south side of the marshes, and what route would best take them there?

'Oh, you've a way to go yet, even before you reach the road.'

'What road?' Canio asked, surprised.

'Why, the road on the high ridge, of course.' Doccia must have seen the puzzled look on his face unchanged by this answer.

'Five or six miles south of here,' she explained, 'there's a ridge of low hills that cuts right across the marshes. I call them hills, though they're nothing like as big as the Lead Hills. Though mind you, they look quite big when you're down in the marshes,' she reflected.

Canio exhaled through his mouth in noisy exasperation.

Doccia gave him a frosty sidelong glance and said to Vilbia, 'Up on the ridge there's a road, a real stoned road built by his lot hundreds of years ago.'

'And I'll bet you sold comforts to the troops while they were building it,' Canio muttered. 'And I don't mean fish stew,' he added under his breath, although loud enough for Vilbia to hear and give him a disapproving look.

Whether diplomatically or otherwise, Doccia gave no sign of having heard him. 'Though before you get to the road you'll have to cross the river.'

'And what river would that be?' Canio asked.

'Why, the Bruella, of course.'

'Perhaps that's the same river we came to at the end of the beach,' Vilbia suggested, turning to Canio.

'Oh, wonderful. Well, if that's so, then all the more reason to be off,' he said briskly. 'How long should it take us to reach this road?'

'Oh, you won't get there by nightfall, and that's a fact.' Doccia shook her grizzled head for emphasis. 'There's no straight path from here; nothing but reeds and meres. And a man can travel ten miles or more on the dry lands in less time than it takes him to travel a straight mile through the marshes.'

But by then Canio was already outside, gathering up Antares' reins and calling out his goodbyes to Doccia, telling her that her fish stew was superb and that he would be sure to recommend it to all his enemies.

Vilbia shook her head in despair of Canio.

Doccia waved one hand as if chasing away a fly. 'Oh, I dare say your man's not so bad really. I've known far worse than him in my time, ones who'd take what they wanted and give nothing, except maybe a knife in the belly if you tried to stop them. And I could see he was fond of you, even though he did try not to let it show.'

Vilbia wondered if she should protest that Canio was definitely not her man. But before she could do so, Canio, who must have been listening just outside the doorway, called out impatiently, 'Stop prattling, Grandmother. Despite what you said, I want to reach that road before dark – if that's all right with you of course, wife,' he added to Vilbia.

Vilbia shrugged her apologies to Doccia. 'I suppose he does have his good points, though I have to look hard to find them.' She felt a reluctance to leave, aware that she and Doccia would almost certainly never meet again. The old woman was like a great scroll on which the knowledge and wisdom of centuries had been written, and brief time had allowed her to read no more than a few of its lines. But she had to go.

As she and Canio were walking away from the village she noticed, out of the corner of her eye, the reeds being eased aside in several places and curious faces peering out at them, faces which vanished the moment she turned to look directly at them.

They walked on southwards, weaving a meandering route as Canio tried to avoid both the densest of the reed beds and the increasingly frequent meres. Beside and over those meres clouds of metallic blue and green damselflies flew endlessly back and forth, their wings making rapid flickering sounds as they skimmed past within a finger's breadth of Vilbia's head.

Passing one mere, she noticed other damselflies, ones with thin blue bodies banded with narrow black rings, whose wings beat so fast as to appear no more than blurs as they drifted like ghosts through the tall meadowsweet which grew by the water's edge, sometimes settling momentarily on a leaf before restlessly moving on.

As if they realise how little of their short lives remain.

CHAPTER SEVENTEEN

After they had been walking for some time, Canio noticed that the reeds were becoming progressively smaller and stunted. He dipped a finger into a pool and licked it. 'Slightly salty,' he informed Vilbia.

Not long afterwards they came to what he assumed was the river that Doccia had called the Bruella. Some miles away downstream he noticed several columns of smoke rising in the still air. 'If those are the salters that the old hag told us about, then they must be using wood today. Charcoal wouldn't make that much smoke.'

Vilbia looked towards the distant columns. 'It must be a terribly hard job in winter,' she mused. 'What with the cold, and the salt getting into the cracks in their hands.'

'It's certainly not a job I'd fancy. Come on, lets find a place where we can get across.' And he set off upstream leading Antares by the reins.

After half a mile they came a point where the Bruella widened and shallowed, and there Antares crossed easily, even with the pair of them up on his back.

By evening, after countless diversions and backtrackings around meres and areas of soft mud, they were both exhausted. Looking south, Canio thought he could make out the ridge that Doccia had told them about, but it still seemed miles distant. Reluctantly agreeing with Vilbia that reaching it by nightfall was impossible, he decided to camp there for the night, on a patch of relatively dry ground beside a desolate mere.

With its pervasive smell of mud and decay the place was far from ideal, but by then he was too tired to care. After seeing Vilbia settle down under her cloak he lay for some time in the long summer twilight, listening to the faint gurgle of a stream emptying sluggishly into the mere, and watching distant sheet lightning as it flickered slowly closer in the darkening sky.

Later, waking in the moonless night, he saw by the position of the stars that dawn was still far away. Vilbia was sleeping peacefully not ten feet from where he lay, but for him sleep would not return. Wondering if something untoward had woken him he lay listening for some time, but heard no sound other than the stream and Antares occasionally shuffling his hooves. Nevertheless, quietly so as not to disturb Vilbia, he stood up and looked all around.

It was then that he noticed them, the faint blue lights out on the surface of the stagnant mere. He saw the most distant ones first, since at that moment they chanced to be the tallest. But as he watched them he became aware of other flames closer to where he stood – wan flames that seemed to rise from pinpricks of light in the gloom until they hovered as tall as a man above the dark mere. He counted nine all told, rising and falling and swaying from side to side like giant candle flames in a slow, silent dance.

Only once had he seen their like before, and that had been in a great tract of swampland in Eastern Gaul. There, a terrified fellow soldier in the *limitanei*, a recruit from one of the Germanic *laeti* that had been settled on the western side of the Rhine, had told him of a belief common among his people. He had said that those flickering blue lights were the ghosts of the wicked dead – men and women condemned for their crimes to haunt such desolate places until the end of time. They had come that night, so the soldier had informed him in an awed whisper, to welcome another lost soul, one soon to leave the body of a man fated to die within days.

But Canio, as he had frequently reminded himself over the

last two weeks, was not a superstitious man. Angrily he searched the edge of the mere for something to throw at the nearest light, but found only the fallen branch of a decaying willow. Nevertheless he grasped it with both hands, swung it around like a discus thrower and hurled it as far as he could out into the water. It was heavy and awkward, and fell some way short of the nearest flame, but he still thought it a satisfyingly contemptuous gesture. And having done it, he lay down again, turned his back and tried to sleep.

But still sleep would not come, and from time to time he felt an irresistible compulsion to sit up and stare out across the mere. Three times he did so, and each time the blue dancers were still there, still swaying from side to side as they slowly rose and fell, calling to him in voices that no-one but he could hear. When he looked for a fourth time he found that they had vanished. Only then did sleep come, although it was a sleep made fitful by dreams in which he saw those same flames becoming ever more numerous and coming ever closer to where he lay, until their massed ranks stood before him like a legion of the dead. The nearest ones even seemed to have vestigial faces.

Most troubling of all, when he awoke just before sunrise he thought he remembered seeing Vilbia standing silently beside the mere, impassively watching both himself and the flames.

In the steel light of dawn he woke her, and after a hurried breakfast they set out again on their journey southwards. On reflection, he decided against telling her about the dancing flames.

The midsummer sun, huge and fiery, rose up in the north-eastern sky and began to warm and hearten him. But still their progress was slowed by the seemingly endless stands of reeds in the less saline areas, by the time-consuming detours around meres, and by having to ford the widest of the slow-flowing watercourses they encountered.

As he paused to allow Antares to crop one of the rare clumps of tasty-looking grass, Canio said with what he thought was studied casualness, 'Going back to what you were saying up on the top of the Lead Hills the evening before last, it must be at least a month now since that trooper of the *Jovii* saw Saturninus, or someone he thought was Saturninus. Being realistic, I suppose the odds must be against him still being at that lake.'

'Yes, I suppose so. But even if Saturninus is gone, perhaps there is something there for us to find?'

Canio froze. 'How's that?' he asked, trying to sound unconcerned.

'Well, perhaps I'm completely mistaken, but I have an idea that you do expect to find something at that lake, even if it's not Saturninus.' She appeared to be waiting for him to reply, but when he said nothing she continued, 'I did wonder whether that trooper might have told you something else about the place, something that you didn't feel able to tell me back near Ovilregis?'

Was she giving him the chance to tell the truth? Or did she already know it? He realised it was possible – perhaps more than possible – that she no longer believed that Saturninus had ever been at that lake. But even if she knew of the existence of the Hecate figurine, how could she possibly know of its connection with the lake? Unless, of course, he had babbled it when the fever was on him. But perhaps he hadn't, and she was only guessing, probing?

The conflicting urges to confess or to keep lying paralysed his tongue. But the silence between them was lengthening and he knew he had to say something. And suddenly, without real conscious intent, the old, atavistic dog-with-a-bone instinct answered for him. 'Something else about the place? Oh, you mean a clue to where Saturninus might have gone from there?'

For a few moments their eyes met. Then she said quietly, 'Yes, I suppose that's what I must mean.'

He saw the disappointment so clearly written on her face. Disappointment with him. Disappointment that he was not more like Saturninus? It hurt. He hurriedly tried to restart the conversation, but her reply was vague and distant as she started walking away. The moment was gone. In the bitterness of regret his mind conjured a distant memory of two yellow leaves being borne along on the surface of a rain-swollen late autumn stream, two leaves caught in a seemingly endless cycle of being brought together by the swirling current, touching momentarily, and then spinning apart.

***

It was a little before noon when Vilbia saw yet another mere blocking their path. Following Canio, she began walking along the bank of the long stretch of open water dotted with patches of light green duckweed, until ...

'Canio, I need to ... you know,' she said, slightly embarrassed.

'Ah ... in that case I'll wait for you by that big willow up ahead.'

She had already spotted a hollow at the edge of the bank, a hollow screened by reeds which afforded some privacy. So she waited until man and horse had reached the willow and halted there in its shade, then stepped down into the hollow. After looking around to confirm that she could not be observed she quickly slipped off her dress.

Afterwards, she removed her shoes and cautiously eased herself naked into the water, finding that there, beside the bank, it only came up to her knees. Conscious of the need to avoid splashing which might attract Canio's attention, she washed carefully, cupping the water with both hands and sluicing it smoothly over her body. Back on the bank she pulled the dress back over her head and smoothed it down over her hips.

As she sat to put on her shoes, the faint sensation of light-headedness she had felt shortly after entering the hollow suddenly intensified. Panicking a little and breathing heavily she

217

stood up, then swayed as a wave of dizziness swept over her. But before she could call out to Canio, something caught her eye – a movement out on the mirror-calm water, where the line of reeds on the opposite bank was reflected. Staring uncertainly towards it, her vision slightly blurred, she saw what appeared to be the figure of an old man in a long brown robe standing among the reeds at the water's edge. Although the glare off the sunlit water made certainty impossible, she thought she knew who it was.

Eutherius ... Eutherius! How could you have known ...?

Almost laughing with happiness, she unlaced her shoes again and kicked them off, then stepped back into the water. The bottom was firm and she felt her bare feet scarcely sinking at all into the smooth silt as she began wading excitedly across the slowly deepening mere.

Canio heard the muted splash as Vilbia entered the water, looked up and saw her wading towards the opposite bank. Mystified, he shaded his eyes against the glare of the sun on the water but could see nothing on that far bank, except the tall, feathery-headed reeds and, amongst them, the hollowing trunk of a decaying pollard willow. He was about to call out to her when he hesitated, overcome by curiosity to discover the reason behind her apparently strange behaviour.

Pausing only to loop Antares' reins over a branch, he trotted quickly and quietly back along the edge of the mere until he was standing immediately behind her. By then she was almost halfway across, the water up to her waist and her gaze apparently fixed upon something on the far bank – although, apart from the reeds and the hollow willow, he still could see nothing there. But what he could see from where he stood, his eyes four feet or more above her own, was a series of bubbles bursting on the surface of the water some yards in front of her.

'Vilbia! What in sweet Venus's name are you up to?'

His voice seemed to startle her, and she halted and slowly

turned to face him. For a few moments she stood looking guilty and irresolute, then called back, 'Don't wait for me, Canio. You go on: I'll catch up as soon as I've spoken with him. I'm sure it won't take long.'

'Spoken with who?' Canio was now both baffled and alarmed. He had seen bubbles like that before and knew what they sometimes gave warning of. 'Come on back!'

But to his consternation she only repeated, 'It won't take long,' and started off again, wading slowly towards that old willow which silently awaited her coming.

Now she was within ten feet of the area where the bubbles were rising. The terror really hit him then, as he realised that even if he rushed into the water he stood no chance of getting to her before she reached it.

'Vilbia! That's quicksand in front of you!' He bawled the warning at the top of his voice, then bawled it again, but to his horrified amazement she gave no sign of having heard him. Wrenching his *spatha* from its scabbard, with one stroke he sliced off a long, slim branch from a nearby pollard willow, then leapt into the water and began splashing wildly towards her, trailing the branch behind him.

And then, without warning, when he was still no more than half a dozen yards out from the bank, on that day which was so still that there was not even breeze enough to quiver the reed heads, he saw a whirlwind born in that patch of reeds immediately in front of her. Tiny at first, he saw it grow at amazing speed into a vortex of howling air that flattened the reeds and toppled the old willow trunk as thoroughly as if an *ala* of cavalry had galloped through them all. And then it died and was gone, as suddenly as it had come.

Vilbia stopped then, stopped as if a spell had been broken. Canio saw her looking at the great mat of prostrate reeds which half-buried the fallen trunk. As he reached her she turned and looked at him, her face a picture of bewilderment. 'Where is he – where's he gone?'

'Who?'

'Eutherius, of course. One moment he was standing there, and the next the reeds started to shake … and he was gone.'

'Eutherius? What in the names of all three *Cucullati* are you talking about – how could that old bastard be here?'

'He ... he just was. Over there, where those reeds are all broken down.'

'So where is he now then?'

'I don't know,' Vilbia replied lamely. 'But I was certain he was here.'

'You almost weren't.'

'How do you mean?' she asked apprehensively.

By way of an answer, he inched past her and began prodding the silty bottom with the cut end of the willow branch that he had intended to use as a makeshift rope. No more than six feet beyond the point where Vilbia had been halted by the whirlwind he felt the branch encounter no resistance. He grunted with grim satisfaction and supported it with one outstretched arm as, under its own weight, the branch slid inexorably downwards.

Vilbia stared at it as it went down, stared until the last leaf was waving feebly under the greenish water before vanishing into the quicksand. Canio, watching her face, saw that it was very composed, very still.

'Thank you,' she whispered, then turned and waded calmly back to the bank. There she sat and carefully washed off all the silty mud from her feet and the hem of her dress, then slowly put on and laced each shoe.

Canio splashed back, climbed out and stood a few yards away from her. He said nothing, sensing that, for the moment at least, she wanted to be alone with her thoughts.

After a little while Vilbia looked up at him, her nerves still feeling taut as bowstrings as she tried to make sense of what had just happened, and to stop her imagination from picturing what would have happened had she walked into the quicksand. Then she noticed that, on his way back, Canio must have waded through a large patch of duckweed, much of which clung to his waist and legs in still-dripping swags.

In an attempt to appear calm she was about to point out the duckweed, of which he seemed unaware, when suddenly it came to her that there was something distinctly comical about his appearance. He looked like a seedy impersonation of Neptune, and it flashed into her mind that all that was missing to complete the picture was a bent and drooping trident in one hand and a frond of the bladderwrack from Moriduno beach dangling over one eye. She felt hysterical laughter rising uncontrollably within her and one hand flew up to cover her mouth in a vain attempt to stop it bursting out.

Time blurred. One moment she was shrieking with laughter, the next she was curling up on the grass, her whole body racked by sobs, tears streaming down her cheeks. Then she was aware of Canio kneeling beside her, cradling her head against his chest, the smell of the mere water in her nostrils as he stroked her hair and murmured words that afterwards she did not remember. What mattered, and what she did remember, was that he had understanding enough to imagine what was going through her mind and cared enough to try, however clumsily, to comfort her. What she also remembered was herself asking him, over and over again, where Eutherius had gone?

But nothing lasts. Good or bad, all things end. Almost as suddenly as it had come the storm passed, and she felt her mask of self-possession slipping back into place.

Uncertain whether she had heard the things he had said, and uncertain too what her reaction would be if she had heard them, Canio rocked back on his heels, rose, picked up the *spatha* from where he had flung it on the bank, and walked back to where he had left Antares, hearing his waterlogged boots squelch with every step. Vilbia remained sitting for a little while longer, gazing out over the mere. Then she herself stood up and began walking slowly towards him. He noticed that she was moving unsteadily, as if she feared her legs might buckle beneath her at any moment.

She seemed to read the concern in his face, because she said, 'I'm fine now, Canio, all the silliness gone. Let's move on.'

He shrugged and did as she asked, leading Antares. She followed behind, and for some time neither spoke. Then, as if thinking with one mind, they both halted beside another mere, where the water was clear and bright and seemingly innocent in the sunlight.

'I don't know about you,' he remarked, as he picked off the last of the duckweed, 'but before I go any further I'm going to lie in the sun and get dry.' By then he was almost sure that the things he had said while she was sobbing had not registered on her consciousness. His initial reaction was a curious mixture of relief and disappointment. Relief, because those words might have embarrassed them both. Disappointment because, if she had heard them, then it would have made telling her about the gold so much easier.

And he knew now that he had to tell her, and tell her soon, because when they reached the lake she would know for certain that he had lied to her and, even worse, kept on lying right up until the last possible moment. Were that to happen … but it mustn't happen: he could not forget what she had told him on the sands of Moriduno beach.

As he was wondering how to begin his confession, Vilbia asked him quietly, 'Do you understand what happened back there?'

'Yes – of course I do: you mistook a tree trunk for your old friend Eutherius, went wading across to say hullo, then almost walked into a patch of quicksand on the way. It's the sort of thing that could happen to anybody.' He winked at her, to show that he was only joking.

'But I truly thought he was there,' she protested, then paused and murmured, 'but it couldn't have been him, could it? So what was it that I really saw, Canio?' He was still wondering how to reply when she added, 'You don't believe a word of it, do you?'

'I believe that you really thought you saw Eutherius.'

'But we both know that he wasn't really there. So what was it that I saw?' she asked again.

'Had you been thinking about the old bas... the old man recently? Perhaps you wanted his advice about something?'

'I ... might have,' she replied guardedly. 'Since Gulioepius died he's been the nearest thing to a father I have.'

Canio picked up the defensive note in her voice. 'Well, there you are then. Knowingly or not, you wanted his advice and encouragement – so in your head the willow trunk became Eutherius. The mind can play funny tricks that way.'

'Yes, I know the mind can play tricks – and I remember that I was feeling rather strange and light-headed when I first saw him.'

'Ah, that's interesting. Tell me, was there an unusual smell in that hollow by the bank?'

'I thought it was just rotting leaves.'

'My guess is that it was marsh gas. You breathed it in and it addled your wits: it can do that. You can't see the damned stuff – sometimes you can't even smell it – but I've heard of it making men go giddy and do strange things. Even suffocating them, if they'd breathed enough of it.'

'And do you think it was just chance that the Eutherius I thought I saw almost led me into the quicksand?'

He recognised the appeal for reassurance. 'Yes, of course it was just chance – you could probably find dozens of quicksands like that in the bottoms of these marshland meres, if you were fool enough to go looking for them.'

'And that strange wind? If that hadn't come when it did, then –'

'But it did come,' Canio interrupted. He could rationalise the rest, but that wind was something else. And yet such things were not unknown: over the years he had seen three or four similar small whirlwinds spring up out of nowhere, and as quickly die.

Suddenly his thoughts went flying back to a June day a year or so after he had first come to Britannia. He had been lying beside a woman in a riverside field where swathes of fresh, sweet grass were drying in the hot sun that made their naked bodies glisten with minute beads of perspiration. Then a tiny whirlwind had sprung up on the far side of the field. Insignificant at first, they had both watched as it rapidly grew until it was a wildly spinning column of hay as tall as a tree. It had moved slowly across the field towards them, swaying from side to side and picking up ever more grass stalks as it went, until, as suddenly as it had been born, the wind had died and all the spinning grass collapsed into an untidy heap.

But as the wind died, so its mad, ecstatic energy had seemed to enter into the body of the woman. And she, who had before been so timid, suddenly became the wanton huntress and made love to him with a passionate, uninhibited abandon that even he had never experienced before. Her name was Tacita, and afterwards she had told him that she loved him. At the time he had not believed her: perhaps had not wanted to believe her. But neither could he forget her, and a few months later he had tried to find her again, but never could.

He stayed sitting beside Vilbia at the water's edge, while the sun dried their skin and clothes. Thin coils of water vapour rose like white smoke from the leather of his boots lying on the grass beside him. He stared at it as it drifted up and vanished – as soon perhaps she would be vanishing out of his life. Quickly, before any doubts could sidle in and change his mind, he said, 'About what I told you, back on the edge of the Hills near Ovilregis –'

But even as he started to speak he realised that Vilbia had got to her feet and was shielding her eyes against the glare of the bright southern sky.

'Look, I can see it again! – that ridge which Doccia told us about. It can't be more than half a mile away now. How strange that we never noticed it before.'

Canio swore viciously under his breath, then he too stood and saw a wooded ridge cutting right across the marshes from east to west. 'About what I told you – ' he began again.

But Vilbia was already a dozen paces away, walking briskly and craning to get a better view of the ridge. It was too late. He realised that the opportunity for telling secrets – hers perhaps, as well as his – had again slipped away. The image of those two yellow leaves bobbing and spinning on the swirling November current came again.

CHAPTER EIGHTEEN

With Vilbia hunting on ahead, finding ways between the reeds and the pools, it didn't take them long to reach the ridge. Following behind her, Canio climbed up the slope, between trunks of great ashes and oaks, pushed through a screen of meadowsweet and found himself standing on the crushed stone of a road which ran along the top of the ridge. The first thing he noticed was that it showed signs of neglect and infrequent use. In places grass was creeping in from the sides, and even growing up through the stones in the centre. But neglected or not, Vilbia seemed astonished that it existed at all. Walking across to the far side, he peered through the trees and saw another great expanse of reeds stretching away southwards.

'Where do you think it goes to – and where on earth does it start from?' she asked, looking up and down the long straight road.

'That way,' he said, pointing eastwards, 'probably leads to Lindinis. The other way, I don't know. To somewhere near the sea, I suppose.'

'How far do you think it is to Lindinis?'

'No idea. Twenty miles – twenty-five, perhaps?'

'So which way shall we go?'

'Towards Lindinis. That way we'll be sure to get round to the south side of these damned marshes quicker than trying to walk through them. The distance will be longer, but the travelling will be much easier. And we've got to find somewhere to buy more food – we've hardly any left of what I liberated from your friend Victorinus.'

'And there's not much barley beer left either,' she observed innocently.

He realised then that climbing up onto this high road had lifted her spirits out of the marshes as well as her body. And yet, such a short time ago ...

'That's true; I really hadn't thought of that. And the wine ran out some way back as well. Come on, you can ride.' He stooped and interlaced his fingers to make a step and she gratefully accepted the offer.

They had only gone a few dozen yards when he noticed a cylindrical stone pillar set into the ground at the side of the road. It was about five feet high, and on it he made out the roughly pick-chipped inscription:

IMP CAES FL VAL CONSTANTINO P FE INVICTO AVG.

From the weathered traces remaining he could see that the letters had once been painted vivid red with cinnabar.

'It's one of those that old Constantine set up to tell the world how wonderful he was.'

'Does it say how many miles to Lindinis?'

He peered all around the stone. 'No, nothing so useful.'

'Why *do* they so rarely show the miles?' she sighed.

'Cheer up; maybe we'll reach some village before sunset.' Impulsively, he decided to try once again to tell her the truth about the lake. Fixing his eyes on the open road ahead, he began, 'Vilbia, back there in the marshes –'

'Hush a moment.'

He caught the note of alarm in her voice and suddenly became aware of the crunch of wheels on the road behind. Swinging round he saw a small enclosed carriage drawn by two black horses and flanked by three riders, all little more than a hundred yards behind and rapidly gaining on them.

'Who do you think they are, Canio?' She sounded nervous.

'No idea – but whoever they are they're not short of a few siliquae,' he muttered. He had noticed that the three outriders and the coachman all wore identical blue embroidered tunics, tight-fitting woollen hose of the same colour and long leather riding boots. 'Leave any talking to me, daughter Claudia,' he whispered.

'Whatever you say, Italicus, my revered father.'

The sounds of wheels and hooves on the compacted stones grew rapidly louder, and moments later the lightweight, two-person carriage and its accompanying riders swept past in a jingle of harnesses and creaking of wood and leather. The riders ignored them, but, as the carriage passed, Canio noticed that its window curtain was being held aside by a hand that wore several large gold rings. Although he only saw it for an instant, he was certain that it had been a female hand, and he found himself staring curiously after the carriage as it began to recede into the distance.

But then, to his surprise, about two hundred yards further on the carriage stopped and the riders first circled back around it, then rode on for some distance before halting again. The carriage remained stationary as Canio and Vilbia slowly caught up and overtook it. The driver remained expressionless, looking straight ahead. But once again Canio saw the curtain held aside by the hand with the gold rings, and also glimpsed the pale blur of a face within the darkened interior. He was barely past its horses when the carriage started off at a rapid pace, only to stop again as soon as it reached the three outriders. One man dismounted and stood for a short while alongside the carriage, apparently in conversation with its occupant. Then the man remounted and started cantering back towards them.

Canio halted and exchanged puzzled looks with Vilbia. 'What in the name of Mercury's ram are they up to?'

'I don't know, but my instinct is telling me to wish they'd kept going,' Vilbia murmured.

'Hope your instinct's wrong,' he replied.

Meanwhile, the carriage and the other two riders had started off again down the long, straight road.

Canio eyed the approaching rider, a big man in his late thirties with fair hair slicked back, a neatly trimmed beard and a generally sleek appearance which suggested that, for him, life was no struggle. Also, he noted, the man's cloak was pinned at the right shoulder with a large silver crossbow brooch with three onion-shaped terminals that sparkled in the sun.

'Greeting!' said the man in a loud, commanding voice.

Ex-army, I'll bet, thought Canio. *He's landed an easy living.* 'Greetings to you my friend. Good day for a ride.'

'You are ...?' said the man.

Not one for wasting time on small talk, are you? Hades, but you remind me of Aemilianus. 'My name is Aulus Claudius Caninus. And yours ...?'

'Flavius Fuscinus,' the man replied briskly. 'May I ask what your business is on this road?'

There was a pause. Canio glanced at Vilbia and raised his eyebrows. Suspecting that she feared he was about to make some extremely rude reply, he decided to surprise her. 'You may ask,' he replied with silky hauteur, 'and I may choose to tell you, when you have informed me why you wish to know. Do not,' he added mysteriously, 'be deceived by my appearance.' And he looked Fuscinus up and down with an expression calculated to imply that he did not particularly like what he saw.

Gratifyingly, Fuscinus appeared somewhat discomfited by this reply. 'I merely ask because my mistress remarked how odd it was that you seemed to have appeared out of nowhere on this road.'

'I frequently do appear unexpectedly. It is the nature of my commission.'

'Your commission? From whom?'

'Why, from the Vicarius, of course,' said Canio, affecting surprise that Fuscinus should not have been able to work this out for himself. 'Surely you've heard that he likes to have first-hand reports on the state of his diocese and its citizens?'

'No, I had not heard that,' said Fuscinus coldly.

'Had you not? I fear that the *Vir Spectabilis* would be most disappointed to learn that his concern for your welfare has gone unappreciated. Perhaps I should mention it when I dine with him upon my return to Londinium Augusta.'

Evidently realising that he was losing this battle, Fuscinus opened another front. 'Perhaps you should. Tonight, however, you will be dining at the table of my mistress, the lady Aelia Aureliana.'

'I will?'

'It is her wish that you should.'

'Indeed? Well, I try never to disappoint a lady, even one whose acquaintance I have never made. Exactly who is she?'

'Surely you have heard the name?' Fuscinus's surprise appeared genuine.

'One hears so many names. Without faces, they mean little.'

'The lady Aelia Aureliana is the owner of the Villa Aurelius: you must have heard of that?'

'Possibly. Near Lindinis, is it not?' Canio guessed.

'A good few miles to the west of Lindinis, actually.'

'And the lady ...?'

'Wishes you to dine with her.'

'So you said. Just myself?'

'And your companion too, of course. Your daughter?'

'This lady is my sister, Claudia. I'm escorting her back to our uncle's villa near Isca, combining imperial and family duties.'

Even as he said it, Canio noticed Vilbia inserting the tip of her tongue between her front teeth, which he had come to recognise as being her way of suppressing a smile. Slightly uncomfortably, he realised she had probably guessed that the changing of their fictional relationship was not unconnected with the gender of their prospective hostess: her metamorphosis from daughter to sister might take years off his age, for anyone attempting to guess it. Fearing that she might actually burst out laughing, he quickly asked Fuscinus, 'Did your Villa Aurelius suffer much damage during the *Conspiratio*?'

'No damage whatsoever,' Fuscinus replied briskly. 'The garrison at Lindinis saw to that. I used my influence with the tribune there to ensure that a detachment of twenty men were stationed near the villa when the invasions were at their height.'

My, what an important person you must be. 'So, how far is it to the Villa Aurelius then?'

'No more than fifteen miles or so.'

'That far? In that case, we'll see you there.' Canio gave Fuscinus a bleak smile and hoped he would take the hint. The invitation was tempting, and he meant to accept it, but first he wanted to resume his interrupted conversation with Vilbia.

'You know the way?' Fuscinus's sarcastic tone implied he was certain that Canio did not.

'No, but I'm sure you could tell us, if you put your mind to it,' Canio replied, trying to keep his temper.

'Of course I could, but after you leave this highway the road to the Villa Aurelius has several branches. Besides, my instructions are to escort you there. So, if you will be so good as to follow me ...' Without waiting for a reply, Fuscinus wheeled his horse and set it ambling in the direction of the now-vanished carriage.

'Jackass,' Canio muttered to his retreating back. But this mysterious woman, the lady Aelia Aureliana, had intrigued him and so he tugged Antares' reins and began following Fuscinus.

To Canio's increasing irritation, for the first mile Fuscinus rode just far enough ahead that he could not be engaged in conversation, but still close enough to prevent himself from talking freely with Vilbia.

Eventually she whispered, 'Why would a woman who owns a great villa want to invite you to dinner, particularly as we both must look as if we've been living in those marshes for months?'

He tried to make light of the unease he heard in her voice. 'For the same reason that any red-blooded woman would want the company of a great handsome buck like me,' he whispered back. 'You'll understand these things when you get older.'

He took her silence for exasperation. 'Don't worry; the worst that can happen is that we'll get a good meal and decent beds for the night.' When she still did not reply, he added, 'Look, if they really wanted to do us harm, there were four of them against one of me back there. They weren't to know that I'm the finest swordsman in all the provinces of Britannia, were they now?'

Turning, he again caught Vilbia trying to suppress a smile. 'Did you know that one of them is now called Valentia,' she murmured.

'Since when?'

'Just before I left Corinium I heard that Valentinian Augustus had renamed one of the northern provinces that *Comes* Theodosius liberated from the barbarians.'

'Which one?'

'I don't know. I'm surprised you didn't know.'

He shrugged. 'I had other things on my mind. Still, renaming a province after himself is just the sort of thing that a meek and unassuming man like our beloved emperor would do.'

'Shssh,' Vilbia cautioned. 'He might hear you.'

'Who might – Valentinian?'

'No, Antares,' she hissed.

'He'd never tell: scattered all over Britannia Prima there are too many mares with foals who'd like to know his whereabouts to risk informing on me.'

'If the things I was told are true, then I have a suspicion that he could say much the same about you.'

'You shouldn't believe everything you hear.'

'No, I realise that now.'

Perhaps by chance, or perhaps because he suspected that he was being discussed unflatteringly, at that moment Fuscinus halted and looked back, and their conversation died. And Canio realised that another chance to confess had gone.

✳✳✳

Some four miles further on they met a train of four empty salt wagons rumbling westwards, each pulled by a team of six mules.

232

Fuscinus made a great show of officiously urging the weary driver of the leading wagon to make faster progress. Recalling what Doccia had said, Canio guessed that the owner of the Villa Aurelius had a proprietorial interest in the local salt industry.

By then the marshes on both sides of the ridge were beginning to give way to an undulating landscape of sheep pastures and occasional small woods. After another mile the line of the ridge turned towards the south-east, and shortly after that Fuscinus twisted around and pointed to a metalled track that led diagonally down the thickly wooded southern side.

'How far now?' Canio called out impatiently.

'Some way yet,' Fuscinus replied. 'Quite a long way, in fact.'

Canio thought he sounded quite relaxed about it, which grated. 'Still, it's a pleasant day for a walk,' he said pointedly.

'Isn't it,' Fuscinus replied.

Evidently sensing the storm clouds gathering, Vilbia quietly slid down off Antares' back. 'You ride for a while, brother. I'm getting stiff sitting up there.'

Canio looked at her questioningly, but she gave him a quick, encouraging smile. In spite of her initial misgivings, he wondered if she too was now curious to see this Aelia Aureliana and her villa?

Several miles down the trackway, whose carefully-filled potholes made Canio think that someone with money still used it regularly, they splashed through a ford across a small river. A few hundred yards further on the track branched, one fork continuing south, the other heading south-west. It was down this latter that Fuscinus nudged his horse. Apparently confident that they would obediently follow, he didn't even bother to look back.

Observing this, Canio decided to have a little amusement at Fuscinus's expense. Noiselessly he brought Antares to a standstill. Vilbia looked at him questioningly, but he grinned and raised one finger to his lips. Waiting until Fuscinus was far enough ahead not to hear, he then turned Antares and retreated behind a dense clump of hazel bushes, motioning Vilbia to follow him.

She had only just stretched out in the long grass beside him when Canio heard the sound of hooves. From behind the screen of leaves he observed Fuscinus arrive back at the junction, look both ways, then set off southwards at a smart trot.

As soon as he was out of sight, Canio said, 'Come on, your turn to ride again.' He helped Vilbia to mount, then started jogging beside her at a smart pace along the track.

They had gone at least half a mile before he heard the sound of a horse approaching rapidly from behind. Turning, he was gratified to see that Fuscinus was red-faced and sweating. The man reined to a halt, but before he could say a word Canio asked indignantly, 'Where in Hades' name have you been, man – I thought you were supposed to be guiding us?'

'What do you mean, "Where have I been?"' Fuscinus almost roared, totally failing to control his seething temper. 'I turned around and you weren't there!'

Canio gave Vilbia a look calculated to imply that they were dealing with some sort of halfwit. 'Of course we were there. We were right behind you – and wondering what you were playing at when you went galloping off like that?' Canio glanced at Vilbia, and was both amused and relieved to see that she was regarding Fuscinus with a suitably displeased expression. They were still acting as a team.

With two against one, Fuscinus must have realised that this was an argument he was not going to win. He half-smothered an expletive, then kicked his horse into motion again to take up what he clearly thought was his rightful place at the head of their little company.

'The Villa Aurelius is another four miles,' he announced curtly as he passed.

When Fuscinus was some twenty yards ahead, Vilbia shook her head at Canio. 'Why?' she asked softly.

He pretended to appear surprised by the question. 'Because

I thought you'd welcome a little amusement, after the things that have happened in these last days. And I'm sure friend Fuscinus didn't really mind: it probably brightened up his dull life.' Noting her sceptical look he added, 'It's years since I've had a chance to play that trick.' The look was still there. He sighed. 'Listen, and I'll tell you a funny story.

'Once, when I was in the army in Germania, we had this cocky little runt of a tribune. Whatever the weather, however muddy the ground, he'd trot on ahead on his big white horse and we were expected to follow, wherever he went.'

'Just like your new friend, Fuscinus?'

'Exactly. Well one day in late autumn, when it had been raining non-stop for a week, we'd had enough. We were marching through this big pine forest when the track forked. Our hero, thirty yards ahead as usual, took one fork. Nobody said a word, but when they reached it, the front men took the other fork, which they knew was the correct one because they'd been that way before. The rest of us kept on marching, all the time expecting the tribune to come flying back, all hot and bothered, and demanding to know who was responsible. But he never did, and when we camped for the night he still hadn't returned. So, in the morning, because his father owned about a quarter of Gaul, we thought we'd better go find him.' Canio paused for dramatic effect.

'And?' Vilbia asked dutifully.

'And at last we found him, wandering lost among the trees, his mind completely gone. The locals said that the forest fiends had got to him. They can be frightening places, those big pine forests – the ones where you can walk for days without ever seeing the sun. After a while men start seeing eyes watching them from the gloom between the tall trunks. They think they see strange creatures too, dark shapes moving high above them in the swaying tops of the trees, especially in the half-light of dawn or dusk.'

He fancied he saw Vilbia shiver slightly. 'What became of the tribune?' she asked quickly.

He suddenly recalled the things she had said, and not said, on the edge of the Hills near Ovilregis, and wondered if she was remembering that dusk at the deserted cemetery on the Sabrina plain? He could have kicked himself: of all the things that he didn't want her to remember ... 'Him? Oh, that night in the woods turned him into a complete drivelling imbecile. So then they had no choice but to make him a *magister militum* – he wasn't fit for anything else.'

'Oh, Canio!'

But he noted with relief that she was unable to check a smile. 'Don't you believe me?' he asked, again feigning surprise. Then, without thinking, he added, 'Would I lie to you?'

She turned in the saddle, and for a long moment they looked directly into each other's eyes.

'Look, about the lake –' But he got no further before Fuscinus, his voice tight with anger, called back, 'In the name of the Good Shepherd, will you be so good as to keep moving! I'm tired and hungry and want to get home.'

Canio felt a murderous rage flare up inside him. Once again the moment had been snatched away, and for the rest of the journey he said little as he plodded along the track beside Antares, at first soothing his anger by contemplating sticking something sharp between Fuscinus's shoulder blades as they jogged up and down on his immaculate black horse.

But as his anger cooled he began taking an interest in the landscape, noticing that to the north the land was flat grassland, while to the south there were low, rolling hills covered with woods and pastures. The grasslands on both sides of the track were dotted with grazing sheep, which displayed the curious illusion of growing increasingly whiter as the evening light faded.

As they rounded a curve in the trackway he saw several yellow lights winking in the twilight ahead. Drawing nearer, he realised that they came from the windows of a substantial building, the dark outline of which was already looming out of the dusk.

So this is the Villa Aurelius?

Moments later he was passing under the wide arch of a stone gateway and onto a gravelled drive that led up to what he assumed was the main entrance of the villa. Just before they reached its impressive portico a slight figure seemed to materialise out of nowhere, silent as a ghost.

'See to that horse as well,' Fuscinus ordered this man whose name he evidently did not deem worth using, indicating Antares with a backwards wave of his hand as he dismounted.

Canio helped Vilbia to dismount. 'And give him a good feed of your best oats – as much as he can eat,' he said to the ostler, prompted as much by a wish to annoy Fuscinus as concern for Antares' welfare.

Before the ostler could lead the horses away, and while Vilbia's back was turned, he deftly extracted the Hecate figurine from one of Antares' saddlebags and slipped it into his belt pouch. Perhaps not deftly enough: as he looked up he saw Vilbia turning quickly away, almost as if she had seen him do it, but did not wish him to know that she had.

Fuscinus led them up the portico steps and into the atrium. 'Wait here,' he said, in much the same voice he had used to the ostler. 'I shall inform my mistress that you have arrived ... At last,' he added under his breath, but loud enough for Canio to hear, as he was no doubt intended to. Further down the atrium, but still within their sight, Fuscinus met a woman and there followed a hurried, sotto voce conversation in which he did most of the talking. He then disappeared into a corridor at the far end of the atrium, but the woman continued on towards them.

Canio judged that she was in her early twenties, neat and slim, her thick, dark brown hair cut just short of her shoulders and framing a pert, attractive face.

She smiled. 'My name is Tertullia – may I offer you the greetings of my mistress, the lady Aelia Aureliana, and all who dwell here in this Villa Aurelius.' Canio realised that she was looking directly at him as she spoke, and got the distinct impression that he was being inspected. 'My mistress thought that you might care to bathe before you dine, to wash off the dust of your long journey.'

Her voice was low and husky, and although he felt uncomfortable for doing so in Vilbia's presence, Canio could not stop himself from wondering what lay beneath the rich but simply-cut cloth of her dress. And he was aware that Tertullia's eyes were still staring boldly into his own.

Just as the silence was becoming embarrassing, Vilbia said, 'Thank you, Tertullia. A chance to bathe would be most welcome, wouldn't it brother?'

'Yes, most welcome. It's been almost two weeks since I last ...'

'Since you last what?' Tertullia enquired, her eyebrows rising fractionally.

'Since I last saw the inside of a suite of baths, of course,' he replied, trying not to grin.

'Of course.' Turning gracefully, Tertullia led them out of the atrium and down a long corridor, past plastered walls painted with brightly coloured frescoes.

One panel depicted an idyllic pastoral scene of long-horned sheep grazing on green hillsides, where shepherds playing panpipes sat in the doorways of small temples.

As she came level with that fresco, Canio noticed Vilbia halt for several moments and gaze at it longingly. But before he could ask why, she had hurried on to catch up with Tertullia, who first turned left into another corridor, then left again and through a doorway into a modest suite of baths.

'The warm pool is through here,' said Tertullia, smiling to Vilbia as she drew aside a curtain to reveal a small room, at the far end of which was a circular bath sunk level with the floor. 'There's oil and a strigil and towels over there,' she added, indicating a low table set against the opposite wall. Canio noticed that it was topped with a carved and polished slab of imported marble, all vivid swirling colours. It must, he reckoned, have cost more than he could earn in two years of soldiering. 'Just call if you want anything else,' Tertullia murmured, as she drew the curtain behind Vilbia.

Canio squatted and began unlacing his boots.

Tertullia knelt and placed a warm hand over his. 'May I suggest that you undress in the tepidarium? I think you'll be more comfortable there.'

There was something in that throaty voice, something that seemed to be saying more than the words themselves. The thought came to Canio that perhaps Tertullia and the lady Aelia Aureliana were one and the same. It was a distinctly pleasant thought. As she led him across the geometric patterned mosaic floor to the tepidarium he asked casually, 'So how old is your mistress – about your own age, perhaps?'

'No. Not my age,' Tertullia replied opaquely. 'Is there anything else you wish to know?'

'Yes, something that's been puzzling me. Why, if your mistress was so keen for me to dine with her, didn't she either squeeze my sister into that carriage of hers, or lend us a horse? That way we could have followed the carriage and got here much sooner?'

'Oh, there could have been any number of reasons,' Tertullia replied airily. 'For one thing, her hair wasn't dressed in the way she prefers it to be on these occasions – and I'm sure you know how particular we women can be about such things.' And before Canio could question her further on the subject she continued, 'If you care to undress here, I'll arrange for your uniform to be cleaned and smartened before you dine with my mistress.'

CHAPTER NINETEEN

Canio had expected her to quickly retreat as soon as he began undressing, quite possibly with a maidenly blush, as he was sure Vilbia would have done. But Tertullia did not retreat or blush. Instead she simply stood there, her bold eyes coolly appraising him, not remotely intimidated. Even when he stood naked before her, her eyes slid slowly upwards, met his and showed not the slightest sign of embarrassment. He noticed the ghost of a smile in the slight upturn at the corners of her mouth, and in that smile he read – what? Desire? Amusement? Perhaps both, or perhaps something else entirely: he simply couldn't tell. Slightly disconcerted, he asked, 'So where is it that I'm supposed to bathe then?'

'Patience – I'll show you in a moment.' She half-turned and clapped her hands three times, before kneeling gracefully and bundling Canio's clothes up into her arms. As she rose she leaned forwards and, for a moment which was over so quickly that afterwards he was not absolutely certain that it had really happened at all, the soft hair of her straightening head brushed against his groin. And in the same continuous upwards movement she inhaled deeply, breathing in the scent of his unwashed body. It was an act of sheer animal sensuality, in piquant contrast to her air of cool self-control.

An instant later and she was standing and walking away, first into the caldarium where, after a brief conversation, she collected Vilbia's dress and cloak, then towards the doorway that led out into the corridor. There Canio heard her talking softly to someone that he assumed her clapped hands had summoned, someone to whom she handed the clothes. He caught a glimpse of a pair of eyes in a vivacious young female face craning over Tertullia's shoulder as if to get a better look at him, before the girl was swiftly shooed away. He thought he heard suppressed giggling.

Then, as if she had at last remembered Canio's question as to where he could bathe, Tertullia returned and said, 'Come – I'll show you.'

She walked over to the far side of the tepidarium, where a curtain hung across what Canio had assumed to be the entrance to the frigidarium. Reaching out, she pulled the curtain aside to reveal a large, semi-circular bath set into an apse in the wall, its stone lip a little above knee height.

Carrying his scabbarded *spatha*, belt and pouches, he padded across, stooped and tested the water with his free hand. 'It's cold as ice,' he declared, letting his disappointment show. He was aware that he was exaggerating: in fact the water had absorbed some of the heat of the day just passed and was merely pleasantly cool.

'Well of course it's cold: it's the cold plunge bath,' Tertullia explained patiently. She paused. 'You have been in a bath suite before, haven't you?'

'I've been in dozens, most of them bigger and better than this,' he replied. 'This one's a trifle poky for a villa of this size.'

'Ah, well there is a reason for that,' Tertullia said mysteriously. 'Get in and I'll tell you what that reason is.' Seeing him hesitate, she added, 'You're not afraid that the nasty cold water will damage your delicate complexion, are you?'

Canio smiled mirthlessly and straddled the lip of the bath. A short flight of steps led down to the bottom, where he stood with the water just above his navel, determined not to show the least sign of discomfort.

Tertullia brought her hands together several times in near-noiseless clapping, as if to show her appreciation of his courage.

Seeing a niche resembling an open sea shell carved into the

stone wall above the bath, he pointed to it and asked, 'So where's the oil and strigil then?'

'They're not usually kept there, it being the cold plunge. Don't worry, I'll get them – don't go away.' She disappeared into the caldarium and he heard the murmur of a brief conversation between herself and Vilbia, a conversation that ended in laughter from both women.

Tertullia returned carrying a polished bronze strigil and an oil flask of the same metal, the latter suspended from a fine chain looped around her wrist. With a faint bow, she handed them both to him.

He shook the flask, noticing as he did so that it was moulded with the figures of a *thiasos* – a procession of drunken maenads and satyrs, with Bacchus and his panther leading the way and a pot-bellied Silenus on a donkey bringing up the rear. Taking his cue from the *thiasos*, he asked, 'Aren't you going to rub the oil on for me?'

'It might splash over my dress,' Tertullia replied smoothly.

'Well, take it off then,' he said, equally smoothly. He had played games like this before, and very enjoyable they had been.

He watched her hands move upwards and toy with the ends of the braided drawstring that closed the demure neckline of her dress, and for several heart-leaping moments he thought she was actually going to undo it.

But apparently it was all part of the game. 'No, I don't think so,' she said slowly. 'I might get cold.'

'If you did, I'm sure I could warm you up again,' he said, trying to keep the leer out of his voice.

'I'm sure you could,' she smiled. 'But I don't want to risk tiring you after your long journey: my mistress would be displeased. So, I think I'll just lie here and tell you why this bath suite doesn't quite meet the high standards to which Your Excellency seems accustomed.'

In the middle of the tepidarium stood a long couch, upholstered in soft leather. He watched as Tertullia sat down on

242

one end, kicked off her openwork slippers, swivelled around and drew her bare feet up onto the leather. Then she slid her body down the couch until she was reclining full length on her side, her head resting on one hand. He couldn't help noticing that the sliding made the hem of her dress ride up to her thighs, but she made no attempt to pull it down. Her legs were lean and well-shaped: dancer's legs, he thought. From where he stood at the bottom of the cold plunge it was what he could not quite see that tantalised.

'Originally,' she began, 'this was only the servants' bath suite – and we still use it of course, when the mistress or her guests don't require it.'

'So what happened to the main suite?' he asked, as he poured a thin stream of olive oil into one palm and began rubbing it vigorously into the dense black hair of his chest and abdomen.

Tertullia smiled, and looked at him through half closed eyes. 'Don't forget the important part.'

'My head, you mean?'

'No, much more important than that.'

'Would you like to do it for me?' Canio asked, ascending the steps far enough to display the part that Tertullia was apparently alluding to.

She smiled again, cat-like, but made no move to take up his offer. 'My mistress lives in what used to be the main bath suite. She even has her bedroom there.'

'Why's that? Has she particularly dirty habits?'

'Certainly not – she's most fastidious in her personal habits. She lives there because that's where the mosaics are, those and the wall paintings.'

'Wall paintings? Paintings of what?'

'Paintings of herself when she was young, or so I've been told. Stark naked in some of them she is. But apparently it's the mosaics that are the main reason for her living and sleeping there. She says they remind her of her previous life.'

'What previous life?'

'Oh, I'm sure she'll tell you at dinner – and I don't want to spoil the surprise. Don't splash so: you'll make your sword go all rusty.'

'No chance of that. I always keep it ready for action at a moment's notice,' he replied as he rubbed more oil onto his shoulders.

'Really? What a reassurance that must be for your lady friends in these dangerous times. Do you practise often?'

'Whenever I get the chance.'

'You must give me a demonstration, if you can spare the time before you leave.'

'I'm sure it would be a pleasure. By the way, how long has your mistress lived here?'

'Since she was a girl, as far as I know.'

'And she actually owns this villa?'

'The villa and all the land around, plus salt workings near the coast.'

'And she's not married?'

'No, and never has been. Ah, but don't think you've struck lucky: under the terms of her father's will, when she dies everything goes to her cousins or their children. And her cousins have lots of children.'

'Is that so?' Canio decided that he had spent long enough in the bath. Ignoring the strigil he crouched down until the water came up to his chin and hurriedly rubbed off all the remaining oil. Then he dipped right under the surface and energetically scrubbed his fingers through his hair and beard before standing up again, spluttering, and scraping the streaming water out of his eyes with both hands.

As he started climbing out of the bath, Tertullia skipped up off the couch and took one of the large towels that lay neatly folded on a small table nearby. As she shook it out he saw her eyes wandering down his body with studied casualness. 'That water couldn't have been quite so cold as you made out,' she observed.

With water dripping off him and pattering onto the mosaic floor, Canio stood and allowed Tertullia to wrap the towel around him and start rubbing his hair gently with a free corner. Wriggling one hand out between the folds he began to stroke her body through the material of her dress.

She gently nibbled one of his ear lobes and whispered, 'Is Claudia really your sister?'

'Yes, of course she is.'

'But your hair's black and she's a redhead.'

'We had different mothers.'

'What, as well as different fathers?'

'Oh, very funny.' But at that moment he heard Vilbia's voice coming from the caldarium. She was talking to someone, probably the giggling girl who had collected their clothes. His fingertips stopped moving in a circular motion over Tertullia's taut belly and he stood there quite still, uncomfortably aware of an unusual feeling of guilt, while she continued to slowly towel him dry. As she did so she softly hummed snatches of a love song that he had first heard as a child more than twenty years before, when Marcia too had hummed it as she energetically ground up the ingredients of her various potions with pestle and mortar.

Lost in an unfamiliar forest of conflicting emotions, he continued to stand there, unresponsive, even after Tertullia had finished towelling. And it seemed that she was perceptive enough to realise that the moment had passed, and perhaps also to guess at least part of the reason.

'I'll go and see if your clothes are ready yet,' she whispered. Feather-lightly she touched her lips on his, then drifted away.

Returning some time later, she set his neatly folded clothes down on the leather couch and scarcely looked at him before walking softly back through the separating curtain into the caldarium, carrying with her Vilbia's own freshly sponged and dried dress and cloak.

Canio dressed quickly, then sat on the couch to await Vilbia's return. He was still sitting there, deep in thought, when an elderly liveried retainer, tall and with grey, thinning hair, came to inform him that his mistress, the lady Aelia Aureliana, was now ready to receive them both.

✳✳✳

He found Vilbia waiting for him in the corridor, and wondered why she had slipped out without taking the opportunity to speak to him while they were both alone in the bath suite. Then a disquieting thought struck him: what if she had spoken, perhaps in a whisper so as not to be overheard, while he had been too lost in thought to hear? Perhaps even now she was wondering why he had ignored her? He wanted to ask her, to reassure her, but she was already walking towards the grey-haired retainer who was beckoning them to follow him down the lamplit corridor.

Canio fell in behind her, passing small windows where, between star-shaped iron lattices that held the small glass panes, he could see out into the dusk-to-dawn twilight of the moonless midsummer night. Once, in that twilight, he was startled to glimpse a motionless figure standing outside only a few feet away, staring in at him through the glass. As he walked on he rationalised that it must only have been a statue; but the staring image lingered and disquieted.

He saw the corridor first widen as another joined it at right angles, and then end in front of a pair of large doors set in an archway. The retainer knocked once on the dark, polished wood, then paused, his head cocked slightly to one side. No sound came from within, or none that Canio could hear. Standing beside Vilbia now, he stealthily reached out, curled his fingers around her left hand and squeezed it gently. He felt her tense momentarily, then relax. She made no attempt to pull her hand away. Grasping the handles, the retainer opened both leaves to reveal a high-ceilinged cavern of a room that blazed with the light of the dozens of oil lamps which Canio could see hanging

246

from rows of ornate bronze stands ranged down the floor on both sides. Standing aside, the retainer bowed and urged them forwards with a stately sweep of his outstretched arm.

Canio still held Vilbia's hand as they walked in together, then stood beside her as he drank in the colours, richness and luxury of the room. He gazed, almost spellbound, at the mosaic floor, the frescoed walls and vaulted ceiling; at the upholstered couches and chairs, the tables inlaid with woods of different hues, and the exquisitely worked bowls, dishes, flagons, goblets, knives and spoons that stood upon them. Most of the tableware was polished silver, but he noticed several pieces which radiated the soft gleam of yellow gold. He caressed them with his eyes.

'I bid you both welcome to the heart of the Villa Aurelius. Do please be seated – you must be tired after your journey.' The voice from the far end of the room startled Canio. It was a strange, arresting voice; not loud, but crystal clear, each word delivered with perfect aristocratic diction.

Dazzled by the lamps and the splendour of the room and its contents, until she spoke he had not realised that their hostess was already present. Now he stared in the direction of that voice and saw an old woman seated on a great chair raised up on a dais of several tiers of steps, as if it were a throne. She was dressed in a dark red robe that left nothing but her head and hands visible. Her fingertips were pressed together, displaying the heavy gold rings he had seen through the carriage window.

In the shadows cast by the lamps her face appeared as wrinkled as a winter apple, although the abundant snow-white hair that framed and darkened that face was elaborately coiffured into a curious style which he had never seen before. It was shoulder-length, swept back behind her ears, and with a large spherical bun at the back of her head. In front, the hair had been pomaded and sculpted into a spike jutting upwards at an angle. He thought the overall effect was curiously inorganic, more like a helmet than soft, living hair.

Seeing him hesitate, the old woman continued, 'Forgive me for not rising to greet you, Aulus Claudius Caninus. It is one of the few privileges that we who have endured long in this world can grant ourselves. Come, sit and eat before the food cools. I trust you like honey omelettes?'

'Thank you, Aelia Aureliana,' Canio replied. He waited just long enough for the old woman to correct him if that were not actually her name, and when she did not, he added, 'Honey omelettes are a favourite of mine.'

'And your sister, Claudia's, too?' Aelia asked.

'They are ... yes,' Vilbia replied. Canio thought she sounded slightly nervous.

'Then begin, begin,' Aelia urged. 'You will find them in that deep silver dish with the domed cover, that one with a faun's head handle.'

'Won't you be joining us?' Canio asked politely, stepping up to the table and lifting the cover. Immediately the delicious smell of the omelettes wafted into his nostrils, reminding him how rarely it was that such delicacies came his way.

'I eat very little in these summer days,' the old woman replied. 'I simply let the unconquered sun suffuse its warmth and life-giving strength into my body.' She stared at Canio and added, so softly that he barely heard her, 'You *are* extraordinarily like him. I really think that this time ...'

'Like him? Like who?' Canio asked casually, settling himself into one of the ornately carved chairs and deftly transferring three of the omelettes from the dish to a silver plate with the blade of a table knife.

As if she had not heard the question, Aelia turned to Vilbia and asked, 'Where were you coming from today, my dear? So few people of quality use that road from the sea these days, not since the unpleasantness with the barbarians.'

Vilbia, by now herself seated at the table, replied that they had come from Corinium.

'Ah, Corinium,' Aelia sighed. 'It's long years since I was last there. Tell me, does the great Jupiter column still stand in the centre of the forum, or have those silly Christians at last done away with it? They were always threatening to do so, even when I was young.'

'No, it's still there,' Vilbia replied. 'Or at least, it was when we left.'

'I am most gratified to hear it. Strange, is it not, that although I have no particular desire to see it again, yet I find it oddly comforting to know that it is still there, a survivor from the better times of long ago. It endures, as I myself do, waiting for those better times to return – as I know they will. Tell me, your people, where did they come from? From far across the ocean, perhaps?'

Vilbia hesitated, but Canio, guessing what she wanted to hear from the way she asked the question, replied smoothly, 'You're right; our ancestors did come from a country far away from Britannia. But how could you possibly have known that?'

'Ah, I just knew.' Aelia nodded contentedly, her eyes half closed. 'And yet ... your voice is somehow deeper, not quite as I remember it.'

Canio exchanged a quick, puzzled glance with Vilbia, and his shoulders moved slowly upwards in answer to her unspoken question.

'But I am forgetting my duties as hostess. You cannot speak and eat at the same time. Eat and drink now: later, there will be time enough for talking.'

So Canio ate and drank as he was bidden, finishing the *gustatio* of honey omelettes and helping himself from a great silver bowl piled high with dark red cherries. Under Aelia Aureliana's enigmatic gaze he then moved on to the *primae mensae*, the main course of spiced roast lamb with peas and carrots and small marrows stuffed with chopped hard-boiled eggs, all washed down with excellent Rhenish wine.

As Vilbia drank, or pretended to drink, holding a silver goblet to her lips, she studied Aelia, sitting so still up there on her throne. She began to realise that the old woman's eyes, half-closed though they were, seemed never to leave Canio's face. Relaxing slightly, she let her own eyes wander around the room.

Between the table where they sat and Aelia's dais was a figured mosaic about five yards square, in red, brown and cream tesserae. Completely free of furniture though it was, with not even a single lamp stand upon it, from where she sat Vilbia could see only parts of the mosaic, and those parts were either sideways-on or upside down to her. Nevertheless, she was sure that she had never seen its like before.

Down the right-hand side she could see three figures on horseback galloping away from her, their cloaks billowing out behind them in the wind. Along the left-hand side was a line of ships with high prows and sterns, tiny flag-like sails, and oversized heads representing their crews peeping above the sides. Of the three central panels, the table and all the things on it prevented her from seeing almost anything of the nearest, and the other two were both upside down. What she could make out was that the panel immediately below Aelia's dais depicted a bearded and helmeted man wearing military uniform. He was embracing a near-naked woman as the pair stood between two stylised leafy trees. Attempting to view it better, she began leaning her head to one side.

'Ah – that scene of the two of us together in the forest as we sheltered from the storm is, of course, my personal favourite. It always has been, through all the long, lonely years.'

Aelia's voice startled Vilbia: it was unnerving to think that those half-closed eyes must have been watching her as closely as Canio. Instinctively she straightened up, and as she did so noticed that the nearest of the riders with the billowing cloaks was the same woman as the one embracing the soldier under the trees. Also, that they shared the same distinctive hair style, which was identical to Aelia's own. The realisation came so suddenly that she could not stop herself from looking up sharply and staring at the old woman.

Aelia smiled. 'And do you recognise them?'

'Recognise who?' The question was Canio's. He had finished extracting the last of the chopped hard boiled eggs from the baby marrows, and was now investigating the contents of another bowl.

'Why, the people in the mosaic, of course.'

Anticipating a puzzled and embarrassing silence from Canio, Vilbia said quickly, 'The woman is you, isn't it?' She fancied that she saw Aelia bestow on her another faint smile.

'And the man bears a more than passing resemblance to myself,' Canio remarked, helping himself to one of the sweet-wine cakes that he had found under a small dish with an ornate fluted cover. 'Though maybe not quite so handsome,' he added.

Vilbia caught his covert wink. 'And the others, who are they?' she asked Aelia, surprised that Canio had even noticed the mosaic. She thought he had been solely interested in the food and wine.

'Doesn't your brother know?' She must have seen Canio hesitate, because Aelia sighed, 'Oh, has it been so long, Aulus Claudius Caninus? Or should I still call you Caius Statius Desideratus? Look at me, and admit that you do not know who the others are.'

Canio admitted that he did not. 'But who's this Caius Stat – '

'And you have no remembrance of me either, do you? No, do not deny it.' She sighed again. 'It is no fault of yours – I myself did not realise who you really were, Caius, until many days after you had gone away. And time does so change the outward appearance of us all. But you, Caius, you have been reborn almost exactly as I remember you, as I knew you would be. And now, time the destroyer will become time the healer, for soon your memories will return and then you will know me for who I really am.' Aelia paused and gazed lovingly at Canio.

Uneasy and puzzled, Vilbia asked, 'From how long ago do you remember my brother?'

'From how long?' Aelia repeated. 'Why, nearly forty years have passed since Caius last held me in his strong arms. Forty

251

summers, all gone. But I knew that he would return to me one day. Not wished, not hoped, not even prayed, you understand, but *knew* – *knew* that he would return. I knew it just as surely as I know that day always follows night, and night always follows day.'

'Knew that *I* would return?'

'Oh yes, I knew ... Aeneas.' There was a long pause, as if, Vilbia thought, Aelia was savouring the name she had just spoken. 'Not at first, naturally, for I was barely eighteen when we met and did not know your true name then.'

'And where did you first meet ... Caius?' Vilbia asked.

'Why here – here in this villa which my father built, my dear. You see, Caius Statius Desideratus – the name Aeneas went by in those days – was a young cavalry officer, a guest of my father. And it was in these very rooms, when they were the main bath suite of the villa, that we used to meet in secret, and where we at last consummated the passionate love we felt for each other ... although my father never knew that, of course.

'Looking back now, from the distance of years, I am sure that it must have been the goddess Venus herself who cast her spell and prompted father to commission this mosaic when I was no more than a little child, long before I met Caius. Father once told me that it was copied from the pictures in one of his treasured scrolls of Virgil's *Aeneid*. I often think how sad it is that he was fated never to understand its true significance to myself.'

Aelia paused briefly, seemingly lost in her memories. Then she said, 'After all too short a time Caius's leave ended, and he had to return to the army. But we wrote to each other – almost every day at first, even when his *ala* was posted across the ocean to fight the barbarians. After a while his letters became less frequent, but I realised that was only because he was kept so busy with his military duties. And then they stopped altogether.

'I begged my father to discover why, which he did, although

it took many months. At first, to spare me, he told a white lie and said that Caius had married some heiress from the Gallic province of Lugdunensis Prima. But I knew that could not possibly be true. So I wept and pleaded with him to tell me the truth, and at last he broke the terrible news that Caius had in fact died in far away Moesia, fighting heroically against the Visigothic hordes.

'The thought that I would never see him again drove me almost insane with grief. But time, healing time, passed, and then, just as I was recovering from my illness, my father also died, and thus I inherited this Villa Aurelius.

'By then I knew that Caius had, of course, been the reincarnation of Aeneas. It was the goddess Venus herself, Aeneas's own mother, who sent the dream that revealed it to me. Oh, such a foolish girl I was not to have realised it when he was still here. To think, I even teased Caius about his resemblance to the man in the mosaic! But when I became mistress of this villa I hired craftsmen from Lindinis and had them convert the suite of baths into the room which you see before you tonight. It became my private living quarters so that, day or night, I would never be parted from him again.'

Aelia looked at them both, but neither spoke. 'Ah, I see that you still do not really understand. You have heard of Aeneas, have you not?' She must have assumed they had not. 'He was a prince of Troy, and when that city fell to the Greeks he escaped and sailed away with his little son, Ascanius – do you see him, there, in the mosaic, standing next to Venus? It was she who arranged that we should fall in love that first time, there in my city of Carthage, when Aeneas's ships sailed into the harbour while travelling along the coat of Africa.'

'In *your* city of Carthage?' Vilbia repeated. 'You mean that your ancestors came from – ?'

'I mean that I was – that I am – Dido, Queen of Carthage ... Do not look so surprised; surely you must have heard the story of our tragic love?'

Quickly, fearing that Canio might bluntly admit that he had not, Vilbia said, 'Yes, of course we have. An old man called Gulioepius once told me the story – of how Aeneas first loved her, and then deserted her, and how in her despair she killed herself.'

'He did *not* desert me!' Aelia's words burst out like a cry of pain. 'Not really ... although I admit that even I believed so at the time. But it was the god Mercury who forced him to leave me. *Forced* him, against his will, to sail away to Italy, there to fulfil his glorious destiny as father of the Roman race – and what mortal can prevail against a god? But he never forgot me, never! When we met again, those forty years ago, I believe he recognised me at once, although I, foolish and inexperienced girl that I was, did not know him. And he could not tell me, knowing as he did that recognition had to come from my own deep-buried memories, just as he had recognised me from his ... and just as I now recognise Aulus from mine. And as the coming days pass, I am certain that Aulus too will come to recognise me for who I truly am – and then we shall become lovers again.'

Canio, who had been munching a honey cake, suddenly stopped.

'But how ...' Vilbia bit her tongue.

'But how could that be, seeing that I am so old?' Aelia completed the question for her. 'It is because only my body is old. The spirit that lives within it will never age, never die.' She appeared to hesitate, then reached down into the folds of her dress and took out what appeared to be a life-sized bronze hand.

Vilbia was too far away to make out all of its bizarre excrescences, but she could see the pine cone at the tip of one of the extended fingers and the crested serpent emerging from another.

'Do either of you know what this is?' Aelia asked dreamily.

CHAPTER TWENTY

Canio gave Vilbia a sideways glance, intended to say, 'What now?' To Aelia he replied, 'It's a hand of Sabazios, isn't it? I've seen one or two in my time.' But, as he dabbed his lips with a napkin, he whispered to Vilbia, 'And very useful back-scratchers they were too.'

'Ah, but this particular hand is unlike any other. With this ...' Aelia hesitated, then said in a lowered voice, 'With this I can summon a being from another world – an immortal being, to whom the future and the past are as one. He can speak of things which are yet to be with the certainty that you and I might talk of events which happened yesterday.'

'Do you mean he's a sort of ... demon?' Vilbia asked. Canio thought she sounded genuinely horrified.

'No, no,' Aelia said quickly. 'At least, I do not think of him as such. He is simply a friend – a friend and comforter in my lonely vigil. A messenger from the gods themselves.'

'So what does he look like, this messenger of yours?' Canio was not himself remotely horrified, not least because he did not believe a word of what Aelia had just said. He only asked because he suspected that Vilbia might want to know.

'Oh, I have never seen him. He only comes to me in the darkest, loneliest depths of the night, and then only after I have drunk the elixir of oblivion.'

'The what?'

'Surely you have heard of it – wine infused with the herb valerian?'

'Yes, of course; I was forgetting. A very useful medication.'

Canio thought it would be unwise to add that, for his own oblivion, he always left out the valerian.

'When the villa and the whole world beyond its doors are silent and still, he comes to me as in a dream. In that strange land between waking and sleeping, when time itself seems first to slow and then to stop altogether, he glides in and whispers to me of things that happened so long ago that even I had quite forgotten them. And sometimes, most longed for of all, he whispers of those things which are still to come.'

Canio saw that Aelia's eyes were closed now. 'And what are those things that are still to come, Aelia Aureliana?'

Aelia opened her eyes and looked directly at him. 'My friend, my comforter, promised me that, on that day of wonders when Aeneas and I consummate our love once more, then I will become young again. Young and supple – as snakes cast off their ancient, worn out skins to reveal the new ones, sleek and glistening, below.'

'And you really do believe that Aulus is Aeneas.' Vilbia sounded diffident, but not questioning, which surprised Canio.

'I am almost, almost sure, my dear. There have been others before him, but none who so perfectly resembled the man I remember. I suspect that Venus has made me endure so long simply to test my steadfastness – waiting until almost the end of my old body's life before returning Aeneas to me.' Aelia smiled serenely at them both before closing her eyes again.

Canio smiled back, then muttered to Vilbia out of the corner of his mouth, 'I'm damned if she's not as crazy as a wolf under a full moon. Just watch: any moment now she'll be throwing back her head and howling – can you see any foam around her lips yet? Hope she hasn't many teeth left.'

'The next full moon is a good two weeks away,' Vilbia whispered. 'It will be the new moon that rises with this coming dawn. Didn't you know that, brother?'

'Just as well; otherwise she'd probably be running around the room on all fours by now.'

'Strange ... that is so strange.' Canio looked up to see Aelia staring at him, a puzzled look on her face. 'As I hold this hand, I feel that my friend from another world is trying to speak to me, something which he has never done before in the light. It is as if there is something that he urgently wishes me to know.' The old woman held the back of the bronze hand against one cheek, rubbing it gently against her wrinkled skin. Her eyes closed, as if concentrating.

Canio looked at Vilbia, rolled his eyes, then tilted his head back until he was looking at the ceiling and pushed out his lips in a noiseless howl.

'Stop it!' Vilbia whispered, shooting him a disapproving look.

He thought she sounded frightened: surely by now she must have realised that Aelia was simply a harmless eccentric? He shrugged and lowered his head, although seeing that Aelia's eyes were still closed, he couldn't resist making rapid paddling movements with both hands, intended to convey the impression of an animal running on all fours.

'Perhaps your messenger from the gods is trying to confirm to you that Aulus really is the reincarnation of Aeneas?' Aelia seemed not to hear Vilbia's voice, remaining silent, her eyes still tightly closed. 'But you said that he only talks to you when you are alone in the stillness of the night,' Vilbia continued. 'So perhaps it is only the presence of Aulus and myself that is discouraging him from speaking clearly to you now?'

'Hush, hush!' Aelia pleaded. There was a long silence, and then she sighed, 'No, he has gone. At the sound of your voice, his own seemed to fade away.' There was another silence, and then she said, 'I think perhaps that you are right. It is the presence of others that is making him wary and reluctant to approach closer to me, however urgent his message may be. Could I ... could I ask you to be so good as to leave me and retire for the night, so that he might return?'

'Of course, of course,' Vilbia said meekly, immediately

standing up and looking at Canio. 'My brother and I fully understand, don't we Aulus?'

Canio certainly understood that Vilbia wanted to leave, although he did not understand why. He gazed longingly at the bowls whose covers he had not yet even lifted.

'Don't we, Aulus?' Vilbia repeated.

'Yes ... of course we do,' said Canio, responding to the tension in her voice. 'May I thank you, Aelia Aureliana, on behalf of us both, for your most generous hospitality.'

Aelia acknowledged his thanks with a smile and a gracious open-handed gesture. 'Tertullia will show you to your rooms. And, Aulus, be assured that we will meet again early tomorrow, in the freshness of the new day.'

Vilbia walked smoothly towards the double doors, then turned and said, 'Drink deeply of your elixir of oblivion, Aelia Aureliana, so that you may speed the return of your friend and comforter.' But as she turned again and opened the doors, Canio heard her murmur, 'Although I pray to Leucesca that nothing but deep and dreamless sleep may come to you this night.'

After he had closed the doors behind them, Canio turned to Vilbia and whispered, 'What in the name of old Rosmerta's tub was all that about? Don't tell me that you really do believe that she can summon up a demon with that metal paw of hers?'

'Are you so sure that she can't?' And before he could think of a suitably sardonic reply, she had added, 'Think of a believable reason that we can give for leaving this place.'

'Leaving? What, you mean now?'

'Yes, now – as soon as we possibly can.'

'But why?'

'Because ... because we have to get to that lake when the new moon is rising. I only realised while Aelia was speaking just now.'

Canio wondered what was coming next. 'You think Saturninus will still be there then?' he asked, groping for understanding.

'No, not Saturninus,' she said wistfully. 'Perhaps nothing but the gold.'

'I see … how long have you known?' he asked softly.

'About the gold? Remember back in the woods, when the fever was on you? You said many things then. Some of them made me like you better, some not so well.'

'Look, I swear that I was going to tell you before – '

'Shssh!'

Canio followed her eyes and saw Tertullia gliding down the corridor towards them.

'Over at last?' she smiled. 'The night must be half gone. And what was it this time that made her decide that you are not her long-lost Aeneas after all?'

'Don't be so sure I'm not – apparently she still hasn't made up her mind on that subject,' Canio replied easily. 'She seems a strange woman, that mistress of yours. Still, at her age I suppose that giving a dinner party after a long day's travelling must have been something of a strain.'

'And when we left her she was behaving slightly oddly,' Vilbia added, looking concerned. 'Saying something about wishing to sleep because a hand of Sab … somebody, wanted to *talk* to her?'

'Ahh,' said Tertullia, as if now she understood. 'Perhaps I'd better go to her.' She made to open one leaf of the double doors.

'Hey, before you go, tell me – was yesterday really the first day before the kalends of Iulius?' Canio put on what he thought was a suitably worried expression. 'It cropped up in conversation with your mistress, and I said, no, it was the second – or the third, properly speaking – but she was adamant that it was the first.'

'This day just gone, you mean?'

'Yes.'

'It was the first day before, of course – *pridie kalendas Iulius*. Does it matter?' It was Tertullia's turn to appear concerned.

'Oh no!' The information appeared to distress Vilbia. 'We told Mother that we'd meet her at uncle Gordianus's villa at noon on the kalends – and that must be today! Somehow, Aulus, you've managed to lose a whole day.'

Canio admired the note of exasperation she injected into her voice. 'Oh that's right, blame me. So who was the brilliant navigator who was *so* certain that there must be a road south through the marshes, eh? Tell me that.'

'I'm still convinced that you could have found a track, if only you'd looked a little harder,' Vilbia replied stiffly. 'And the worst of it is, you promised Mother faithfully that we'd be with her by the kalends. The gods alone know what she'll think has happened to us when we don't arrive.'

Canio gave her an irritated look. Turning to Tertullia he asked, 'Just how far is it to Isca from here? Our uncle's villa is about fifteen miles north-east of the city.'

'Isca? It must be all of forty miles.'

'Right, that settles it then. I'm afraid we won't be having the pleasure of breakfasting with your mistress this morning, because now we'll be setting off for uncle Gordianus's villa.'

'You mean literally now – this very moment?' Tertullia looked at him as if he were mad.

'I'm afraid so. If we travel through the night we might reach uncle's villa by noon. It'll be a long, hard journey, but if it means that Mother will be spared the least anxiety, then it'll be worth every weary moment, won't it, Claudia? Come noon, we'll be there – just in time to greet her as she slithers out of bed.'

Vilbia shot him a look that he thought was somewhat deficient in sisterly affection. 'If you say so.'

'Right, that's settled then,' he said briskly. 'Tertullia, if you would be so good as to point us in the direction of the stables, I'll collect our horse and we'll be away into the night.'

'Certainly – if that's what you really want,' Tertullia replied hesitantly. 'But first, I'd better see if my Lady Aelia requires assistance in preparing for sleep.'

Perhaps thinking that Canio might be about to object, Vilbia said quickly, 'Yes of course; we'll wait here.' Then, as an apparent afterthought, she added, 'Tell me, does she often pretend to contact a strange being from another world with that metal hand of hers?'

'I ... couldn't say,' Tertullia replied cautiously, and hurried into Aelia's chamber, shutting the door behind her.

When she had gone, they stood together in silence for a few moments. Then Canio grinned at Vilbia. 'We make a good team: you're almost as fine a liar as I am.' Anticipating her reply, he added, 'But I swear I'm not lying when I say that, back there in the marshes, and on the road to this Villa Aurelius, I was several times on the point of telling you about the gold, but every time I tried, something –'

'Not here,' Vilbia murmured, pointing to the doors. 'You never know who might be listening.'

'No, you never know,' Canio sighed.

Sooner than he had anticipated he heard the muffled sound of pattering feet. Then the doors swung open again and Tertullia reappeared. 'My lady is already fast asleep – it seems that she has taken one of her valerian sleeping draughts.' She moved past them and started walking quickly down the corridor, before turning and giving Canio a sly look. 'I wonder if she really will decide that she's found her Aeneas at last?'

'And why shouldn't she? Me looking even more handsome than the man in the mosaic.'

'And yet so modest too. Follow me – the stables are this way.' Tertullia led them down the corridor and out through a side door into a courtyard, where the night air was fragrant with the scent of herbs growing in neat beds set between paths of fine, raked gravel that crunched softly underfoot. At the far side of the courtyard was an elaborate openwork screen of carved white stone. After passing through an ornamental gateway in this screen the path widened and carried on towards an extensive range of stables and other outbuildings. There Tertullia woke the ostler and told the sleepy man to saddle Antares.

As they waited, Canio asked Tertullia, 'Will the road beyond the villa take us towards Isca?'

'Yes, more or less. The road heads south for a mile, down into a small valley where there's a ford across the river – '

'What river?'

'The Uxela, of course, Aeneas.' Tertullia turned to Vilbia and smiled. 'Don't worry, it's only a small river.' To Canio she continued, 'And then the road turns and heads south-west.'

There was something in her voice that Canio couldn't interpret: one moment he thought it was displeasure, the next suppressed laughter. However, south-west was definitely the direction that he wanted to go. 'But won't we get into the marshes again if we go that way?' he asked, fishing for more information.

'You shouldn't. The road follows a low ridge that runs just beyond the southern edge of the marshes and lakes.'

'Oh no, don't tell me there are more lakes for you to get lost among, brother dear,' Vilbia sighed.

Tertullia purred with amusement. 'Don't worry: there aren't many lakes, and you wouldn't even know they were there unless you looked, and then all you'd see would be glimpses of water between the trees. Just stay on the road and you'll be quite safe.'

When Antares was saddled, Vilbia took hold of one of the stiff leather horns and sprang lightly up onto his back, twisting in mid-air so that she sat side-saddle. Canio took the reins and followed Tertullia, who walked silently out in front as she guided them back to the road.

There she halted, turned, blew him a kiss and said, 'Now you will hurry back, won't you? I'm sure my mistress will want to see her Aeneas again very, very soon.'

Canio assured her that he would return as quickly as the gods would allow, then started walking rapidly along the road. After some thirty yards, as he turned to speak to Vilbia, he saw

Tertullia still standing at the spot where they had left her. The embroidered belt, which had been buckled around her waist, now dangled from one hand. Before he could even begin to wonder why, he saw her slowly cross her arms and draw her dress smoothly up and over her head.

For a moment she stood there, naked, with the crumpled dress raised high above her head, posing motionless as a statue, her skin pale and perfect in the ethereal half-light. He glimpsed the small, dark-tipped breasts, the curves of her slim waist broadening out into wide hips, and the triangular smudge at the base of her flat stomach. Then she lowered her arms, blew him another kiss, turned and skipped away into the night.

Canio stared after her. 'Too late,' he murmured. 'Three days long as years too late.' He became aware that Vilbia was looking curiously at him, but before she could ask he had jerked Antares' reins and started the horse trotting forwards again. For some time he said nothing, and he guessed that she was assuming that his thoughts were on the lake and the gold. But in truth, they were on her.

※※※

The road that might eventually have led to Isca turned out to be little better than a track, often no more than one wagon wide, and stoned only in those low spots where it would otherwise have become a sea of mud in winter. For the first mile, until they had forded the Uxela, and then for some time afterwards, neither Canio nor Vilbia spoke, and the only sounds he heard were the rhythmic clopping of Antares' hooves, the fitful whispering of the cool night breeze through the trees and grasses, and the occasional furtive rustle as some small nocturnal creature sensed their presence and scurried away through the long grasses at the roadside.

He looked up at the moonless sky, scattered with stars. To the north he made out the box and tail of the Great Bear and the double "V" of Cassiopeia. Even with no moon the sky was several degrees lighter than the land, the nearby trees outlined black against it.

Time was running out now. He wondered if he should make one last attempt to convince Vilbia that he really had intended to tell her about the gold? A fatalistic realisation that it was simply too late decided him against it. She either believed him or she did not, and if not then nothing he could say now would convince her otherwise. And there was no point in telling her that the supposed sighting of Saturninus was a lie. She knew that now: of that he was certain.

And did she also know about the Hecate figurine? If he had talked about the gold when the fever was on him, then perhaps he had babbled something about the Dark Lady too? But it was possible that he had not. So if he were to tell her now, might she see it as some sort of atonement for all the lies and evasions that had gone before?

'There's something else you should know,' he began slowly, looking straight ahead, not back at her. Far away to the west he saw sheet lightning flicker, momentarily illuminating dark, unknown hills.

'Something else? Besides the gold, you mean?'

The darkness, Canio thought, made the confession easier. 'Besides the gold. And besides what I told you about Saturninus – although it is connected with the lake.' He waited for her to tell him that she knew about the Hecate figurine. He waited until the silence between them was almost tangible, and then he said, 'The man who told me about the gold was dying – '

'Dying of what?' she asked sharply.

'A stab in the guts. Not by me – it was one of the regular army bastards supposedly under my command who did it. I've never killed anyone I didn't really hate, give or take the odd goat-shagger.'

'And the raven,' she softly reminded him.

'Who was killing you ... Anyway, this man who died gave

me something that he wanted thrown into the lake where the gold is hidden.' Trying to sound casual, he went on, 'It was a little figurine of the goddess Hecate. Perhaps you noticed it when you came to my room in Corinium?'

She said nothing.

'Dying men sometimes say strange things. Orgillus – that was his name – made me swear to take the figurine back to the lake and throw it in.'

'Why?' she asked.

'Because the jackass had convinced himself that if I did so, then Hecate would somehow bring him back to life again. He thought he must have offended the Dark Lady by not throwing it into the lake himself when he had the chance.'

'And when was that?'

'When he and his fellow deserters threw the gold in after they had looted it from the same temple that the figurine came from.'

'Which temple – did he say?'

'No; he never did ... that's the truth.'

'But what possessed them to throw the gold into the lake anyway?'

'To evade the army. Apparently the gold was slowing them down. They meant to go back for it later, of course.'

'How do you know they didn't?'

'Because they're dead.'

'All of them?'

'That's what Orgillus heard.' *And I hope they are.*

'Dead of what?'

'The army: apparently it did catch up with them after all.'

'I see. Have you got the figurine with you now?'

'Yes.'

'Can I hold it?'

Wordlessly, Canio unbuckled his belt pouch and handed the brass goddess up to her. In the night-long twilight of midsummer he watched as she ran her fingertips over the hound curled at the base, over the crossed arms holding torch and sword, and finally over Hecate's grim face. He saw her head silhouetted against the lighter sky as she held the figurine close to one ear and gently shook it.

Then she said quietly, 'You suspected that there was something fearful about this little thing, didn't you? Is that why you wanted me with you – to deflect whatever malign influence you thought it might possess?' He did not reply, and she added, 'Remembering what you told me about Marcia, I can understand why you would have done that.'

Understand perhaps, but not forgive? Canio wondered. 'How long have you known?'

She reached down and handed the figurine back to him. 'As time passed, I guessed that you had to have some secret reason for wanting me with you ... and also that what you told me about Saturninus being seen at the lake was ...' She shrugged, and left the rest unsaid.

'But you never turned back. Why?'

'At first I was unsure.'

'And now?'

'And now ... perhaps I don't want to be sure.'

Canio wondered what she meant by that, and waited for her to say more. But she did not. The silence between them grew longer, and the conversation died.

Letting her take the reins, he dropped back a few paces and surreptitiously shook the figurine, listening as she had done. And for the first time he heard it – a faint rustle, as if there were something trapped inside. He rationalised that it was nothing more than a tiny shard or two that had become detached as the molten metal cooled. But if that were all it was, then why did it interest Vilbia? And she had seemed to know it was there. How could she have known that?

'What will you do with your share of the gold?'

'My share?' She sounded even more astonished than he thought she would be. 'I don't want any part of it!'

'Why not; do you like being poor?'

'I have all I need.'

'Do you? All you really have is a little old temple in a wood up on the edge of the Long Limestone Hills, miles from anywhere, in a time when belief in your old gods seems to be going out of fashion. Not much of a future, is it?'

'Can either of us see into the future, Canio?' When he did not reply, she asked, 'So what do you plan to do with the gold, assuming of course that you do actually find it?'

'Buy a villa somewhere up in those Hills. I've heard there are several to choose from, now that the *Conspiratio* has frightened their owners into moving permanently into their big town houses in Corinium – just so that they can sleep soundly at night without wetting themselves every time a mouse squeaks outside their windows.'

'But you'd need a fortune to buy one of those.' He didn't need to see her face to read the scepticism.

'I reckon no more than eight thousand solidi.'

'Eight *thousand*!'

'It sounds a lot, but do you know how many solidi there are to a pound of gold?'

'No, I don't. Strangely, I've never had reason to find out.'

'Seventy-two, that's how many. So even eight thousand of those little beauties would only weigh about a hundred and ten pounds. Add, say, a fifth for the various ... let's call them expenses ... of converting bullion into coin, and that's still only a hundred and thirty pounds of bullion. No heavier than you, I'd guess.'

'That's still a lot of gold, Canio,' she said reflectively.

'But there's a lot of gold in that lake. There must be – Orgillus said that all five of them struggled to carry it.'

'You really have got it all planned, haven't you?'

Perhaps she didn't mean it to sound like an accusation, but to Canio's ears it did. It was time to tell her. 'No, not quite. There is something that I hadn't planned.'

'And what's that?'

'You.' Canio paused, took a deep breath and said, 'Look, whether or not you decide to keep some of the gold for yourself, come and live with me in that villa in the Hills.' Against the faint lightness of the eastern horizon he saw her head move from side to side in slow rejection. 'But think about it,' he urged. 'I could probably buy a villa not far from that temple of yours, so you could go back to it as often as you liked. And you'd have your own rooms in the villa – everything you could want.'

'And what would I be at that villa, Canio? Your wife, your mistress – what?'

'You'd be my sister, just like you are now – I promise I wouldn't lay a finger on you. Look, in the new life I've got planned I want someone with me that I like and trust. Be that someone, Vilbia. It would be a good life, and you could go on serving that goddess of yours without worrying where the next siliqua was coming from.'

'No Canio, I don't want any part of that gold, or anything bought with it. By rights it should be returned to the temple it was stolen from.'

'It can't be returned: Orgillus said the temple was burnt and all its priests died.'

'Died? Died of what?'

He hesitated. 'Not of old age, apparently.'

'So there's blood on that gold?'

He shrugged. 'At some time or other there's probably been blood spilt over every little silver siliqua you take at that temple of yours. Does it really matter? When you and I get our hands on that gold it'll just be pieces of yellow metal, as innocent as buttercups in a summer meadow.'

'No. I don't want it.'

'But perhaps Leucesca wants you to have it – have you thought of that? Whether you realised it or not, perhaps that's the reason why you never turned back? She knows that money is power, Vilbia. Power to resist any zealous jackass of a

Christian who one day soon might decide to polish his halo by turning your temple into a neat little pile of stones.'

'No, Canio, I'll never take any of that gold. Please don't ever ask me again.'

He shrugged. 'All right, I won't – but come and live with me anyway. All I want is companionship and someone to talk to, someone I can trust. That's all, I swear.'

'How strange: I'd never thought of you as a man who feels loneliness, Canio. A man alone, perhaps, like Saturninus was – but not a lonely man.'

'Hadn't you? I'll be thirty years old some time next year. Last November I found myself standing on a bridge over a flood-swollen stream. Yellow leaves were floating by, their one and only summer gone. Sometimes a couple would drift along side by side, coming so close that for a few moments they touched. But then the current would speed one up or hold the other back, so that they went spinning apart. And they never touched again, just floated on alone until I suppose first one, and then the other, disappeared under the dark water for ever. Have you ever found yourself looking at such things, Vilbia – and maybe thinking how much like those leaves we are?'

'Why Canio, I do believe that you might be turning into a philosopher,' she replied with what seemed unforced lightness. 'If you go on saying things like that, then even Antares will start wondering what to make of you, won't you my hero?' She leant forwards and patted the horse between the ears and Antares whinnied softly in response.

'So will you come and live in that villa?'

'As your sister?'

'As my sister – free to come and go whenever you please.'

She hesitated. 'Perhaps – ask me again tomorrow.'

'I'll do that,' Canio assured her, turning to try and read her face. As he did so he noticed the first orange streaks low in the eastern sky behind them. 'Dawn's coming. That lake can't be far away now.'

They journeyed on in silence, their heads turning with increasing frequency towards the north as they sought the first glimpse of the lake that they had come so far to find. And as the sky slowly lightened, Canio noticed a pair of small bats flitting silently and erratically backwards and forwards overhead as they hunted the last of the night-flying insects.

CHAPTER TWENTY-ONE

The fiery disc of the sun was just beginning to show above the north-eastern horizon when Canio saw the first lake, alerted by Vilbia who, from her perch up on Antares' back, had spotted flashes of sunlight reflected off the water.

He halted and peered northwards through the thin belt of woodland that flanked the road.

'Do you think it's the one?' she asked.

He was uncomfortably aware that he had no idea. 'Could well be,' he said, trying to sound confident. 'Orgillus said it was near a road.'

As Vilbia slid down out of the saddle, he looked cautiously up and down the road to make sure that they were unobserved by any other early morning wayfarer. Then he took Antares' reins and began leading the horse down the wooded slope. Although it was twenty-four hours since he had last slept he felt no tiredness: the exhilaration of the chase had possessed him now. Glancing back at Vilbia's watchful face he wondered if it was possessing her too?

Night and its shades of grey still lingered under the trees, and he passed briefly through a twilight world where clumps of luxuriant hart's tongue ferns grew, their corrugated strap-like leaves fully two feet long.

At the foot of the slope the trees ended, and he found himself standing beside Vilbia in a wilderness of tall grasses interspersed with clumps of great sedges and sprinkled with yellow buttercups and mauve vetches. A hundred yards away he saw an expanse of greeny-brown water, its surface ruffling in the dawn breeze.

'So … is that it?' Vilbia asked again.

'I don't really know,' he admitted: the time for lies and evasions was past. He gazed from side to side, searching for something – anything – which would tell him that this lake was indeed the chosen one. But nothing he could see spoke to him of hidden gold.

The lake was roughly circular and some three to four hundred yards across, its margin fringed with reeds. Feeling slightly uncomfortable with Vilbia watching him, he took the Hecate figurine from his belt pouch and held it up towards the lake. But still he felt and saw nothing, the figurine remaining cool, lifeless metal in his hand.

'Perhaps if we were to walk around the edge you might see something to show where the gold was thrown in?' Vilbia suggested.

Unable to think of a better idea, he set off around the reedy margin holding the figurine in one hand and Antares' reins in the other. He walked slowly, his eyes flickering between the figurine and the greeny-brown water, impatiently trampling down those reeds that obscured his view.

When he was about a quarter of the way around he heard a dog howl. It came from some distance away to the west, and he thought little of it. On the far side of the lake he heard it again, but it was only when he heard it for a third time that he realised its possible significance. The insight came so suddenly that it stopped him in his tracks. 'That's it! That's got to be it!'

'You think this is the place?' Vilbia asked, studying the spot where he had halted.

'No, not here – this is the wrong damned lake! The one we want is further over that way.' He pointed westwards with the hand that still clutched the Hecate figurine, and tugging Antares he started walking quickly back along the way they had come.

'How can you know that?' Vilbia asked, as she trotted after him.

'That hound of course! Didn't you hear it?'

'Yes, I heard it, but what – '

'I didn't think to tell you,' he interrupted, 'but after Orgillus died this big black hound appeared and followed me for miles as I rode back to Corinium.'

'But surely that couldn't have been the same dog that's howling over there?'

'Couldn't it? Orgillus said that somehow the Dark Lady would lead me to the right place, and look – the clue was here all the time!' He held out the Hecate figurine so that Vilbia could clearly see the hound curled at the goddess's feet. 'Oh sweet Venus, it's so obvious now – I can't understand why I didn't think of it before and keep a lookout for that damned dog! Come on, it can't be far. Let's get there before the world is properly awake.'

Almost running, moving so fast that he slipped and stumbled several times, but too excited even to curse, he started forging his way westwards through the wilderness of grasses and sedges.

After half a mile he came to a second lake, but before he could even begin searching he heard the hound again, still some distance away to the west. He swore under his breath and started off again.

Several hundred yards further on he reached the third lake. It was smaller than the first two, no more than two hundred yards across. Dropping Antares' reins he stood, panting slightly, listening for the hound as his eyes swept across the lake from side to side and back again. To his disappointment he heard nothing, saw nothing. But before he could say as much to Vilbia, he became aware that the cool morning air was full of a sweet, delicate scent.

Turning, he saw a riot of honeysuckle bines climbing up saplings and scrambling through the branches of the trees at the foot of the slope that ran down from the road. So profuse and vigorous was it that in places it completely hid the leaves of the trees themselves, a hanging curtain of rich yellow and white flowers stretching for some fifteen yards, countless slender trumpets diffusing their perfume out into the morning air. Never before had he seen honeysuckle growing quite so exuberantly, or smelt its fragrance in such pervasive strength. He stared up at it, mesmerised.

'Canio ... look, over there!'

He swung round to see Vilbia pointing towards the lake, where a large black hound was rising up out of the long grass in which it had been crouching unseen.

The beast seemed to look directly at him as he stood beside Vilbia, its flanks quivering slightly, as if it were tensing to attack. Its eyes were a dull dark red, the colour of old blood, and Canio felt a stab of primeval fear as those eyes stared balefully straight into his own.

But the hound did not attack. Instead it turned abruptly and walked the few yards to the water's edge, where it lowered its great head and appeared to drink briefly. Turning again, it looked at him for one last time, before trotting away westwards, slipping soundlessly through the tall grasses and scattered clumps of sedge like a shadow until he lost sight of it.

'That must be the place,' Vilbia said, so softly that he barely heard her.

'What?' The malevolence he fancied he had seen in the hound's stare had chilled Canio like frost, despite the growing heat of the rising sun.

'Where it drank – that must be the place where the gold was thrown in.'

'Yes ... do you think so?' With an effort he quelled the doubts and fears that had suddenly beset him. He walked slowly over to the spot where the hound had drunk, and looked into the calm greeny-brown water, seeing only a patchy carpet of weeds growing just below the surface. But he also noticed that, several feet out from the edge, the lake appeared to deepen, so that the bottom and anything lying on it rapidly became invisible.

'Yes, this must be the place,' he said, echoing her words. 'But it looks so ...'

'So ordinary?' Vilbia murmured. 'Maybe that's why they chose it?'

'Maybe. Only one way to be certain though.' Memories of the hound's stare were receding quickly now, replaced by tantalising images of what might be under the water, only a few short yards away. Quickened, he handed the Hecate figurine to Vilbia and then, hopping on each leg alternately, pulled off his boots and started wading out into the lake. No more than six feet from the edge, where the water came to just above his knees, he felt something prickle under his bare left foot. Taking a step back, he stooped and groped across the silty lake bed until his fingers made contact.

'Oh you little beauty!' he whispered exultantly. He swished it through the surface water to wash off the last traces of silt, then held out for Vilbia's inspection a crumpled piece of wafer-thin sheet gold.

Taking it from his outstretched hand she unfolded it back to its original triangular shape, and as she did so he saw that it was about six inches long and vaguely resembled a feather, with a raised central spine and ribs radiating outwards from it.

'I've seen plaques like this fixed to the walls inside temples,' she said, 'but they've mostly been of copper, or occasionally silver. This is the first one I've ever seen made of gold. Gulioepius told me they're made to look like feathers because feathers come from birds, and birds fly up to the heavens and so can carry messages between gods and men – did you know that?'

'No, I don't think so.' Canio wasn't really listening now, as he restlessly waded backwards and forwards in the shallows, searching for whatever else might be there. After a while he reluctantly concluded that there was nothing else.

'But it proves that this must be the right place,' Vilbia said encouragingly. 'I suppose the plaque didn't go far when it was thrown because it's so light. The rest of the gold must be further out.'

'Yes, the gold must be here – it really must be.' Of all the emotions Canio felt at that moment, the predominant one was surprise. He had suddenly realised that, in a dark, pessimistic corner of his soul, he had never more than half-believed that he would ever find the longed-for gold. And even now, perhaps, something might still …

As he splashed out of the water, Vilbia handed the Hecate figurine back to him. He stared at the figurine as it lay on his open palm. 'So, it would seem that the time has come for this lady to go for a swim.'

Even as he spoke he was struck by the disquieting thought that, in these last moments, he might see the figurine come to life. Perhaps her head would turn, or her arms move, or the hound at her feet uncurl and stretch? Something, anything, before it was to pass out of his sight for ever. But nothing happened. The grim face stared blankly up at him, and he felt a strange mixture of disappointment and relief; of somehow being both rejected and spared by her quiescence.

He glanced at Vilbia. She was still as a mouse now, watching him intently. He forced a grin, then looked down at the figurine. 'Well, goodbye then, dear lady. I hope you'll be happy, living with the fishes.'

But as he drew back his arm to throw, Vilbia abruptly reached out and laid her hand gently on his. 'Are you sure you should be doing this? I mean, absolutely sure?' she asked softly.

Canio hesitated, recognising a warning but seeing no obvious reason for it. In any case, surely he had to throw the figurine into the lake?

Because Marcia believed that Hecate existed and had power over the living and the dead, and Orgillus believed that Hecate wanted the figurine thrown into the lake … And I believe, against my will, that if I don't throw it then I'll never find the rest of the gold, however near it might seem now.

'Why shouldn't I throw it in?'

'Because that little figurine is …' She hesitated, then said, 'Far more valuable than you realise.'

276

He relaxed. 'Valuable? No, it's not gold – not even gilded bronze. Melted down it'd only make a couple of belt buckles.'

'Those who think they know what it really is would say it is far more precious than all the gold in the world,' she said slowly, as if giving him time to work out what she meant.

'Oh, priests, you mean?' He thought he understood now. The gold feather plaque she held in her other hand, still wet with lake water, sparkled as it caught the rays of the rising sun. That decided him. He winked at her, gently disengaged his hand from hers, and before she could say another word he had drawn back his arm again and sent the figurine spinning high into the air.

Out of the corner of his eye he noticed Vilbia watching it intently, momentarily black against the bright sky, then falling in a smooth arc before it splashed into the lake some thirty yards from the bank. Then he saw her staring at the concentric circles of tiny ripples as they spread ever outwards from the spot where it had disappeared.

Puzzled, he muttered, 'It should have gone further than that – I put some muscle into the throw. Still, it's done now.'

'Yes, it's done.' He thought she sounded wistful; sad even. But, before he could ask why, she said, 'How deep do you think it is out there?'

'Oh, chest deep at most I should think.' He unbuckled his broad leather belt and handed it to her, complete with leather pouches and scabbarded *spatha*. 'Here, hold these for me and I'll soon find out.'

He waded out into the lake again, feeling around with his bare feet, moving slowly as the water rose up first to his waist, then to his chest. Suddenly he felt something move under his left foot. Instinct took over and he rapidly stepped back, but slipped and overbalanced – and despite flailing his arms wildly in an attempt to steady himself, he fell over backwards with a tremendous splash, plunging right under the cold water. It was in his nose and ears and mouth, and for several long moments he felt the panic of the drowning, before managing to scramble upright again, spluttering and cursing and feeling a sharp pain in his left shoulder.

'Damn, damn, damn, damn!' he snarled furiously as he struggled back to Vilbia, clutching his left arm with his right.

'Is it broken?' she asked apprehensively.

'No – I think I've just wrenched the damned shoulder, that's all.' He extended his left arm sideways and tried several times to rotate it. He didn't say anything, but realised that Vilbia must have noticed him wince as he did so.

'So how will you get to the gold now?' she asked. 'The water out there's too deep for wading, and you can't swim with that arm.'

'I can if I have to,' he said defiantly.

'With only one good arm? Won't you go round in circles?'

He showed his teeth. Half grin, half scowl. 'No I won't. Anyway, what's the alternative?'

'To let me get it for you.'

'You? Can you swim?'

'Yes, I can swim – probably better than you.' She must have seen his still-doubtful look, because she added, 'It's either me or say goodbye to the gold.'

She was right, and he knew it, but still he asked, 'Are you sure you can do it?'

'Quite sure,' she said patiently. 'One thing though ...'

'What?'

'The figurine – can I have it?'

He stared at her, mystified. 'But it's out there at the bottom of the lake now. You saw me –'

'I know. But will you give it to me anyway? And promise never, ever, to take it back?'

Why would she ...? 'Yes, you can have it ... of course you can have it, if that's what you really want.'

'Say it – say that you give it me,' she urged.

'I give it you ...'

'And ...'

'And I promise never, ever, to take it back. But why in the name of old Hades himself didn't you ask before I threw it in?'

'Because you wouldn't have given it to me then, would you?' And before he could reply, she murmured, 'In any case, I suppose she wanted it to be this way. I don't know why.'

***

She took off her cloak, unbuckled her belt and handed him the large purse that had hung from it, then crouched and unlaced her shoes and kicked them off. She shortened her dress by hitching it up and securing it round her waist with the belt, so that now the hem came to well above her knees. Then she walked into the water. After only a couple of steps, when the water had barely reached above her calves, he saw her hesitate.

'What's the matter?'

'Will you keep this safe for me?' She pulled over her head the cord from which the large copper coin of the emperor Julian was suspended and handed it to him. 'I wouldn't want to lose it – Saturninus asked me to keep it safe for him until he returned.'

He heard sadness in her voice, and wondered again what Saturninus had been to her, and she to him? 'Don't worry, I'll look after it,' he assured her, and dropped the coin into his own belt pouch.

She waded until the water was up to her waist, then leaned forwards and swam quickly out into the deep water. There he saw her dive at the spot where, as far as he could recollect, the Hecate figurine had dropped into the lake.

He started to feel uneasy, and instinctively began counting. Five … ten … fifteen … but just as he reached twenty she bobbed back up, waving something clutched in her right hand.

For those first few moments he was so relieved to see her safe that he didn't even care what she had found. And although, when she stood waist-deep in the shallows to throw the object to him, he could not help but notice how the soaking wet dress had moulded itself to the contours of her body, he felt no physical desire. She was his sister now. Or perhaps even – ?

'Catch!' she cried.

He shot out his arms and grabbed the flattened lump of yellow metal, cursing under his breath as his left shoulder jabbed. The piece was roughly four inches square, but very heavy for its size. Rocking it to catch the sun he made out, between the dents and gouges, most of the head of a bearded man surrounded by several small, deer-like animals.

Once it had been part of an object of mystery and great beauty; a broad, shallow dish, made perhaps for receiving offerings to a god. Then Orgillus, or one of his fellow deserters, had hacked and folded and refolded it, simply to make it easier to carry. He was not insensible to the fact that something wonderful had been destroyed to produce a lump of gold bullion. But it was now *his* gold bullion, and that was a wonderfully consoling thought.

Almost before he had finished rummaging in the depths of one of Antares' saddlebags for the stout sacks he had brought all the way from Corinium, Vilbia had returned with another much-folded lump of gold.

'How much is down there, do you think?' he asked excitedly, as she lobbed it to him.

'Lots, I think,' she replied, scraping the streaming water from her face with both hands. 'The water's too cloudy to see properly, but both times I dived I touched two or three pieces, all of them at least as big as that one.' She hesitated, then added, 'It's strange, isn't it, how they all seem to be near the place where the Dark Lady fell?'

'Yes, strange,' he replied, as he stared distractedly down at the lump of gold in his hand.

This second lump seemed once to have been a bowl with a flanged base. Actually, only half of a bowl he reflected, as he turned it over in his hands and saw how something, probably an axe, had been used to hack it apart. On the much-folded portion which he held, the front half of one horse appeared to be eternally chasing the back half of another, whose faceless rider's cloak streamed out behind him.

Impatient to know what Vilbia would bring him next, his sodden clothes were at first ignored and then forgotten completely, as he watched her repeatedly diving down through the greeny-brown water to the silty bottom of the lake. Sometimes she surfaced empty-handed, but more often bobbed up clutching another flattened piece of what had once been part of a magnificently decorated dish or bowl or cup or flagon. And he weighed each piece thoughtfully in his hand, before dropping it into one or other of the two sacks which, now joined by a short length of rope, hung on either side of Antares' saddle.

Afterwards, as he went over the sequence of events again and again in his mind, he reckoned that it must have been while he was holding the fourth or fifth creased and folded lump of gold that the waking dreams began. And they were such pleasant dreams that the idea of driving them away never even occurred to him.

Each pound of gold would become seventy-two solidi ... No, say sixty, allowing for those palms which would have to be greased along the way as he turned the bullion into coin and forged a legitimate title to it. And each sack, when full, would weigh, what? – eighty pounds, he guessed, grasping the thick, coarse cloth with both hands and lifting one momentarily, now all but oblivious to the sharp pain that jabbed through his left shoulder as he did so.

If he could fill both sacks, then he would have at least one hundred and sixty pounds: something over nine and a half thousand solidi. Perhaps six thousand for the villa, two thousand for more of the surrounding land, and around fifteen hundred to do with exactly as he pleased. He fancied a mixture of woodland and pasture, costing maybe a solidus for two *iugera* ... an estate of over four thousand *iugera*. How wonderful to think that at that very moment he was holding in his hand at least two hundred of them.

As time passed he barely noticed that the intervals between Vilbia's returns were steadily becoming longer. He was absorbed in caressing each misshapen lump of gold as it arrived, its soft, sensual touch beguiling him, warming in his hand to the temperature of his body until it was almost part of him, as all the while it spoke of the cornucopia of good things that it could buy. In a voice not unlike Tertullia's he heard each successive piece whisper to him of a villa at least as luxurious as the Villa Aurelius.

A villa nestling in a secluded, fertile valley in the Long Limestone Hills, a villa where room after room was clean and sweet-smelling, warm and dry and radiant with light, even on the coldest, darkest winter days. Of an endless supply of good food and wine, of fine clothes and of servants – pretty, young female servants who would do anything that he asked of them. Anything. And above all, those flattened lumps of yellow metal would set him free forever from the shackles of the harsh world into which he had been born, and which he had endured (whenever he could not evade them) for nearly thirty years.

So hypnotic were those dreams that he scarcely heard Vilbia's first shout of alarm. She cried out again, and he slowly looked up – as if waking from a drugged sleep – to see her treading the deep water and waving and pointing to the south-west. He turned and saw, little more than a hundred yards away, a man coming towards him. A man who seemed to have appeared from out of the tree-covered slope that led down from the road.

The man looked back and called out, apparently to others not yet visible. Canio could not make out the words, but they scarcely mattered because, moments later, another half dozen men were emerging like shadows from out of the cover of the trees. Several of them were dressed in what were still recognisable as army uniforms. One even wore an iron helmet, and they all had swords which, even as he watched, several drew and raised above their heads. The first man was now no more than eighty yards away, close enough for Canio to clearly see his grinning face.

What happened next came to seem like the imperfectly remembered fragments of a terrible dream. One moment he was looking at Vilbia, now swimming rapidly back towards the edge of the lake. The next – suddenly, and with no knowledge of how he got there – he was sitting up on Antares' back, reins clutched in both hands, and gazing eastwards, gazing into the great golden disc of the morning sun. He recalled kicking his heels into Antares' flanks and the horse refusing to move. And then kicking again, and keeping on kicking, harder and harder, until Antares stumbled jerkily forwards under the combined weight of his rider and the two full sacks of gold.

As if from far away he heard Vilbia scream his name. He slowly turned his head and looked back, seeing her standing mid-way between himself and the lake, wild-eyed, her wet dark-copper hair dishevelled and clinging to her cheeks and shoulders. He remembered thinking that he had never seen her looking so beautiful. In one hand she held something small and dark, and he knew instinctively what it was. She screamed his name once more – only his name – but in that one word there was such an intensity of bewilderment and hurt and accusation that it would return in memory to claw his very soul.

Then his eyes were irresistibly drawn back to the bent and folded lumps of yellow gold that leered so seductively from the tops of the sacks, and memories of the Villa Aurelius flooded into his mind, driving out everything else. In front of him he saw, in rapid succession, visions of Aelia Aureliana's luxurious great hall, and then Tertullia, first stretched out on the couch in the bath suite, then naked in the starlight. This last vision lingered. And then someone – not him – was kicking savagely into Antares' flanks again, sending the reluctant horse plunging eastwards into the brightness of that golden sun.

Somehow – he could never recollect how – he forced Antares up the wooded slope and across the road along which he and Vilbia had so recently travelled together, then headed due south at a laboured gallop, then trot, then walk. He rode on and on, until many blurred and unremembered miles separated him from the lake, stopping only when Antares was so exhausted that the horse could scarcely take another step.

It was only then that he recalled, as a distant, dream-like memory, that as he had been crossing the road there had come, from the direction of the lake, the eeriest sound he had ever heard. He remembered it as being like the growl of an angry dog, but so thunderously loud and deep that the very earth had seemed to tremble. But perhaps, he rationalised later, it had only been inside his head – an agonised howl of remorse from some still-unbeguiled part of his brain.

CHAPTER TWENTY-TWO

January AD 370 – Eighteen Months Later

Canio saddles Antares himself. He had bought the horse when he left the civil guard, but never gave a reason for wanting him, not even to himself: now more than ever he tries to avoid introspection. During the late summer of 368, in the course of several visits on official business to Londinium Augusta (courtesy of a well-bribed Vitalinus), he had, by devious and unlawful means, first turned the gold bullion into anonymous ingots, then exchanged the ingots for lovely gold solidi.

He had also arranged for the production, discovery and authentication of the will of a spinster lady, recently deceased, leaving a considerable legacy and naming him as her sole heir. The lady had had an existence as real as the solidi, although their paths had, of course, never crossed. With the money he had bought his way out of the civil guard and purchased a large villa up in the Long Limestone Hills to the north of Corinium. He should be happy, but the dark, accusing dreams still come, undiminished by the passage of time. And now, tonight, that scent of honeysuckle.

He checks the tightness of the girth, then horse and man set off into the frigid night, heading north along old tracks which lead out of the little valley that he now calls home. The cloudless, moonless sky glitters with myriad stars, and nothing disturbs the unnatural silence of the cold except the soft clopping of Antares' hooves and, occasionally, the far-off unearthly screams of mating foxes. Further north, as the ground steadily rises, he comes into a country where light snow has fallen, creating

285

starkly contrasting landscapes of white grasslands and black woods.

The long miles pass slowly, but eventually he finds himself high on the north-west escarpment of the Hills, following much the same route towards the temple of Leucesca that Saturninus must have taken those two and a half years before.

At last he comes to the spot where the temple stands in the woods below him. He knows where it is because, several times in the past eighteen months, he has come this far – and each time turned back, never able to face what he might learn by venturing those few extra yards down to the temple itself. Now, peering into the darkness, he makes out several faint streaks of light escaping from the high-level windows of the cella tower. Stiff with cold he dismounts, stamps around in the snow to get some life back into his legs, then begins leading Antares down the slope.

Inside the ink-black wood man and horse blunder their way along the path until they emerge into a snowy clearing. To his right he sees the temple, on the far side a small stone house, and in the centre of the clearing, sitting in a large, throne-like chair, an old man who is looking directly at him. Though he had never met him in life, for a heart-stopping moment Canio thinks it must be Gulioepius, instantly remembering what Vilbia had told him on that day when they first met – that Gulioepius had died in a November now over two years gone. And if ever there was one, this surely is a night when the dead might return to this world.

'Greetings to you, Canio. It's been a long time since we last met.'

Canio knows that voice, sees the short-lived cloud of breath in the frosty dark. 'Eutherius! What in the names of the Mothers of the Hills are you doing here?'

'I might ask you the same question, Canio, wealthy man that you are these days. Surely there is nothing here that you could possibly want?'

He hears derision in the old man's words. Dropping Antares' reins he walks towards him. 'Is she here?' he asks abruptly.

'Who?'

'Vilbia, of course. Is she here?'

'No, Canio, she's not here.'

'But she is still ...?' For a moment he cannot bring himself to say the word.

'Still what, Canio?'

'Alive – she's still alive?'

'Is that what you've come all this way to find out?'

'Yes. That and ... Where is she?'

'I'm surprised you don't know, Canio. I thought she was a friend of yours.' Canio says nothing, and the old man adds, 'Tell me, why would you be wanting to see her now? To invite her to a dinner party at your fine villa, perhaps?'

He realises that the old man has no intention of giving him the answers he craves, even if he knows them. Anger rises, but he curbs it, knowing it will achieve nothing. 'I wanted to return something she once left with me, something she wanted kept safe.'

'Indeed: and what might that be?'

Canio hesitates, then reaches under the collar of his tunic for the cord and draws the Julian coin over his head. 'This,' he says, holding it out so that it swings gently to and fro a few inches in front of the old man's face, not caring whether or not he can see in the gloom the great bull standing beneath its twin stars.

But it seems that Eutherius does not need to see it clearly to know what it is. 'Ah, that. Isn't that the coin which Saturninus gave her?'

He suspects that the old man knows full well it is. 'That's what she told me.'

'I'll have it now.' Eutherius reaches out to take the coin, but Canio jerks it away.

'No, I want to give it back to her myself. That way I'll know that she's alive and well.'

287

'Have you any reason to think that she isn't, Canio?'

'Don't fool with me, Eutherius. You know full well what happened at that lake.' He is bluffing of course, but if Eutherius does not deny knowing what only Vilbia could have told him …

'Do I, Canio? Perhaps you'd better remind me.'

Canio hesitates, then realises that now he has little choice. But perhaps a confession is the price that Eutherius requires? Confession for information. So he tells Eutherius everything that happened at the lake, and when he has finished he says, 'But I couldn't help myself, Eutherius – I swear I couldn't. I haven't even any memory of doing half the things I must have done. It was as though something came out of that gold like a cloud of marsh gas – something which spread over me and took possession of my body and mind and made me do what I did.'

'Really, Canio? Are you absolutely sure that it wasn't simply fear of losing that gold which possessed you?'

And Canio is not sure. It is one of the demons that are driving him.

'From what you've just told me,' the old man continues, 'it seems that you came to a fork in the path of life; to a three-way crossroads, so to speak. Vilbia stood on one fork, and the gold stood on the other. But you couldn't take both forks, so you had to choose. And you chose the gold. To you, the gold was more valuable than she was. Wasn't it as simple as that?'

Eutherius's face is in near-darkness, illuminated only by the pale glow of the starlight reflected off the snow, but in his mind's eye Canio can clearly see the contempt written on it.

'I don't condemn you, Canio. Each of us is what he is, and acts according to his nature,' the old man adds, twisting the knife. 'But one thing puzzles me: when this "marsh gas," or whatever it was, had left you, why didn't you go back to that lake to discover what had become of her?'

Canio has been trying to find a convincing answer to that question for the past eighteen months. He still hasn't found one. 'I don't know why – not for sure.'

Eutherius says nothing, letting him wriggle on his own hook.

'I was almost certain that she would have escaped – she must have been able to run faster than those deserters.'

Still Eutherius says nothing.

'And between the lakes that place was thick with tall grass and great patches of sedge that she could have hidden in.'

'It doesn't sound like the sort of place where anyone could run very fast, Canio – particularly in a sopping wet dress,' Eutherius observes reflectively, as if the point has only just occurred to him.

But it has occurred to Canio. Many, many times. 'All right, so perhaps I did think that there was a chance – a tiny, tiny chance – that she hadn't escaped. And if she hadn't, then I couldn't face ...' He cannot bring himself to say the words.

'Face what, Canio – finding her body? Her rotting body? Is that what you were about to say?' But before he can answer, Eutherius continues disarmingly, 'Still, that does at least sound like an honest answer. It almost convinces me.'

'I had no other reason for not going back. She didn't want the gold – I offered to give her some of it, but she only wanted that Hecate figurine, nothing else ... Surely she must have told you that herself?'

But Eutherius does not take the bait. Canio is unable see the old man's eyes clearly, but he knows that they are staring intently at him. 'You chose the gold, Canio. You took it and left her to die.' His voice is as cold as the frigid night air.

'How many times do I have to tell you! I didn't *choose* to desert her. Something made me do it, damn you.' Canio hears his words, harsh and angry, echo around the clearing. Then the silence between the two men slowly lengthens, and to end it he asks, 'Why did she want it?'

'Want what?'

'That figurine, of course. She must have told you, seeing as you were like father and daughter.'

'I suspect that she's another's daughter now,' Canio thinks he hears Eutherius murmur. Then, louder, the old man says, 'The new moon must have risen when you were at that lake.'

'I never saw it.'

'No one sees the new moon rise, Canio. Surely you know that?'

'Yes, of course I know … what in sweet Venus's name are you talking about now?'

'Another new moon will rise when this dawn comes. Think of that, Canio.'

Canio thinks that Eutherius is only trying to avoid answering his question. 'Perhaps I know anyway.'

'Why she wanted that figurine? Then tell me.'

'She wanted it because she believed that there was some sort of truth in a silly old story.'

'And what story would that be?'

Canio is sure that Eutherius knows what story, but …

'The story that tells of how, back near the dawn of time, a girl is supposed to have been picking flowers in a meadow on the island of Sicilia, when she came across the most beautiful flower that she had ever seen. So she hurried over to it and found that it had a scent sweeter even than …' He stops, realising that he had been about to say "honeysuckle."

'Sweeter than what, Canio?'

'Dog roses, Eutherius. Sweeter than a thousand deep pink dog roses in the full sun. But before she could so much as touch it, the ground beside her opened up with a tremendous roar and out of the earth – '

'Came a golden chariot drawn by four night-black horses,' Eutherius interrupts. 'And in that chariot was King Hades himself, and he snatched the girl and carried her off to be his queen, down in the land under the earth where the ghosts of the dead wander forever. The girl's name was Persephone, or Proserpina, and she was the daughter of Ceres, sometimes called Demeter, the goddess of corn and summer, who was so distraught at her daughter's abduction that she roamed for years over all the world looking for her. And throughout all those years it was an endless winter, a time when summer never came.' Eutherius draws breath and sighs. 'Yes, Canio, as you say, it is a silly old story – so why would Vilbia believe that there was any truth in it?'

Probably because you told her so, you old bastard. Canio ignores the sarcasm in Eutherius's voice and says, 'But do you know who's supposed to have helped Ceres to search for Persephone?'

'I'm sure you're going to tell me.'

'Hecate, that's who. And later, when Persephone was escorted up out of the Lower World for the first time by Mercury, after Jupiter told Hades to set her free for a while, the story goes that it was Hecate's torches that lit their way back up into this world, carrying the pomegranate seeds.'

'The pomegranate seeds? What pomegranate seeds?'

But behind the old man's mockery Canio thinks he can perceive a slight tension. 'Don't pretend you haven't heard that part of the story. While Persephone was in the Lower World, Hades tricked her into eating some pomegranate seeds – some say four, some six. That's why she had to return to Hades and spend four or six months of every year with him in the Lower World, or so the story goes.'

'Oh, *those* seeds – of course I know about them: it's what mothers tell their children to explain the changing seasons.' And with exaggerated earnestness, as if explaining to a slow-witted child, Eutherius says, 'When Persephone is in the Lower World, then it's winter. When she's getting ready to journey into or out of the Lower World then it's autumn or spring, and when she's back in this world then it's summer. But why, Canio, on this bitter cold night, are you telling me a silly story that everybody knows and only children believe?'

'I told you why – because I'm certain Vilbia believed that at least part of the story was true.' Actually, Canio isn't certain. He has a suspicion, but nothing more.

'So what has the figurine got to do with it?'

'There's something inside that rattled softly when I shook it. Vilbia knew that: I think she knew it long before I did.'

'And you think that something was – what?'

'Pomegranate seeds – Vilbia thought they were pomegranate seeds.'

'Oh, I see – the ones that Persephone ate. Did she sick them up afterwards? I don't remember that part of the story.'

Canio almost smiles, thinking he detects something forced in Eutherius's mockery – surely confirmation of his suspicion that the old man already knows what he is about to tell him? 'They were the ones that Persephone *didn't* eat, of course. Listen to the second part of the story, the one that not so many people know about.'

Eutherius sighs. 'I'm listening, Canio, I'm listening.'

'Good; then listen well, Ancient One, and tell me if I've left anything out.

'The tale I heard was this: when old Hades released Persephone from his kingdom for that first time, long, long ago, he took the eight or six remaining pomegranate seeds and sealed them inside a little brass figurine of Hecate. Then he gave it to Persephone to carry with her back into this world. And you know why he did that, don't you?'

'If I did, there would be no point in you telling me – and you are going to tell me, aren't you, Canio?' Eutherius replies tonelessly.

'Oh, I am Eutherius, I am – just to make sure that you know that I know. There were two reasons. First, Hades reckoned that whenever Persephone shook the figurine she would hear the rustle of those seeds and remember that – in a few short months, or weeks, or days – she would have to return to him: that there was no escape. And second, it would be Hecate herself who would come for her, come with the torch to guide her back down into the Lower World. The torch to guide her, the sword to threaten her. It was perfect, or so he thought.

'It wasn't until Persephone had returned to this Upper World that Hades had second thoughts. If, somehow, he could have tricked her into eating those remaining pomegranate seeds, then she would have been compelled to stay with him for all eternity. But he never got the chance to trick her for a second time because, when they were journeying out of the Lower World, Persephone showed Hecate the figurine and told her what it contained. She told Ceres too, once they were back in this world. And then the figurine disappeared, and neither Persephone nor Hades ever saw it again.

'Persephone swore that she had no idea where it had gone, and Hades believed her. He reckoned that Ceres had taken it, but he never knew for sure. And as the years passed, so the knowledge that somewhere in this world must be those seeds that would keep Persephone with him forever came to obsess and torment him. It's only a child's foolish story, Eutherius, but even now some people still believe such stories are true. And they act on what they believe.'

'So Ceres is supposed to have taken that little figurine?'

'No, Eutherius. In the version I heard it was Hecate who took it and hid it.'

'But what would be the point of hiding it? Why not simply destroy it?'

Canio suspects that the old man knows the answers to all these questions; that he is only asking them to probe the limits of his own knowledge. But it doesn't matter: the more he appears to know, then the more Eutherius might be willing to tell him. 'I was given two reasons. The first was that only Hades himself can destroy what he had created.'

'Hmm, I suppose that makes sense. And the second?'

'Is that Hecate fears that if those seeds were ever to be destroyed, then the world would be plunged into an everlasting winter, and spring would never come again. Were they the reasons that you were given?'

Canio fancies he sees the old man smile sardonically. 'But

why run the risk of hiding it? Why doesn't the Dark Lady simply carry it with her?'

'Because she's a creature of both worlds, Eutherius, and daren't risk carrying it when she goes down into the Lower World. I've heard it said that she can't even touch it, for fear that Cerberus might scent it when she crosses the Styx. I'm surprised you didn't know that,' Canio cannot resist adding.

'Know, Canio? What do any of us really know? Tell me, how much truth do you think there is in those two stories?'

'Not a single word, Ancient One.'

'And you're probably right … but, there again,' the old man muses, as if it were some abstract philosophical point, 'perhaps the stories really *are* true, every word of them: did you ever consider that possibility, Canio?'

Canio has considered it. Since he was a little child he has never really believed in the existence of all the other gods and goddesses – of Hades, Ceres, Persephone and the rest. But Hecate is different. Marcia had sown an uneasy belief in her into his child's mind at too early an age for him ever to succeed in ridding himself of it completely, no matter how hard he has tried over the years.

'Well did you, Canio?' Still Canio does not reply, and at last Eutherius says, 'Perhaps it's time for me to tell you a story that I heard about that little figurine.'

'Another old story?'

'Oh no, not old at all, but I think you ought to hear it.'

'Why?'

'Because, if you intend to continue asking questions about the figurine and what it's supposed to contain, then you should at least be aware of its recent history.'

Canio feels his muscles tensing. He has no idea what Eutherius is about to say, only a leaden certainty that whatever it is will not be welcome.

'It began in the early May of the year 367 – the month that

saw the beginning of the *Conspiratio* – in the remote, hilly country that lies some way to the south-west of the Great Marshes. There, in the heart of a rich temple dedicated to Apollo, god of the sun – that's ironic, isn't it? – among all the treasures which it had accumulated over the years, was a small, insignificant casket. It had been there for so long that no memory remained of what it held, or even of who had brought it there. It was locked, and the key, if there had ever been a key, had long since disappeared. What had survived, through generations of priests, was the warning that no attempt should ever be made to open it.

'One day a man arrived at the temple asking for food and a bed for the night. He was dressed in the robes of a priest, though ragged and stained, and so the priests fed him and agreed to let him stay. But it soon became obvious that he was brainsick, because several times they found him muttering to himself about how arbitrarily cruel the gods could be.'

'Is that madness?' Canio asks.

'The priests thought so. But mad or sane, during the night he crept into the cella and began rooting through the treasures. Eventually he came to the casket, managed to pick the lock … and do you know what he found inside?'

'The Hecate figurine? Just a wild guess, you understand,' Canio says, with a studied casualness he does not feel.

'It was *a* Hecate figurine, Canio – though not necessarily the one that was once in your possession, of course. However, it seems that the priest was deluded enough to think that what he had discovered was the actual one that Hades is supposed to have given to Persephone. And so it follows that he thought he knew what it contained.'

'How did he know?'

'Ah, who can say? Perhaps he'd been told the story by the same person who told you?' Canio thinks he can see the old man actually grinning. 'And he'd been seeking her for several years.'

'Why?'

295

'Because he knew that if the stories about it were true – and apparently he was crazy enough to believe that they were – then the Rich One would give a great deal for it.'

'The Rich One? Who – ?'

'Surely you've heard the name before, Canio?' Eutherius interrupts impatiently. 'Dis? Pluto? Orcus? The Lord of Erebus? ... Hades? – he has so many names.'

'I see,' Canio says slowly. 'So what did that priest want from the Rich One: eternal life, perhaps?'

'A life, certainly, Canio – but not eternal, and not even his own. The story I heard was that, some thirty years before, when he was young, our priest had an affair with a married woman. In those far-off days he lived at a small temple a few miles from Ovilregis. A woman, young and quite pretty, but still childless after three years of marriage, had come to the temple seeking reassurance from the gods that her husband still loved her, still desired her. It was summer, the sun was hot, the temple was surrounded by hay meadows full of flowers, and the priest thought that he was but the instrument of the gods ... I'm sure you can imagine the rest.'

Canio can vividly imagine the rest. In another time and place he might have been grinning broadly. But not this night.

'The following spring a child, a daughter, was born, and although the priest tried to deceive himself that he was not the father, in his heart he believed that he was.'

'And belief is what drives men ... Like winds drive clouds across the sky,' Canio observes.

'Quite so. And in such matters belief is all. From time to time he chanced to see the child, something which gave him both pleasure and pain – pleasure in knowing who she really was, pain that she would never know him as her father. So the years passed, and when the girl was about ten years old the woman and her husband fell on hard times. And, as sometimes happens in such situations, they sold her to a rich man, a wine merchant. At Abona, I think it was. Now the priest could have stopped the sale, if only he had possessed the courage to take and sell one or two of his temple's treasures, such as they were. Two or three solidi, no more, would have allowed the couple to keep the girl. But the priest hesitated too long, terrified by the fear of discovery. And then the girl was gone, carried away, first to Abona and then to far-off Londinium.

'More years passed, and the girl grew into a woman. And by and by the merchant married her so that she could legally act as partner in his business, for he was now a widower, no longer young and in failing health. And when the priest eventually heard of this he told himself that, despite what he had done, and not done, in the end the Parcae had smiled upon his daughter and good fortune and happiness were to be hers. But the Parcae rarely smile, do they Canio?'

'No, they rarely do. So what happened then?' He is already near-certain that this story will not have a happy ending.

'In the summer of 364 – over five years ago – there was a great storm off the coast of western Gaul, a storm in which many ships were lost and all aboard them believed drowned. At the time it meant nothing to our priest. But then he heard a rumour that one of those ships had belonged to a wine merchant and his wife, who had been sailing back from Burdigala. And then all the priest could do was wait and hope. So he waited and he hoped, and of course the rumour turned out to be true.'

'The evil ones always do,' Canio mutters, as much to himself as Eutherius.

'I'm sure the priest would agree. He was getting old, and now his only child was dead and gone, and all that he was left with were the memories and the guilt. A guilt which, like his brain sickness, grew rather than diminished as another three winters came and went. And then he found the figurine.'

'So what did he do with it?'

Eutherius pauses, then murmurs, 'They say that somewhere in the Lead Hills there is a certain cave which is one of the entrances to the Lower World. Did you know that?'

'No, I didn't – you don't really believe that, do you?' Canio certainly doesn't want to believe it himself.

Eutherius shrugs. 'The cave exists,' he replies obliquely. 'And it seems that our priest certainly believed it was an entrance to the Underworld because, as quickly as he could after discovering the figurine, he journeyed north to the Lead Hills. At the entrance he lit a torch and walked into the cave. Deeper and deeper he went, until at last he came to the point where the cave ends in an underground river which flows towards the very centre of the earth.

'Some say that river is a tributary of the Styx itself, but whether it is or not, on the edge of that black river, almost fainting with terror, his feeble torch lighting up little more than the eternal night which was all around him, the priest actually tried to bargain with Hades. In that echoing cavern he called out that he knew where the figurine was hidden. And that, if his daughter were to be returned to him, alive and well at a place he named, then he swore that he would give Hades the figurine before the rising of the first full moon following her return.'

'What was the place he named?' Canio is unable to stop himself from asking.

'Abona, or so I heard,' Eutherius says carelessly. 'And then, terrified that his torch would burn out while he was still deep inside the cave, our priest turned and fled, and didn't stop running until he was back out in the sunlight again.'

'And did his daughter return?'

'Oh, the priest never knew, Canio. You see, he went back to that temple of Apollo, intending to steal the figurine and carry it with him to Abona. He nearly succeeded too, but one of Apollo's priests spotted him sneaking out of the temple. They chased and caught him, recovered the figurine, and beat him so badly that afterwards he crawled away to die. But he didn't die. His wounds healed, and a month or so later he managed to make his way to Abona. By then, of course, the town had been sacked by the Hibernians, but nevertheless he stayed and waited. But his daughter never came while he was there, and in the chaos of that wasted town he could find nobody who could say if she had ever been there.

'Eventually the priest persuaded himself that Hades had not returned her simply because he hadn't believed his claim to know the figurine's hiding place. And so, in his madness, he decided to try again. But this time he was determined to steal the figurine first and carry it with him into the cave. So he returned to the South Country, and for much of that year, while the *Conspiratio* was blighting the land, he skulked around in the wild, hilly country near the temple, always on the lookout for an opportunity to steal the figurine again. And then, in the April of the following year –'

'Three sixty-eight?'

'Yes of course, Canio – three sixty-eight. Sometime in the April of that year he fell in with a small band of army deserters and struck a bargain with them. He would lead them to the temple – that temple which, ironically, the barbarians had never chanced to find – so that they could rob it of its treasures. And in return they would give him the figurine.'

'And did they?'

'Perhaps – I really don't know what happened after that,' Eutherius replies smoothly. 'Do you?'

Canio turns away and kicks viciously at the snow, sending a spray of small lumps flying across the clearing. 'And I suppose you don't know the name of that mad priest, or where he is now?'

'Canio, I'm not even sure that he ever really existed. It was just a story I heard.'

But Canio, remembering what Orgillus told him, is sure. 'Who did you say told you the story?'

'I didn't say.'

'No you didn't, did you. Just like you didn't say the name of that priest's supposed daughter.' Too late, Canio wishes he hadn't said that. He is already near-certain, but dreads actually hearing it confirmed.

'But Canio, I assumed you knew,' Eutherius replies, managing (Canio thinks) to sound surprised. 'Her name was Pascentia – the same name as the woman Saturninus met at Ovilregis on that night of the May full moon in 367, just before the beginning of the *Conspiratio*. The woman he rode away with into the night, before they both disappeared without trace near that old cemetery on the Sabrina plain.'

'Where the Caelofernus tombstone stands,' murmurs Canio, remembering what Vilbia had told him when he met her that dawn near Ovilregis.

'Does it indeed. I didn't know that,' Eutherius says blandly. 'Of course, it probably wasn't the same woman,' he continues, in that tone of a pedagogue mulling an abstruse point of philosophy. 'But, on the other hand, if it were, then I suppose it's reasonable to assume that Hades would have been very angry, him having kept his part of the bargain but not received the figurine. Which could, possibly, account for her disappearance that night – and Saturninus's too, of course. And I would hazard a guess that, even now, Hades wouldn't look charitably on anyone who he might chance to learn has had that figurine in their possession. You say that Vilbia had it, briefly. But if she's now … I suppose that leaves just you. That must be a terrible thing to live with, Canio.'

'What must be?'

'Why, the knowledge that at any time – day or night – the ground might suddenly open up and swallow you.' Eutherius's voice is honeyed with a solicitude that Canio knows he does not even begin to feel.

***

He feels the rage welling up inside him. He thinks that Eutherius has been playing cat and mouse with him, telling him things – probably lies – that he never wanted to know, but not the one thing he longs to hear – that Vilbia is alive and well. For the space of several pounding heartbeats he is on the point of beating the truth out of the old man, and it is only the thought that Vilbia would hate him for doing so that stops him. He decides to try one last time. 'Vilbia *is* here – I know she is. I saw a light in the temple as I was coming down from the high ground.'

'That means nothing, Canio. In winter a candle always burns there on the night before the new moon rises.'

Why then? Canio wonders, but decides not to ask. 'But *is* she in there?'

'No, Canio, she isn't in there – but go and see for yourself, if you don't believe me.' And Eutherius gestures towards the door of the temple.

Canio hears the challenge in the old man's voice, hesitates, then walks quickly over to the temple. At the door he pauses, then impulsively turns to where he can still see Eutherius sitting motionless in the snowy dark. 'On what day of the month was she born?'

'Who – Vilbia?'

'Of course, Vilbia. On what day was she born?'

'Why, on the nones, Canio – the nones of December in the year three fifty-one, as I recall. Didn't she tell you? Or perhaps,' Eutherius adds reflectively, 'she didn't know herself. I don't remember ever telling her, and she never asked.'

Of all the days in that month that it could have been, Canio had prayed to the Dark Lady that it would not be that one. Perhaps in his heart he already knew – had known since that day on Moriduno beach – but to hear it confirmed shrivels his soul.

Staring at the old man he grips the bone-achingly cold iron latch so tightly that its impression will stay on his palm for hours afterwards. Still he waits, but it seems that Eutherius does not intend to say more. Turning again, he lifts the latch, pushes open the heavy door and peers inside. A large candle burns in a sconce driven into a mortar joint in the stone wall, its slowly wavering flame casting light and shadows around the ambulatory and into the cella itself.

'Are you in there, Vilbia?' he calls softly. 'Won't you talk to me?' He repeats the words, louder this time, but still there is no reply. All he can hear is the muted lapping from the stone font as the ever-upwelling waters of Leucesca's spring overflow into the lead pipe that carries them away to the little stream that winds its way down through the wood, their constant motion preventing them from freezing, even on a night such as this. Canio twists the candle out of its socket. Carrying it, he eases between the columns and walks into the cella. There is no one there. Then he notices the door of the small room formed by walling-off the far side of the ambulatory. Slowly he reaches out and opens it.

By the candle's flickering light he sees the pale shape of a faceless woman hovering no more than a yard in front of him. For a moment fear rushes unchecked through his veins, before he realises that it is nothing more than a long white robe hanging there. With his free hand he gently caresses the robe, stroking the soft cloth between finger and thumb. Then abruptly he releases it and slams the door closed, vainly attempting to shut away behind that door all the memories that had come flooding back. The draught snuffs out the candle.

Standing in the darkness beside the low font in the middle of the cella he gazes upwards into the inky blackness of the roof, seeing slivers of starry sky through the narrow windows under the eaves. He shakes his head, re-crosses the mosaic floor and gropes to replace the candle in its sconce, opens and shuts the door behind him, and finally walks back out into the snow.

'All right, so she's not in there now – but you do know where she is, don't you,' he says harshly, making no attempt to hide the bitter disappointment he feels. He stops, suddenly realising that he is talking to an empty chair: Eutherius has vanished. 'Where in the names of the Mothers of the Hills have you gone, damn you,' he mutters.

The only logical place is the little house on the other side of the clearing. He stamps over to it, trying to make out clear footprints in the snow. At least one set of prints appears to head towards the Stygian darkness of the wood, but in the gloom it is impossible to see whether they are coming, or going, or both. He finds the house locked, a thin unbroken feather of snow across the junction of door and frame. An obscenity rises to his lips but he does not utter it. Instead, he turns back towards the temple, then stops as he sees something moving above the chair. He takes several paces towards it, before realising that it is a raven, perching on the chair back. For a long moment bird and man stare unblinkingly at each other, then the raven spreads its wings and flies noiselessly up, disappearing almost instantly into the oblivion of the frigid night.

And now Canio knows that there is nothing left for him here. Yet even so he lingers for a while, slowly circling and re-circling the perimeter of the clearing, hoping against reason. Hope slowly dies, and then at last he gathers Antares' reins and leads the horse up through the black wood and out onto the undulating plateau, where he mounts to begin the long ride home.

A mean wind whips stinging granules of frozen snow into his eyes, making them fill with tears. And with the wind, but colder far, there comes a crushing sense of loneliness and emptiness and loss. Now he sees only one yellow leaf being carried along by the current of that November stream, a solitary leaf spinning slowly on its journey to dissolution. Looking towards the south-east he sees the heatless, blood-red midwinter sun beginning to struggle above the horizon, bringing light back into the world behind that unseen new moon.

And then he sees her. She is standing about a hundred yards away, beside a large patch of gorse. At first he cannot believe his eyes, thinks that she is no more than a product of his own longings, that at any moment her image will fade away. Then the awful thought comes that it might be her ghost, sent by Hecate to – what? For a moment pure terror floods into his mind. Then Antares gives a soft whinny of apparent recognition, and without urging starts ambling forwards. Though still fearful, Canio does not attempt to check the horse. He has to know. Whatever the cost, he has to know. Ever nearer he approaches, and when he is no more than a couple of yards away the woman steps forwards, stretches out one arm and strokes Antares' nose.

'Hullo, boy,' she says softly. 'It's been a long time. Has he been treating you well?'

'Vilbia?' He slides down off Antares' back and hesitantly reaches out to touch the hand that is still stroking Antares. At the last moment his nerve fails him, and instead he slides his hand against her heavy winter cloak. To his profound relief his fingertips feel the slightly bristly nap of the cloth. 'It really is you … isn't it?'

'Of course it's really me, Canio. Did you think I was a ghost?'

But she is no ghost. She is flesh and blood, and with that realisation his heart starts singing like a bird in spring. 'I … what else could I think? From what Eutherius said … Why couldn't that old dung beetle have told me you were alive?' he cannot stop himself blurting out, anger mingling with the euphoric relief.

'Perhaps because he thought you deserved to be punished, Canio?'

He cannot even begin to deny that. 'And do you think so too?'

'Haven't I reason to?'

'Yes, all the reason in the world. But Vilbia, I swear to you that I truly couldn't help myself at that damned lake. Something weird came over me, the same way the marsh gas beside that mere in the Great Marshes affected you when you thought you saw Eutherius there.'

'I know, Canio. I heard what you said to Eutherius.'

'You heard? How?'

'I was in the wood, just beyond the edge of the clearing.'

304

And before he can ask, she adds, 'Eutherius didn't know I was there.'

'I see ... And did you believe what I said?'

'About being possessed by something which came out of the gold? I don't know, Canio. Are you quite sure you believe it yourself?'

She is looking directly into his eyes now, and he cannot lie. He doesn't even want to lie. 'No, I'm not sure – I don't think I'll ever be sure.'

'No,' she says sadly. 'There are some things that neither of us will ever know for sure, no matter how much we may long to.'

He is uncertain how to answer that. Instead, he asks, 'How did you escape from those men at the lake?'

'I ran, Canio. I simply ran as fast as I possibly could. And fear lends men wings, as Gulioepius once told me – I think it was a quotation from somewhere. Besides, I don't think they were really interested in catching me. They were deserters, weren't they – Orgillus's surviving comrades, come with more of their kind to recover the gold? In those first moments I don't think they realised that we'd already found it. Perhaps they never did.'

'But where have you been this past year and a half?'

'Oh, wandering. Here, in Britannia – and other places. And on my wanderings I learnt many things. But now I've come home.'

'To your temple?'

She nods.

'But it's so cold there. Why not come and live with me in my villa – as my sister, like I wanted you to on the road to the lake? I could give you a horse or a saddle donkey, so you could come back to this place as often as you wanted. It's not so bad a journey in daylight.'

'I don't seem to feel the cold, Canio. Or weariness, or the summer's heat. And besides, this is my home.'

'But it must be so lonely at this time of year. At least stay with me through the winter months.'

'Like Persephone, you mean?'

She smiles, but the allusion makes him shiver. 'I hate to think of you here, all alone – I can't bear the thought of losing you again.'

'I won't be alone.'

'Eutherius?'

'No, not Eutherius.' She claps her hands and, from where it had been crouching unseen among the gorse, a large black hound springs up and bounds to her side.

It growls threateningly at Canio, who instinctively steps back several paces.

She laughs merrily. 'Don't be afraid of Cerberus – he's gentle as a lamb really.'

Canio suspects otherwise, and some of the old fears suddenly return. 'But isn't that the same dog that was at the lake, the one that … '

'The very same, and he's followed me ever since. But don't worry, he's no supernatural creature – despite the name I've given him. He eats and drinks, and does all the other things that dogs do. He also catches his own dinners, don't you boy?' and she pats the hound on the head. 'Say hello to him, Canio.'

Gingerly, Canio reaches out and rubs the dog's head, and this time it doesn't growl. Then, remembering, he asks, 'Do you want this back?' And he lifts over his head the cord from which the Julian coin is suspended.

She takes the coin and looks wistfully down at it. 'No, you keep it,' she says quietly.

'Are you sure?'

'No – but keep it for now. Some day I may ask for it back.'

As she passes the coin back to him he gently takes her hand in his. It feels warm against his own cold palm, and she does not attempt to pull away. 'I really meant it when I asked you to come and live in my villa. You should at least see it – it's quite something.'

'I know: Eutherius told me. But no, Canio. Thank you, but no. And now I must be going.' She gently disengages her hand from his and starts walking towards the wood.

'No, don't go, not so soon! Will I see you again?'

'You may come and see me whenever you wish. I'll often be here ... Is there anything else you wish to know?'

He has to ask. He doesn't want to, but if he doesn't ... 'Have you still got it – that little brass figurine of the Dark Lady?'

By way of reply she reaches inside her cloak and holds it out for his inspection.

He gazes uneasily at the figurine. Remembering Eutherius's words, he does not attempt to touch it. 'You truly believe that this is the real one, don't you – the one that Hades is supposed to have given to Persephone?'

Her answer surprises him. 'Was there ever a real one, Canio? In this past year I've talked to men who are quite sure that story about the pomegranate seeds is nothing more than a tale told to explain the changing seasons to children – just like Eutherius told you it was. And if that is so, then all the other stories associated with the seeds are simply myths too. Which means that this little piece of brass is probably just a fake, perhaps one of several made to sell to the gullible.'

'But at the lake, surely you must have believed – '

'At the lake I believed many things that now...' She shrugs. 'Now I'm older. And perhaps wiser.'

'If you think that, then why keep the figurine?'

'Because although I may suspect it's a fake, can I ever be sure? Sometimes, in those matters where we most long for certainty, in the end we have to accept that we'll never find it, or if we do it will only be an illusion.'

'Aren't you even certain of the existence of your goddess, Leucesca, any more?'

She smiles again, and he realises how much he has missed that smile. 'That's the one certainty I still possess.'

'Why?'

'Because I'm still convinced that she was protecting Saturninus and Pascentia on that May night in 367, just before the *Conspiratio* began.'

'Even though they disappeared without trace? Even though to this day no one knows what became of them?'

She is silent for several moments, as if trying to decide. Then she says, 'Last summer I sailed across the ocean to Gaul.'

And at once he guesses why. 'Looking for Saturninus?'

She nods.

'And did you find him?' Canio feels his stomach muscles tensing.

'I found them both; him and Pascentia. At a little villa surrounded by endless rows of vines, way down in the south-west of Gaul. It was the place where I thought they might be.' Perhaps seeing the scepticism lingering on his face, she says, 'That's the truth, Canio. Unlike yourself, I have no reason to lie about finding him. Some day, perhaps, I'll tell you about our meeting ... I liked Pascentia: it was easy to see why Saturninus fell in love with her on that day beside the Moselle.'

But Canio is still taking in the implications of what she has just said. 'So Pascentia really did survive the shipwreck. Which means they weren't ...'

'Weren't what – dragged down to the Underworld by a vengeful Hades, perhaps? No, Canio. I think that was just Eutherius's little ... well, perhaps joke isn't quite the right word.'

'The old bastard!'

'He thought you'd left me to die, Canio. How would you have felt towards him if he'd done the same? But now I really must go.'

'To Eutherius?'

'Perhaps.'

'Am I forgiven?'

'Do you need forgiveness?'

'I need your forgiveness.'

She hesitates, before saying simply, 'Then you have it.'

He watches her walk away, the black hound trotting after her. When she reaches the edge of the wood she turns and waves. He waves back, and is still waving after she has disappeared into the darkness under the trees. And as he remounts Antares he notices for the first time that, in the middle of the expanse of winter-dulled gorse, one bush is smothered with the rich, yellow pea-like flowers that usually only appear in such profusion in spring and early summer. He feels happiness welling up inside him, wildly, unstoppably. Everything has come right. Still smiling, he twitches the reins and man and horse start the journey back to the little valley they left earlier that night, now such a long time ago.

The miles pass contentedly, unhurriedly, and he is still some way from home when, out of nowhere, there suddenly returns the memory of something which Vilbia said: that she did not seem to feel either the cold, or weariness, or the summer's heat. In the exhilaration of their meeting he had barely noted it, but now ... Uneasily he pulls out from beneath his tunic the Julian coin, the coin which she had so recently touched. And he is still slowly turning it over and over between his fingers, staring first at Julian's inscrutable bearded face and then at the great bull standing beneath its twin stars, when the roofs of his villa at last come into view.

***

THE MOON ON THE HILLS

The Sower of the Seeds of Dreams is the sequel to *The Moon on the Hills*. The main characters from *Moon* who also appear or are mentioned in *Sower* are as follows:-

Saturninus: Main protagonist of *Moon* and Canio's predecessor as primicerius of the Corinium civil guard. At the opening of *Moon*, in May 367, he had a dream in which he saw, by the light of a full moon, a standing stone bearing the carved name Caelofernus turn into a living man who then stabbed him with his own sword. He tracked down and killed the man whose face was that of the Caelofernus of his dream, but nevertheless went on to vanish in mysterious circumstances soon after, just before the beginning of the *Barbarica Conspiratio*.

Pascentia: Wife of a wine merchant, and once Saturninus's lover, she was believed drowned in a great storm off the coast of Gaul in 364. But having apparently survived the shipwreck, she met Saturninus again at the town of Ovilregis on the evening of the May full moon in 367. She rode off with him that same night in the direction of the Sabrina Estuary, and neither was ever seen again. Next morning, Saturninus's horse, Antares, was found wandering near a deserted cemetery containing a large tombstone bearing the name Caelofernus.

Canio: Saturninus's second in command in *Moon*. Accompanied him on his search for Caelofernus. Appointed acting primicerius following Saturninus's disappearance and remained in this post throughout the *Barbarica Conspiratio*.

Vilbia: As the fifteen year old priestess of Leucesca, she met Saturninus for the first (and only) time when he came to consult Gulioepius on the meaning of his dream. Before leaving, Saturninus gave her a large coin of the pagan emperor Julian which he wore medallion-like around his neck, saying that she should keep it safe for him until he returned from his search for Caelofernus.

In *Sower*, her motives for wanting to know what became of Saturninus are complex, although she would deny (even, or perhaps especially, to herself) that they are romantic.

Aemilianus: Prefect of the Corinium civil guard and thus Saturninus's and Canio's immediate superior. A political appointee, not overburdened with brains.

Caelofernus: The man Saturninus dreamed would kill him beneath the May full moon in 367.

Carausius: The man whose face Saturninus saw in his dream and subsequently tracked down and killed. Assumed by him to be an alias used by Caelofernus

Eutherius: Old apothecary living in Corinium. Father-figure to Vilbia after Gulioepius's death. Possible magus. Regarded with suspicion by Canio.

Gulioepius: Elderly priest of the goddess Leucesca. Vilbia's original mentor.

Leucesca: Water goddess (fictional) whose sacred spring rises inside a temple in a wood on the north-west escarpment of the Cotswold Hills.

HISTORICAL NOTES, GAZETTEER AND MISCELLANEA.

1. Historical Accuracy.

I have tried to make both novels reasonably historically accurate, but Late Roman Britain is still very much an unknown land. This may appear paradoxical in view of the vast numbers of stone, metal, fired clay, etc. artefacts from the period that have survived, but the fact is that very few personal documents have come down to us. Thus the millions of people who lived and died here in those times are virtually silent, their thoughts and the stories of their lives now lost forever. All that is left are a few inscribed or scratched names on those surviving artefacts and the mute records of toil, injury and hard living etched into their bones.

What little is known of contemporary events in Britannia was recorded by historians who had probably never been anywhere near these islands, and their surviving writings are often tantalisingly incomplete, enigmatic or their accuracy disputed.

For example, some historians have cast doubt on whether the *Barbarica Conspiratio* of AD 367 was really the momentous event that the historian Ammianus Marcellinus, originally an army officer from Antioch, makes it appear.

They point out that he was writing in the reign of the emperor Theodosius I (379-395), who was the son of the *Comes* Theodosius who Ammianus paints as the hero who rescued Britannia from the invading barbarians. It is of course possible that he was flattering the emperor, but there is no real evidence to support this contention. We will probably never know for sure, but at the time of writing his account (early 390s?) there must have been many people still alive with personal memories of the events of 367-8 and who could have criticised any serious distortion of the facts.

✵✵✵

2. Would the Greek myth of Persephone and Hades have been known in fourth century Roman Britain?
Certainly. Consider the following:

(a) Persephone and Hades were adopted into the Roman pantheon as Proserpina and Dis respectively (although in the novel I have used the Greek names, simply because they are perhaps more familiar today).

(b) The most complete surviving Latin version of the Persephone myth was written by the Roman poet Claudius Claudianus (Claudian) in the late fourth century AD.

(c) As an example of the continuing currency of Greek myths generally in fourth century Britain, the Hinton St Mary (Dorset) mosaic of circa AD 350 depicts both (i) the Greek myth of Bellerophon slaying the Chimaera and (ii) a bust of Christ flanked by two pomegranates – symbols of resurrection and immortality which, ironically, have their origins in the Persephone myth.

✵✵✵

3. Emperors mentioned in the novel.
Hadrian: 117-138 (ie. some 230 years before the time of this novel).

Constantine I (The Great): 307-337. The first emperor to convert to Christianity. Most emperors after Constantine were at least nominally Christian, the most important exception being Julian (see below).

314

Constantius II: 337-361. Son of Constantine I. An Arian Christian. Ruler of the eastern half of the empire 337-350, then of the entire empire following the murder of his brother Constans by Magnentius.

Magnentius: 350-353. Probably pagan (but sought the support of Catholic Christians against the Arian Constantius). An outstanding military commander of barbarian origin, he seized power in Gaul in 350, but after initial successes which gave him control of much of the western half of the empire he was defeated at the bloody battle of Mursa in September 351 (see below). He retreated back into Gaul, but after further defeats committed suicide in August 353. He enjoyed considerable support in Britain, which resulted in reprisals against his followers after his fall.

Julian: 360-363. Pagan. Appointed Caesar (junior emperor) by his cousin Constantius II in 355. Rebelled against him in 360, but Constantius died of fever in November 361, sparing the empire another civil war. He invaded Persia, but was mortally wounded and died on 26th June 363.

Valentinian I: 364-375. Christian. Arguably the last really competent emperor to rule the western half of the empire, but a harsh, cruel man with a horror of sorcery and a violent temper which was to cause the stroke which killed him.

✻✻✻

4. Historical Events.
AD 350: January. Magnentius proclaimed himself emperor in Gaul.

AD 351: September. Battle of Mursa Major (modern Osijek, 100 miles north-west of Belgrade). It was said to have been the bloodiest battle of the fourth century, with Magnentius losing 24,000 men and Constantius II 30,000.

AD 353: August. After a final defeat at Mons Seleucus in Gaul, Magnentius committed suicide at Lugdunum (Lyons).

AD 367: The *Barbarica Conspiratio*, when Britain was invaded by waves of apparently co-ordinated barbarian tribes from beyond the frontiers of the Roman Empire – Picts from north of Hadrian's wall, Saxons and Franks from across the North Sea, and Scotti and Attacotti from Hibernia (Ireland) and the Western Isles.

Following the *Conspiratio* came a period of near-anarchy, with bands of army deserters roaming the countryside, the situation further complicated by a short-lived bid for power by a Pannonian exile called Valentinus.

***

5. Fourth Century Army Ranks, etc.
Comes: An officer usually commanding *comitatenses* units of the mobile field army, ranging from substantial army corps to a couple of the small (1000 men) fourth century legions. (See also Comes Theodosius below.)

Dux: An officer commanding static frontier troops (*limitanei*). (Although in medieval Latin texts *comes* is translated as count and *dux* as duke, in the Late Roman army a *comes* outranked a *dux*.)

While the old-established army units retained their ranks of *centurion, optio*, etc, in the new army units of the fourth century, the NCO ranks were (in descending order of seniority):-
   Primicerius
   Ducenarius

Centenarius
Biarchus

The 'Civil Guard': in the absence of hard facts, I have conjectured:-

(a) That there must have been some organisation responsible for policing the civilian population. I have called it the Civil Guard and assumed that it was a paramilitary organisation, largely staffed by ex-soldiers or men seconded from army units.

(b) That it was the successor to the corps of *beneficiarii consularis* of the earlier empire.

(c) That the titles of its ranks were *primicerius, ducenarius,* etc.

***

6. Gazetteer

(Names marked * are my fictional names for real places whose Roman names are now lost)

(Portum) Abona: Roman port settlement on the north bank of the Bristol Avon in what is now the Sea Mills district of Bristol.
(Flumen) Abona: The Bristol Avon, which flows into the Severn at Avonmouth.
Aquae Sulis: Bath.
*(Flumen) Bruella**: River Brue, Somerset.
Burdigala: Bordeaux.
Calleva (Atrebatum): Silchester, Hampshire.
Cambria: Wales.
Corinium (Dobunnorum): Cirencester, Gloucestershire. Capital of the province of Britannia Prima.
Durnovaria: Dorchester, Dorset.
Fosse Way: Roman road running from Exeter to Lincoln, passing through Lindinis (Ilchester), Aquae Sulis (Bath) and Corinium (Cirencester).

Fretum Gallicum: The Strait of Dover.

Glevum: Gloucester.

Great Marshes*: Formerly a large area of what is now Somerset, south of the Mendip Hills and also extending some way south of the Polden Hills. It was apparently marsh in the Late Iron Age, was at least partially drained in the early Roman period, but later reverted to marsh when the sea level rose. As with so much of Romano-British history, there is uncertainty as to the date of this reversion (the so-called Late Roman Marine Transgression). In *Sower* I have assumed that the process was already under way by the late 360s.

Isca (Dumnoniorum): Exeter.

(Flumen) Iscalis: River Axe, Somerset, flowing just south of the Mendip Hills.

Lead Hills*: The Mendip Hills.

Lindinis: Ilchester, Somerset. The Roman road which runs along the Polden Hills (see below) joined the Fosse Way at Lindinis.

Londinium: London. The title *Augusta* may have been bestowed on it by Valentinian in 368, following the crushing of the *Conspiratio*.

Long Limestone Hills*: The Cotswold Hills.

Lugdunum: Lyons.

Maglocrouco*: Belas Knap Neolithic long barrow, above Winchcombe, Gloucestershire.

Moesia: Two Balkan provinces on the south bank of the Danube, mainly in Serbia and Bulgaria.

Moriduno*: Brean Down promontory on the Somerset coast.

Mursa Major: A city in the province of Pannonia (now Osijek, eastern Croatia, 100 miles north-west of Belgrade).

Noviomagus (Regnensium): Chichester, Sussex.

Oceanus Britannicus: The English Channel.

Oceanus Germanicus: The North Sea.

Ovilregis*: Roman town near Kingscote, Gloucestershire.

Rotomago: Rouen.

(Flumen) Sabrina: River Severn.

(Flumen) Tamesis: River Thames.

Treveri: Trier, Germany.

(Flumen) Uxela: River Parrett, Somerset.

Vadumleucara*: Bourton-on-the-Water, Gloucestershire.

Venta Belgarum: Winchester.

Via Erminus*: Roman road (Ermin Street), running from Calleva (Silchester) to Glevum (Gloucester).

Villa Aurelius: is loosely based on the Low Ham villa, Somerset.

❊❊❊

7. Miscellanea.

Agrestis: Rustic (adjective).

Ahura-Mazda (also known as Ormazd): The Mithraic creator god and god of light. The eternal opponent of Ahriman, god of darkness and chaos.

Ala: A unit of cavalry.

Ballista (pl. ballistae): In the later Roman Empire this name was applied to the large, mounted, bolt-firing crossbow.

Burning at the stake: Burning alive was apparently a not uncommon punishment in the later Roman Empire. It is mentioned at least nine times in Ammianus Marcellinus's history, which covers the period 354–378. In 372, for instance, by order of Valentinian himself, a charioteer called Athanasius was burnt at the stake for practising sorcery (Ammianus 29.3).

Caldarium: The hot room of a Roman bath suite.

Centenionalis: The names of the copper coins of the fourth century are generally unknown. The sole exception is the centenionalis, which may have been the name of the 2p sized coin introduced in circa 346. This coin rapidly diminished in size, but I have assumed that the name continued in use and may even have been applied to the 1p sized copper coins minted in vast quantities in the 360s and 370s.

Charon: Ferryman who carried the shades of the newly dead

across the Rivers Styx or Acheron, which separated the world of the living from the Underworld.

Chi-rho monogram: Monogram made up of the first two letters of Christ's name in Greek (Xpistos) – x (chi) and p (rho). Constantine the Great is said to have dreamed that he should paint it on his soldiers' shields before his victory at the battle of the Milvian Bridge in 312, and henceforth it appeared with increasing frequency in Christian contexts.

Cinnabar: Mercury sulphide, an ore of mercury called *minium* by the Romans. This red pigment was sometimes used to pick out the lettering of monumental inscriptions.

Classis Britannica: A fleet of war galleys stationed at various points around the coast of Eastern and Southern England and (possibly) South Wales to intercept pirates and barbarian raiders. It may have been under the command of the *comes maritimi tractus* (see Nectaridus below).

Comes Theodosius: The father of the future Emperor Theodosius (reigned 379-395), this officer was sent to Britannia by the Emperor Valentinian in 367 to restore order following the invasions of the *Barbarica Conspiratio*. He brought with him four units of the Gallic *comitatus*, namely the Batavi, Heruli, Jovii and Victores. Over the course of the next year Theodosius crushed the *Barbarica Conspiratio*, induced or forced deserting soldiers to return to their units and later captured the Pannonian exile, Valentinus, who was apparently plotting rebellion. He may also have put down an insurrection in that northern province which was henceforth renamed Valentia (see below).

Comitatenses: Units of the elite mobile field army, the *comitatus.* There were also *pseudocomitatenses*, units of *limitanei* seconded to the mobile field army.

Cursus publicus: The state-run service by which officials and documents were transported across the Roman Empire. The use of this service was supposed to be restricted to persons with the appropriate *diploma*.

Diocese (pl. dioceses): By the fourth century the large provinces of the early empire had been subdivided, to avoid concentrating too much power in the hands of any one provincial governor. These small provinces were aggregated into dioceses under the command of a *vicarius*. The diocese of Britannia was divided into four(?) provinces (but see *Valentia* below), and its *vicarius* was stationed in Londinium and reported to the Praetorian Prefect of Gaul, who in turn reported directly to the emperor.

D.N. (Dominus Noster): "Our Master". Title frequently used by Late Roman Emperors from the time of Constantine the Great onwards. Usually abbreviated to D.N. on the obverse of their coins.

Follis: A leather bag or purse. (Also applied to a large bronze coin introduced by emperor Diocletian in 295 or 296.)

Frigidarium: The cold room of a Roman bath suite.

Ganymede: In Greek mythology, a handsome prince of Troy snatched up by Zeus / Jupiter in the guise of an eagle to act as his cupbearer in Olympus.

Gustatio: The first course of a Roman banquet.

Hades / House of Hades: Properly speaking, Hades was the god who ruled over the Underworld, which was itself sometimes referred to as the House of Hades.

Hecate: In early Greek myth this goddess played an important and benevolent part in the Persephone / Hades story, first helping Demeter (Ceres) to search for her abducted daughter, and then (according to one version) lighting Persephone's way out of the Underworld with her torches. It was only in the later Hellenistic period that she began to be represented with three faces / heads / bodies as *Hecate Triformis* and to be associated with magic, witchcraft and curses.

Hippocamps: Fabulous sea monsters with the heads and forelegs of horses and coiling eel-like hind parts terminating in fishes' tails.

Honestiores and Humiliores: In law, the inhabitants of the later Roman Empire (free, not slave) were classified as either high class honestiores or low class humiliores. Humiliores, the bulk of the civilian population, could be tortured as witnesses, flogged and executed by the cruellest means. For the same crimes, honestiores could usually escape with banishment. In time, humiliores working for the great landowners, either directly or as tenant farmers, came to be legally bound to the land, much like medieval serfs.

Iugerum (pl. iugera): A Roman unit of land, approximating to 0.625 of an English acre.

Jovii: See *Comes* Theodosius, above.

Kalends: The first day of all Roman months.

Laeti: Barbarian peoples allowed to settle within the Empire on condition that they supplied a regular quota of recruits to the Roman army.

Limes Germanicus: The Germanic frontier of the Roman Empire. In the fourth century the *limes* followed the line of the rivers Rhine, Iller and Danube.

Limitanei: Lightly armed frontier garrison troops, generally considered to be of inferior quality to the *comitatenses* units (see above).

Mansio (pl. mansiones): Government-maintained hotels for persons travelling on official business. Usually sited at about 15 to 18 miles apart along major roads.

Maenads: Female followers of Bacchus, god of wine. They formed part of the *thiasos*, the retinue of frenzied revellers who followed the god.

Nectaridus: An officer, described by Ammianus as *comes maritimi tractus* (count of the maritime region), who was killed in the early stages of the *Barbarica Conspiratio*. His command included the forts on the south and east coasts of Britannia, and may have also extended to those on the Welsh, Lancastrian and even the north Gallic coasts. Later officers who held what was probably the same post were listed in the *Notitia Dignitatum* as *comes litoris Saxonici* (count of the Saxon Shore).

Nones: The seventh day of the Roman months of March, May, July and October (but the fifth day of all other months).

Notitia Dignitatum: An early 5th century document listing the posts involved in administering the Late Roman Empire, including officials of the imperial court, vicarii, provincial governors and military commands. Only incomplete copies dating from medieval times survive.

Orantes: Early Christians praying with outstretched arms, as depicted in the reconstructed fresco from Lullingstone villa, Kent.

Orichalcum: A gold-coloured copper alloy, as used for the sestertius and dupondius coins of the early empire.

Paganus: A countryman or rustic. Probable derivation of the term "pagan", the spread of Christianity being more rapid in urban areas than in the more conservative countryside.

Parcae: Roman name of the Fates.

Polden Hills: A ridge of low hills in South Somerset, running roughly north-west to south-east and carrying along its crest a Roman road (now the A39) which ran from Crandon Bridge near Bridgwater to Lindinis (Ilchester). This is the ridge that Canio and Vilbia come across when travelling south through the Great Marshes.

Pound (Roman): The Roman pound (327 grams) weighed only 72% of an English pound (454 grams). See also *siliqua* and *solidus* below.

Praetorium: By the fourth century this term had come to mean the residence of a provincial governor.

Priapus: The ancient Greek and Roman god of fertility, the protector of orchards and gardens, bees and herds. He was often depicted as a wizened elderly man with disproportionately large genitalia.

Primae Mensae: The main courses of a Roman banquet.

Rosmerta: A Celtic goddess of fertility and abundance. Of Gallic origin, she is often portrayed as the consort of Mercury. On limestone reliefs from the Cotswolds she is frequently depicted with a magic tub of food and drink, the contents of which never decreased no matter how much was taken out.

Sabazios: Originally a Thraco-Phrygian sky god; a rider god who carried a staff of power. The Romans identified him variously with Jupiter and Bacchus, and bronze hands bearing symbols to avert the evil eye were offered to him.

Siliqua (pl. siliquae): The standard small silver coin of the Late Roman Empire, tariffed at 24 to the solidus. It was introduced by Constantine the Great soon after the solidus and struck at 96 to the (Roman) pound of pure silver.

Solidus (pl. solidi): The standard Late Roman gold coin, introduced by Constantine the Great in 312, replacing the aureus of the earlier empire. It was struck at 72 to the (Roman) pound of pure gold.

Sol Invictus: The unconquered sun (god).

Spatha: Long sword with a rounded tip, used by Roman cavalry.

Stabulum): An inn for the general public, incorporating stabling for horses (cf. mansio).

Styx: One of the five rivers of the Underworld. See also Charon, above.

Taberna: Tabernae were basically shops. Some sold cooked food and wine and so functioned as takeaways.

Tegula: A large, flat, fired-clay roof tile with flanged edges.

Tepidarium: The cool heated room of a Roman bath suite.

Valentia: The current theory is that Valentia was a pre-existing fifth province (original name unknown) located somewhere in northern Britain. It is not mentioned among the other four provinces of Britannia named in the Verona List of 312-4 (ie. Britannia Prima, Britannia Secunda, Maxima Caesariensis and Flavia Caesariensis) and so is assumed to have been created some time after that date but before 367, by which date it had "fallen into the hands of the enemy," according to the contemporary historian Ammianus Marcellinus. (Enemy in this case may mean either the invading barbarians or rebellious provincials, possibly led by exiles from elsewhere in the Empire). The emperor Valentinian renamed it Valentia after it was recovered by the *Comes* Theodosius in 367/8.

Valerian: The flowering plant *valeriana officinalis*, a native perennial of Britain and Europe, was recommended by Galen as a cure for insomnia.

Vicarius: A high ranking civilian official of the later Roman Empire, in charge of a *diocese* (group of provinces).

Vir spectabilis: Literally "Admirable Man." One of the titles given to holders of high office from the fourth century onwards. I have assumed that a vicarius would have been granted this title.

Visigoths: The westernmost of the two main branches of the Goths, a Germanic people. In the fourth century, under pressure from the migrating Huns, they began to invade Roman territory from the east.